THE
EINSTEIN
PURSUIT

BY CHRIS KUZNESKI

CHRIS KUZNESKI

THE EINSTEIN PURSUIT

headline

First published in 2013 by
HEADLINE PUBLISHING GROUP

1

Cataloguing in Publication Data is
available from the British Library

Hardback ISBN 978 0 7553 8651 2
Trade paperback ISBN 978 0 7553 8652 9

Typeset in Monotype Garamond
by Palimpsest Book Production Limited, Falkirk, Stirlingshire

Printed and bound in Great Britain by
Clays Ltd, St Ives plc

Headline's policy is to use papers that are natural, renewable and
recyclable products and made from wood grown in sustainable
forests. The logging and manufacturing processes are expected
to conform to the environmental regulations of the country of origin.

HEADLINE PUBLISHING GROUP
An Hachette UK Company
338 Euston Road
London NW1 3BH

www.headline.co.uk
www.hachette.co.uk

Central Europe

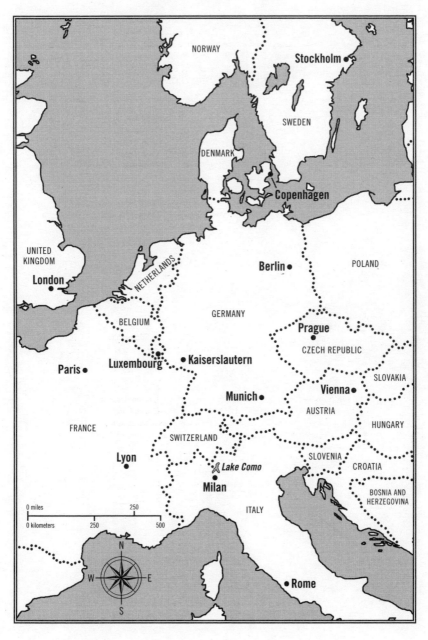

I

The lab was packed with many of the brightest minds in their field, all focused on a secret project that would change mankind for ever.

In a matter of seconds, they would all be dead.

Of course, none of them knew why they had been called to the facility in the middle of the night. Most had assumed a major breakthrough had occurred, and they had been brought in for an historic announcement that simply could not wait until morning.

Instead, they had been summoned to their slaughter.

The assault had started hours earlier, long before the researchers were misled. Guards had been killed. Locks had been breached. Specimens had been located and stolen. All had been done with a surgical precision the scientists might have appreciated under different circumstances – circumstances that wouldn't lead to their deaths.

Dr Stephanie Albright was the last to arrive at the sprawling warehouse. Not because she was running late, but because she had the furthest to drive and was on the verge of exhaustion. Over the past few months she had averaged less than four hours' sleep per day, a figure that included the naps she took when she was on the verge of passing out in the lab. But she never complained. Neither did the others. They knew how important their project was, and they were willing to forgo food and sleep if it meant reaching their goal a little sooner.

Tonight, they would give up more than that.

They would sacrifice their lives.

Albright rushed into the lobby and took the elevator to the third floor. She was so lost in her thoughts, she failed to notice the vacant guard station. And the blank security monitors. And all the other things that weren't quite right. Most importantly, she overlooked the man in the boat who had watched her every move from the calm waters of Riddarfjärden Bay.

He had waited nearly twenty minutes for her arrival.

It was time to finish the job.

His detonator included a state-of-the-art transmitter. It was capable of igniting multiple devices from up to a thousand meters away. Explosives had been placed throughout the warehouse near load-bearing walls and columns. His goal was to collapse the floors, one after another, with no time for escape. A smoldering coffin of steel and concrete for those trapped inside.

The assassin smiled at the thought.

He had killed many times before, but never so many at once.

This would be his masterpiece.

With the touch of a button, the charges erupted with so much force, he felt it in the bay. Chunks of stone and shards of glass filled the air before crashing to the earth like hail. Columns cracked and walls crumbled as the warehouse screamed in pain. Amplified by the water, the deafening roar forced him to cover his ears, but he refused to cover his eyes.

The show was just getting started.

Acetone is commonly used in laboratories around the world

to clean scientific instruments. Most of the time it is stored in polyethylene plastic containers, but this particular lab was equipped with a customized delivery system that would pump the acetone throughout the building to a multitude of cleaning stations. This set-up required large drums of acetone to be housed in the upper floors of the building.

The assassin knew this and used it to his advantage.

To cover his tracks and to prevent survivors, he had rigged the barrels of acetone to rupture from the initial force of the blast. The flammable liquid rained down on the destruction below. Within seconds, the fumes ignited and a flash fire occurred. Flames swept through the warehouse like a blistering flood, killing everyone in its wake. The heat from the blaze was so intense that bodies and evidence literally melted.

Like a crime-scene crematorium.

On most jobs, he preferred to work alone. But that wasn't the case tonight. This project was far too complex for a single cleaner, even someone with his experience. To pull it off, he needed the help of a local team – men to do the lifting, and the drilling, and the grunt work.

Men to do the things he didn't have time to do.

Men who were expendable.

He had thanked them for their service with gunfire.

Then he had left them to burn with everyone else.

2

Interpol Headquarters
Lyon, France

Nick Dial was miserable. Absolutely miserable.

He hated his office. And his desk. And the stacks of paperwork on his desk. He hated going to sleep after midnight and waking up before dawn. He hated the brown gruel the locals called coffee and the miniature mugs they served it in. Worst of all, he hated wasting his days in meetings instead of doing what he did best: finding clues and catching killers.

He was a cop at heart, not an executive.

Unfortunately, his business cards disagreed.

Dial was the director of the homicide division at Interpol, the largest international crime-fighting organization in the world. His job was to coordinate the flow of information between police departments any time a murder investigation crossed national boundaries. All told he was in charge of 190 member countries, filled with billions of people and hundreds of languages.

One of the biggest misconceptions about Interpol was their role in stopping crime. They seldom sent agents across borders to investigate a case. Instead they used local offices called National Central Bureaus in the member countries. The NCBs monitored their own territory and reported pertinent facts to Interpol's headquarters in Lyon. From there, information was entered into a central database that could be accessed by agencies around the globe.

Interpol's motto: *Connecting Police for a Safer World.*

Dial was fully committed to a 'safer world', and he was more than willing to do his part. That was why he had left his position at the FBI to work for the Europe-based organization. At the time, the decision to accept the job was a no-brainer. Not only was he the first American to be named as a department head at Interpol, but he had been asked to run the new homicide division.

How could he possibly turn that down?

Initially, Dial was thrilled with his position. He wrote the rules. He set the budget. He hand-picked the personnel in his department. On a few occasions, he even went into the field to work on high-profile cases. Not because he had to, but because he wanted to. It was his way of staying sharp while he transitioned from a field agent to an administrator.

Plus, he loved doing it.

Being a cop was in his blood.

Over the years, Dial had never seen the harm in working on an occasional case – especially if he followed the local laws and customs. However, the new secretary general disagreed. He felt the personal involvement of a division head in an open investigation could lead to bad press or, even worse, an international incident. Dial had protested fiercely but was told in explicit terms that his participation in an active case would lead to his suspension and/or termination.

That was four months ago.

Since then, Dial had written and rewritten his resignation several times.

The wording still wasn't right, but it would be soon.

After all, there are only so many ways to say *shove it.*

Dial had just entered Interpol headquarters, an impressive fortress overlooking the Rhône, when he spotted a familiar face sneaking outside. Unlike most of the analysts who roamed the hallways in pressed shirts and polished shoes, Henri Toulon stood out from the crowd.

And not in a good way.

Known for his gray ponytail and his horrible disposition, the hard-drinking Frenchman had been cited for so many work violations over the years he should have been fired long ago. Sleeping during important meetings. Coming and going as he pleased. Using the nearest restroom, regardless of its intended gender. All were worthy of discipline, but Dial had overlooked his bad habits and promoted him to assistant director because he realized something that few people did: Toulon was a brilliant son-of-a-bitch.

And that wasn't just an expression.

Dial had met Toulon's mother on three occasions, and there was little doubt she was the meanest person on the planet. Like Darth Vader in a dress. In fact, her looming presence explained nearly everything about Toulon – from his bad attitude to his drinking problem.

The only thing it didn't explain was his greasy ponytail.

There was *no* excuse for that.

Dial glanced at his watch and realized it was awfully early to be taking a break, even for a misfit like Toulon. Dial immediately assumed something tragic had happened in the world, something so bad that the son of the Antichrist had to sneak outside for a breath of fresh air.

That is, if it was possible to get fresh air while smoking.

Dial followed him to find out.

By the time he caught up to Toulon, the Frenchman was sitting on a bench with a half-burned cigarette in his mouth.

How he had smoked it so quickly was a mystery. His body was slouched, his head hung low. His eyes were closed, and he was humming a song to himself. As he did, ashes landed on his shirt like dirty snow.

Dial stared at him for several seconds, but Toulon didn't notice. He didn't think Toulon was reckless enough to drink at work, but he still had to ask. 'Are you drunk?'

'Not yet,' Toulon answered without raising his head. The cigarette bobbed in his mouth as he spoke, threatening to fall from his lips at any moment. 'I'm saving that for later.'

'Troubles at home?' Dial wondered.

Toulon straightened his back and cracked his neck. He took a long, final drag from his cigarette, then stamped out the ember with his tennis shoe. 'No. At work.'

'But you just got here.'

'No,' he said sharply, 'I've been here all night.'

'Really? Why's that?'

Toulon squinted at him quizzically, wondering whether Dial was feigning his confusion. Eventually he realized that he wasn't. 'Because *you* scheduled me for the late shift.'

Dial laughed. He had completely forgotten about that week's schedule. Toulon was being punished for a disgusting incident involving a co-worker's lunch. 'Well, you deserved it.'

Toulon cracked a mischievous smile. '*Oui.* You're right, I did.'

'If you agree with me, why are you pouting?'

'I'm not pouting; I'm relaxing. I foresee a long day.'

'Why? What happened?'

Toulon reached into his pocket and found his pack of cigarettes. He lit up a second time and inhaled the smoke deeply. 'Large explosion in Stockholm. The fire is still burning. We don't have many details – at least not yet – but it appears to be intentional.'

8

'When did this happen?'

'While *you* were sleeping.'

Dial knew if the homicide division had been notified, someone must have been killed. He only hoped casualties would be limited at that late hour. 'How many dead?'

'It's too soon to say,' Toulon said in between drags. 'But if my hunch is correct, the morgue will be full of Swedes.'

Dial groaned at the thought. Not only for the loss of life, but also because of the paperwork. 'Let me see that pack of cigarettes.'

Toulon did as he was told. 'Careful, they're a bit stronger than what you Americans prefer. And why do I not know that you smoke? What else have you been hiding from me?'

Dial took the cigarettes and tucked them inside his jacket. 'I don't smoke. And neither do you until we have some more answers.' With that, he turned and walked back toward the entrance. 'I'll see you upstairs in five minutes.'

Back inside the building, Dial took a deep breath and headed upstairs to start his day. He sensed it would be a rough one. In his office, he hung his suit coat on the wooden rack in the corner, then made his way to his desk. In the front center of the workspace, where most people would have put an engraved nameplate, Dial kept a plastic milk crate filled with hanging green folders. It had served as his inbox for years.

He stared at it, wondering what horrors it held today.

Important cases were loaded into the back end of the crate and slowly made their way toward him as he worked through the never-ending stream of information supplied by police forces from around the world. Reports were collected by his division, organized by his secretary and funneled into this murderer's row for his analysis.

He wondered if the Stockholm blast was lurking in the lineup.

He shook his head, realizing that it didn't matter.

Right now, he needed to focus his full attention on the first file.

In his mind, it was the least he could do.

After all, someone had been murdered.

3

Dial had just finished reviewing his second file of the day when Toulon barged into his office without knocking. He slammed the door behind him.

'Nick,' Toulon said – which sounded like "Neek" when the Frenchman tried to say it. 'The early reports were true.'

'Stockholm?' Dial asked, making sure they were on the same page.

'*Oui*. It appears the entire staff was in the building at the time of the explosion. The parking lot was filled with cars.'

'How many dead?' Dial asked.

'At least twenty, probably more. We won't have a solid figure until they have had a chance to sort through the rubble.'

'Any survivors?'

Toulon shook his head. 'Not likely. From what I've heard, nothing could have survived. The place was an inferno. It's still smoldering now.'

Dial nodded in understanding. Fire scenes were the worst. 'Let's get the list of names they put together from the cars. Check the nationalities of everyone involved.'

'*Oui*.'

'And get me a list of our top agents in Sweden. I want to know who we have in Stockholm who can answer our questions.'

'Of course. Anything else?'

'No. That's it for now.'

Toulon nodded, but he didn't leave the room. Instead, he just stood there, staring at Dial as if it would be rude to talk without his permission.

'What is it?' Dial snapped.

'I have yet to determine how this incident hit our radar so quickly. If this happened overnight and they haven't identified a single victim, why were we notified?'

Dial shrugged. It was a good question, one he hadn't considered until that very moment. Based on preliminary reports, he had assumed the case had been brought to his attention because it had met the basic criteria for Interpol's involvement, meaning it was an international incident of some kind. But Toulon was correct: if the explosion had occurred in Stockholm and no borders had been crossed in the commission of the crime, then Dial had no authority in the case.

This was a matter for the Swedish police, not Interpol.

'Start there,' Dial said. He opened the top drawer of his desk and grabbed Toulon's cigarettes. He tossed them back to Henri as if they were a reward for his insight. 'But first, go home and get some sleep. You look like shit.'

Toulon placed the Stockholm file at the back of Dial's inbox and headed for the door. When he opened it, he inadvertently collided with a young man who was attempting to enter. As they stepped back from one another, Toulon bowed and tipped an imaginary cap. 'So good to see you, *mademoiselle*.' Then he pushed by the visitor and continued forward without waiting for a response.

Dial knew Toulon well enough to detect his sarcastic tone.

Then again, Toulon did little to hide the way he felt.

For his part, the young man looked equally disgusted by the encounter. He set his jaw and crumpled his nose, as if his unplanned interaction with Toulon was both the most insulting and the most repugnant thing he could envision.

'Sebastian,' Dial said drily. 'Why are you in my office?'

Sebastian James was the special assistant to the Interpol secretary general. He was the product of some of the world's finest educational institutions, and he had worked his way up through the ranks of Interpol by means of successful politicking, rather than years of field service. Few people could place his nationality, as he spoke several languages without the hint of an accent. He would regularly demean those he considered beneath him in a tongue they couldn't understand – and he considered nearly everyone to be beneath him.

To reinforce his 'holier than thou' demeanor, he was always impeccably dressed. From his Hermès ties to his Bruno Magli shoes, he made every attempt to exude importance. He was angling for Interpol's top post – at least for starters – and everyone knew it.

In short, he was the type of guy that Dial despised.

'You're going to Stockholm,' James announced.

'On whose orders?' Dial demanded.

He knew James didn't have the authority to send him out for coffee, much less a trip to Sweden, and he wanted James to admit it.

'The secretary general,' James clarified. 'He's sending you there . . . *today*. Pack your bags. Your plane leaves in less than two hours.'

Dial leaned back in his chair. 'I think I'll wait to hear from him, if it's all the same to you.'

'He sent me to tell you, and my word is the same as his.'

'Is that so? Does *he* know you feel this way?'

James's face turned bright red. He was about to clarify his

remark, but Dial cut him off before he had a chance. 'What's so important in Stockholm?'

'There was an explosion,' James informed him. 'At least twenty dead. Maybe more. It's all over the morning news.'

'I'm familiar with the incident,' Dial said, thankful that Toulon had brought it to his attention. The last thing he needed was to be briefed by James. He didn't have the time or patience to wade through the asshole's long-winded explanation. 'I'm waiting for the NCB report. I'll have it by the end of the day.'

'You're not getting it,' James countered. 'The secretary wants *your* report by the end of the day. We're not leaving this to the NCB. There's too much at stake.'

Dial didn't flinch. There was nothing about his body language that suggested he had any intention of going. 'Once again I ask: what's so important in Stockholm?'

James realized Dial wasn't going to jump to attention without a full explanation, so he pulled up a chair and sat down. 'It would appear the victims of last night's tragedy represent a multitude of nations from around the world. And I'm not referring to tourists. It seems that several highly respected scientists somehow found their way to the same laboratory in Sweden. We've been fielding calls all morning. Delegates want to know why their countrymen were targeted, and by whom.'

The General Assembly, the controlling body that governed Interpol, was comprised of delegates from every member country, and was responsible for most aspects of Interpol's operation: finances, staffing, agenda, and so on. Its power in the organization was virtually absolute.

Dial nodded in understanding. 'Everyone feels they've lost their best and brightest. That they've been robbed of the next super-genius. Is that it?'

James grinned, relishing his sense of superiority. He might

have been younger than Dial, but right now he knew something that Dial didn't. 'It's almost *nothing* like that. These men and women weren't the fresh-faced new generation of scientific prodigies. They were the old guard. Relics of a bygone era whose research, while once cutting edge, had seemingly reached its inevitable conclusions.'

'Relics, and yet the secretary's phone has been ringing off the hook?'

James nodded. 'They've all had their moment in the sun. They've all furthered the understanding of their respective disciplines. It's simply that nature has run its course, thrusting their once proud achievements into the realm of obscurity, if not complete obsolescence.' He paused, if only to set up his final remark on the subject. 'An ancient vase may be cracked and serve no useful purpose, but it still has some value in a museum.'

Although the last comment bothered him, Dial ignored it. His goal was to get to the heart of the investigation as quickly as possible, if for no other reason than to get James out of his office. 'You said respective discipline*s*, plural. Which scientific fields are in play?'

'A mix of studies – botany, zoology, anthropology, genetics, and so on. You can educate yourself on the plane. You now have . . .' he checked his watch, 'ninety minutes.'

'Tell the secretary I'll be ready in three hours,' Dial countered. He guessed the difference wouldn't upset the secretary general in the slightest, but he knew that delivering the news of a scheduling change would more than ruffle James's finely groomed feathers.

James glared at him. 'I suggest you take that imbecile Toulon with you. You're the only one who tolerates his nonsense. Heaven only knows what havoc he would wreak in your absence.'

Whatever disregard James felt for Dial paled in comparison to the utter contempt he felt for Toulon. He simply could not stand to be near the Frenchman – and interacting with him was entirely out of the question. Ultimately, if Dial took Toulon on the trip, it would be nothing less than a personal favor to James.

'I'll inform the secretary about your adjustment to his schedule,' James said as he stood.

'You do that,' Dial said. 'But before you do, close my door behind you.'

Dial waited for privacy before he stared at the inbox again. At the back of the row was the file Toulon had left for him.

Botanists, zoologists, and many other fields.

What the hell was going on in this lab?

He picked up the phone and dialed a familiar extension. After one ring, he was connected to Toulon's office voicemail.

'Henri, it's Nick. Things just got a lot more interesting. The director wants me in Stockholm to handle the case. While I'm gone, I'm putting you in charge.' He stared at the empty chair across from him and smiled. 'I need you to update Sebastian James on a daily basis.'

Then he grinned wickedly. 'No, scratch that. I'll need you to meet with him *hourly.*'

4

The main focus of Interpol had little to do with the day-to-day investigation of criminal activities. Instead, that responsibility was left to local law enforcement officers (LEOs) in Interpol's member countries. Local LEOs collected the evidence. They arrested the suspects. They also held the trials and carried out any punishment according to local laws.

All in all, a pretty straightforward procedure.

Unless, of course, a case involved multiple countries.

That was when things got messy.

Interpol's primary role was to coordinate the flow of information gathered by the local LEOs and to make it available to member nations. That way, if someone was arrested for assault in Vienna, the Austrian police could quickly check Interpol's database to see if the suspect was wanted for crimes in other parts of the world. If, for instance, he was wanted for murder in Toronto, arrangements could be made to transport him to Canada, where he would stand trial for a more serious charge. At the very least, it might help the Austrian police track down known associates or other details that might help them solve their case.

But sometimes that wasn't enough.

Sometimes the head of a division (Drugs, Counterfeiting, Terrorism, etc.) was brought in when a case involved multiple countries. Possibly to cut through red tape. Or to handle a border dispute. Or to deal with the international media. Dial realized all of these situations were in play, or else the secretary general wouldn't have sent him to Stockholm on such short notice.

Dial reviewed the case file during his flight and confirmed what he had been told earlier. Everyone trapped inside the burning warehouse had been burned beyond recognition. It would take days, possibly weeks, for all the victims to be positively identified by their dental records.

In the meantime, the police were forced to make assumptions about the victims based on the cars found in the warehouse parking lot. The Swedish authorities ran the license plates of the cars and came up with a list of names that read like a United Nations roll call:

Gerwick van Hooseldorf
Kenoshi Yakamura
Viktor Eisen
Stephanie Albright
Juan Carjego
Mustafa Yussaf
Abioye Owusu

And many more . . .

Several phone calls were made to verify the names, but the language barrier between the police and the victims' families had hindered the flow of information. Translators were brought in to help the investigators, but that only seemed to produce more drama than answers. Dial knew from experience that it was something the LEOs should have anticipated. Most people reacted poorly to the death of a loved one, but throw in some uncertainty – we *think* your husband is dead but we're not really sure – and emotions tended to rage out of control.

Within hours of the inferno, the wife of a German scientist

had contacted her embassy. Minutes later, an Interpol delegate from Berlin had been notified of the situation. That sparked a flurry of activity in which other delegates were informed of the tragedy, and the secretary general was roused from his peaceful slumber. To quell the growing uproar and to make sure all the delegates received updates as quickly as possible, the director selected the one man he knew who could keep his cool and handle a tragedy of this magnitude.

Not that it sat well with Dial.

To him, this part of his job was like being a traffic cop. He was told to stand out in the open, a target for everyone, and direct the flow of information in order to prevent collisions. It wasn't exactly what he had envisioned when he accepted the post. In his line of work, the only thing that mattered was *justice* – righting a wrong in the fairest way possible. That was the creed he had lived by as an investigator and the creed he followed as director.

But justice was rare in cases like this.

There were too many moving parts.

*   *   *

Dial stepped out of a taxi at the scene of the crime and was surprised by the setting. He knew the building had been described as a warehouse with a vast laboratory inside, but he had pictured a modernized industrial park on the edge of town, not a picturesque building on the water's edge. The charred walls and broken windows didn't help its curb appeal, but nothing about the exterior gave any indication that scientific research had been conducted inside.

'Chief Dial,' a voice yelled. 'You'll want to see this.'

Dial turned and saw a gray-haired man in thick-soled rubber boots and a dirty poncho waving him over. The weather was warm and dry, so Dial rightly assumed the rain gear was to protect the man's clothes from the ash-filled water that often leaked from ceilings after a major blaze. The fact that this guy knew enough about fires to dress accordingly gave Dial hope. He nodded at him and headed his way.

'Johann Eklund,' the man announced. 'Stockholm police.'

'Nick Dial,' he said as he shook the man's hand. 'Interpol.'

Eklund laughed. 'I know who you are. I've been waiting for your arrival.'

With that, he turned and led Dial to the far side of the building.

Based on Eklund's hair, his walk, and his slightly withered features, Dial concluded that he was well into his fifties, maybe even his sixties. Dial liked to think he was seldom surprised, but this caught him off guard. Not because detective work was a young man's game – he realized that most cops were better in their golden years than they ever were as rookies – he simply had never seen an Interpol NCB agent with this much experience. The hours were long, the paperwork was tedious, and the money wasn't great. Typically, Interpol got five, maybe ten good years from an NCB agent before he or she moved on to something else, but it seemed Eklund had made a career of it.

Dial pointed at the smoldering warehouse as they walked. 'I know everyone's treating this like a homicide, but how can we know for sure?'

'Because the secretary general sent you,' Eklund replied. 'If it wasn't a homicide, I really doubt he would have sent someone of your stature.'

Normally Dial would have ripped into a subordinate agent for such a sarcastic remark, but it was different with Eklund. Dial sensed the Swede was a kindred spirit, someone who fully understood the concept of bureaucratic bullshit, so he let the comment slide.

'That being said,' Eklund continued, 'I suppose I should show you the evidence that led your boss to such an obvious conclusion.'

To avoid the police tape and any members of the media that might be lurking, Eklund led Dial around the far corner of the building to an emergency exit that had been hidden from view. Two local cops flanked the door, their hands tensely gripping assault rifles as if they were expecting an ambush.

Eklund nodded to the men and half introduced Dial. 'Chief Dial, Interpol Homicide.'

The men relaxed, but only slightly.

Eklund led Dial through the door, past emergency stairs that led up into the lobby. He stopped in front of the two elevators along the far wall. 'When the first response team arrived, they conducted a thorough sweep of the area. This elevator was disabled when they got here. They pried the door open looking for survivors. They found this instead.'

Dial noticed three bodies inside, each covered by a police-issue plastic sheet.

'The body on the far left is a security guard. The other two are suspects – *and* victims. We think they might have killed the guard right away and stashed him inside for safe keeping. Like I said, they knocked the elevator out of service so no one would stumble across his body.'

Dial looked at the floor. He didn't see a blood trail from the security desk to the elevator. If the guard was killed outside and then dragged inside, it was done by someone smart enough to make sure that evidence had not been spilled to the ground.

'Depending on how technically savvy they were,' Eklund continued, 'they could have even used this elevator to rig the explosives on the upper floors while it appeared to be out of service. Anyone else that arrived would have simply used the second elevator to get to the lab. We really can't be certain. All we know is that when they were done, someone killed them and left them here to burn.'

'How can you be sure?'

'See for yourself.'

Eklund pulled back the plastic sheets to reveal the bodies underneath. They weren't charred; they were *cooked*. Their skin was swollen and blistered, a result of the fire that had raged a few floors above them. The steel walls of the elevator had served as an oven, baking the bodies in the extreme heat.

It took Dial a moment to look past the gore, but then he saw it: bullet holes in their heads and chests. 'You're right. These men were dead before the fire.'

Eklund nodded. 'The elevator became a chimney, allowing the fire to go up and down the shaft. The outer doors kept the flames from reaching the lobby, but the elevator would have been subjected to unbelievable heat.' He knelt beside the second body. It barely looked human. Using his knife, he peeled back the man's jacket to reveal a diagonal line of polymer draped across his body like a melted sash from a beauty pageant. 'That's nylon.'

Dial glanced toward the floor and spotted a metal fastener with a burned end connected to the same type of melted nylon. He recognized the assembly. 'Was this a sling?'

Eklund nodded. 'Judging from its width, I'd say it was heavy firepower – probably an assault rifle of some kind. If I had to guess, I'd say their original plan went to shit. That's when someone shot them dead and took their guns.'

Dial disagreed. 'Unless their deaths were a part of the original plan. Maybe they were hired thugs who knew too much and were left to burn with all the others. Why risk a second crime scene when you can kill two birds with one stone?'

'Trust me, it's a lot more than two birds.'

'Really?'

Eklund nodded. 'We found an entire zoo.'

5

Normally this section of the laboratory would have been bathed in the soft glow of fluorescent light. Today it was filled with the blinding glare of several halogen lamps. They had been hastily erected by the Swedish police because the overhead lights had burst from the explosion and the extreme rise in temperature. The fire had burned so hot that the fixtures themselves had actually started to melt.

Despite their brightness, the halogen lamps weren't enough to illuminate the entire space. Those who had prepped the scene had little sense of exactly what they should be focused on, so the lamps were randomly scattered throughout the floor and pointed haphazardly in different directions. The dimly lit sections that fell between the lamps only added to the sense of dread, as if every shadow might be concealing the monster responsible for this heinous act.

Eklund reached under his poncho and pulled out two flashlights, one for himself and one for Dial, who wondered what else the Swede might be hiding under there.

'Sir, may I ask you a personal question?'

'That depends,' Dial said. 'Does it involve the case?'

'It does.'

'Then fire away.'

'Are you an animal-lover?'

'I like some, not all. Why do you ask?'

Eklund shined his light toward a series of metal grids that comprised the opposite wall. 'Come see for yourself.'

Dial raised his flashlight and climbed over the rubble that blocked his path. As he did, the acrid stench of seared flesh suddenly became overwhelming, so much so that he was forced to cover his nose and mouth as he examined the first grid. Much to his surprise, it was all that remained of a cage. A thick Lucite plate had once covered it, but that had melted away in the blaze. Inside the box, Dial could see the charred skeletons of dozens of mice.

Eklund sidestepped to the right, his light still focused on the wall.

Dial followed and saw a similar cage. This one contained something bigger. They could have been rats, they could have been hamsters – he could no longer tell. 'Are those squirrels?'

Eklund said nothing. Instead, he stepped back and swept his beam of light down the aisle. Dial could see that the entire wall was lined with cages of progressively larger sizes.

'Fuck me,' he mumbled under his breath.

As they made their way down the row, Dial's stomach churned. The burned remains of rodents gave way to larger mammals. There were cats whose last acts were to paw frantically through the metal grate, dogs whose teeth had become hopelessly lodged in the mesh as they tried to gnaw their way out of their enclosures, and primates who had died clinging to the heavy bars that separated them from their captors.

All had been reduced to little more than blackened skeletons.

Dial couldn't help but feel for these animals. It was a sense of sorrow mixed with rage and confusion. They were defenseless, and he knew their deaths had been painful. He wanted answers as to what they had been used for. Why were they even there? And who was responsible for their demise?

'Where are the scientists?' he asked.

Eklund led Dial up some stairs and into a maze of

overturned lab tables and scorched equipment. Stone and glass crunched underfoot. In the center of the back wall of the laboratory there was a section of the room that was deeper in width than the main floor, as if the concrete walls had been specifically laid to create two thirds of a room. What remained of the fourth wall – the wall that separated the room from the rest of the laboratory – was badly scorched.

'We have no idea how many people worked in the lab, but so far we have found more than twenty. Most were gathered here.'

Eklund pointed his light toward the rear of the room, his nostrils flaring as he tried to stave off the pungent scent of roasted flesh. His years as a homicide detective had prepared him for many things, but not something like this. Despite the scent, he stood steadfast, as if turning away in disgust would dishonor those who had died.

Unprepared for sights and smells, the first cops on the scene had vomited in the middle of the floor – and who could blame them? The scene was horrific. Like a protective father, Eklund straddled the spot where the young officers had purged, preventing Dial from accidentally stepping in it and further contaminating the crime scene.

In truth, a pool of vomit was the least of Dial's concerns.

He turned a halogen spotlight from the main floor and pointed it into the room, adding to the single lamp that had already been placed inside. He saw bodies piled against the farthest wall, and in an instant, he knew exactly what had happened there.

After the blast, those trapped on this floor had backed away to avoid the heat. As the fire swept through the laboratory, they huddled against the back wall – the farthest they could run from the flames. In the growing inferno, they covered their exposed skin with clothing or anything else they could find, including each other, hoping to shield themselves from the intensely radiating fire.

Dial grimaced and thought back to the wall of cages.

Down there, the fire had washed over the animals, incinerating their fur and flesh and leaving only their bones. Horrible as their deaths were, the animals were the lucky ones. The flames would have engulfed them quickly, and their suffering would have been short and merciful.

In here, it was far worse. It wasn't the explosion, or the smoke, or the fire itself that had killed the humans; it was the heat. These unfortunate souls were literally roasted alive. Every fluid in their bodies – their eyes, their blood, the moisture in their lungs – would have slowly begun to boil. Their tissues would have broken down, causing intense bleeding from the eyes, ears and nose, and eventually their organs. Each breath would have grown more agonizing until they could breathe no more.

In a fire, nerve endings are burned away quickly. The pain is severe, but it is fleeting.

In a slow burn, the victim feels every agonizing moment. Only death brings relief.

Dial stared at the shriveled remains of the scientists. They looked like they had undergone a badly executed mummification – or worse. A few looked like meat that had been left on the grill for too long.

'I want to know everything. What was the ignition source? What was the accelerant? Did this go down as planned, or did a small fire get out of hand?'

Eklund motioned skyward, to where the ceiling once was.

Now it was nothing but a gaping hole.

'Best as we can tell, it started up there. They knocked out the upper two floors with a charge and let everything come crashing down. Whatever survived the blast and the falling debris was destroyed by the fire.'

'And the accelerant?'

Eklund shrugged. 'Possibly acetone, but we won't know for sure until we run some tests.'

'How long will that take?'

'Probably a day or two.'

'Screw that. We can find out right now.'

Eklund furrowed his brow, wondering how they would accomplish that feat in the blackened lab. He hoped it didn't involve a taste test of any kind. Although he wanted to impress Dial, there was no way he could lick a corpse without vomiting.

'How?'

Dial pointed at Eklund's poncho. 'Do you have a UV light under your skirt?'

Eklund nodded and pulled a small ultraviolet light from his utility belt. It was often used to detect blood spatter at crime scenes. He handed the device to Dial, who asked one of the cops to turn off the nearest halogen lamps.

The room quickly grew dark.

'I learned this trick at Quantico,' Dial said as he turned on the penlight. As if by magic, the rubble around them started to glow like the flowers in *Avatar*. 'Acetone fluoresces in the right conditions. One of them is ultraviolet light.'

Eklund stared with amazement. 'I'll be damned.'

'Based on this, I'd say that your theory is correct. They blew the upper floors, and the acetone fell from above like a waterfall. It burns *really* hot, so there was no need to bring in gasoline or any other accelerants.'

'They used the lab against itself.'

'Exactly.'

Dial hated to admit it, but he was impressed with the planning. He had seen a lot of creative ways to kill, but this was really ingenious. 'Run a history of every scientist working here. I mean a *full* history. I want to know what their specialties were, where they went to school, what they did in their personal lives, all of it. Find out who might be targeting them.'

'Already on it,' Eklund assured him.

'Good,' Dial said as he glanced around the grisly room. 'I get the sense these bastards aren't done killing yet. The sooner we get to them, the better.'

6

Duquesne Heights
Pittsburgh, PA

When Mattias Sahlberg first arrived in America, he had every intention of settling in one of the few communities in Pittsburgh with a recognized – albeit small – Swedish population. Friends who were familiar with the city's ethnic composition had suggested Homestead, Munhall or Braddock: all Monongahela riverfront communities east of the city. There he had hoped to find a pocket of his countrymen, people he could turn to if he ever felt homesick or craved Swedish delicacies like *köttbullar* (meatballs) or *inlagd sill* (pickled herring).

But his new employer had other ideas.

They wanted him to focus on his research.

To encourage his loyalty and to reward his talents, they bought Sahlberg a nice house in the hillside community of Duquesne Heights. With sweeping views of Pittsburgh's skyline, its three rivers and dozens of bridges, the house was far more expensive than anything he could have afforded on his own. Having grown up in squalor, he jumped at the chance to live there, even though he was the first and only Swede in the neighborhood.

Not that it really mattered.

Once he'd settled in, he realized that Pittsburgh was an exceptionally friendly city, filled with immigrants who had left their war-torn countries for steady employment in the steel mills and, more importantly, a chance to pursue the American dream. Before long, he had made dozens of friends from around the world, most of whom had thick accents and calloused hands and a burning desire to give their children a better life than they'd ever had. And even though he had none of those things – thanks to his first-rate education, his job in academia, and his relative youth – he felt comfortable with those that did.

So much so that he had lived there for nearly six decades.

Sahlberg's day started as it almost always did. After a restless night, he rose late to a tangle of sweaty sheets. The noonday sun was waging war against his air conditioner and was temporarily winning the battle. He adjusted his thermostat and waited for the ageing compressor to fight back. A few seconds later, he felt the rush of cold air on his face as he combed his hair and brushed his teeth. It reminded him of the winter winds that used to seep through the thin walls in his childhood home in Sweden.

Sahlberg headed to his kitchen, where he made a sandwich and poured himself a glass of iced tea before carrying both to the living room table, where he would eat his lunch while surfing the web. It was all part of his daily routine. First he looked at the weather. Then he checked the headlines on several scientific websites. There were a few tidbits about the Human Genome Project, but nothing that really kept his interest.

Finally he turned his attention to his homeland.

Sahlberg had come to embrace modern technology in a way that few others of his generation had. Much of that acceptance had come through his work, but it had trickled down to other aspects of his life as well. He carried an iPhone. He owned an iPad. More importantly, he knew how to use both. He streamed music through his computer, downloaded movies frequently, and even kept a hard-to-find folder on his hard drive labeled ANATOMICAL STUDY – only the images had less to do with physiology and more to do with naked bodies in motion.

But his favorite technological advancement was his ability to peruse Swedish newspapers the instant they were published. He would read everything from sports to obituaries to the latest social gossip. He always started at the website for the *Dagens Nyheter*, one of Stockholm's two daily newspapers, and then followed links from there.

The incident at the laboratory was front-page news.

He gasped when he saw the headline.

According to the article, a devastating fire had swept through a warehouse, destroying a lab and killing everyone inside. Strangely, no one was sure why the staff had been working so late or what type of lab it was. The article explained that it had no apparent affiliation with any pharmaceutical company or biological research facility in the country, but they hoped the ongoing investigation would eventually make a connection. Police were unwilling to release an official body count, but they confirmed that more than twenty victims had been found so far.

Sahlberg was saddened by the news.

Even though he did not know the purpose of this particular lab, the death of any scientist in Stockholm was sure to affect him personally. Sahlberg had never married, but a tragedy at a facility in his hometown was nearly certain to involve someone from his other family – his *scientific* family. He was sure he would soon learn that someone in the fire had either worked for him or with him, or was associated with someone who would fit into one of those categories. The research community was surprisingly close-knit, despite its worldwide distribution.

He immediately checked his email. He was searching for any first-hand information from his colleagues back home. All he saw were standard messages from the various mailing lists he subscribed to. He breathed a momentary sigh of relief. Unfortunately, the feeling was short-lived. He knew it was far too early to assume that no news was good news, so he went back to his browser and searched for more details.

Stockholm's other major newspaper, *Svenska Dagbladet*, echoed the details from the other report, with one notable addition: an unnamed source in the fire department said that the scene had the look and feel of a controlled burn, intentionally contained to this specific building.

Sahlberg's mind raced with questions.

The scientists were murdered? By whom?

For what possible reason?

No longer in the mood to eat, he decided to walk off the growing tension in his shoulders with a quick lap around his neighborhood. He figured the exercise in the warm summer air would do him some good.

Despite his advanced age, Sahlberg didn't need any assistance to get around. He still walked with the brisk stride of a man in his early thirties. Maybe even his twenties. Whatever the case, he was far more nimble than anyone his age had a right to be. When people asked him for his secret, he always smiled and answered truthfully: genetics.

As an expert in that field, he knew it to be true.

Strolling past the rows of homes that dotted his street, he thought back to the first few years after his arrival. Back then, the community was mostly Germanic. He couldn't walk more than a few feet from his house before being overcome with the smell of curing sausages or fresh-baked streusel. God, he loved that smell. At least on the days when the air wasn't heavy with the soot from the area's mills.

Today the air was clean, but the only smell he could detect was the faint waft of garbage that had cooked too long inside the neighborhood's waste cans. It was trash day, and he could hear the hum and whirl of the garbage truck from two streets away. Sahlberg smiled, knowing that the odor would be gone by the time he returned.

He walked away from the river, where the houses gave way to apartments and condominium complexes. He stopped briefly at one of the neighborhood's small parks. It wasn't that he needed the rest – even in the heat he had yet to break a sweat. Instead, it was the class of preschoolers who had invaded the playground that had caught his eye. He watched for a while as they played. They chased each other everywhere, an endless cycle of constant motion as they climbed up the jungle gym and slid down the slide. Up the stairs and down the slide. Over and over again. Kid after kid after kid. As they did, they laughed and giggled without a care in the world.

How refreshing, Sahlberg thought.

Nothing worries them at all.

They have no fear of the future.

Suddenly he was struck by the dichotomy of the last hour: the joy of these children and the lives they had in front of them versus the horror of the lab fire and the lives of his peers cut needlessly short. His physical tension was gone, but his anger and curiosity remained. So much so that he decided to head back home to search for answers.

As he rounded the street corner nearest his house, he noticed something peculiar. A delivery truck was parked at his curb, and two men in jumpsuit uniforms were walking toward his front porch. The first man approached empty-handed, followed by a man carrying a large package. But when they arrived at the door, they didn't knock or ring the bell. Instead, they peered through the slit windows on either side of the door as if they were casing the joint.

Sahlberg slowed to a halt. The sight of two strangers on his front porch – either of whom could have delivered a package on his own – tripped an alarm in his mind. Something about this didn't seem right. With his heart pounding in his chest, he ducked behind a row of hedges to see what they did next.

The first man picked the lock on the front door while the second man concealed the crime with the large box in his hands. As soon as the door was open, he placed the package on the porch and pulled a pistol from his jumpsuit. He waited for his partner to draw his own weapon before the two of them slipped inside the house.

Sahlberg gasped at the sight.

Who were these men? What did they want with him?

Less than a minute later, they reappeared in the doorway. The first man shook his head toward the delivery truck and pointed left. Then he pointed to himself and motioned right. As they hustled from Sahlberg's house, two more men stepped from the truck. They were dressed in suits and had shoulder holsters.

Until that moment, Sahlberg hadn't even known they were there.

Now he knew they were after him.

Sahlberg had to act fast. He cut through his neighbor's yard and retreated to the relative safety of a nearby market. He knew it wasn't perfect, but at least he wasn't by himself.

'Mr Matty, how are you!' shouted the twenty-something behind the counter. Sahlberg had known the young man since he was a child, back when *Mattias* had been too difficult for the boy to pronounce. He had been Mr Matty ever since.

'I'm fine,' he lied. 'Except I seem to have left my cell phone at home. Would you mind terribly if I made a call? Local, of course.'

'No problem at all,' the young man said as he handed Sahlberg a cordless phone. 'Help yourself.'

Sahlberg grabbed the phone and stepped away from the counter so he would not be overheard. Then he dialed a number from memory. At a time like this, there was only one person he thought he could trust. He only hoped the stranger would listen.

The call was connected on the second ring.

'Please don't hang up,' Sahlberg pleaded. 'Someone is trying to kill me.'

7

Payne Industries Building
Pittsburgh, PA

During his highly decorated military career, Jonathon Payne had survived gunfire, terrorists, and several forms of torture, but none of that compared to the nails-on-a-chalkboard agony he suffered whenever his board of directors gathered for their quarterly meetings.

For a man of action, it was cruel and unusual punishment.

Borderline inhumane.

If given the choice, Payne would rather rappel down the side of the building in a blizzard while completely naked than listen to a bunch of geezers in custom-tailored suits drone on and on about his company's debt-to-equity ratio, its market capitalization, or whatever the hell they were talking about, because the truth was he had stopped listening an hour ago. If not for the love and respect he felt for his grandfather – a self-made millionaire who had risen from steelworker to mill owner before willing the company to his grandson – Payne never would have left the military to take over as CEO of Payne Industries.

What did he know about the business world?

A lot less than anyone else in this room.

And yet he was technically running a multinational corporation when all he wanted to do was run back to the life he had trained for, the life he had chosen for himself.

The one where he made a difference.

A graduate of the United States Naval Academy, Payne had excelled in all aspects of his training but was particularly adept at leadership and hand-to-hand combat. He was such a skilled officer he was asked to lead a newly formed special forces unit known as the MANIACs, an elite counterinsurgency team comprised of the top soldiers the Marines, Army, Navy, Intelligence, Air Force and Coast Guard could find – hence the acronym. Whether it was unconventional warfare, personnel recovery or counter-guerrilla sabotage, the MANIACs were the best of the best and Payne was the alpha dog – the unquestioned leader of the military's top team.

Now he was little more than a figurehead.

An insider who wanted out.

He glanced down the mahogany conference table and surveyed his board of directors. They were arguing about something he didn't understand. His eyes shifted to the chestnut-lined walls and intricately carved molding. He noted the state-of-the-art audiovisual system of plasma screens and 3D projectors. Everything was first class. The best that money could buy. He leaned back into the soft leather of his executive chair and wondered how much the company had paid for it and all the others chairs that were spaced around the table.

Probably several thousand each.

But that paled in comparison to the building itself.

It was an architectural marvel, a sparkling tower of glass and steel.

Located atop Mount Washington, high above the city of Pittsburgh, the Payne Industries building had a magnificent view of the city's skyline, its two sports stadiums (PNC Park and Heinz Field), and the confluence of Pittsburgh's three rivers (the Monongahela and Allegheny flowing together to form the Ohio). If the motorized shades in the conference room had been up, Payne would have gladly spent the entire morning staring at the scenery below. Unfortunately, the shades were down to protect the company's secrets from telephoto cameras, radio-controlled drones and laser-guided listening devices.

Payne realized the precautions probably weren't necessary. After all, he was *inside* the room and he wasn't even listening. He couldn't imagine why an outsider would want to eavesdrop. Unless, of course, they had insomnia.

Payne sighed from boredom and tapped his fingers on the yellow legal pad on the table in front of him. He knew he should probably be taking notes like those bickering around him, but the message he was tempted to write would have had major repercussions:

I quit.
Sincerely,
Jonathon Payne

Those closest to Payne knew he had been considering this option for several years. They also knew he would have left the company long ago if not for the debt he felt he owed his grandfather. After all, this was the man who had raised Jon after the death of his parents. The man who had taught him right from wrong and the value of hard work. The man who had given him the keys to the kingdom because he wanted him to live longer than his parents had, something that probably wouldn't have happened if Jon had stayed in the special forces.

Eventually, the risks he took would have caught up with him. He knew it. His grandfather knew it. Everyone knew it.

Then again, what good was life if you weren't doing what you loved?

Before Payne could ponder that question, he was distracted by the conversation in the conference room. He only heard the tail end of the statement – something about the declining reputation of Payne Industries – but it was enough to warrant his attention.

'Can you repeat that? What about our reputation?' he asked.

A short, squat man with an absurdly large head cleared his throat. 'Our reputation has been suffering in recent years. It simply isn't what it used to be.'

The room fell silent, waiting for Payne's reaction.

'How so, Sam?' he asked without a hint of ire.

Samuel McCormick was one of the board's longest-serving members. He was a carryover from the final years of Payne's grandfather. A company historian of sorts.

'This company was founded on established industry. Yes, we made the manufacturing of steel safer and more efficient, but we didn't try to reinvent the wheel. Today we've diversified into technologies undreamed of in the early years. Robotics. Artificial intelligence. Nanotech. We're on the cutting edge of emerging sciences.'

'And you think we've overstepped our bounds?' Payne asked.

'Not at all,' McCormick replied. 'I'm all for these advancements. But there are those who believe that our eagerness to uncover the next big thing is hurting our bottom line.'

'In other words, we can make more money *selling* wheels than reinventing them. Is that what you're trying to say?'

McCormick nodded. 'Again, it's not me that's saying it. It's *them*.'

'*Them?* Who is *them*? The public? The press? Our competition?'

'Me for one,' said Peter Archibald, who was seated directly across from McCormick. 'We have a responsibility to our shareholders, to our employees. We can't meander into flights of fancy just to explore the science. We make things that people need. And for that service, we are able to employ many thousands of people around the world. You start banking on things that people *might* want, and suddenly you're playing with lives. What if we keep expanding into these fringe areas and nothing pays off? What then?'

Then our stock dips three points, Payne thought to himself.

In the Fortune 500 world in which these men operated, the risk of unpopular products and unproductive facilities was 'playing with lives'. Of course, that was nothing like his former career, where lives truly were in jeopardy.

Still, he hated the thought of possible layoffs.

As he weighed the arguments, everyone in the room turned their attention toward him. They could discuss the merits of both sides for days, but it would be fruitless to decide the preferred course of action among themselves if he had no plans to endorse their decision.

'Jonathon,' McCormick said gently, 'your thoughts?'

As if on cue, the double doors of the conference room swung open and Payne's elderly secretary shuffled into the room. In her left hand she carried Payne's personal cell phone, which she had confiscated when he had first arrived to prevent him from playing *Angry Birds* during the meeting. In her right, she held a slip of paper.

She handed both to Payne without saying a word.

Payne read the note and instantly snapped to attention. 'Gentlemen, I need to take this. We'll have to continue this discussion at a later time.' He rose from his chair and headed for his office. The secretary followed, closing the double doors of the conference room behind her. His board of directors was left to stare across the table at each other.

It wasn't the first time he had excused himself.

And it wouldn't be the last.

At least this time he had a valid reason.

In his mind, the name of the caller was merely a formality, since Payne could count on one hand the number of people who had his personal number. If someone from that list needed his immediate attention, he was going to take the call regardless of what it interrupted. He was a loyal person, who valued his friends and his country above all else.

However, this situation was different. Not only was Payne unfamiliar with the name on the note, but the caller had stressed that his life was in danger. Normally his secretary would have dismissed the whole thing as a prank, but there was something about the urgency in the caller's voice that led her to believe that he was telling the truth.

'Hello,' Payne said as he headed toward his office. 'This is Jon.'

'I know this is going to sound terribly odd – I realize that – but I need you to trust me. My name is Mattias Sahlberg. I worked with your father for many years.'

'You have my attention,' Payne replied.

'Your father spoke of you often. He never doubted that you would someday grow into the man that you are now. He always said you were special.'

'I appreciate the compliment, but I'm not sure—'

'Jonathon, I need your help. I'm being followed. Four armed men broke into my home, and now they're searching the streets, trying to locate me.'

'Where are you?'

Sahlberg ignored the question. 'Meet me at the upper end of the Monongahela Incline in twenty minutes. Can I trust you to do that?'

'Sir, if you're in some sort of trouble, I can send the police.'

'No police. Neither of us wants that.'

'Neither of whom? You and me, or is someone else with you?'

'Please. The incline. Twenty minutes.' Sahlberg looked down at his clothing. 'I'm wearing khaki pants and a blue shirt. Please, I need your help.'

A second later, the phone went dead.

Payne sat down at his desk and entered Sahlberg's name into a program on his office computer. His company employed tens of thousands of people worldwide, in more than forty countries. This program could instantly list any and all employees, where they worked, and their entire histories with Payne Industries.

A few seconds passed before he got a result.

ZERO MATCHES.

He broadened his search to include all employees, past and present. He also tried different spellings of Sahlberg's name, just in case. But the result didn't change.

ZERO MATCHES.

Payne growled at his screen. Given what he was seeing, he didn't know what to make of Sahlberg's claim. The system had been designed by Randy Raskin, a trusted friend who also happened to be the Pentagon's top computer genius. If *his* program said that no one by the name of Mattias Sahlberg had ever worked for Payne Industries, he knew it was true.

And yet . . .

Payne pushed back from his desk and raced to the

conference room. The board was still there, still challenging each other on the best course for the company's future. Payne ducked inside and interrupted the debate. 'Sam, can I have a word with you?'

'Can it wait? We're right in the mid—'

'Now, Sam.'

The request put McCormick in a tough position. He didn't want to be seen as Payne's lackey, at his beck and call – especially not in front of the entire board. However, he trusted the CEO's judgment. He knew Payne didn't care for the politicking in their board meetings but always respected the process. Excusing himself to take a phone call was one thing, but Payne had never asked anyone else to step away from the room. At least until now.

His curiosity piqued, McCormick nodded his agreement.

'Excuse me,' he said as he stood. 'We'll make this as quick as possible. Please, carry on.' He followed Payne into the hallway and closed the door behind him.

'Can they do any damage in there?' Payne asked, only half joking.

'To each other, maybe,' McCormick answered, 'but they can't *vote* on anything. Not with the two of us out here.'

'Good. Because this might take a while.'

8

McCormick's office was on the same floor as the conference room. Payne entered first, followed by the flustered senior executive. Unsure of Payne's intentions, McCormick closed the door for privacy then hustled to his seat behind his desk. Payne pulled a chair close. He sat down and leaned even closer, as if he were about to deliver a hushed threat, a whisper so that no one else could hear what he was about to say.

McCormick's face turned red and he started to sweat.

'Jonathon,' he said defensively, 'I thought we were of the same mind on this. Ultimately, there is nothing to gain by treading water. We *must* continue to push our research in new directions. Otherwise, this company will become stagnant!'

'Relax,' Payne said in a calming tone. 'We're on the same page.'

'We are?'

'We are.'

McCormick breathed a sigh of relief. 'Then what did you need?'

'You've been an executive here longer than anyone, myself included. How much do you know about my father's involvement with the company?'

'Not much. No more than what I've seen in the files. His name pops up every now and then when I'm running through the background on this project or that, but it's never anything noteworthy.' McCormick thought better of his last remark. 'I didn't mean that in the negative sense. I meant no disrespect.

Your father was a brilliant man. He truly was. What I meant to say is that there's nothing out of the ordinary.'

'Ever heard of a man named Mattias Sahlberg?'

'The name rings a bell, but I don't know why. Who is he?'

'He claims to be a former employee who worked with my father. But I can't find any record of him in our system.'

'If he's a former employee, he might not be in the system.'

Now it was Payne's turn to be confused. 'I was told it covered everyone, even after they left the company. That's not correct?'

'It is, and it isn't. It covers everyone who was hired after 1970. If they worked for us before that, their records haven't been digitized yet.'

'But do we have their records?'

'We do. In fact, *I* do.' McCormick spun his chair to face a wall of file cabinets. He patted his hand against the nearest drawer. 'They're all in here.'

'Great. See if you have a file for him.'

McCormick stood, opened the drawer, and then flipped through the alphabetical files. 'What was that name again?'

'Mattias Sahlberg.'

'S . . . SA . . . Here it is!' McCormick opened the folder to make sure it contained the paperwork they were looking for before he handed it to Payne. 'It seems kind of thin.'

Payne had seen hundreds of employee files. They typically included the applicant's initial résumé, health records, performance reviews, and tax documents. They were *usually* a complete, comprehensive history of the employee's entire time at Payne Industries.

Mattias Sahlberg's file contained only two pages.

The first page was a copy of his work visa. It listed his full name and birth date, his Swedish personal identification number – the equivalent of the United States' social security number – and his home address in Sweden.

The second page was his contract of employment with Payne Industries. Curiously, it listed a salary that was well above that of other researchers employed at the time. But what interested Payne even more was that his position was simply listed as 'Research and Development', and that it was Jon's father's signature on the contract, not his grandfather's. The revelation should not have been surprising – after all, it was his father that had initially steered Payne Industries into the area of emerging technologies – but it had been years since Payne had seen his father's handwriting.

'That's really not much to go on,' McCormick said as Payne showed him the contents of the file. 'It's odd that his records have never been updated.'

'It's enough for now,' Payne said.

So far, everything Sahlberg had told him on the phone had been true. He was a former employee of Payne Industries, and it did appear that he had worked with Payne's father. If Sahlberg was being honest about everything else, it meant he really was in fear of his life.

Payne checked his watch. Sahlberg would be waiting for him at the Monongahela Incline in less than ten minutes.

If he hurried, he just might make it.

*   *   *

Nowadays, the Monongahela Incline is equal parts commuter railway and tourist attraction – like the cable cars in San Francisco or the streetcars in New Orleans.

But it wasn't always this way.

When the steel industry took hold of western Pennsylvania, the lands near the riverbanks were the prime locations to establish the steel mills. The access to the waterway allowed

49

supplies such as iron and coal to be shipped in on large barges. The steel produced by these mills could likewise be transported via the rivers to finishing plants that crafted the steel into girders, coils, or other needed forms, as well as cargo ships in larger ports.

The manpower that operated these factories lived high above the water's edge on the bluffs that overlooked the rivers. In order to safely and efficiently traverse the hillside – the typical commute involved worn roads or footpaths that zigzagged to the mills below – German immigrants proposed the concept of an incline, based on the *sielbahns* of their homeland. But instead of traveling from peak to peak over treacherous terrain, these cable cars simply went up and down the hillside.

The Monongahela Incline was completed in 1870, and was a godsend for the weary workers. Its two enclosed passenger cars served as counterbalances on a continuous loop of cable. As one car traveled down the slope, its weight helped pull the other toward the top of the hill. Its primary purpose was to shuttle the mill workers between their hilltop neighborhoods and the factories below. It wasn't glamorous – the soot and dirt from the workers fell from their faces, clothing and boots, creating an ever-present layer of filth – but it was spectacularly efficient. What used to take hours if the weather was poor now took only minutes in any conditions.

The incline system was such a rousing success that at one time the city of Pittsburgh had seventeen of them in operation. The Monongahela Incline was so proficient at moving people up and down the hillside that a separate system was built directly alongside it in 1883 to accommodate larger items. The Monongahela Freight Incline ran on a track that was ten feet wide instead of five. Rather than enclosed cars, it used covered platforms that could carry pallets, crates and even vehicles between the upper and lower stations.

Despite their prominence in the late 1800s and early 1900s, only two Pittsburgh area inclines remained in service today. The Monongahela Incline, the steepest and oldest in America, rose 370 feet above the river below. To cover this elevation, its tracks ran only 635 feet in length, resulting in a noticeably steep thirty-five-degree slope – and spectacular views.

Sahlberg couldn't possibly remember how many times he had traveled up and down the hillside on the incline. Ten thousand? Twenty thousand? It wasn't an unreasonable guess. He had lived above the city and commuted into it for over sixty years, and while he occasionally drove himself to work, he actually preferred public transportation because it gave him time to think.

During all those trips, he had never worried about what might happen to him once he stepped aboard the cable car. Not once. Not even for a second.

Today that streak would end.

9

Omar Masseri was furious.

After retiring from the Egyptian army, he had made quite a name for himself as a mercenary/assassin/bounty-hunter. If it involved money and guns, he was willing to listen. Over the past decade, he had tracked and killed guerrillas for kidnap and ransom companies in South America, he had found deadbeat gamblers for the crime lords in Hong Kong, and he had shot two Mafia informers in the witness protection program.

He could find anyone . . . for the right price.

And yet, an eighty-year-old man had managed to elude him.

How could that possibly happen?

On the surface, his assignment could not have been simpler. He had been given a complement of additional soldiers – presumably mercenaries like him, though he had never met them before that day – an SUV full of weapons, and a state-of-the-art tracking system. Their goal was to capture an elderly scientist named Mattias Sahlberg and to seize any work materials at his house, preferably without being noticed.

The delivery truck had been Masseri's idea. It was a gambit he had used before, one that had been highly effective in the past. People got packages all the time. The United States Postal Service, United Parcel Service, Federal Express and several other companies used box trucks to route their packages. Their appearance was so commonplace that people rarely gave them – or their employees – a second glance.

Cops had been known to stop suspicious vehicles out of curiosity.

He had never known them to arbitrarily stop deliveries.

Unfortunately, he hadn't counted on Sahlberg's departure. Masseri had been warned that the video surveillance of the neighborhood had a 'slight' data lag while being streamed to his phone. In actuality, that delay was fourteen minutes long. He had expected to find Sahlberg inside the house because that was where he had appeared on the satellite image, but by the time Masseri and his team had arrived, Sahlberg had left for his walk and hadn't returned.

Facing a tight deadline, Masseri was forced to alter their plans. The delivery truck was parked on a side street. The deliverymen changed from overalls into business suits before they jumped into two SUVs. The uniforms had helped them blend into the background at Sahlberg's house, but they would do the opposite if they had to chase him on foot. A man in a suit was just another white-collar worker on his way to a meeting. If necessary, they could even pose as detectives if anyone witnessed Sahlberg's capture. It would be much harder to convince a bystander that the old man was being detained for insufficient postage.

Masseri had scouted the area in advance of his mission. For him, it was a habit as common as brushing his teeth at night. After calculating the length of the satellite delay by tracking his own movements, he returned his focus to his target. From the looks of things, Sahlberg was headed toward the Monongahela Incline, which would give him access to the city below.

If that happened, Masseri's job would be much harder.

He rushed to prevent that from happening.

* * *

Sahlberg had been waiting inside the doors of the incline's upper station for several minutes. The small area to the left of the ticket booth was hardly a lobby, but it did provide shelter from the elements for the passengers awaiting the next cable car – though he only used it when it was raining or cold enough to see his breath. In the summer, he preferred to stand outside in the warmth until the arriving passengers had exited, then he would duck inside and find a seat.

Today, he was grateful that he could see people on the street before they could see him. It gave him a minute's warning before he would have to face the men from his house or explain himself to Payne.

Unfortunately, it was his pursuers who arrived first.

Sahlberg saw the black SUV as it crept along Grandview Avenue. Its slow, deliberate speed was the first indication that something was wrong. The driver was looking for something . . . or someone. When the SUV inched past the station and rounded the sharp bend near the incline, he felt a glimmer of hope that he was mistaken. His feeling was crushed when the SUV pulled to the curb and two men exited.

Sahlberg recognized them both.

They were the men who had entered his home.

Thinking fast, he turned toward the ticket counter to see who was working that day. He was pleased to see a familiar face smiling back at him.

'Darla, my sweetheart, I didn't notice it was you.'

'Well, you would have if you weren't so preoccupied with that window.' She eyed him curiously, her smile still beaming. 'What'choo lookin' at anyhow?'

'I'm supposed to meet a lady friend of mine,' he lied, not wanting to reveal the true nature of the threat, 'and I—'

'Is she younger than you?' Darla pried.

'She'd have to be, wouldn't she? Any older and she'd be dead.'

Darla burst out laughing, so hard she almost fell off her stool.

'Anyway,' he continued, 'I'm supposed to meet her here, but I think I just spotted her husband's car outside. Needless to say, I'm slightly concerned.'

'You horny old dog,' she said with affection. 'I should be disgusted by your cheating, but I'm glad to hear that a man your age still has some lead in his pencil.'

'Excuse me?'

'Some blood in your bone. Some pop in your tart.' She stood and unlocked the door to the ticket booth. 'There's an office in back. I'll let you know when the coast is clear.'

Sahlberg thanked her profusely as he made his way through the booth. Darla closed the door and turned back toward the ticket counter just as Masseri and his partner entered the station.

Masseri scanned left, then right. The space was small, with nowhere to hide. He approached the ticket booth and pressed a picture against the glass. 'Have you seen this man?'

Darla pretended to study the picture for a moment, even going so far as to adjust her glasses for a better look. All the while, it was clear the man in the photo was Sahlberg. 'Yeah, he looks familiar. He walked by about ten minutes ago. Headed down toward the city.'

'Two tickets,' Masseri demanded. He slid his money under the Plexiglas that separated him from Darla. In return, she handed him two passes and his change.

'Enjoy the ride,' she said as Masseri and his partner made their way toward the waiting cable car. A minute later, they were on their way to the lower station.

Sahlberg watched it all unfold on the small video monitors in the office. From there, he could see the outside of the upper station, the ticket booth, the cable car entryway, and the exit at the lower station. All were covered by closed-circuit video cameras. After the cable car left the upper station, Darla knocked on the door. He opened it sheepishly, not completely sure how to explain his actions, but nevertheless thankful for what she had done.

'Honey,' she said, 'you need to get yourself a new girlfriend, because her husband looked as angry as Ike Turner.'

*   *   *

Payne sprinted the two blocks from his building to the Monongahela Incline, but he was still behind schedule for his meeting with Sahlberg. The last thing he wanted was to miss this opportunity. If Sahlberg had already left, he would have to wait for him to make contact again . . . *if* he made contact again. Who knew when that would happen?

Payne slowed to a jog as he approached the station, hoping to spot the older man. In many ways, the physical exertion helped to control the adrenalin he had been fighting since he had left McCormick's office. It wasn't just the excitement of meeting someone who had known his father – although that certainly had piqued his interest – it was the possibility of danger.

The rush was something he missed.

It made him feel alive.

10

As he neared the entrance to the incline's upper station, Payne passed two men in business suits who immediately grabbed his attention. They weren't doing anything out of the ordinary, and yet he noticed a few minor details that most people would miss.

The first thing was their positioning. They were standing next to a platform that looked over the city and the river below, yet they were facing in the opposite direction. This might have been understandable if they were waiting for a bus or trying to hail a cab, but they were focused on the front of the station, not the traffic on Grandview Avenue.

Next was their posture. Both men were rigid and alert, as if they were standing at attention on guard duty. They kept their heads raised and backs straight as they subtly scanned the area – like hungry wolves looking for prey.

The last and most important thing was their clothes. Those gave the duo away. Though their linen suits were appropriate for the season, they didn't drape as well as wool. Given his background, it was easy for Payne to spot the telltale bulges of shoulder holsters.

Both of these men were armed.

Payne's suspicions were confirmed as he made his way to the entrance. He was close enough to overhear a snippet of their conversation. It was more than damning.

'Is this our backup?' the first man asked.

'No,' the second man replied. 'He's sending four guys, not one.'

'All of this for an old man?'

*　　*　　*

Masseri was finished with the cat-and-mouse approach. He had a cadre of personnel at his disposal, and it was time to use it. Why hunt with only two pairs of dogs when he could unleash the whole pack?

He ordered four more men to the incline's upper station. Once they arrived, the two men already in position had instructions to join Masseri in the lower station. He also put a third team on standby. They were to wait in a separate SUV – fully armed – until Masseri could give them Sahlberg's location. Once his whereabouts were known, all three teams would spring into action. With several men in pursuit, Masseri knew it was only a matter of time before they caught up to their target.

Masseri stared at the delayed satellite feed on his phone.

He watched as the image of Sahlberg entered the upper station.

They were getting closer.

*　　*　　*

Payne burst through the station's door like a late commuter rushing to catch his train. The first thing he saw was Darla. She had a half-terrified, half-exhilarated look on her face. Before she could react further, Payne was already standing at her ticket booth.

Her heartbeat pounded, as she wondered what else this day might bring.

'I'm looking for my neighbor,' Payne lied. 'Mid eighties, wearing a blue shirt and khaki pants. He wandered away from home, and we're worried sick. Any chance you've seen him?'

'Your neighbor?' she challenged. She looked Payne up and down. He seemed awfully familiar, but she couldn't quite place him. 'Um, let me think . . .'

Payne sensed she was stalling. 'I know you don't know me, but if you could just point me in the right direction, you'd be helping us out more than you know.'

Before she could respond to Payne's plea, Sahlberg emerged from the back room. He had been watching the front entrance on the monitors. He smiled at Payne, grateful that he had finally arrived. 'Allow me to introduce you. Darla, this is my neighbor, Jonathon.'

'Jon is fine. Nice to meet you, Darla.'

She turned her back to Payne and focused on Sahlberg instead. 'What's really going on? Are you sure you're all right?'

He patted her on her shoulder as he exited the booth. 'I appreciate all you've done, my dear, but I believe we can take it from here.'

Darla shrugged and nodded.

'To your car, then?' Sahlberg asked Payne.

'We can't,' Payne whispered. 'First of all, I didn't drive. Secondly, there are two men looking for you outside with four more on the way. We have to go down.'

'There are two men waiting for me at the lower station.'

'You're sure?'

'I'm positive. They followed me here from my house. I managed to hide in the back in the nick of time. Darla told them I continued down the incline, and they believed her. They took the last car.' Sahlberg paused. 'Jonathon, both men were armed.'

'So are the men outside – with four more on the way. I suck at math, but I'll take two over six any day of the week. Better odds.'

61

Payne reached into his pocket and pulled out his wallet.

'No need,' Darla said with a smile. 'You're good.'

'Thank you,' Sahlberg replied.

Payne nodded his thanks and made a mental note to send Darla some flowers and a box of chocolates. Heck, if she could somehow keep the six men stranded up here while he dealt with matters below, he would buy her a whole candy store, but he knew that was too much to ask.

Besides, she had done enough for their cause.

Payne led Sahlberg down the small flight of stairs to the loading area, where the next car was waiting. Three doors were standing open in the oddly shaped cars.

Rather than a simple rectangle that would restrict the view of some passengers, the unique tiered design of the incline cars created three viewing areas. The cars might look a bit strange in transit – like three steps in an escalator – but the design gave all the passengers a magnificent view without the need to look past, over, or through the other riders.

Each separate tier had its own door that opened on to two rows of bench seating. These benches were on opposite walls of the compartment, so that passengers sat facing one another. Inside the car, the tiers were separated only by a small railing and a steep ledge.

Payne and Sahlberg stepped into the top compartment.

There were only three other passengers on board. A couple in their fifties sat on the bench directly below them in the middle section of the car. Across from them, a teenager had spread out on the entire bench with his back to the city. Two small cords sprouted from his ears, and he drummed furiously on his backpack as the music from his headphones buzzed faintly throughout the cabin. His eyes closed, he was oblivious to the world around him.

Sahlberg took a seat against the far wall, opposite the doorway.

Payne instinctively sat in the middle of the bench, where he could survey the entire car. Taking advantage of the moment, he pulled out his cell phone and fired off a quick text to his best friend, who was already in the city:

911. MEET AT MON. INCLINE LOWER STATION. GAME ON.

It meant to come fully armed, ready for battle.

Things were about to get messy.

Just before the cabin doors closed, two more passengers jumped aboard the incline – the two men Payne had passed on the street. They sat in the empty lower level, with their backs turned to the passengers above. Payne cursed his luck. So far, they hadn't noticed Sahlberg tucked into the corner of the upper compartment, but the journey down the hill was just starting.

For the next three minutes, they would be locked together in a moving box.

With nowhere to run. Nowhere to hide.

David Jones had faced death on every continent and in every condition imaginable. He had been shot in the mountains of Afghanistan, stabbed in the Bolivian rainforest, and left for dead in the desert grasslands of the Gobi. He had endured pain that would cripple a battalion of lesser men, but he kept going back for more because it was his job, his duty, his calling.

He was a MANIAC. A warrior. A killing machine.

One of the baddest motherfuckers on earth.

And yet he had a weakness. A major weakness.

David Jones was scared of the dentist.

Make that *petrified.*

Years of soda and sugary treats had left him with more than a few cavities. Couple that with his high tolerance of pain, and he would often let things fester for weeks until he was unable to eat. To him, each filling in his mouth was a battle scar. Each represented another time he had survived the horrors of dentistry. The excruciating bright lights. The sadistic tools. The tortuously small paper cups. Just thinking about it made his heart beat faster.

'You have nothing to worry about,' the technician assured him as she lowered the chair into position. From his medical history, she knew that Jones was a graduate of the Air Force Academy. 'Just try to relax. Think about flying one of your airplanes. Just floating through the sky.'

Screw that, he thought to himself. *I'd rather be in a fighter jet. At least you can pull the ripcord in an F-16 and eject!*

'Deep breaths,' she said calmly. 'It'll all be over soon.'

What'll be over soon? My life?

'Relax. I'm just going to kill the pain with a shot of Novocain, then the doctor will be in to drill the tooth and fill the cavity. Kill, drill and fill, as we like to say.'

Did she just say 'kill'?

What kind of bedside manner is that?

She tilted the chair all the way back and sat next to Jones's head. She looked down at him – albeit upside down – as she spread a cloth bib across his chest. Then she prepped the syringe that would be used to anesthetize the affected area.

Jones could only see her eyes – the rest of her face was hidden behind a surgical mask – but they were a remarkable shade of green. Somehow the color gave Jones a deep sense of calm . . . until he saw her tap the syringe. Then her eyes grew dark, and cold, and sinister. Suddenly she was a beast and he was her victim.

He was half tempted to bite her hand to defend himself, but she was too quick. He felt the pinch of her needle as it pierced his gum. A moment later, the slow burn of anesthetic started to spread throughout his mouth. He felt the poison take hold.

'There,' she announced. 'All done with the first step. That wasn't so bad, was it? The drug will take a few minutes to take full effect. We'll be back then to finish the job.'

He groaned in anticipation.

She looked down at him, concerned. 'Are you okay?'

'Do I *look* okay?'

'Not really. You look kind of pale.'

'*Pale?* You think I look *pale?* What kind of bullshit is that? Never call a black man *pale!* Look in the damn mirror – you're the one who's *pale!*'

66

She stood there stunned, unsure how to respond.

Jones quickly realized his mistake. He knew he had over-reacted. 'Sorry, I didn't mean to snap at you. I really didn't.' He took a deep breath and tried to calm down. 'I swear, I'm normally not like this. You're catching me at my absolute worst.'

She nodded and backed away.

'Seriously, I didn't mean it. You're the perfect amount of pale.'

She ignored his comment. 'Oh, one more thing. Try to keep your mouth closed. The anesthetic is going to numb your mouth and the lower half of your face. The last thing we want is for you to accidentally bite through your tongue. I've seen it happen many times. Boy, is it messy! You wouldn't believe the blood. We'd have to bring in a mop to clean it all up.'

With that, she closed the door behind her.

It was her way of getting even.

Most patients would have freaked out over the thought of blood, but not Jones. He had spilled enough over the years to become immune. Too bad the same didn't apply to power tools, because the thought of a high-speed drill in his mouth made him nauseous.

'Calmm dowwn,' he said to himself, his words suddenly slurred by the Novocain. 'Whaatt the fuckk?'

He poked his lips with his finger. They were already growing numb. He slipped his finger inside his mouth and pressed down on his tongue. Strangely, his finger could feel his tongue, but his tongue didn't feel the finger. He moved it around, trying to illicit even the slightest sense of touch. There was nothing. It felt like a dead fish in his mouth.

Just then his cell phone started to vibrate.

He was so unnerved, he nearly bit his finger in two.

'Shiiitttt!' he screamed as he yanked the damaged digit from his mouth. It took a moment to wipe the saliva on his bib and pull the cell phone from his pocket. Once he did, he read the text message from Payne.

911. MEET AT MON. INCLINE LOWER STATION. GAME ON.

'Gaamme onn?' he mumbled. 'Thannkk Godd!'

A jolt of adrenalin shot through his body, as if his nerves were on fire. His best friend was in danger and needed his help. Nothing, absolutely nothing, would keep Jones from coming to his aid – especially if it meant getting out of a root canal.

He leapt from the dental chair, grabbed the tray of tools that was blocking his path, and flung it against the wall. They clattered to the floor as he bolted from the examination room and hurried down the hallway toward the reception desk.

'Mr Jones!' the technician shouted. 'You can't leave yet!'

'I hawf to go! We'll hawf to rethedual.'

'But we're not done!'

Jones ignored the comment, completely focused on his escape. He threw open the next door with so much force that it crashed against the wall and ricocheted back against his face. If not for the Novocain, he would have felt his bottom lip splitting against his teeth. For the time being, it was merely a minor inconvenience as blood poured from his mouth.

'Sonnoffabitchh!'

He pushed the door open again, this time with a lot less force, stepped over the threshold and found himself in the waiting room, surrounded by several frazzled patients. He tried to assure them that everything was okay, but a spray of blood and several incoherent words did more damage than good.

'Mr Jones!' the dentist yelled from behind. 'I know you're wary of the drill, but trust me, the hard part is over.'

Jones ignored him and ran outside like a condemned man

fleeing the gallows. Never in his life had he been more thankful to get a life-or-death text from a friend.

Back in the waiting room, a hush fell as everyone wondered what they had just witnessed. A madman on the loose, or a procedure gone wrong?

The dentist smiled to reassure them. 'Okay, who's next?'

Not a single patient moved.

12

Three minutes.

That was how long it would take the incline to reach the lower station.

Three agonizing minutes.

It wasn't a lot of time in the grand scheme of things, but Payne knew it was an eternity in close-quarters combat. And that was what he would be facing if the two men turned around and spotted Sahlberg in the upper level of the car.

At least, that was what he *thought* he would be facing.

For the time being, he had no way of knowing if Sahlberg was telling the truth. Sure, he had been able to verify that the old man was a former employee of Payne Industries who had worked for his father, but that was only part of the story. Sahlberg also claimed that these men had broken into his house and meant to do him harm. But Payne had no way of knowing if that was true.

The thought had crossed his mind that these men might actually be the good guys. After all, what did he really know about Sahlberg? Regardless of his former employment, there was no guarantee that he hadn't turned to a life of crime. Maybe that was why his employment file was so thin. Maybe his paperwork had been shredded to protect the company. Sahlberg might simply be using his connection to the company to pull Payne to his aid.

What a disaster that would be.

If Payne helped a wanted fugitive, the impact of his actions would be severe. He didn't like the prospect of a jail cell. Even worse, he hated the thought of negative publicity for his grandfather's company. Abetting a criminal would not go over well at the next board meeting.

Nevertheless, Payne's gut told him that he was on the side of right. If these men were detectives or federal agents, they could have invaded Sahlberg's house in the dead of night, catching him while he slept. Even if they had been forced to act immediately, without the chance to wait until the wee hours of the morning, he could not understand the need for secrecy.

Why pretend to be deliverymen?

Why not just storm the house?

Sahlberg wouldn't stand a chance against a SWAT team.

Still, even if Payne's intuition was correct, he knew it was a risk to attack the men now. If something went wrong, the only escape routes were treacherous: climbing the steep tracks to one of the stations or jumping from the incline entirely. It was several feet to the hillside below, with little more than shrubbery and rocks to break the fall. Even if they survived the drop – and Payne had to assume Sahlberg wouldn't survive uninjured – they would be easy targets.

Payne didn't like his options. He truly didn't. But if the two men in the lower station had called in reinforcements, there was a good chance he was heading into a hornets' nest. And if that was the case, he preferred to squash two of the insects now. He knew the maneuver was risky, but he decided to use the only tactical advantage he had: the element of surprise.

He calmly reached under his jacket and withdrew the pistol he had tucked in the small of his back. Sahlberg stared at him, unsure of what would happen next.

Payne pressed the gun into Sahlberg's hand. 'Do you know how to use it?'

Sahlberg gripped the weapon. 'Yes.'

'Good. If this goes to hell, protect yourself. Understood?'

'Yes,' Sahlberg whispered. 'But what about you?'

Payne handed Sahlberg his cell phone. 'If anything happens to me, call the first entry in the speed dial. Tell him what happened. He'll know what to do.'

With that, Payne removed his jacket and stepped toward the opposite bench. The middle-aged couple were gabbing in the level below him, and the teenager was still in a world of his own, his eyes closed and his head bobbing as he beat out the rhythm of his music on his backpack.

Payne climbed on to the bench and eyed his targets on the bottom level. His muscular physique strained against his fitted shirt. Silhouetted against the sunlight and the city below, he looked like a gargoyle preparing to swoop down upon its prey.

A moment later, he was airborne.

Payne launched himself over the passengers in the middle section and landed between the gunmen with a thud. The car lurched slightly and the woman screamed. Before his targets knew what was happening, he struck both men in the head with his elbows. His goal was to knock them out before they could pull their weapons.

It didn't work.

His elbows landed hard, but they didn't have the desired effect. Instead of knocking them out, he transformed his targets into the skilled soldiers they were.

Though dazed by the blow, the larger of the two men flailed wildly at Payne, hoping his counterpunch would find its mark. He missed, and Payne was able to lock on to his forearm as he stumbled into his follow-through.

Payne twisted his grasp and bore down with all his might. He hadn't been able to drop the man with a single punch, but now he hoped to disable him. A few seconds more, and the bones in the gunman's forearm would splinter and snap. Unfortunately, Payne didn't have that much time.

The second mercenary wasn't about to take on Payne with his fists. Not when he had a Beretta 92 under his jacket. In a flash, he reached for his weapon.

Sensing what was happening, Payne spun the man in the arm-bar toward his colleague, using him to knock the pistol from his partner's hand. The weapon fell to the ground, but not before the mercenary had managed to get off a shot.

The bullet tore through the larger man's hand like a spike at a crucifixion, cutting through the soft flesh and tendons with ease. Blood squirted as he shrieked in agony.

The thunderous blast of the gun snapped the teenager out of his daze. He sat upright as if he had been hit by an electric current. The scene would have terrified most people. The middle-aged man in the second tier was using his body to shield his wife from the gunfight below. She continued to scream at the top of her lungs as shock and terror overwhelmed her. But the teenager's reaction was different. To him, it was as if he had awoken inside his favorite video game. His eyes lit up, and he actually squealed with delight as the larger mercenary stared through the hole in his bloody hand.

It looked like a scene from a horror movie.

The gaping wound made the large man even more enraged. He charged recklessly toward Payne, who countered the move by jumping on to the bench and delivering a knee to his opponent's chest. The blow had the dual effect of dropping the larger soldier on top of the smaller one and at the same time dislodging his weapon from his holster. Both fell to the ground, the larger man pinning his partner beneath him.

But the larger man was unrelenting. He couldn't rise, but

he had the presence of mind to grab the nearest pistol. He smiled as he aimed it squarely at Payne's chest.

Payne had nowhere to run – and he knew it.

The gunman pulled the trigger, but nothing happened.

He tried it a second time, still nothing.

The mercenary glanced at the gun and realized his mistake. Each of the thug's weapons had been fitted with a palm-print reader on the grip. This biometric safety prevented anyone but the authorized user of the gun from firing it. In his haste, he had reached for the first weapon he saw and had grabbed the wrong one. In his hand, his partner's gun was basically just a hunk of steel. He threw it at Payne's face, hoping to do some damage.

Payne ducked just in time.

Unarmed and one-handed, the thug was at Payne's mercy. Payne grabbed him by his suit collar and slammed him into the far wall. The glass cracked from the impact. A moment later, he swung his elbow into the man's throat, crushing his windpipe. Suddenly unable to breathe, the thug slumped to the floor as blood poured from his nose and mouth.

The smaller man realized he'd be next if he didn't act fast. He dove to the ground and grabbed both weapons just as Payne spun to face him. The gunman didn't know which gun was his, but it didn't matter. If he squeezed both triggers, he knew *one* would fire.

Payne saw everything in slow motion.

The guns. The gunman. The triggers.

Ka-boom! A shot thundered in the cable car, but he didn't see a muzzle flare. Instead, the front window exploded into a thousand shards as a bullet cut through the glass.

Payne instantly recognized the sound of his own gun. He didn't have to look to know that Sahlberg had pulled the trigger.

But the mercenary had no idea who had fired the shot. As he glanced to find the shooter, he took his eyes off Payne for a split second.

It was a reaction he couldn't control.

An instinct that cost him the fight.

Before the gunman could re-aim, Payne lowered his shoulder and exploded from his stance. Years of American football had taught him how to turn his body into a battering ram. The impact was violent. He lifted the mercenary off the ground and kept his legs churning forward until the man slammed into the wall. He felt ribs breaking in the man's chest.

The mercenary fell limp against the wall.

As the world sped up to real time, Payne turned toward the upper level of the car. Sahlberg was standing at the edge of the railing, Payne's gun shaking in his hand.

The room was moving forward but also still.

There was no more violence.

No more gunshots.

The only sound was the wind.

'Everyone okay?' Payne asked.

'We're all right,' the husband answered.

Sahlberg nodded. So did the woman.

Only then did the teenager react, leaping to his feet with so much vigor that Sahlberg momentarily pointed the gun his way. He pumped his fist several times and screamed at the top of his lungs, 'That . . . was . . . AWESOME!'

13

Payne checked the fallen gunmen for signs of life. Both were breathing, but the larger one was in bad shape. He would need medical attention to survive the day.

But it wouldn't come from Payne.

Not with Sahlberg's life still in jeopardy.

Payne searched their pockets for identification. He found nothing useful. It was further proof that Sahlberg had been telling the truth. Almost everyone in law enforcement – local police, FBI, ATF and so on – carried a badge or some sort of ID. But Payne only found cash. No wallets. No credit cards. No personal items. These guys didn't want to be identified.

He took a moment to examine their high-tech pistols. The palm-print scanners were almost perfectly integrated. The only thing that gave them away was a slight thickening of the grip and a noticeable change in texture. The scanner was smooth and shimmery; the rest of the grip was pebbled and dull. He had seen biometric locks before, but nothing like this. Even the prototypes he had used in the military were clunky and cumbersome.

But not these.

These were streamlined and sophisticated.

They were damn near perfect.

Payne glanced through the shattered window and saw the lower station getting closer. He had less than a minute before they reached the bottom. He had to work fast.

He looked up at the couple in the second tier. 'Ma'am, I'm going to need the strap from your purse.'

She nodded nervously and threw the purse to him.

'Sorry about this.' He ripped off the strap before he tossed the purse back to her. He shifted his gaze to the teenager. 'Same with you. Throw me your backpack.'

The teen tossed his bag without hesitation. Payne removed the bungee cord that held the bag closed and used it to tie the larger gunman's hands to the bench. He did the same to the smaller thug using the strap from the purse. He knew the knots wouldn't hold for ever, but it was better than nothing.

'Listen to me,' he said to the passengers. 'Everything's going to be fine, but I need you to stay in here with these two until the police arrive. There are more gunmen in the station, so it's safer in here than there. Understood?'

'Yes,' the husband replied.

'Good. Do you have a cell phone?'

'Yes.'

'Call 911 and tell them there's been a shooting on the Monongahela Incline. Tell them you need the police and multiple ambulances. You don't need to explain anything else or identify anyone. Just make sure these two are taken into custody. Okay?'

'Okay,' the husband said.

Payne ran through the best-case scenario in his head. The couple would call 911, and the police would arrive inside of ten minutes. That gave him enough time to get Sahlberg clear of the lower station. He knew they would have to speak with the authorities eventually – and he wouldn't mind being there for the interrogation of the two men tied up in the cable car – but he had questions of his own that had to be answered first.

'What about me?' the teenager shouted. 'What can I do?'

Payne stared at the young man. He was practically bouncing up and down with excitement. It was clear the kid was relishing this. 'Did you enjoy the fight?'

'Hell, yeah! That was some *Call of Duty: Black Ops* shit!'

'Do you want to learn how to fight like me?'

'Fuck, yeah!'

'Then quit playing video games and join the navy.'

* * *

The lower station was a two-and-a-half-story building sitting at the foot of Mount Washington, across the street from the Station Square shopping complex. Made of brick and painted auburn, it had a peaked roof with a turquoise spire and was designed to capture the feel of the old-time train stations of the past century. The structure might have looked spacious from the outside, but its appearance was deceiving. The back half of the building was used to shelter the two loading bays from the elements, and the rest was little more than a waiting area, a set of two staircases that led to the cable cars, and a second floor with a few small offices.

Other than that, it was mostly storage space.

On a busy weekend or during rush hour there would have been a line of people waiting for their chance to board at the lower station. There would have been little time, if any, for Payne and Sahlberg to make their way to the exit before panic set in and all hell broke loose. Thankfully, today Payne could only see five people waiting.

The doors opened, and he led Sahlberg down the staircase toward the main exit. He scanned the station for any signs of the gunmen from the previous trip. He hadn't seen their faces, but Sahlberg had described them in detail. Furthermore, Payne knew they would be watching the passengers as they passed through the station. Seeing only tourists in shorts and sandals, he felt confident they weren't walking into an ambush.

'Follow me closely,' he said to Sahlberg.

They moved steadily toward the front exit, walking past the five tourists who strolled toward the cable car. He was tempted to warn them about the wreckage inside, but what could he possibly say? *I just beat the shit out of two men in the lower level, so unless you want to get blood on your shoes, you might want to find a seat in the upper section.*

He knew a warning like that was just as likely to cause panic as the scene itself, so he put his head down and kept moving, hoping to make it outside before anyone noticed.

But he wasn't quick enough.

The instant Payne opened the front door, a scream emerged from the loading platform behind him. It was a blood-curdling wail that echoed through the building and blared out into the street. At a time when Payne was trying to avoid attention, the scream might as well have been a siren imploring everyone within range to take notice.

Thankfully, the only people nearby were across the street.

Unfortunately, it was Masseri and a hired thug.

Payne instantly knew it was them. Not only because they were dressed like the two men he had knocked unconscious, but because the goon raised his pistol and opened fire.

That made things pretty obvious.

Payne dove back inside the building, knocking Sahlberg to the floor for his protection. The old man landed hard on his right hip, but a few seconds later he was back on his feet and ready to run for cover. Meanwhile, Payne darted across the lobby and grabbed a heavy iron bench from the waiting area. He dragged it across the tiled floor and shoved it against the front entrance. It wasn't perfect, but the improvised barricade would at least slow their pursuers. Then he turned from the door and sprinted up the steps toward the cable car, urging the five tourists to get in the car with the teenager and the married couple. They'd be safer riding up the hill than hanging out in the lobby, which would soon resemble a shooting gallery.

Sahlberg, however, was the exception.

He would be safer with Payne.

As the tourists crowded into the incline, Payne crouched low on the stairs, pulling his pistol and facing the doorway below. From this vantage point he was protected by the geometry of the door and the stairwell: the men would have to be on their knees if they wanted to shoot him, such was the line of sight between the doorway and his position. The drawback was that Payne couldn't get a clear shot at the men if they tried to enter; he would only be able to see their feet as they came toward the stairs.

The moment the door swung open and a leg stepped into view, Payne took aim. He waited for the intruder to step over the toppled bench, then fired once. His bullet found its mark, shattering the goon's shin like a porcelain doll.

He immediately fell to the floor.

Writhing in agony, the man tried to locate the son-of-a-bitch who had shot him in the leg, but it was all for naught: he spotted Payne just in time to see him pull his trigger again. The resulting shot hit the man in his face, popping his skull open like a piñata. But instead of candy, it showered Masseri's shoes with bits of bone and clumps of grey matter.

Payne hoped that shot would deliver a message.

If you want to live, you better leave now.

You don't know who you're messing with.

14

If the numbers had been even, Masseri might have reconsidered his tactics against an accurate shooter like Payne, but due to the seemingly unlimited supply of men and weapons at his disposal, he decided to escalate the attack on the Monongahela Incline.

The black sedan roared down the opposite side of the street from the station, as if it were approaching a pit row. Masseri backed away as the car accelerated toward the curb in front of him. At the very last second the driver slammed on the brakes and the wheels squealed in protest. Three men dressed in suits jumped out of the vehicle. With their buzz cuts and stern demeanors, all three looked like soldiers from central casting.

These weren't men who dealt in subtlety.

They were here for a battle.

Despite stopping on the side of a busy road, the driver opened the trunk of the sedan to reveal their arsenal: shotguns, rifles, grenades, rockets and even a flamethrower. If they couldn't draw Sahlberg out, they could sure as hell bring the building – or all of Mount Washington – crashing down on top of him. Too bad they needed him alive, or they could really have fun.

'The old man's inside,' Masseri announced. 'He picked up a bodyguard along the way. So far he has taken out three men by himself. The guy is a crack shot.'

The driver considered the situation. 'Let's gas 'em out.'

His two associates nodded in agreement. They dug into the trunk and emerged with an armful of weapons including a modified grenade launcher that could fire multiple canisters of pepper spray using a rotary magazine. The police commonly used this type of 'riot gun' to disperse crowds. These men would use it to flush out their target.

Masseri stared at the three soldiers, who were wired and ready for action. 'Remember: we need the old man *alive*. The bodyguard you can kill. Anyone else, use your discretion.'

The men smiled. There would be no discretion.

Wasting no time, the driver launched three tear-gas cartridges through the first-floor windows. A moment later, the cartridges detonated and noxious smoke began to fill the building.

Now all they had to do was wait.

*　*　*

Payne recognized the odor immediately. He knew everyone in the building would be choking and wheezing as soon as the gas made its way into their lungs.

'Cover your nose and mouth,' he ordered as the passengers began to panic.

The entire group – minus Sahlberg and the teenager – crowded into the upper tier of the car. They all wanted to put as much distance as they could between themselves and the tied-up men in the lowest level. The teenager sat alone in the middle section, brazenly taking pictures of the fiasco with his cell phone.

Sahlberg stayed in the stairwell with Payne, who waved his arms in front of the closed-circuit video camera, hoping someone would see him in the control booth at the upper station. After a few frantic gestures to get their attention, Payne pointed up the hillside. The doors instantly closed, and before long the cable car was leaving the station toward Mount Washington above.

That left only Payne and Sahlberg in the lower station.

'Now what?' Sahlberg asked.

Payne tore off his sleeve and held it up to Sahlberg's face. 'Breathe shallow, and keep your eyes shut as much as possible. And whatever you do, don't panic. That's when you suck in the most gas.'

'What about you?'

'I've been through so many drills over the years, I'm practically immune to this shit. Stay with me, and you'll be fine.'

Then he took Sahlberg by the arm and led him up a narrow passageway to the storage area above the lobby. The air was better up there, but it wouldn't stay that way for long.

*   *   *

'You, to the left,' the driver demanded as he motioned for one of the other men to take position along the left-hand wall of the building. 'You, to the right.'

The men scurried in opposite directions, leaving Masseri and the driver to guard the front of the station.

Masseri knew the tear gas would force Sahlberg to flee the building, but he was worried that it would take too long. The actions of his team – the gunfire, the broken glass, the rising gas billowing from the windows – were sure to attract attention. It was only a matter of time before the police arrived to investigate. If the old man didn't appear soon, he would order the men to go inside and drag him out.

Masseri watched as the two soldiers flanking the building crept along the painted brick wall, searching for any sign of Sahlberg or his bodyguard. Suddenly, the man on the left crumpled to the ground as a plume of pink mist erupted from the top of his head.

*   *   *

The shot from above was almost too easy. The man had stopped directly underneath the second-floor window that Payne had opened to get some fresh air.

If he had looked up, he might have seen Payne.

But he didn't, so now he was dead.

Payne smiled and hustled to the front of the building. He peeked through the window and confirmed what he already knew: the reinforcements had arrived.

He took aim and fired again as the enemy retaliated.

*　*　*

Masseri watched as another soldier dropped to the ground.

Four shots, three kills, he thought.

Who the hell is this guy?

Suddenly, the parameters of the mission had changed. Whoever was protecting Sahlberg was much more than a bodyguard. For each of his team's moves, the guardian knew how to counter. It had taken the horrors of war for Masseri to develop these abilities, and he wondered if the shooter inside had survived similar atrocities.

'Fall back,' Masseri ordered.

'We can take him!' the driver argued.

'Collect their weapons and leave,' Masseri demanded. He didn't care about the bodies. These soldiers were expendable fodder that couldn't be traced back to him. The next-generation pistols, however, were a rare technology used by only a few manufacturers. It would take some digging, but a thorough investigation into the source of the equipment might lead back to him. Even worse, it might lead back to his boss.

Masseri feared few things in life.

His employer was one of them.

He slowly backed away, leaving the driver to retrieve

the weapons from his dead colleagues before the police arrived.

*   *   *

Jones rounded the corner and spotted smoke drifting out of the lower station. The building seemed to ooze as tear gas found every crack in the windows and every bullet hole through the siding. He wondered if Payne was trapped somewhere inside.

Then he noticed the driver. He had scrambled from the side of the building and was halfway across the street. Jones had seen soldiers from around the globe, but few carried the sheer number of weapons this man did. He was holding a pistol in each hand. An Uzi dangled from a strap across his chest, bouncing against a bandolier of rocket-propelled grenades. The launcher itself was slung around his back.

Despite the numbness in his lower face, Jones recognized the enemy when he saw him. Even if he hadn't been a trained operative, he had watched enough movies to know that a man with that much firepower on a city street was up to no good.

Their eyes locked, and the other man reacted. Jones accelerated just as the man opened fire. Bullets shattered the windshield and hit the grill of the SUV as Jones ducked for cover. But he never took his foot off the gas.

Frozen in a fit of rage, the driver of the sedan never stood a chance. Jones's SUV slammed into him at more than fifty miles per hour, instantly shattering most of the bones in his body. His chest and face exploded as the impact whiplashed him into the hood of the truck. Blood and gore splattered over the front half of the SUV.

The instant he heard the thump, Jones tramped on the brakes. The sudden stop launched the assassin – well, most of the assassin – through the air as if he had been shot from a catapult. He landed several feet in front of the vehicle, just as Jones stole a peek over the dashboard.

The bastard was definitely dead.

Jones tried to smile in victory.

When he did, drool leaked from his mouth.

*   *   *

Masseri watched events unfold before he calmly walked toward the nearby shopping complex. Once inside, he would disappear into the crowd.

But he would return soon.

*   *   *

Payne had watched the incident from his position on the second floor. He had glanced out the window just as the gleaming white SUV had slammed into the gunman.

He hoped his best friend had survived unscathed.

Less than a minute later, he and Sahlberg emerged from the haze and hurried over to Jones, who was crouched next to the victim, searching for an ID.

Payne saw the blood on Jones's shirt. 'Are you okay?'

Jones nodded.

'What happened? Were you hit?'

Jones shook his head, still silent.

'DJ, look at me. Is that your blood?'

Jones nodded a second time.

'Where'd it come from?'

Embarrassed by the injury from the dentist's office, Jones decided to lie. 'I bitt mmyy lipp whenn I hitt thaa bastarrd!'

15

It was just after 11 p.m. when Henri Toulon returned to the parking garage at Interpol headquarters in Lyon. Technically, his shift didn't begin until midnight, but Toulon was typically on his second pot of coffee by then. It wasn't a lack of things to do that brought him in so early; it was the fact that he actually enjoyed his job. Or at least he did most nights.

Tonight would be one of the exceptions.

Toulon could deal with death. It was a prerequisite for the homicide division. Any new employee who couldn't stomach the incessant barrage of victims would file for a transfer before the end of his first week. Sometimes the end of his first day. Toulon had seen it happen to several promising detectives. Some people simply weren't built for this kind of work. But he was.

Of course, Toulon was used to seeing *people* in the homicide case files. Over the years, he had become desensitized to human-on-human crime, but tonight he would be forced to study something different: the charred remains of several species.

The thought sickened him.

He opened the Stockholm file on his computer to review the latest, scrolling past the preliminary report and scanning the details that had been added while he was asleep. Several phrases caught his attention. *Unknown explosive compound. Barrels of acetone. Probable remote detonation.* And yet the item that intrigued him most was merely a footnote in the file: the

Swedish police had been unable to produce the name of the property's owner.

How was that possible?

They should have been able to find a name from a simple search of the tax records or the registry of local land deeds, but so far they had come up empty. Toulon knew that if he found the name of the owner before the Swedish police did, it would be a huge help to Dial in the field – which, in turn, might be enough to make up for the indiscretion that had landed him on the graveyard shift to begin with, plus a few more that Dial hadn't found out about.

At least not yet.

Toulon poured himself another cup of coffee and cracked his knuckles. There was work to be done. But first he needed to make a phone call. He smiled as the phone on the other end of the connection rang once . . . twice . . . a third time. He checked his watch: 11.47 p.m.

Finally, someone answered. He did not sound happy.

'Good evening, Sebastian!' Toulon announced spryly. 'Time for your hourly update!'

*   *   *

Eklund rolled his neck as he rode the elevator, trying to stave off the tension in his shoulders before it developed into a headache. It had been another long day in a career filled with long days. He thought back to the time before he was a cop and wondered if he had made the right decision all those years ago.

He had grown up in one of the poorest sections of Gothenburg, on the western coast of Sweden. His upbringing had been 'uneventful' in his words, though it was often described as 'deprived' by others. Both his mother and his father worked

90

hard just to put food on the table and keep a roof over their heads. Holidays meant working only single shifts. They had little, but they wanted for less. Extravagances such as a family car were so far removed from possibility that they were never considered. They had each other, and that was enough to make them happy.

His teachers thought Eklund was destined for great things in college because of his high marks at school, but he never enrolled. The simple truth was that he had yet to find any course of study that interested him. Instead, he had taken the only job that appealed to him after graduation. He became a longshoreman in Gothenburg Harbor.

More than forty million metric tons of freight passed through the harbor each year, making it the largest seaport in Scandinavia. As such, there was always a need for laborers. It was backbreaking work for minimal pay, and Eklund had no sooner started the job before he was reconsidering his decision. It took him more than three years, but he finally found a reason to quit.

During his third year as a longshoreman, he was working alongside a young Swede by the name of Gustav Vaso. It was quite early, well before dawn, and Vaso had been working straight through since Wednesday night, trying to earn a few extra dollars to buy a gift for his mother's birthday. Fighting through the yawns and heavy eyelids, he had failed to secure a dock line properly to its mooring. When the wind shifted and the ship was pushed away from the dock, the heavy line had broken free and snapped back toward the ship, the tension causing it to crack like a bullwhip. Vaso had been caught in its path. The impact of the speeding rope had split his side like a sword. Blood and entrails had gushed from the gaping wound and flooded the dock with gore. Eklund and others had rushed to his aid, but there was nothing they could do. Vaso had bled out within minutes.

Later, Eklund loaded the body into the coroner's van. Then he rode with the body on its way to the morgue. He even made the call to notify Vaso's family.

He performed these tasks because Gustav was his best friend.

It was his first glimpse of death, and the experience had changed him. He realized that fate could take a life at any time, and he wanted his efforts to mean more than they did now. If his death was unavoidable, the least he could do was to help people before his time was up. He had walked from his friend's funeral to the nearest police station. Two weeks later, he enrolled in the Swedish National Police Academy.

Eklund had been an exemplary cadet who had made quite an impression on the academy's top brass. For his first assignment, he had been selected for service in the National Task Force, a tactical unit known to accept only the best of the best. An elite SWAT team, the National Task Force dealt exclusively with high-risk situations such as kidnappings, hostage negotiation and acts of terrorism. It was during this time that Eklund first started to make a name for himself among his colleagues. He was seen as tenacious, a guy who didn't understand the concept of failure. He also had no qualms about putting his life on the line when the time came. Some even went as far as to say that he had a death wish.

Those closest to him understood the truth.

He respected death; he simply didn't fear it.

Unfortunately for Eklund, rappeling from helicopters and storming drug dens was a younger man's game, and his years quickly got the better of him. Looking to use his tenacity to its best advantage, his superiors placed him in the International Police Cooperation Division of the National Bureau of Investigation. His duty was to coordinate border issues such as witness protection and criminal intelligence between the Swedish National Police Board and Sweden's neighboring countries. He was also charged with assisting local authorities in their cooperative efforts, which included operational control when necessary.

He excelled at his job, and when Interpol requested names to consider for the post of National Central Bureau agent, Eklund was at the top of the list.

Technically speaking, Dial had been his boss for several years.

But they had never met before this case.

16

Because of the gunfire and the smoke that was oozing from the lower station, 911 operators notified the police department, the fire department and the city ambulance division. All three groups of emergency responders converged on the scene to find a scarred historic landmark, a bloodstained SUV, a sedan carrying enough firepower to outfit a small army, several gunshot victims, and a mutilated body lying dead in the street. The three primary witnesses were a muscular man who was missing a sleeve, an elderly Swede who was struggling to catch his breath, and a 'drunk' guy who kept slurring his words.

Needless to say, traffic was backed up for miles.

While Jones and Sahlberg were treated in the back of an ambulance, Payne took charge of things, as he often did. He identified himself as the CEO of Payne Industries and explained that Sahlberg, a former colleague of his father's, had called him earlier. They were heading to Station Square for a drink or two – taking the incline into the city in case they overindulged – when the gunmen in the cable car sidetracked their plans.

Payne had noticed them – and their weapons – outside of the upper station, and the way they had sized him up had raised his suspicions. As the CEO of one of the most profitable corporations in the nation, he knew he was a potential target for kidnappers, and as a former commando, he also knew there were foreign entities that had placed a bounty on his head. When the men jumped aboard the cable car at the last possible second, ensuring that he had no time to escape, he knew he had to act fast. He admitted to being the aggressor, but he made it clear that he had only used his fists until he found himself trapped in the lower station.

For his part, Jones could offer even less. After convincing the police that a sobriety test wasn't necessary, he told them that he had received an urgent text from Payne asking for his assistance. He had known Payne for most of his adult life, ever since they were both assigned to the MANIACs. There was little, if anything, that took precedent over his friendship with Payne, and he had left the dentist's chair in the middle of a procedure and hurried to the incline. He had arrived just as the man crossing the street opened fire. Seeing no other alternative, he had made the split-second decision to counter the attack with the only weapon he had at his disposal: his Escalade. The man's death had been an unfortunate result, but it had been unavoidable.

Even though Sahlberg had actually instigated the entire mess (albeit unintentionally), he was the one who got off the easiest. The police simply asked him to confirm Payne's story that he had made contact earlier that day, and that they had agreed to meet at the Monongahela Incline. After assuring them that he had never seen any of the attackers before that day, Sahlberg was free to go. In the eyes of the police, his participation was little more than bad timing. Had his call not been placed on the same day as the assault on Payne, he would never have been involved in the ordeal. Apart from making sure he had survived the tear gas and the firefight unscathed, the police had no further need for him. He was only a footnote in their investigation.

Sahlberg had played the role of the innocent victim to perfection.

In any other city, Payne and Jones would have been brought to the local police station for questioning, but there was little chance of that happening in Pittsburgh. Because of his respect for the profession, Payne made sure that his company provided continuous contributions to Pittsburgh's law enforcement community, and he put pressure on other titans of industry to do the same. Jones's contributions were on a smaller scale and often under the table, but they were appreciated nonetheless. He regularly hired off-duty police officers and recent retirees for odd jobs at his private investigation firm, and he always paid well for their experience.

Over the years, the duo's combined efforts had not only saved countless lives by outfitting the men and women of the police force and the fire department with the latest life-saving equipment; they had also helped those who couldn't make their mortgage payments or afford holidays or presents.

Gotham might have Batman and Robin.

Pittsburgh had Payne and Jones.

The irony of the situation – at least with regard to how the duo was perceived – was that their roles should have been reversed. Payne was the more reserved of the two. If anyone would prefer to stand in the shadows and do his good deeds anonymously, it was Payne. Jones, on the other hand, was much more flamboyant. He gladly embraced the public spotlight, so much so that Payne was often forced to reel him in.

Yet somehow their friendship thrived.

Jones watched from his seat on the curb as Payne shook hands and said some final goodbyes, then headed to the ambulance where Sahlberg was resting. Three hours had passed, and the Novocain had fully worn off. In one way that was a bad thing, because his bottom lip was throbbing despite the ice pack he had used to control the swelling. To make matters worse, he was starving. He had asked several cops if they had any donuts, but all he got were dirty looks. Probably because he couldn't pronounce 'donuts'.

A minute later, Payne and Sahlberg made their way to where he was sitting. Until that moment, he hadn't actually met the Swede. He stood as Payne introduced them.

'DJ, this is Dr Mattias Sahlberg. He used to work with my father.'

'Pleased to meet you, sir. I'm David Jones. I used to work with Jon, back when he was young.'

Sahlberg shook his hand and said hello.

Jones quickly turned his attention to Payne. 'Listen, I can't wait to hear about your dad and the good doctor, and I *really* can't wait to hear why I just killed someone with my Cadillac, but right now, let's focus on what's most important. Can we get something to eat? I'm starving, and if I know you, you're starving too.'

Payne laughed.

No one knew him better than Jones.

17

The moment Masseri was clear of the chaos at the Monongahela Incline, he tried to figure out where everything had gone wrong. He had ordered the guards at the upper station to descend as soon as their backup arrived, yet they had never appeared below.

He soon understood why.

Masseri called the backup team, and they told him that Sahlberg's bodyguard – whoever he was – had dealt with the men on the trip down the hillside. While Sahlberg and his protector exited the car to face Masseri and the sedan, the men – now bloodied, battered and tied to the bench inside the cable car – were sent back to the upper station with several passengers. A short while later, the backup team had watched as the smaller goon was dragged to a waiting squad car. The larger one was taken from the station in a body bag.

After that, they had followed the police to determine where their colleague would be booked. They got word to Masseri, who arranged for one of his men to speak with the prisoner. Less than an hour later, the associate was walking into the police station.

'My name is Marcus Lindo,' he told the officer at the front desk. 'I understand you have one of my clients in custody. A Mr Derek Paulsen. As his attorney, I am requesting that any and all questioning cease immediately, and that I be allowed to see Mr Paulsen in private.'

After filling out some paperwork, Lindo was led into an

interrogation room. Derek Paulsen, the smaller of the two thugs that Payne had left tied up in the cable car, sat inside.

'Your lawyer's here,' the officer informed him.

For the first time since he had been taken into custody, a glimmer of hope spread across Paulsen's face. 'Thank God.'

'This isn't going to work,' Lindo informed the officer.

'What isn't?'

'This room. I asked for a private meeting. You and I both know that if I ask for such accommodations, you have a legal obligation to provide them.' He tapped the mirrored wall of the interrogation room. 'Something without one-way glass. This conversation is privileged. That means you don't get to listen or watch.'

Paulsen smiled at the exchange.

'Fine,' the officer grunted. 'Give me a minute. I'll see what I can do.'

He closed the door behind him.

'Don't say a word,' Lindo said to Paulsen. He pointed at the mirror. 'Not until we're completely alone.'

A few minutes later, the officer reappeared and motioned for Lindo to follow him to a small room with cinder-block walls. The only things inside were two chairs. The only way in or out was a heavy iron door.

'Does this work?' the officer asked.

'Yes, this is fine. Thank you.' In contrast to his earlier indignation, Lindo's response was polite, even grateful.

The officer wasn't the least bit moved by Lindo's tone. He simply stared at him blankly and whistled loudly. Moments later a second officer led Paulsen into the room. Before leaving, the officer unshackled Paulsen's handcuffs.

'Thank you for your kindness,' Lindo said.

The cop sneered. 'This isn't kindness; this is wishful thinking.

If your client decides to attack you, that's one less lawyer we have to worry about.'

The first officer laughed loudly and patted his buddy on the back as the two cops left the room together.

Once the door was shut, Lindo was free to talk. 'Are you okay?'

'Better now. Did the Egyptian send you?' Paulsen was referring to Masseri in the only way he could. He didn't know his name; he only knew him by nationality.

'He did.'

'Great. So what's the plan? How soon can you get me out of here?'

'It won't take long. But first I need to ask you a few questions. What happened at the incline?'

'We got jumped,' Paulsen said.

'What do you mean?'

'One minute we were sitting on the bench, riding the car to the lower station, and the next minute there's a guy punching me in the face. He was an animal. He broke my ribs. My partner got it worse. Much worse. How's he doing?'

'He's dead,' Lindo replied. 'But we can't worry about that. Right now, let's focus on you. Let me get this straight: this guy just picks you out of a crowd and starts swinging? That doesn't make any sense. Had you seen him before?'

'Yeah. When we were waiting for our backup to arrive, he passed us on the street outside the upper station. He was running to catch the next car down.'

'Wait. The two of you spoke?'

'No, I'm just guessing from the way he was hurrying.' Paulsen wiped his brow with the back of his hand.

'Why are you sweating?'

'Why? Because I've got a bunch of broken ribs and I'm

sitting in a police station facing weapons charges. Why the fuck do you think I'm sweating?'

Lindo stared at him. 'Are you sure you want to snap at me? If I leave, you're facing several years in Western Penitentiary. On the bright side, it has a lovely view of the river.'

'Sorry. I didn't mean to yell. It's just – it's been a long day.'

'And it's going to get even longer if we can't figure out why you were jumped. Were you talking about the mission on the cable car?'

'No! Of course not. We aren't *that* stupid.'

'Then what did you do to get noticed?'

Paulsen sensed that Lindo wouldn't spring him from jail unless he gave him something, so he decided to pin the blame on his dead partner. 'I didn't do anything, I swear I didn't. But when the guy was running to the incline, my dumbass partner asked me if this was our backup.'

'He said that? Did the guy overhear it?'

Paulsen shrugged. 'He might have. I can't say for sure.'

'Shit. There's his motive. If he thought you two were plotting something, he can use it to defend his actions. As far as he knew, he was preventing a crime, not committing one.' Lindo shook his head dejectedly. 'Did you mention the Egyptian by name?'

'How could I? I don't even *know* his name.'

'What about the old man? Did you mention him?'

Paulsen shook his head. 'No, but he knew we were coming.'

'Why do you say that?'

'Why? Because the geezer was armed.'

'Really?'

'Yes! At one point I had the drop on the other fucker, but before I had a chance to take him out, the old geezer shot at me. I'm lucky to be alive.'

Lindo nodded. 'Yes, you are.'

'So what now?' Paulsen demanded.

Lindo looked at his watch. 'At this time of day, it's probably too late to get you released. I'm guessing they'll want to schedule a bail hearing for first thing tomorrow morning.'

Paulsen had figured as much. 'Any chance you can get me a night in the medical ward? My ribs are fucking killing me.'

'No, but I brought in something to take the edge off.' Lindo glanced over his shoulder, just to make sure the cops weren't watching. Then he reached into his suit coat and pulled out a single white capsule. 'Take this. Quick. Before the guards return.'

Paulsen grabbed the pill and popped it in his mouth. A moment later, he had worked up enough saliva to wash it down. 'What was it?'

'High-dose pain relief. Ten minutes from now, you won't feel a thing.'

*   *   *

The black SUV was parked in an alley three blocks from the police station. Masseri sat in the shadows of the back seat, waiting for Lindo to return.

Despite his slick suit, polished shoes, and extensive knowledge of the legal system, Lindo was not an attorney. He was actually a member of a backup team sent to assist Masseri. Thanks to his sadistic ways, Lindo jumped at the chance to kill Paulsen – not only to impress Masseri, but because he thought it would be fun to kill a suspect in police custody.

Waiting in a nearby car, Masseri watched Lindo as he turned the corner and made his way into the alley. As far as he could tell, no cops had followed him from the station.

'We're good,' Lindo said as he opened the car door.

Masseri needed more than that. 'Define "good".'

'I questioned him. He took the pill. No problem at all.'

'What did he know?'

'He said the guy on the incline was the first to act. He knew who they were and tried to stop them.'

'How?'

'They were talking about backup while they waited outside the upper station. The guy came jogging by, and he might have overheard them.'

'What about names?'

'He didn't say anything about Sahlberg, and he had no idea who the other guy was.'

Masseri's jaw clenched. He desperately wanted to know the identity of the man who had ruined his plans at the incline. He had been hired to secure Sahlberg, but the mission wouldn't be complete until he had eliminated the man protecting him.

'Anything else?'

'No, that's it. He took the pill. He'll be dead soon. No more loose ends.'

'Exactly,' Masseri replied.

Before Lindo could process the remark, Masseri reached forward and pressed his pistol to Lindo's temple. The silenced round split through Lindo's frontal lobe and ricocheted off the inside of his skull. As the slug careened back into Lindo's brain, Masseri fired twice more. He knew that Lindo was dead after the first bullet, but he wanted this to look like something other than a professional hit. To help steer the police toward the conclusion of a drug deal gone wrong, he took on the mindset of a junkie.

He reached a gloved hand into Lindo's suit and pulled out his wallet. Satisfied that there was nothing in the vehicle that could be linked to him or the other members of his team, he calmly opened the door and stepped outside.

The ambient noise of the city had masked what little sound had escaped the silencer. Even the birds perched on the fire escapes and power lines overhead had not been disturbed.

Masseri smiled as he walked into the shadows.

18

Eklund was confused and more than a little frustrated. He was standing in the middle of *his* crime scene at the charred laboratory in Stockholm, and yet he was waiting for Dial to tell him what to do, even though Dial had no authority at the scene. He was merely there as an official observer – an observer who was technically Eklund's boss at Interpol.

Well, not really his boss. More like his superior.

No, that wasn't quite right either.

The truth was, Eklund didn't really know what their relationship was, which was why he was confused and frustrated to begin with. Eventually, he decided the best way to rectify the situation was to simply voice what was on his mind.

'Nick, may I ask you a question?'

'Of course,' Dial replied.

'What's your role here?' he blurted.

Twenty years ago, Eklund wouldn't have even thought about challenging one of the division heads at Interpol. Ten years ago, he would have considered it for a few, fleeting moments before pushing it to the back of his mind and keeping his mouth shut.

But today was a different story.

Eklund had reached the point in his career where nothing mattered more than solving crimes, and if someone wanted to challenge his authority, he would deal with it then and there. It didn't matter if it was a colleague at his local station, the chief of an elite unit, or the Interpol secretary general himself.

One way or another, Eklund needed to know that everyone was on the same page – even if it put his career in jeopardy.

As it turned out, Dial was more impressed than insulted. To him, one of the things that separated good cops from bad was the willingness to ask the questions that needed to be asked, regardless of the person being questioned. Dial had seen far too many good leads go to shit because the investigator's priority was to *keep* his job rather than *do* his job.

'You want me to get out of your way?' Dial asked.

'Not at all. If you want to stay, then stay. I just want to clear the air before anyone starts stepping on anyone else's toes.'

Dial smiled to lighten the mood. 'As you know, Interpol can't run a crime scene. It's in our charter. I'm here for the sole purpose of making sure the right information gets distributed to all the nations involved. The investigation itself must be conducted by local law enforcement. That's you, not me.'

Eklund stared at him. He was usually good at reading people, but right then he had no idea if Dial was testing him. 'You're staying out of it?'

'I never said *that*,' Dial teased. 'But it's your show. I'm just along for the ride.'

'In that case, I'd like to shift our focus to something else.'

'To what?'

'The science.'

'You think we can learn anything from this equipment?'

Eklund nodded. 'I think the equipment, the specimens and whatever else remains from their experiments gives us a very good place to start.'

'I completely agree. Where do you want to begin?'

Eklund checked the equipment list he had been given by the forensics team. It was like reading a foreign language. 'Do you know anything about science?'

'Not a damn thing.'

'Me neither,' Eklund admitted with a laugh. 'Let's find someone who does.'

*   *   *

The Karolinska Institute was located in the Stockholm suburb of Solna, just north of the city. It was one of the most highly regarded medical schools in Europe, and its work in the fields of clinical medicine and pharmacology was regularly lauded by academics around the world. The Karolinska Institute was responsible – through its facility or its graduates – for a full third of all the medical research being carried out in Sweden.

This wasn't the first time Eklund had visited the campus in search of help. Years earlier he had spent an entire week working in a cadaver lab in order to better understand a case. Back then, he had been attempting to identify the particular weapon being used in a series of grisly murders. He was hoping that today's visit wouldn't require a butcher's apron.

'Dr Olsen?' he said in Swedish as he pushed open the saloon-style double doors of the laboratory. 'We saw the light on and figured that you were working late.'

'When am I *not* working late?' Olsen asked from the adjoining room.

Before they could locate the source of the sound, a wispy beanpole of a man came bounding through the doorway to meet them. He stood six and a half feet tall, yet weighed well under two hundred pounds. His shirt draped over his skeletal frame, and his belt was cinched comically tight, as if it closed a pouch of marbles instead of holding up a pair of pants. His skin was pale – almost white – and his shoulder-length hair was jet black.

Dial tried not to stare. To him, Olsen looked like he belonged on a slab, not in a lab.

'Dr Alexander Olsen, this is Chief Nick Dial,' Eklund said in English. 'He's here from Interpol's main office in France to help us work through a case. Chief Dial, this is Dr Alexander Olsen, professor of anatomy here at the university. Though I assure you his knowledge covers a wide array of other topics.'

'*Bonjour. Ravi . . . de . . . vous rencontrer,*' Olsen said in broken French.

Dial shook his hand. 'I'm actually an American.'

'An American from France in Sweden?' Olsen said, as if trying to work things out in his head. He stared at Dial for an awkward moment before finally accepting the situation. 'I assume you're here because of the explosion?'

'Unfortunately, yes.'

Olsen turned away and busied himself with a box of specimen jars. They were filled with formaldehyde and a wide assortment of body parts from cadavers. The gangly doctor gave no indication that he was at all intrigued by Dial's visit. It was as if unannounced visitors from foreign law enforcement agencies were a daily occurrence.

Dial leaned close to Eklund. 'Is he always like this?'

'Admittedly, yes,' Eklund said. 'I don't think he gets out much. The bodies are his life, and everything else is secondary. I know, it's sort of off-putting at first, but you get used to it.'

'Like I said, it's your show.'

Dial had met nearly every type of personality over his years of service, and an obsessive scientist barely registered on his intolerance scale. To be honest, what struck him more was the way in which Olsen had dehumanized the corpses. To Dial, every body meant a life lost, a future unfulfilled. But to Olsen, they were simply pieces of meat to be studied. He didn't disapprove of Olsen's approach; it was the nature of his job.

'What do you know about the incident?' Dial asked. He

knew the media had reported the explosion, but many of the details about the laboratory had not been released.

'I know that more than a handful of scientists lost their lives,' replied Olsen. 'People talk. Someone says that an explosion destroyed a lab in Stockholm, and suddenly my phone is ringing off the hook. Half the callers were checking to make sure I wasn't one of those caught in the flames, the other half were people wanting to know if I knew anyone that was.'

'Did you?'

'Not that I'm currently aware of, but these things take time. I'm sure once you have sorted through all the bodies there will be a name or two that I'm familiar with.'

'Why do you say that?' Dial asked.

'Because the scientific community in Sweden is a tight-knit group, and the Karolinska Institute is the center of their universe.'

'So I've heard.'

Olsen looked up from his specimens, suddenly concerned. 'Wait! Is that why you're here? To tell me all the people from the institute who were killed?'

'No,' Eklund said in a calming tone. 'We're here for the science. Nothing more.'

'Oh, good . . . Wait! What science?'

'That's what we were hoping you could tell us. If we showed you a list of supplies and equipment, could you explain what it might have been used for?'

'Sure, where's the list?'

Eklund opened a folder and handed Olsen a sheet of paper. But before he reviewed it, Olsen made a point of putting on his extra-long and way-too-wide lab coat. He obviously thought it made him look intelligent; Dial thought it made him look like Gandalf.

Of course, at this point of the investigation, they could use a little magic.

Olsen studied the list for nearly a minute without muttering a single word. Eventually, he shrugged his shoulders and sighed. 'I've *never* seen a lab like this. *Ever.*'

'Meaning what?' Eklund asked.

'Labs like this simply don't exist. These chemicals. This equipment. It's like someone took every area of science known to man, put them into a blender, and poured the resulting concoction into this list. To run a lab like this, you would need a chemist, a molecular biologist, and I don't know – experts in at least a dozen other fields.'

'Well, we have experts like that at the scene,' Dial said.

'Then why are you talking to me?'

'Because all of them are in body bags.'

19

The Payne Industries building was guarded around the clock by a security force that had been hand-picked by Payne and personally trained by Jones. It was the safest place in the city to keep Sahlberg until they figured out what was going on.

Not only did the building house hundreds of offices for the company's employees, it also had a magnificent penthouse on the highest floor. The scenic residence gave Payne the option of staying in the building when his meetings ran late or whenever an early flight had been scheduled. From here, he could wake up, grab a quick bite, and be taken by chopper to the airport instead of having to fight rush-hour traffic from his house in the suburbs.

It was also a great place to entertain.

On this night, the only person they were worried about was Sahlberg. He was nursing a glass of wine at the dining room table, well out of earshot of Payne and Jones, who were preparing dinner in the kitchen. Though both of them could cook, neither was in the mood after that day's events, so their preparations involved little more than pulling a pizza out of its box and dumping the cartons of takeout pasta and salad into serving dishes.

Though it wasn't a two-man job, it gave them a chance to speak in private.

A chance to debrief. A chance to honor the dead.

Jones stuffed a piece of garlic bread into his mouth. 'Holy

shit! Did you see that guy fly through the air? He flew, like, fifty feet. I knew I hit him hard, but that's ridiculous.'

Payne shook his head. 'You didn't hit him. Your Escalade did.'

'But I was driving.'

'Is that what you call it? From where I was standing, it looked like you were ducking, not driving. You're lucky you even hit the guy.'

Jones rolled his eyes. 'Speaking of ducking, isn't that what you were doing when I arrived? I don't remember seeing you in the middle of the street when I risked my life and car to kill the gunman who was trying to kill you.'

'You didn't see me because I was inside the station – you know, the one filling with tear gas – taking out several gunmen on my own.'

'That's not true.'

'What's not true?'

'You didn't do *anything* on your own. From what I understand, the old Swede saved your ass on the incline. Then I saved your ass on the street. How embarrassing is that?'

'Not as embarrassing as your lip. It looks like a Snickers bar.'

Jones pretended to be insulted. 'Despite your malicious, unprovoked and possibly racist comment, do you know what bothers me the most?'

'The fact that I'm younger, taller and richer than you.'

Jones shook his head. 'Unless I'm mistaken, you haven't thanked either one of us yet.'

'Actually, I planned on doing that over dinner – an Italian feast that I ordered myself and paid for with my hard-earned inheritance – but you had to ruin the moment by questioning my gratitude. You should be ashamed of yourself.'

Jones stared at him. 'So where does that leave us?'

Payne arched an eyebrow. He knew exactly what his best friend was referring to. 'Where does that leave us? Do you really want to compare how many times you've saved my life versus how many times I've saved yours? Really?'

'No,' Jones grunted. 'You're still ahead.'

'DJ, it's not a competition – but yeah, I'm *way* ahead.'

Most people would have been traumatized by the events at the incline, but Payne and Jones were able to joke about it with ease. It was a defense mechanism they had developed over their years of service in the military. Even in the direst of situations, they never lost their sense of humor. Besides, a few dead men and some tear gas paled in comparison to the horrors of war.

Payne and Jones carried the food and water to the table where Sahlberg was sipping his wine. He was staring aimlessly out the window, captivated by the panoramic view.

'Dr Sahlberg, are you okay?' Jones asked.

Sahlberg snapped to attention and turned to face Payne and Jones. 'Yes, yes, I'm fine. Thanks to you. Thanks to both of you.'

'Happy to help,' Payne replied.

'Says the guy who's going to have my Cadillac detailed,' Jones teased.

'Nonsense!' Sahlberg said. 'Whatever the damage, I'll pay for the repairs.'

'That isn't necessary,' Payne clarified. 'He was joking. But I do have a few serious questions for you, if you don't mind?'

'Not at all,' Sahlberg replied.

'Well, for starters, who the hell is following you?'

'I wish I knew. I went for a walk this afternoon, and when I came home there were four men waiting at my house. Actually, they weren't waiting; they were breaking in. They were disguised as deliverymen, but I watched them pick the lock and pull guns. At that point, I fled.'

'Why?' Jones wondered.

'Why did I flee?' Sahlberg asked, confused.

'No. Why are you so valuable that someone would send a team of heavily armed thugs to track you down at any cost?'

'Probably my work,' he said cryptically.

'What does that mean?'

'I've spent the last six decades working with some of the finest minds in the world. Not working with them personally, at least not every day, but working in the same circles.'

'In what field?'

'Biomedical research, mainly. With forays into the associated fields: engineering, chemistry, things of that nature.'

'What does any of that have to do with Payne Industries?' Jones asked.

'And why call me?' Payne added. 'When people feel threatened, they don't usually turn to their former employer for help. They go to the cops.'

Sahlberg stared at him. 'I've heard the stories. I know what you're capable of.'

Payne returned his stare, unsure how much Sahlberg knew about his past. As a former employee, he would definitely know about Payne's military career, since it was mentioned on the company's website, but only his closest friends – those with very high security clearances – knew about his time with the MANIACs. 'What stories are those?'

'I know about your time in Greece, and your recent adventures in Mexico.'

'You mean *our* adventures,' Jones blurted. 'Not just his. *I* was there too.'

Sahlberg nodded. 'I also know you're someone I can trust.'

Payne arched an eyebrow. 'How do you know that?'

'Because your father spoke of you often.'

Payne's father had died when Jonathon was in the eighth grade. As a kid, he knew his father was being groomed by his grandfather to take over the operation of Payne Industries, but he never fully understood his father's role in the corporation. His memories were more personal. Things like the backyard football games on Thanksgiving with the other families in the neighborhood, and the days they would play hooky from work and school and head over to Kennywood, an amusement park in the Pittsburgh suburbs.

That was how Payne remembered his dad.

Those were the memories he clung to.

As Payne's involvement in the company grew, he had reviewed many of the files relating to his father's work there. He had hoped to better understand what his father had accomplished, but what he had found provided little insight. Most of the projects his father had worked on had been short-term undertakings, usually in conjunction with numerous subcontractors. Few people within the company could remember any meaningful interaction with his father, and those that could described him as Payne Industries' jack of all trades: a man who would bounce from project to project as needed, helping when he could but mostly keeping to himself.

Sahlberg, on the other hand, appeared to know his father personally, yet until that morning, Payne had never heard of Sahlberg or his research.

He was eager to learn why. 'Please start from the beginning. I want to know everything about you, your research for the company, and your connection to my father. The more I know, the sooner I'll be able to figure out today's events.'

Jones cleared his throat. 'What Jon meant to say is: the more *we* know, the sooner *we'll* be able to figure out today's events. Sometimes he forgets about me.'

Payne grabbed the bowl of pasta and scooped some on to Sahlberg's plate. 'Actually, I didn't mean that at all. Besides, how could I forget about you? Your lip is the size of a bagel.'

Sahlberg laughed at their banter. It had been several weeks since he had spoken to his own best friend, and he missed their late-night conversations. 'I studied both biology and medicine at Lund University in Stockholm. I won't confess to the year, but suffice it to say that it was long before either of you were born.'

'Good school,' Jones offered.

Payne glanced at him, silently asking for clarification.

Jones recognized the look. 'It would be like Princeton or Harvard.'

Payne nodded his understanding. 'Go on.'

'I was a bit of a scholar – what you might call a nerd or a geek these days – and was courted by the Royal Swedish Academy of Sciences. Though top of my class at Lund, I would have been just another drone at the academy. There, only a Nobel Prize earns you recognition among your peers. Perhaps it was arrogance that led me in another direction, or maybe it was fear that I would never live up to their expectations. Whatever the case, I was far more intrigued by the offer I received from the young entrepreneur at the American steel company.'

'My father,' Payne said.

'Yes,' Sahlberg replied, 'your father.'

20

Payne hadn't realized that his father had traveled overseas to recruit scientists to work at Payne Industries. The mere thought of it was intriguing – and confusing.

Sahlberg continued. 'He came to me upon my graduation and invited me to dinner. He said he only wanted an hour of my time, and if I wasn't convinced by then, he would never bother me again. Though I couldn't see any connection between the steel industry and my work, I was young and poor, and the offer of a free meal was enough to bring me to the table.'

'What was your field of expertise?' Payne wondered.

'Molecular biology. Particularly with regard to cellular manipulation.'

'You were a geneticist?' Jones asked.

'Not until much later,' Sahlberg replied. 'At the time, my studies were primarily based on notions of cellular immunity. For instance, is there a way to kill the agents that cause cells to become cancerous without killing the entire cancerous cell? And if so, is it possible to condition cells so that they are able to detect such agents and destroy them *before* they have caused the cells to become cancerous? A sort of cellular self-defense, if you will.'

'What did that have to do with the steel industry?' Payne wondered.

'Absolutely nothing,' Sahlberg said with a smile. 'Absolutely nothing at all. It seems your father simply saw the writing on the wall. He knew the demand for steel could not possibly keep to the levels it was reaching, and he wanted to make sure that Payne Industries remained solvent – even prosperous – long after the demand had dried up. To that end, he began to diversify the company's interests. And rather than switch the focus to established fields, he was looking toward emerging technologies.'

Jones laughed at the statement. 'That's kind of confusing.'

'What is?' Payne demanded.

'We're talking about emerging technologies in the past tense, which means we're actually discussing things that have already been invented. I'm tempted to smoke a joint just so I can follow the conversation.'

Payne rolled his eyes. 'Obviously he's kidding about the drugs, and yet he brings up an interesting point. What was considered cutting-edge tech in that era?'

'Let's see . . .' Sahlberg rubbed his chin. 'Fiber optics came along in the mid 1950s, and shortly after that the microchip and the computer modem were introduced. Techniques for data storage, such as audio and video cassettes, were still being tested. And the first video game – a game called *Spacewar* – was invented by a computer programmer at MIT.'

Sahlberg took a sip of water before he continued. 'From a medical perspective, you had studies concerning the hepatitis B vaccine, rudimentary versions of artificial skin and advancements in grafting techniques, and of course, the release of oral contraception.'

Jones grinned and stuck up his hand for the doctor to slap. 'High five for that!'

Sahlberg laughed and willingly gave him a high five. 'Yes, I have to admit, that's a personal favorite of mine, too.'

Jones pointed at him. 'Hell, yeah. The doc's a playa!'

Payne ignored the comment – for now – and got Sahlberg back on track. 'Which field interested my father?'

'All of them,' Sahlberg replied. 'Your father was a visionary. No one knew which of these would bear the most fruit, so he explored them all. By keeping his options open, he ensured that Payne Industries would survive the eventual decline of the steel boom, that it would even survive its total collapse. And he succeeded. Just look at this place! Every advancement this company has made – every technology it has studied, improved and perfected – is a direct result of your father's foresight. From the moment we met, I was certain about one thing: your father was a man ahead of his time.'

Sahlberg turned his head and stared out the window at the glistening lights of the city. He wanted to say more – something that conveyed how much he'd respected Payne's father and how truly sorry he was that he hadn't come forward years ago to share these memories – but he didn't know how to put it into words.

'Thank you for that,' Payne said.

Sahlberg looked at him and smiled, grateful that Payne understood his sentiment.

Payne nodded once, then grabbed his water bottle from the table and took several large gulps as he reviewed the details in his mind. Something about it didn't make sense.

The only Payne Industries research and development facility in the Pittsburgh area was located in the nearby city of Ambridge. It was a sprawling billion-dollar complex that housed countless scientists, engineers and computer wunderkinds, all of whom were working on top-secret projects in a variety of fields. It was exactly the kind of place that his father would have used to entice Sahlberg, if it had actually existed back then.

However, the Ambridge facility was brand new.

Before the new building opened its doors, the R&D division was run out of an industrial complex in nearby Sewickley. The location was built into a grassy hillside, and many of the offices were completely underground. For that reason alone, the facility was affectionately known as 'the Mine'.

'Were you one of the mole men?' Payne asked. It was the preferred nickname of the scientists who worked inside the Mine.

'No, I never worked in Sewickley, nor in Ambridge for that matter. In fact, my retirement coincided with the opening of the new facility.'

'Then where did you work?'

'I ran my own facility on the University of Pittsburgh campus.'

'At Pitt? I didn't know you had a facility there,' Jones said.

'Neither did I,' Payne admitted.

'Good!' Sahlberg said, laughing. 'Then my colleagues kept things quiet like they were supposed to.'

Jones smiled. 'Why there?'

'Fifty years ago, the University of Pittsburgh was the center of the scientific universe, so your father felt it was the perfect place for me.'

'Any idea why?' Payne asked.

'Your grandfather kept him on a very short financial leash. He was happy to invest in technologies applicable to the steel industry, but he wasn't about to waste his fortune on flights of fancy. Our research was significant, but it had no relevance to the company as your grandfather envisioned it. As such, there was no room for us at the Mine.'

'Given that it didn't have my grandfather's support, how many years did your laboratory last?'

'More than fifty,' Sahlberg said proudly.

'How is that possible?' Jones asked.

'Jonathon's father established means for my work to be funded in perpetuity. I don't exactly know how he did it – I never asked, and he never mentioned it – but I've had access to the same credit line for half a century.'

Payne's curiosity was piqued. He leaned forward, bringing himself closer to Sahlberg. Though they were in the privacy of his penthouse, he actually felt the need to lower his voice to a whisper. 'Doctor, what *exactly* is your area of expertise?'

Sahlberg grabbed his glass and gulped his wine.

He had been dreading this moment for many years.

21

Sahlberg knew the general public had an uneasy relationship with the scientific community. People clamored for safer, more effective drugs, but they preferred the testing to be done in a way that didn't put anyone (or any animal) at risk. And that was just for starters. When the topic turned to something more controversial, like stem cells, emotions tended to flare.

Stem cells were essentially 'blank' cells that could grow into any number of specific cell types, depending on how and where they were introduced to a larger organism. Many scientists believed that they offered the best possibilities for combating or eliminating conditions such as Parkinson's and paralysis, and yet some people were completely against this research because certain types of stem cells could only be obtained from human embryos, and since the extraction process destroyed the embryo itself, they regarded it as tantamount to murder.

Sahlberg understood their position – he just didn't agree with it. Such was the nature of his work. 'Are you familiar with perpetual cell lines?'

'Assume for the moment that I have no idea what you're talking about,' Payne said.

'Because he doesn't,' Jones added.

Payne glared at him.

'What?' Jones said, laughing. 'It's nothing to be ashamed of. I'm not exactly sure what he's talking about either, and I'm *a lot* smarter than you.'

Payne rolled his eyes and told Sahlberg to continue.

'As you probably know, cells are the basic structure of all living things, but within those cells there are even smaller structures called telomeres. Think of them as a tiny chain. Each time the cell divides, a link of the chain is knocked off in the process. When the last link is destroyed, the cell essentially withers and dies. The telomeres serve as a biological clock, if you will. A device that counts down to the cell's inevitable death. Sometimes that countdown can last for decades – for instance, the cells in your brain – while other cells, such as those that form your skin, only last for a few hours. The length of a cell's lifespan is determined by the Hayflick limit, which refers to the number of divisions, or cell cycles, a cell can undergo before it has used up all of its telomeres.'

Sahlberg paused to give Payne and Jones a moment to digest everything. He raised an eyebrow, looking for permission to continue.

'With you so far,' Payne said.

'Me too,' Jones assured him.

Sahlberg nodded. 'However, some very special cells are able to produce an enzyme that prevents the links in the telomere chain from shearing off. With no biological clock to signal the end of its lifespan – or, perhaps more aptly, a *malfunctioning* clock that never counts down – the cells never stop dividing. They replicate indefinitely, for ever.'

'I'm not sure if I like where this is headed,' Payne said.

Jones tried to lighten the mood. 'Doc, if you have a ten-thousand-year-old monkey man living in your basement, I've got to meet him!'

'It's nothing like that!' Sahlberg protested. 'We're only talking about *clumps* of cells that continue to proliferate.

Extending the longevity of something as simple as tissue is well beyond the scope of what we're capable of achieving, much less the continued existence of an entire organism. And even then, the cells that have been discovered with the necessary enzymes to inhibit the telomere breakdown are limited to an extremely narrow range of material. Three-T-three: a cell line from the fatty connective tissue of a mouse. Jurkat: a cell line from the lymphocyte of a leukemia patient. And HeLa: a cell line from a cancer patient in Maryland.'

Payne nodded. 'You're talking about Henrietta Lacks.'

'Indeed I am. Are you familiar with her story?'

He nodded again. 'Back in the early fifties, a woman named Henrietta Lacks was admitted to a hospital in Baltimore because of extreme stomach pain. After finding a large tumor on her cervix, the doctors did a biopsy and discovered that it was cervical cancer. They also discovered that the cancer cells from her biopsy continued to replicate long after they should have stopped. Properly incubated, the cells simply wouldn't die. This meant they were perfect for scientific studies, because you could run test after test after test and know that the subject material was identical in each experiment. Even if the process took years, the cells used as the base of the study remained exactly the same, which eliminated one important variable in research: the "what if the differing results were caused by a small difference in the sample cells?"'

'Exactly,' Sahlberg said. 'Lacks's cells were mass-produced and shipped all across the world so that everyone's experiments could use the same subject material. These cells allowed for monumental advancements in the study of cancer, AIDS, gene mapping, and so on. Over the years, so many of her cells have been produced that if they were amassed together they would weigh more than *five hundred times* her original body weight.'

Payne glanced at Jones. 'Still with us?'

'Who, me?'

'Of course *you*. We're saying all this for your benefit.'

'For *my* benefit?' Jones said, half insulted. 'Sorry, I thought you guys were just thinking out loud, not lecturing me. As an educated black man, I'm quite familiar with Henrietta Lacks and the billion-dollar industry that her body spawned. I also know that her impoverished family was never paid a single cent for the mass production of her cells – or even notified that her cells were being used for research – even though every HeLa cell in the world is traceable back to that original biopsy in Baltimore. The only thing I don't understand is why *you're* familiar with her – your knowledge base is generally limited to the sports section.'

Payne winced. 'First of all, *ouch*. That was uncalled for.'

Jones smiled but didn't apologize.

'Secondly, I know about HeLa cells because of Jonas Salk. He was hired by the University of Pittsburgh in 1947 and was tasked with finding a polio vaccine. Less than a decade later, Salk announced the creation of a successful vaccine, one that would save millions of people from the crippling effects of the disease. One of the keys to his discovery was the use of HeLa cells in his experiments.'

Sahlberg nodded. 'Do you know how Salk got the HeLa cells to begin with?'

Payne shrugged, unsure.

'They were sent to him by George Otto Gey, a Pitt alumnus who was the head of tissue culture research at Johns Hopkins Hospital in Baltimore. He was the doctor who first studied the tissue sample from Henrietta Lacks, and because of his association with the University of Pittsburgh, he was quite familiar with the research that Salk was conducting. If not for the Pitt connection, who knows how many more lives would have been lost?'

Payne smiled with pride. 'My dad used to talk about that stuff all the time. Salk's discovery actually happened while my father was a student at Pitt. He used to tell me stories about all the great scientific minds that worked in Pittsburgh during that era.'

Sahlberg nodded. 'It truly was an amazing time to be a scientist. In fact, that was one of the main reasons that I was willing to move to Pittsburgh from Sweden – to work with and learn from many of the pioneers in their fields. It changed my life for ever.'

The smile on Payne's face lingered for a few more seconds before it began to fade as he shifted his focus from warm memories of his father to the violence of that afternoon. Stories about Jonas Salk and the golden era of research were entertaining, and yet Payne was smart enough to realize that the gunmen weren't after Sahlberg because of the polio vaccine.

They were after him for something current.

He looked Sahlberg squarely in the eyes. 'I'm going to ask you this one more time, and your answer needs to be clear and concise. No ramp-up. No side stories. The point, and only the point. Am I understood?'

'You are,' Sahlberg answered.

'Good. Now tell me, what exactly were you working on before your retirement?'

'I wanted to know the limits of perpetual cell lines – specifically, what is the connection between unchecked cell division and immunity.'

'And how could that research be used?'

Sahlberg raised his palms. 'I suppose it could have implications in several fields, but the science is still decades away. Certainly not in my lifetime. Why?'

'I think someone out there is a fan of your work.'

22

After finishing their meal, Payne and Jones tried to piece together the details of Sahlberg's attempted abduction.

Payne started the questioning. 'Since we don't know why the gunmen came after you, let's concentrate on the timing of things. Why now? What prompted them to act today?'

'It doesn't have to be specific to your work,' Jones added. 'It could relate to any one of the people you're connected to. Any new developments that caught your eye?'

Sahlberg thought back to his morning routine and the articles he had read online. 'There was a troubling event in Sweden last night. A laboratory in Stockholm was destroyed. The newspapers are reporting it as a deliberate act that targeted the scientists who worked there.'

'Did you know any of the victims?' Jones asked.

'Maybe, maybe not. No names were listed in the paper.'

'But it is a possibility.'

'Yes, of course it's a possibility since it occurred in Stockholm, but I don't have any connection to the lab. As far as I know, my troubles here and the explosion in Sweden are entirely coincidental. It wasn't until you asked about any noticeable developments that I even remembered reading about it! It's four thousand miles away. Surely you don't think—'

'I don't know what to think,' Payne interrupted. 'But I've seen enough in my life to know that nothing can be dismissed as coincidence. We need to know more about what happened in Stockholm.'

'If you have a computer available, I'd be happy to pull up the most recent news reports. The Swedish media has taken a keen interest in the story.'

Jones nodded. 'Jon, why don't you get your laptop, and I'll take Dr Sahlberg—'

'Mattias,' Sahlberg said.

'I'll take Mattias into the living room where he'll be more comfortable.'

Payne did as he was asked and retrieved his laptop from his bedroom nightstand while Jones directed Sahlberg to a plush, oversized recliner in the corner of the penthouse.

'Would you like some coffee?' he asked.

'Tea, if you have it.'

'Tea sounds great – I'll see if we have any.'

Payne returned with his computer and handed it to Sahlberg. 'Here you go, Mattias. Take your time. Be thorough. We want to know everything that's available.'

'I'll see what I can find,' Sahlberg assured them.

'Jon,' Jones said, 'I'm going to make Mattias a cup of tea. Can you show me where you keep your supplies?'

Payne raised an eyebrow. 'No problem.'

The two of them walked to the opposite end of the penthouse, where they ducked into a large, mostly empty pantry. Jones closed the door behind them for privacy.

'What gives?' Payne blurted.

'What do you mean?'

'Is there a reason we're leaving him alone?'

'Relax,' Jones said. 'He's in your living room, using your laptop, with every keystroke being logged. Two of America's most decorated and highly skilled soldiers are fifty feet away, and there's a full detail of security guards ready to strike at the push of a button. Also, by the way, did you happen to notice that he's like a hundred and twelve years old? I think we're covered either way. He's not going anywhere, and no one's getting to him here.'

'Still, if it's all the same to you, I'd prefer to be in the same room as him . . .' Payne paused and scrunched up his face. 'Wait, did you say the keystrokes are being logged? Since when?'

'Details,' Jones said, avoiding the question. 'You can go back in a bit. Right now, I don't want him to hear us talking.'

'About what?'

'I doubt he's going to find any leads regarding who's responsible, but that doesn't mean we don't have angles to work with.' Jones reached under his shirt and pulled out a pistol. He handed it to Payne. 'What do you make of this?'

Payne examined the weapon, rolling it over in his hands. 'This is the same type of pistol the guys in the cable car were using. Where'd you get it?'

'Took it off of the bastard I flattened outside the station.'

'You don't think the police will notice that he's missing his weapon?'

'His weapon? The guy was draped with weapons. Besides, did you see the shit he had in his car? I could have taken a ballistic missile without anyone noticing. Between the Uzi and the grenade launcher, I doubt anyone will question why he didn't have a sidearm.'

'And if they do?'

'I'll play the "oops" card.'

'What's the "oops" card?'

'I'll go, oops! I must have picked it up by mistake.'

Payne grimaced. 'I'm serious.'

'I am too,' Jones insisted. 'I mean, bullets were flying and blood was flowing. Shit got crazy. Somehow I must have grabbed his gun thinking it was mine. Oops! My bad.'

Payne shifted his focus to the weapon in his hand. 'What am I looking at?'

'At first I thought it was a Beretta 92, but it's not. It only looks like a Beretta. Same interchangeable grip and accessory rail to attach lights, laser sights, you name it. Same nine-millimeter semi-auto capabilities. Same seventeen-round-capacity magazine.'

'If it's not a Beretta, what is it?' Payne asked.

'It's a one-off. A one-of-a-kind custom job.'

'You mean someone modified a base model?'

'No, I mean someone said, "I like the Beretta 92, so I'll base my design on that." They built this weapon from scratch.'

'How can you be so sure?'

'Aim it at something.'

Payne did as he was told.

'What do you notice?' Jones asked.

In the heat of the moment on the incline, the only thing Payne had noticed about the gun was the palm-print safety feature. Now, as he examined the weapon more thoroughly, he understood what Jones was talking about.

'It's awkward,' he said. 'There are things about it that are just . . . *off*. The way the grip feels in my hand. The way I have to cock my hand to line it up to the scanner. Bending my finger to reach the trigger. Even the balance seems off.'

'Have you ever held one as awkward as this?'

Payne had been trained on virtually every weapon in the military's arsenal, from single-shot micro-guns that could be concealed inside a shirtsleeve to guided missile-launching systems that were mounted on the deck of aircraft carriers. He was proficient with all and highly skilled with most. Still, this weapon was uncomfortable in his hands. 'No, not this awkward.'

'Me neither. That's because this wasn't designed for either of us,' Jones said as he took back the weapon. 'The palm scanner is just the icing on the cake. Everything about it is unique. This whole piece was crafted for one specific user. Someone with narrow hands and short fingers. Someone who likes to hold his gun tilted just ever so slightly, like this.' He pointed the gun at the pantry door and rotated his hand a few degrees. 'Personalized in every way.'

'Can you trace it?' Payne wondered.

'Maybe, but it won't be easy. Obviously there's no serial number, but it's also missing a craftsman's mark of any kind. Whoever designed it didn't do it for show. In fact, I'm guessing he'd rather stay anonymous. Fortunately, we know some people who know some people who know some people. Hopefully someone might be able to point us in the right direction.'

'Just from looking at the craftsmanship?'

'Actually, we have more than that.'

'We do?'

Jones nodded. 'The palm-print scanner isn't standard. It's not even close. That's a next-generation modification.'

'Can you find out who deals with that kind of technology?'

'Like I said, we know some people . . .'

'Like who?'

'Like Kaiser,' Jones replied.

Payne groaned. He should have known where this was going. 'Are you sure you want to get him involved with this?'

'I don't see why not.'

'Well, for one, he's a black marketeer.'

'Yeah, but he's *our* black marketeer.'

'And two, the last time we dealt with him, he lost an eye.'

'No worries, Jon. I bet he's forgotten all about that.'

'Somehow I doubt it.'

'I'm telling you: when it comes to us, he'll be willing to turn a blind eye.'

Payne groaned even louder. 'How long have you been waiting to say that?'

Jones laughed. 'About a year.'

23

Tuesday, 23 July
Stockholm, Sweden

During his time with Interpol, Dial had slept in more hotels than he cared to remember. It was a necessary part of the job. Over the years he had developed an immunity to uncomfortable beds, scratchy pillows, noisy air conditioners, and all the other obstacles that kept the typical traveler from enjoying a good night's rest. But the one thing he could never ignore was his cell phone.

Even while dreaming, Dial could distinguish his cell phone's ring from other ambient sounds. In many ways he was like Pavlov's dogs, but instead of salivating in anticipation of food whenever their master rang a bell, Dial would force open his eyes whenever he heard his phone, locate his bifocals, and then grab the pen and paper that were always at his bedside.

It had become a reflex.

The expectation of food excited the dogs, regardless of the hour.

But Dial was rarely happy to take the call.

'Dial,' he announced without bothering to look at the caller ID.

'Nick, it's Henri. How are you?'

'*How am I?*' Dial snapped. He checked the clock. 'It's four in the fucking morning. How do you think I am? I'm tired.'

'Then you should get some sleep,' Toulon teased.

Dial growled into the phone. Literally growled. 'Henri, there's a popular expression in America that applies to this situation: *don't poke the bear*. Do you know what that means?'

A hundred different responses flashed through Toulon's head, each more obnoxious than the last, but he knew a warning when he heard it.

'*Oui*. It means I should get to the point.'

'Either that, or start updating your résumé.'

Toulon nodded in understanding. 'Did the Swedish police ever identify the property owner?'

Dial flipped through his notes. 'Not to my knowledge. Why?'

'Well, I think I did.'

'Really? How'd you manage that?'

'They were looking at tax records and deeds. I took another approach. I looked into insurance records.'

'And?' Dial asked.

'I found an old policy from the previous landholder of that address. The policy was terminated in 1990 because of the sale of the land, and someone noted that they should approach the new owner to offer continued coverage. The new owner is listed as Asgard Rhymä.'

Dial shook his head and grinned. Sometimes cases were broken through sheer luck. This time it was the note of an insurance salesman hoping for new business. 'Asgard Rhymä. Is that Swedish?'

'It's Finnish. It translates to "the Asgard Group" in English.'

Dial scribbled the name in his pad. 'Should that mean anything to me?'

'I'm not sure. Asgard was the home of the Norse gods of Æsir. It was one of the nine worlds of their mythology, ruled by the god Odin and the goddess Frig. It was the location of

Valhalla, a beautiful palace that served as the reward for Norse warriors who died valiantly in battle.'

'In other words, it means *nothing* to me.'

'If you say so.'

'Who owns the Asgard Group?'

'A shell company. Actually, it's a shell company owned by a shell company owned by a shell company, but if you look deep enough, you eventually find a real person. The land and the building are owned by Dr Tomas Berglund.'

'And he is?'

'A scientist,' Toulon replied. 'And a brilliant one at that. Since you've been in Sweden, has anyone mentioned the Karolinska Institute?'

'I was there last night. My liaison has a connection there.'

'Great. Ask him if he's ever heard of Berglund – I bet he has. Apparently he was a wunderkind at the institute. Graduated at eighteen with highest honors. Then he bounced around for a couple of decades, jumping from field to field and mastering them all. The guy has more than fifty published articles to his name, on subjects ranging from ethics to endocrinology.'

'Where's he now?'

'Nobody knows. Two months ago he just disappeared. No papers, no speaking engagements, no anything. The only indication that he's still alive is his tax returns. Apart from that, it's like he dropped off the face of the earth.'

'How'd you get his returns so quickly?'

'Scandinavian tax returns are public records. Sweden, Finland and Norway actually publish every citizen's return online. It's just a click away. Berglund filed a recent return with a very modest salary, listing his current residence as the address of his childhood home. It's a small community outside of Turku, Finland.'

'He's probably just using his parents' house as cover,' Dial said.

'That's what I figured, too.'

'Either way, send me the address. In fact, send me everything you have on the guy. I'll mention his name around here and see if anyone has anything to add to his file. In the meantime, notify the Finns. Ask them to send someone to Berglund's address. If they happen to find him there – which I doubt – tell them to make him comfortable, but give him as few details as possible. Finland is only an hour by air. If he's there, I'll fly over for the interrogation myself.'

'Sebastian is going to love that,' Toulon said sarcastically.

'While you're at it, see if the Finns can secure a warrant to examine Berglund's bank records. He wouldn't be the first person to lie on a tax return, and I highly doubt that a genius who has multiple shell companies to protect his identity only earns a modest salary.'

'On it.'

'Good. Call me back if you get anywhere.'

'Of course,' Toulon replied.

'And Henri . . .'

'*Oui?*'

'Good work.'

*   *   *

Dial wanted to go back to bed after his call with Toulon, but he knew it would be pointless. His mind was too busy mulling over the details of the case. As it was, it had taken him most of the night to get any sleep at all.

With nothing better to do, he showered, got dressed, and headed to the lobby. He had a rough idea of where he was in the city, which was to say that he knew he needed to go north to reach Eklund's office at the police station. Normally he would have simply hailed a cab and given the driver the address. But knowing that he had a few hours to burn before his morning meeting with Eklund, he decided against the cab.

Today, he would walk.

Familiarizing himself with a place was part of Dial's normal routine. He preferred to understand the geography and demographics before drawing any conclusions about the situation that had drawn him there. But on this trip he hadn't yet had much of an opportunity to look around. Although he had visited Stockholm once before, that tour had introduced him to little more than the airport, the hangar at the airport that had become a crime scene, and his hotel near the airport. He had never truly seen the city.

The Swedish capital was comprised of fourteen islands situated in Riddarfjärden Bay, where the water of Lake Mälaren met the Baltic Sea. When the first of these islands was settled more than nine hundred years ago, the only way to visit the central city was by boat. Today, the sprawling metropolis was connected by a vast network of ferries, subways, buses and commuter rails that were the envy of most other European cities.

Despite these modern advancements, Stockholm remained one of the cleanest cities in the world. For nearly two centuries, the governing factions of the city had sought to keep the air and water as pristine as possible. The ecological impact of every construction project was considered before any permits were granted, and factories – especially those that burned fossil fuels – were strongly discouraged. Instead of manufacturing, Stockholm was focused on the service industries. It was the financial capital of Sweden, and most, if not all, of the country's major banks were headquartered there, as well as many of the nation's biggest insurance companies and its busiest stock exchange.

To alleviate the urban feel, nearly a third of the city's land had been reserved for parks, recreational areas and nature reserves. The city's government had certified more than a thousand of these 'green spaces', which had resulted in minimal pollution and a well-earned reputation as Europe's first 'green capital'.

Dial checked his map and walked east, toward the oldest part of the city. A few minutes later he turned north and crossed the main bridge in Skeppsbron into the neighborhood of Gamla stan, which was strangely spelled with a capital 'G' and a lowercase 's'.

Here he could see the roots of the city.

Cobbled streets and narrow alleyways crisscrossed the small island of Stadsholmen. They led Dial past Stockholm Cathedral – the city's oldest church – and the royal palace. Though the king and queen did not call the palace home, it remained the Swedish monarch's official residence and housed the offices of the royal family.

Dial noticed the prominent gothic brick styling of north German architecture at nearly every turn, a carryover from the fledgling days of the town. In the middle of the community he found a large square known as the Stortorget. In the early morning light the scene was calm and serene, with no trace of the massacre that had taken place on that very spot centuries ago, when Danish invaders executed nearly a hundred clergymen in the streets. The site of the Stockholm Bloodbath, as it came to be known, was now a tourist attraction surrounded by shops.

Dial meandered through these streets for more than an hour before continuing on his path toward the police headquarters. As he walked, he marveled at the clear blue waterways and the pleasant demeanor of those enjoying their daily commute.

Everything here felt welcoming and secure. He couldn't think of anywhere he had ever been that projected the same vibe.

It made his investigation that much more troubling.

As if the sanctity of the city was now his to defend.

With a renewed sense of purpose, he practically jogged the last few blocks to Eklund's office. He didn't need the map to identify his destination. He remembered the recessed entrance and glass-enclosed lobby from the day before. The facade was almost warm and inviting, very different from the majority of police buildings he had visited.

He arrived a full hour before his eight o'clock meeting, hoping to get a snack before the others arrived. He flashed his ID at the door and was shown to Eklund's office.

He expected to find an empty room.

Instead, Eklund was already hard at work.

24

Eklund immediately stood from his desk. 'Nick, I didn't expect to see you so early.'

'I was just thinking the same thing about you. Did you even sleep?'

'A little, here and there.'

Dial could see from the wrinkled shirt Eklund wore and the rumpled cushions on his office couch that he hadn't made it home the night before. 'But you're good to go?'

'Fit as a fiddle, as you Americans say.'

'Actually, we stopped saying that about fifty years ago.'

'Really? Why's that?'

'We stopped playing fiddles.'

Eklund laughed as he smoothed his hands across the front of his shirt, trying to make himself look more presentable. 'Now that you mention it, it is rather dated.'

Dial nodded and glanced around the office. He immediately focused on a large magnetic dry erase board that covered most of the back wall, opposite Eklund's desk. The middle third of the board was plastered with photos from the crime scene and scribbled notes.

'What's all this?' he asked.

'That's my version of a touch screen,' Eklund joked. 'The younger guys enter all their information into a computerized display that spits it out and lets you pull it around the screen however you want.'

'I'm familiar with the technology. If you'd like one for your office, I can make a call and have one here by noon. Budget be damned.'

'With all due respect, I'd like to throw that stuff off a goddamn bridge. All that tapping and dragging and squeezing and spreading your fingers – what a bunch of nonsense! Give me some pictures, a whiteboard and some markers. That's all I need.'

'No need to convince me,' Dial said, laughing. 'I still use a corkboard.'

The more he got to know Eklund, the more he liked him. When it came to evidence, Dial was old-school like Eklund. He preferred the simplicity of a bulletin board to the functionality of a high-tech gadget. To him there was no better way to organize a case. He could move things around whenever he wanted until everything fit into place – like a giant jigsaw puzzle that revealed the identity of the killer.

'So, what do we have so far?' Dial asked as he examined the evidence.

'Not enough,' Eklund replied, pointing to the various columns on his board. 'This is the list of the registered owners of the cars in the warehouse parking lot. Unfortunately, half of the vehicles were rented, which means we have to track down the drivers' names through the rental agencies – and some of them require court orders.'

Dial saw a second list of names on the opposite side of the board. 'What about them?'

Eklund glanced at the list. 'Believe it or not, we were actually able to get a few usable prints from the scientists who were trapped in the back room. The science is beyond me – something about rehydrating the fingertips to expose the ridge patterns – but I can get a tech up here to explain it if you'd like.'

'No need. I'll take your word for it.' Dial shifted his focus to a photo of the two men who had been killed at the scene. 'What about the gunmen? Were you able to get their names?'

'Unfortunately, no. At least, not yet. We're running their dentals and prints through every database we can access, but so far nothing has given us a match. It's really not that uncommon, to be honest. If they were covert military or government, there's a better-than-good chance that their records have been expunged.'

'The perfect hit men,' Dial offered.

'You're right. This doesn't look like a hack job. But until we figure out what was going on and who was doing what, there's no way of knowing which one of these people was the target. It could be any of them, or it could be all of them.'

'Speaking of names, I've got one to add to your board.' Dial grabbed a blue marker from the plastic tray and wrote DR TOMAS BERGLUND in capital letters.

Eklund wasn't familiar with the name. 'Who is he?'

'The owner of the building.'

'Really? How did you manage that?'

Dial smiled. 'I'm good at what I do.'

'You must be better than good, because my guys have gotten nowhere with the paperwork. They said it's one shell company after another.'

'I managed to get a few details about him, but not much. Apparently, he's a well-known Finnish scientist who dropped off the face of the earth a few months ago. My assistant is trying to track down some additional information about his past, but my guess is we'll have more luck at the Karolinska Institute.'

Eklund checked his watch. 'Olsen and his colleagues should be arriving soon. If you'd like, we can stop by my favorite bakery for some coffee and pastries before we head over there. Do you like fruit tarts?'

Dial licked his lips in anticipation. 'I bet I will.'

*   *   *

After picking up their breakfast in a charming old-world bakery, they climbed into Eklund's car and headed north toward the institute.

Although the trip was a short distance in miles, it felt like a long journey through time as they left the ancient streets for the modern part of the city. Dial was startled by the contrast between the historic feel of the old town and the futuristic architecture of the adjacent islands. He envied the way that Stockholm had been able to preserve its history while still embracing innovation. It truly was spectacular.

'You know,' he said as he sipped his coffee, 'I've traveled all over the world, to every continent on the globe, but I've never seen a country like this. Sweden is simply gorgeous.'

Eklund beamed with pride. 'Thank you. It is a wonderful place to call home.'

'Maybe I will someday,' Dial offered.

Sensing an opportunity, Eklund mustered the courage to ask a question that had been weighing on him for some time. 'Nick, why are you doing this?'

'Doing what?'

'The investigation,' Eklund clarified. 'Why are you involving yourself? I'm not saying I don't want you here, or that you're in the way – of course I'm not saying *that* – but I would like to understand why. You could coordinate the information from the station. Hell, you could probably do it from France. But you're *here*, in my car, on your way to hear what these scientists might have to say, rather than reading their conclusions later.'

Dial sat back in his seat. He rarely discussed his life – personal

148

or professional – with those he met on the job. But Eklund's question was legitimate, and Dial felt that he somehow owed him an explanation – especially since Eklund had paid for breakfast.

'Back in '93, I was stationed in the southwest United States when a religious sect called the Branch Davidians faced off against the ATF and the FBI near Waco, Texas. For fifty-one days their leader, a self-proclaimed prophet named David Koresh, held us at bay. They were well armed, bunkered in, and threatening the lives of twenty-eight kids, so we tried to wait them out as long as we could. Eventually, orders were given to raid the compound, but everything went to shit when the Davidians started three fires, thereby blocking the exits. In the end, four ATF agents lost their lives, and eighty-two church members were killed in the blaze. It was a horrible scene.'

'Did you know them? The agents?'

'Conway LeBleu, Todd McKeehan, Robert Williams and Steven Willis . . . I didn't know them before they died, but I'll never forget those names. They'll stay with me for ever.'

Eklund nodded in understanding.

'Exactly two years to the day, an American terrorist named Timothy McVeigh parked a rental truck filled with five thousand pounds of ammonium nitrate outside the Federal Building in Oklahoma City. He did it in protest at the government's actions in Waco. Most employees had just started their workday when McVeigh lit the fuse. The blast tore through the north face of the building. One hundred and sixty-eight were killed. Eight hundred more were injured. I arrived less than two hours later.'

Dial had worked non-stop, all day and all night, pulling victims from the rubble and collecting evidence in between.

Based on blast patterns, his team had figured out where in the smoldering wreckage they should be searching for the suspect's vehicle. When they found an axle and pieces of a license plate, they were able to link the truck to a rental agency in Junction City, Kansas. The agency's owner remembered McVeigh and provided a detailed description to the FBI, who used the sketch to implicate him in the bombing.

'I remember that,' Eklund said. 'He was convicted on multiple counts.'

'And he was executed for his crimes on June 11, 2001. Maybe the best night of sleep I've ever had.'

It wasn't an exaggeration. Dial had slept like a baby that night. For the first time in years, he was able to close his eyes without seeing burned and mangled corpses, their lifeless faces staring back at him in a plea for help that wouldn't come. They had haunted his dreams since the day of the bombing, as if their final journey could not be completed until the man who had killed them had been sent to hell.

'I'm not a religious man,' he said in summation, 'but I do believe in justice. It's the reason I became a cop. It's the reason I work for Interpol. And it's the reason I'm in this car. As much as I'd like to pack my things and head back home, that is no longer an option. Now that I'm a part of this investigation, I plan on sticking around until the case is solved.'

25

The parking lot near Olsen's office had been empty the night before except for the doctor's white Volvo. Today, six vehicles – four cars, a scooter and a bicycle – were parked outside the building. Dial hoped it was a positive sign. With any luck, it meant Olsen had come through on his promise to deliver a panel of experts to explain the science in the investigation.

Before leaving the institute, Eklund had arranged for some of the animal remains to be transported to Olsen's lab, along with several tissue samples, pictures of the crime scene, and anything else he felt was appropriate. Since that time, the doctor's car hadn't moved an inch.

Dial pointed at the Volvo. 'Apparently, none of us got a good night's sleep.'

'I told you: give him a project, and his focus is absolute.'

'I just hope he has something to tell us.'

Eklund led Dial into the lobby and down the long corridor toward the small lecture hall where they had agreed to meet Olsen. Twenty meters from the doorway, they found the young police officer that Eklund had left to protect the chain of evidence. He was sitting on the floor with his knees pulled close to his chest. His head was buried in his folded arms.

'Is he asleep?' Dial asked.

'Not asleep,' the young man said without raising his head. 'I just couldn't take it anymore.'

'Gunnar, what are you talking about?' Eklund asked.

Hearing his name, the cop's head jerked upward. He was

stunned to see his boss and his boss's boss standing in front of him. He jumped from the floor and stood at attention. 'I'm sorry, sir. I thought it was *them* again. They've been squawking all night like parrots.'

Eklund leaned forward and sniffed the air. 'Have you been drinking?'

'No, sir! Of course not, sir! I've been standing guard all night.'

'Then why are you babbling about birds?'

'It's *them*, sir. The *scientists*. They won't stop their incessant bickering. And they keep saying the same things over and over again like parrots – really smart parrots.'

Eklund glared at the youngster. 'And the evidence?'

'My partner took it back to headquarters, sir, after Dr Olsen had completed his examination. For everyone's protection, I decided to stay until you arrived.'

Eklund nodded his approval, a sign that pleased the rookie cop. Unfortunately for him, the moment was short-lived. 'What have they learned?'

Gunnar's smile faded. 'I honestly don't know, sir. Most of the science terms are things I've never heard before, and I didn't want to interrupt for an explanation. They kept talking, faster and faster, using words and concepts that I didn't understand. Eventually it all became a blur.' He hung his head. 'I came out here to get away from it and clear my mind.'

'No shame in that,' Eklund offered. 'Your job was to safeguard the evidence. You did that and more. Now go home and get some rest.'

Gunnar lifted his head. 'If you need me to stay . . .'

'A bit of advice,' Dial said as he patted the rookie on his shoulder. 'If you're offered a chance to sleep, you sleep. No matter what.'

'Yes, sir. I will, sir. Good luck with . . . well . . . *them.*' With that, Gunnar turned and practically ran toward the lobby before his superior changed his mind.

Eklund and Dial continued down the empty corridor. As they approached the meeting room, they could hear a cacophony of voices inside. The steel doors of the hall muffled the sound in such a way that they could not tell if topics were being discussed, debated, or outright argued, but one thing was certain: there was intensity to the tone.

Side by side, they pushed open the double doors and stepped into the hall. Their entrance caused the group inside to fall silent. The scientists turned and stared warily at the strangers. For a moment, Dial felt like a sheriff in the American Old West, sauntering into a rowdy saloon. Everyone stopped and waited for him to make a move.

Instead, the two lawmen just stood there and glared.

No words were spoken, but their point was made.

They were in charge of the meeting.

Olsen broke the tension with an introduction. 'Everyone, this is Special Agent Johann Eklund of the National Police, and Director Nick Dial of Interpol's homicide division.' He turned toward the officers and smiled. 'Rather than introduce my colleagues en masse, let's save their names until they offer their opinions on the crime scene.'

'That'll be fine,' Eklund said.

Olsen turned and faced his peers, who were settling into their seats in the first row of the lecture hall. 'Suffice it to say, the men and women gathered here are at the top of their respective fields. We've been discussing your findings for several hours now, and while we're not prepared to draw any definitive conclusions about the laboratory, we are fairly certain we can provide the background information that you seek.'

Dial furrowed his brow. There was a drastic change in Olsen; he was like a different person in the lecture hall. Now in his element, he had transformed from the detached scientist he had been in the lab into a verbose academic. Of course, it only stood to reason, since lectures were an integral part of a professor's work. Whether information was being conveyed to students, colleagues, or the investigators of a murder, the basic skills remained the same.

Olsen continued. 'Let's start with Dr Cassandra Larsson.'

One of the two women in the room – and by far the youngest scientist in the group – rose from her seat and walked to Olsen's side.

Dial guessed her to be in her early twenties, and she looked nothing like the biology teachers he'd had in school. Tall and slender, with short blond hair and piercing blue eyes, her snug-fitting shorts and T-shirt would certainly turn heads on the street, but here no one seemed to notice but Dial. Though her body was extremely fit, she somehow made her outfit look wholesome, not indecent – as if she was striving for comfort rather than compliments.

'Dr Larsson is our resident zoologist,' Olsen explained. 'When your associates arrived with the specimens last evening, it became clear that my specific expertise in human anatomy would have to be supplemented by someone with a far broader understanding of mammalian anatomy. Dr Larsson was the logical choice.'

I'm sure she was, thought Dial.

'Working together through the night, we were able to identify and categorize most of the remains.'

'What did you find?' Eklund asked.

'A menagerie,' Cassandra answered. 'The live specimens included mice, rats, guinea pigs, rabbits, cats, dogs, monkeys and chimpanzees.'

'Wait. What do you mean by *live* specimens?' Eklund was momentarily horrified by the suggestion that any of the scorched victims had still been alive when they had been found sealed in their cages.

'These animals were alive when the fire broke out. Their deaths were caused by a combination of smoke inhalation and traumatic thermal decomposition of their organs.'

'Put another way,' Olsen clarified, 'the fire caused their innards to burst.'

Cassandra nodded. 'Unfortunately, yes.'

'And that's in contrast to what?' Eklund asked.

'The animals that were already deceased,' Cassandra answered. 'We have samples – bones and teeth mainly – from animals that were not alive at the time of the fire. This list includes pigs, turtles and juvenile gorillas, and all the other animals on the first list.'

Dial shook his head in confusion. 'We'll get back to the lists in a moment, but first I want to know how you're sure these animals were not alive when the fire broke out. Is there a difference between how a live bone and a dead bone burn?'

'If there is, I'm not the right person to ask about the distinction,' Cassandra replied. 'Our assumption that these animals were dead prior to the fire is based upon a number of factors: what little remained of the bodies, where these remains were located, their spatial arrangement, and an inspection of the equipment available.'

'I'm not following,' Dial said.

'With the other animals – the mice and rabbits and so forth – we found complete, intact skeletons. We were told that these skeletons were found in cages, and that each species was housed separately.'

'Go on,' Dial said.

'With regard to the second list of animals, there were only fragmented remains: the bits of bone and teeth I mentioned earlier. These remains were delivered to us exactly as they were found in the laboratory: layered inside a large metal box.'

'Layered?' Eklund asked.

'Yes, layered. The bone at the top of the box was the brow ridge of a young gorilla. As we dug deeper, we discovered the foot of a pig. Next was a series of turtle bones, then some more pig, some rodents, some more gorilla, and a mix of the other animals.'

'What separated the layers?' Eklund asked.

'Ash,' Cassandra replied. 'All that remained of their bodies.'

'We compared this theory with the inventory of items found at the scene, and the photos,' Olsen explained. 'Your men determined that two large canisters of acetylene were destroyed in the fire. Acetylene is a flammable gas. It is certainly *possible* that this laboratory used it as fuel for their Bunsen burners and other equipment, but it's highly improbable.'

'Why not?' Dial asked.

'Acetylene burns at nearly twenty-four hundred degrees centigrade. It's way too hot for use with standard experimentation. It's also relatively unstable and expensive. Given the alternative of using the natural gas that is already piped into the building, acetylene is an illogical choice to use as everyday fuel. It is much better suited for short bursts of incredibly high heat.'

'Like for incinerating a body,' Dial concluded.

'Precisely,' Cassandra said. 'Whoever was running this lab had built themselves a crematorium on site. Whenever they were done with a test subject, they simply incinerated the evidence.'

The words struck Eklund hard. Until that moment, he had been working under the assumption that the scientists who had died in the fire were innocent victims. But Cassandra's comment made him wonder if he was seeing things from the wrong perspective.

What if the explosion was retaliation for their sins?

And if so, what sins had they committed?

26

Dial knew that mice and rats were used in laboratories throughout the world. He imagined a huge factory in the middle of nowhere filled with millions upon millions of fertile rodents, their offspring serving as an endless supply of test subjects. The mere thought of it gave him chills. He quickly blocked the image from his mind and focused his attention on the larger animals.

He said, 'Tell me about the monkeys, pigs and turtles. Can those species be traced? And if they can, does the supplier require information about the testing itself?'

'They can be traced,' Olsen said, 'but only if they were procured through legitimate means. In Sweden, the European Council determines the method of procurement. It governs the buying and selling of animals that are to be used in testing, and regulates the entities involved.'

'However,' Cassandra said, 'there's no reason to believe that a rogue laboratory such as this would adhere to EU standards. They could have easily imported these animals from countries outside of Europe, or obtained them through the black market.'

Olsen spoke again. 'And even if they used EU-approved sources, I doubt they would have shipped the subjects directly to the lab. Since no one knew of its existence, it appears likely that the animals were delivered to a separate location, then moved to the facility.'

Dial made a note to contact the companies that were certified by the EU to provide animals, but he knew Olsen was right: having test subjects delivered direct to a secret laboratory would be a massive oversight on the part of whoever was running this operation.

Eklund picked up from there. 'Since we know which species they were using in their testing, does that help us determine what field they were studying?'

Cassandra shrugged. 'I don't know. I mean, it's pretty obvious they weren't studying astronomy, but we were able to figure that out from the equipment alone.'

'What about disease?' Dial asked as Cassandra returned to her seat. 'Is there any chance they were using these animals to test infectious agents?'

The question hung in the air like a contagious pathogen.

No one was willing to handle it.

Dial had seen some horrible things in his life, but they were always isolated incidents. He knew they paled in comparison to a worldwide epidemic, which was one of his biggest fears. Given what he still didn't know about the lab, he had to at least consider the possibility.

What if they were cultivating the newest super-disease?

What if they were designing the perfect biological weapon?

Finally, after several seconds, a balding scientist in his mid forties addressed Dial's question. 'The animals were clean. In fact, the evidence leads me to believe that every effort was taken to keep them that way. The chemical traces suggest a full series of vaccines and immunizations. They didn't have so much as the common cold.'

Dial nodded his appreciation. 'And you are?'

'Dr Alton Miles, microbiologist.'

'And what do the vaccines tell us about the lab?'

'That's for you to determine, not me. I deal in facts, not speculation.'

Dial glanced at Olsen to see if he knew why the micro-biologist had just snapped at him like an insolent child.

Olsen apologized on behalf of his colleague. 'Sorry. It's been a long night.'

Dial forced a smile. 'No apology necessary. You're doing us the favor, not the other way around.'

Olsen spun toward the group. 'Dr Norling, perhaps you could speak next.'

Dr Hanna Norling was the other female in the group. She was Cassandra's opposite in nearly every way imaginable. At seventy-four years of age, she was the matriarch of the insti-tute's science departments. Despite her age, her hair was a darker shade of brown than her eyes. A shade under five feet tall, she was forced to use a step stool when speaking from behind a lectern or else her audience wouldn't know she was there. Today, however, she simply tapped the ground twice with her cane. It was her way of letting them know that she would not be rising.

She launched into a long, rambling explanation in Swedish. Nearly a full minute passed before Dial found an opportunity to cut her off.

'I'm sorry,' he said, 'but I don't speak Swedish.'

A scruffy man who had not yet spoken translated for him. 'She says there's a chance they created the animals themselves. They have large quantities of growth medium and Petri dishes, as well as microsurgical scalpels and the other implements needed for artificial embryonic division. Basically she's saying they could split one embryo into two.'

Hanna nodded her agreement of the translation, yet she continued in Swedish.

This time it was Olsen who related her words to Dial. 'She also says they had the right equipment – microscopic needles and what not – needed to pull the nucleus from its original cell and transplant it into another cell. A second cell without any genetic material of its own. They also had the equipment needed to incubate the newly created recombinant cell.'

Dial pondered the new information. 'Is she talking about *cloning?*'

'Yes,' answered the scruffy scientist. 'That is what she is saying. They had the means to clone their own animals.'

'Just animals?'

'No. Anything they liked. It's all the same science. Dolly the sheep is no different from a human being. It's the same procedure.'

'But it's an entirely different world of ethics,' Dial challenged.

'I suppose to some,' the man argued.

'But not to you?' Eklund asked.

'It is a luxury I can enjoy: not choosing sides. I am only an engineer. I simply build the machines. How they are used is not for me to decide.'

'And your name?' Eklund asked.

'Magnus Hedman. Pleased to meet you both.'

Hedman was dressed like a lumberjack, as if he were about to go out and cut wood for the winter ahead. Even though it was summer, he wore long work pants and a flannel shirt with the sleeves rolled above his elbows. His hair was grey and unkempt. His face was ruddy and weathered. Dial's first thought was that he looked like someone's drunken uncle – the one who was always playing practical jokes. He certainly wasn't what Dial thought of when contemplating an engineer at one of the world's finest institutions.

'Nice to meet you too,' Dial said. 'What's your take on things?'

'Whatever they were doing, it was cutting-edge,' Hedman

answered. 'Some of the recovered samples were not organic, they were bionic. Are you familiar with nanotechnology?'

'Let's assume we're not,' Eklund said truthfully.

'Nanotechnology concerns the order of things on the microscopic scale. We're talking about machines and devices that are fully functional, yet no bigger than a human cell. In fact, there are those who believe we will someday be able to create machines that can be used to replace the very components of a cell. It would be like a heart transplant, only instead of something as big as a baseball, we'd be replacing a faulty nucleus a thousand times smaller than the head of a pin.'

'And you found these devices in the lab?' Dial asked.

Hedman laughed. 'No, we're not there yet. Perfecting machines that can operate on that small a scale is some time away. But what I found was still ahead of the curve.'

'How so?'

'Most nanotech in the market today relates to "passive" technology. For instance, microscopic particles that are added to sunscreens to make them more effective. The particles don't change; they simply are what they are. That being said, the goal of nanotechnology is "active" technology, where a device could function as a sort of mini-mini-mini-*mini*-submarine that could be programmed to carry out a specific task, such as seeking out and destroying cancer cells before they propagate.'

'And . . .'

'I didn't find that. What I found was somewhere in between. If I'm correct, it appears to be "reactionary" nanotech. It's too soon to understand the trigger mechanism, but it seems they had created an inorganic microscopic delivery method.'

'You're saying it can't seek out cancer, but it could react if it ever encountered it? Not so much a guided missile as a landmine.'

'Theoretically, yes. That's a very good analogy. But of course, there's nothing that limits its target.'

'What do you mean?'

'Programmed differently, it could just as easily be used to destroy healthy cells.'

Dial furrowed his brow. 'It would attack healthy cells? Correct me if I'm wrong, but aren't people mostly made up of healthy cells?'

'Yes,' Hedman said. 'Theoretically, if you were to introduce a device like that into a human body, the result would be less like a landmine and more like a nuclear bomb.'

27

Dial took a moment to digest the new information. A pile of cremated animals that were in perfect health before their deaths. A bunch of dead scientists who had the ability to clone. Microscopic machines that could hurt or heal at the whim of their designer.

What the hell was going on at this lab?

With several crazy theories running through his mind, he decided to shift the focus to something different. If the property owner was as famous as Toulon had claimed, then someone in the room would have heard of him. 'Tell me about Tomas Berglund.'

In a flash, the room grew still.

No movement. No sound. No breathing.

As if the air had been sucked from the lecture hall.

Dial and Eklund exchanged glances. With decades of experience between them, they instantly knew when a question resonated with an expert or witness.

This was one of those times.

Dial repeated the name. 'Dr Tomas Berglund . . . Does the name ring a bell?'

Miles, the balding microbiologist, was the first to speak. 'What would you like to know?'

'Let's start with the basics. Have you heard of him?'

'Of course we've heard of him.'

'And?'

'Berglund is brilliant. A man ahead of his time.'

'In what way?'

Miles sat up in his chair, as if slouching while talking about Berglund would be a mortal sin. 'There are scientists in several fields who stumbled into greatness, men and women who made incredible breakthroughs without any forethought. Fortuitous accidents, if you will.'

'You mean like penicillin,' Eklund said.

He was referring to the unplanned discovery of *Penicillium notatum*, which was made when Dr Alexander Fleming returned to his laboratory after an extended absence and noticed that a culture of staphylococcus bacteria had been overrun by a strange mold. Upon closer examination, he noticed circular areas around the mold where the bacteria would not grow. He concluded that something in the mold was inhibiting, or possibly even destroying, the staphylococcus. Further studies showed that the mold was effective against bacteria while at the same time non-toxic to the host organism.

Eventually, the *Penicillium notatum* mold was purified and approved for medical use. The resulting drug – penicillin – had been used to treat bacterial infections since the mid 1940s.

It was the most popular antibiotic in the history of the world.

It was impossible to determine how many lives it had saved.

And it was discovered because someone forgot to put the lid on a Petri dish.

Miles approved of the reference. 'That is the perfect example. Penicillin wasn't a mistake, but it certainly wasn't planned. Accidents like that happen all the time. You set out to prove one thing, and you end up making a discovery that is totally unrelated.'

'And that's what happened with Berglund?'

'Not at all. In fact, that is the exact opposite of Berglund.

He looks for the solutions before anyone has even identified the problems.'

'I don't follow,' Eklund said.

Miles paused in thought. 'Let's pretend that we, as a collective group, manage to invent a revolutionary form of glass. Something that never smudges, just for the sake of argument. Well, Berglund is the type of guy who would go to his desk and pull out a notebook from a decade ago that would be filled with applicable uses for our new glass and theories about its limitations.'

Hedman chimed in with further explanation. 'For instance, someone asks if the glass can be used in space. Well, we don't know. We've never even *thought* about space. We were just trying to make a piece of glass that wouldn't smudge. But Berglund – not only has he thought about space, he's determined the issues with our new glass in sub-zero, non-atmospheric conditions, and he's already established a treatment to correct these flaws.'

'And he did that ten years before we even met,' Miles stressed.

Dial nodded in understanding. 'He's a visionary.'

'Yes,' Hedman said, 'and Picasso was just a painter.'

Dial smiled. It was a funny line. 'What field does he work in?'

'All of them. He's dabbled in a variety of sciences,' Hedman replied. 'He has made unparalleled contributions in biology, chemistry, physics, you name it.'

Olsen rejoined the conversation. 'Why do you want to know about Tomas?'

Hedman turned to face his host. 'Isn't it obvious? This was Berglund's lab.'

Once again the air was sucked from the room.

Miles, who was clearly smitten with Berglund's accomplishments, seemed particularly stung by the revelation. He stared at Dial and Eklund, hoping that one of them would refute Hedman's claim, but neither did. In fact, after several awkward seconds, Eklund did the opposite.

'Yes,' he said. 'According to property records, Berglund owned the facility.'

Miles was visibly crushed. The others – even Hedman, who had put forth the theory in the first place – remained speechless. No one knew quite what to make of the news.

Hanna eventually broke the silence, abandoning her native Swedish and speaking in thickly accented English. 'Is he dead?'

'Sorry. We're not at liberty to discuss it.'

The answer did not sit well with the matriarch of the group. She showed her anger by smacking her cane on the ground in front of her. The sound echoed through the hall. 'Without us, where would you be? We have given you every explanation. We have walked you through the science. We have answered *all* of your questions. Surely you can answer one of ours.'

Eklund shook his head. 'With all due respect, Dr Norling, you're asking about an open, ongoing investigation. I can understand your interest, but unfortunately, I'm not in a position to provide any more details at this time.'

'With all due respect, Special Agent Eklund, you're not in a position to *keep* all the details at this time. You asked for our help, and we obliged. If Dr Berglund or *any* of our colleagues have been murdered in our city, we have a right to know. Otherwise, you may find yourself without the assistance of the Swedish scientific community.'

Hanna's threat was clear. Olsen had gathered the best minds that the institute had to offer, and their continuing support was vital to the investigation. If the experts decided to withhold their participation, Eklund was certain that something would get overlooked.

He glanced at Dial, who subtly nodded his head.

Sometimes rules were meant to be broken.

Eklund cleared his throat. 'In appreciation of your help and guidance, I can confirm that Dr Berglund has *not* been found at the scene.' There was a collective sigh in the room. Miles's face brightened with hope. 'That does not mean he is out of danger. The building was large, and the damage was extensive. There is always a chance that we will find more bodies as we continue our examination. However, for the time being, we remain hopeful.'

'Thank you,' Hanna said in a warmer tone. 'And what of the others?'

Eklund frowned. 'I'm afraid they weren't as fortunate.'

He opened his notebook and read two lists of names: the presumed dead and the confirmed dead. As Eklund spoke, Dial studied the reactions of the gathered scientists. What he saw was a mix of recognition, shock and horrified speculation.

Eventually Hedman said what the others were thinking. 'Whatever they were doing, I assure you it was *way* bigger than you realize.'

'What makes you say that?' Dial asked.

'Those names. Most of them should be running their own labs. To find them working side by side is remarkable. It would take something extraordinary to bring them all together.'

Olsen added more. 'They represent the top percentages of their respective disciplines. Take everyone in this room and convince them all to put aside their own research and come together. Set them to work on a common goal. Your lab in Stockholm represents a similar endeavor.'

The implications of Olsen's statement were not lost on the group. If someone had murdered such a collection of scientists – scientists who, like them, represented diverse areas of interest and, like them, were well known in their fields – what was to stop him from hunting them down next? Suddenly, their presence in the same room took on an ominous feel.

But Dial wasn't concerned. 'Tell me, could Berglund have brought them all together? Did he have that kind of pull?'

'Almost certainly,' Hedman replied. 'Year after year he's on the shortlist to win a Nobel Prize – the only question is the field in which he will be honored. Who wouldn't want to be a part of that?'

Eklund grabbed a chair from against the wall and slid it to the front of the lecture hall. 'Everyone get comfortable. It looks like we're going to be here for a while.'

The group looked at him quizzically.

'I want to know everything you can tell me about Dr Berglund. Every discovery he's made. Every theory he's put forth. Every rumor anyone's ever heard about him. If someone wanted him dead, I want to know why. The same goes for any of the scientists on those lists. If you know anything that can help my case, I need to know now.'

Dial fought the urge to smile. He continued to be impressed by Eklund. It was the exact move he would have made had he been leading the investigation. He too wanted to hear more about Berglund and the other scientists.

He took a chair for himself and was about to carry it over to Eklund when he felt his phone vibrate in his pocket. He put the chair down and glanced at the screen.

He grunted when he saw the name. It wasn't Toulon, or anyone else from his department. Instead, it was a friend of his who rarely called to chat. In fact, their conversations almost always led to something interesting. Or life-threatening. Or both.

Dial looked at his phone again, just to make sure.

But the name hadn't changed.

JONATHON PAYNE.

28

Dial glanced at his watch and realized it was the middle of the night in Pittsburgh. Given Payne's background and resources, there was no guarantee that he was stateside, but if he was, Dial knew the odds were pretty damn good he wasn't calling to talk about baseball.

'Just a second,' Dial said into the phone as he excused himself from the lecture hall. 'You haven't even said a word yet, and I'm already dreading this call.'

'Screw you, too.'

'Sorry, it's just—'

'No,' Payne teased, 'I don't want to hear an apology; it's too late for that. I take time out of my busy schedule to see how your chin is doing, and you give me nothing but attitude.'

Dial couldn't help but smile. Payne was referring to Dial's most prominent feature; the finely chiseled lines of his chin gave him the look of a movie star rather than a detective, and Payne was always quick to give him shit about it.

'The chin is fine – even after that sucker punch.'

'Sorry, man, I couldn't resist.'

'It helps if you try.'

'Good point. I'll remember that the next time.'

'Sadly, you said that the last time.'

Both men laughed at the exchange.

'Well,' Dial said, 'if you're at home, you're either up awfully early or awfully late. That means you're either in trouble or something is troubling you. Spill it.'

'At home. Couldn't sleep. Too much on my mind.'

'Go on.'

'Yesterday I got a call from a man who used to work for my father back in the sixties. This guy was a total stranger to me, but he called me out of the blue because he needed my help.'

'Money problems?'

'People problems.'

'Meaning?'

'Some people were after him.'

'What kind of people?'

Payne cleared his throat. 'Dead people.'

Dial raised his voice. 'Jesus, Jon! I hope you mean he's being haunted, because if you're telling me that you killed some people and want my help, I'm going to hang up the damn phone.'

'Not really your help, but . . .'

'Let me guess,' Dial said rhetorically, 'they were all foreign nationals, and now you've got the makings of an international incident on your hands.'

'Wait a second. Did DJ call you already?'

Dial growled into the phone. 'Seriously, is there ever going to be a time you call just to say hello? Every time I hear from you, it's to tell me about someone you killed.'

'Not *every* time. Just *most* of the time.'

Dial didn't find the statement funny.

Payne continued. 'If it makes you feel any better, I have no idea where the gunmen came from. There's a decent chance they were Americans.'

'Then what does this have to do with me?' Dial asked.

'Maybe they weren't foreigners, but the scientist who worked for my father is.'

Dial bristled at the word *scientist*. He sensed their two worlds were about to collide. 'What's his name?'

'Dr Mattias Sahlberg. He was born and raised in Stockholm, but he's been living in the States longer than I've been alive. I think there might be a connection between the gunmen who showed up yesterday and a bombing in his hometown the night before. Any chance you've got someone in Sweden who can fill me in on the case?'

'Yeah . . . me.'

'What are you talking about?'

'I'm currently in Stockholm. I've been here since yesterday.'

'You went personally? I didn't think you were allowed to do that anymore.'

'I'm not supposed to investigate, but I was assigned to this case.'

'By whom? The director?'

'Jon,' Dial stressed, 'this is bigger than we thought. Even before you told me about Sahlberg, I didn't think this was random. Someone targeted these people.'

'Why?'

'That's what we're working on. The men you killed, what can you tell me about them?'

'They were pros. These guys weren't messing around.'

'The attack in Stockholm was brutal but efficient. Very little wasted effort, with no loose ends. Sound familiar?'

'Tough to say, since we took them out before they could finish their job. But they brought an arsenal when they went after Sahlberg. Weapon tech like I've never seen on the street.'

'How so?'

'Their pistols had biometric safeties – palm-print scanners to be precise. DJ thinks one of our sources might be able to give us some leads on the guns. If so, you'll be the next to know.'

Dial wasn't sure if Payne was referring to one of their military contacts or one of their criminal sources. He didn't know, and frankly he didn't care. The only thing that mattered was whether Payne trusted them. If he did, that was good enough for Dial.

'Speaking of contacts, do you know anyone who can rig explosives?'

Payne laughed. 'I know a thousand people who can rig explosives, including myself. What exactly are you looking for?'

'The design of the laboratory explosion was beautiful. It brought down the whole inner structure without collapsing the building. What's more, they used the lab's own chemical supply to ensure that no one survived. This wasn't an amateur job. Whoever planned this has experience.'

'You're thinking military?'

'Military. Government. Can't be sure. But he certainly knew what he was doing.'

'Any leads?' Payne asked.

'On the bomber?'

'On anything.'

'Not as many as I would like. I'm currently interviewing a bunch of scientists here in Stockholm. No one knows what was going on at the lab, but according to them, the people who were killed were at the top of their fields.'

'If you can, send me their names. I'll run them by Sahlberg and see what he says.'

'You'll have a list within the hour. In the meantime, see what he can tell you about a Dr Tomas Berglund.'

Payne jotted down the name. 'Who's he?'

'He is the missing link in our investigation. Right now, we

don't know if he's a suspect, a target, or merely the guy who owned the lab. Knowing my luck, he's probably all three.'

'Actually, I hope he *is* all three.'

'Why do you say that?'

Payne grinned. 'That'll make it more fun to find the bastard.'

29

With two armed guards posted inside his penthouse and Sahlberg sound asleep in the guest bedroom, Payne hustled down a few flights of stairs to the other business in the Payne Industries building. At one point, the entire operation had consisted of a single employee working from a small, rent-free office, and yet over the years it had steadily grown into one of the premier detective agencies in America. With forty-two full-time employees and hundreds of subcontractors around the globe, the David Jones Agency now occupied an entire floor.

Jones paced back and forth in his office because he was too uneasy to sit still. There were simply too many things running through his mind. Too many questions that needed to be answered.

His first order of business had been to initiate contact with Kaiser. In the past, it had been as simple as firing off an email or even tracking him down on the phone. But that was before Kaiser had lost an eye in a battle with an adversary. That episode with a competing 'businessman' had cost him half his vision. It had also driven him even further underground than he was before.

His location had always been hard to pin down, but now it was virtually impossible. He never checked his email, for fear someone might use the embedded server information to track him, and no one knew his cell phone number. The only way to reach out to him was to post a message on a specific online message board, the name of which was a closely guarded secret.

The World Wide Web was an endlessly vast place to hide these coded exchanges, and only a handful of Kaiser's most trusted associates – including Jones – knew where to look.

Paranoid? Yes.

Effective? Definitely.

It was also frustrating. Jones had posted his message an hour earlier and was still waiting for a reply from Kaiser, even though it was late morning in Germany.

'Wow,' Payne said as he entered the room. He glanced around and noted all the souvenirs. 'This isn't an office, it's more like a shrine. All hail the conquering hero.'

On one wall a Mayan dagger.

On another a Spartan shield.

There was even a letter from Nostradamus.

It had been a while since he had visited Jones's office, and he had forgotten just how many artifacts his friend had collected over the years. Even though their lives had been in danger more often than he would have liked, Payne still smiled at the memories. He pulled a small model of Neuschwanstein Castle from one of the shelves. 'Look at this shit.'

'It's not shit,' Jones countered. 'It's stuff. And don't touch it. It's exactly as I want it. A place for everything, and everything in its place.'

While it contrasted with the clean lines of Payne's office, Jones was not lying. He did in fact have a highly complex organizational system, one that allowed him to locate anything he needed in a matter of seconds. And ultimately, that was what mattered the most.

The same could be said about their friendship.

On the surface, they were nothing alike.

And yet they fit together like a well-oiled machine.

Payne was white; Jones was black. Payne had been an All-American athlete at the Naval Academy; Jones, a former nerd, had been a 'math-lete' in high school. Payne had chiseled features and a ripped physique; Jones had the wiry build of a runner and was prettier than most girls. Not feminine, just pretty – like a young Chris Kuzneski.

Some viewed them as the Odd Couple, but they didn't care.

Their friendship would endure until the end of time.

'So,' Payne said, 'have you been working or pacing?'

'A little of both,' Jones admitted as he stepped over a stack of folders that was taller than a hobbit and headed toward his desk. 'Come take a look.'

Two large computer monitors, a wireless keyboard, and a host of other electronic gadgets littered his desktop. On the wall behind him, looming over everything like a shiny monolith, was a massive flat-screen television that had been mounted at a downward angle, so that clients could view surveillance videos, work proposals, or anything else he wanted them to see.

Payne stood across the desk from Jones and watched as he clicked away on his keyboard. A few seconds later, the television lit up with a panoramic image of Bavaria.

'Is that Linderhof Palace?' Payne asked.

Jones tapped his mouse and the photo disappeared. 'Not anymore.'

A moment later, a virtual police report opened in its place. Jones used his cursor to click on the thumbnail image in the corner of the file, and a mug shot of a man named Kenneth Dalton suddenly appeared in the middle of the screen.

'Who's that?' Payne asked.

'The guy I hit with my SUV.'

'He looks better with a face.'

'I can't argue with that.'

'Wait. Where'd you get this?'

'From a friend at the department. He sent it to me as soon as the body was processed.'

Payne focused on the name. 'And what do we know about Mr Dalton?'

'We know he's dead.'

'We knew that before.'

'Good point,' Jones said as he sat in his leather chair. 'It seems Mr Dalton has been a troublemaker for years. First as a teen – he bounced around the juvenile system for years – then in the military – he received a disorderly discharge from the Marines back in '93.'

'What'd he do?'

'He hit his commanding officer in the face with a shovel.'

'Ouch. I bet that hurt.'

'Not as much as getting hit by an Escalade.'

Payne laughed. 'Touché.'

'After a short stint in military prison, Dalton brought his skills – and shovel – to Pittsburgh, where he made a reputation as a collector for some of the guys running numbers on the Southside. If you forgot to pay, he'd beat a reminder into you. He was locked up for eighteen months when one of the guys he smacked around turned his name over to the police. Three days after he got out, the guy who put him away was found dead in his apartment. The cops could never link Dalton to the crime, but they don't have any other suspects.'

'In other words, a real sweetheart.'

'Exactly,' Jones said as he changed the image on the screen. 'Next up is Mr Derek Paulsen.'

Payne recognized him at once. He was the smaller gunman

from the incline. 'Him I know. The two of us go waaayy back. I'm talking, like, several hours.'

'Well you can cross him off your Christmas list, because he didn't survive the night.'

'Come on! That can't be right. I hardly even hit the guy.'

'You mean compared to how hard I hit Dalton?'

'Exactly.'

'Don't worry. He didn't die from your fists of fury. He died at the police station. Someone killed him before he could talk.'

'Do they know who did it?'

'That would be this gem,' Jones said as he changed the image to a third police report. 'Mr Marcus Lindo. They found him inside a parked car two blocks from the station. Someone popped him with a small-caliber to the temple. No witnesses. No suspects.'

'Do Lindo and Paulsen have anything in common?'

'Not before yesterday.' Jones clicked his mouse again. This time the screen split into several smaller windows, each displaying a separate police file, including some they hadn't discussed. 'In fact, I can't find a connection between any of these guys.'

Payne stepped closer for a better look. He recognized the larger gunman from the incline and the man he'd shot inside the lower station. The two remaining men were the goons he had shot from the second-floor window. Along with the first three, it brought the total to seven.

Noticeably absent was the Arab who had been running the show at the lower station. Payne had only seen him briefly, but he wasn't one of the dead men on the screen.

'So,' Payne said, 'where do we go from here?'

As if on cue, the phone started to ring.

30

Dial stood in the hallway of the institute jotting a few notes. His conversation with Payne had brought new details to light – namely Sahlberg and those pursuing him – and he wanted to get the information down while it was still fresh in his head.

He was about to push through the double doors of the lecture hall when they swung open toward him instead and Eklund barged into the hallway, his cell phone pressed tightly to his ear. With his free hand he reached out and grabbed Dial's arm.

His message was clear: *Don't go back in. You need to hear this.*

Dial watched and listened as Eklund launched into a long conversation in his native Swedish. He didn't understand anything except for an occasional name, but he could tell from the wide range of expressions on Eklund's face that something important had happened.

Eventually Eklund hung up the phone and filled him in. 'That was my office. They just heard from the Rättsmedicinalverket—'

'The what?'

'Our doctor from the National Board of Forensic Medicine.'

Dial furrowed his brow. 'The what?'

'The coroner.'

'Oh.'

'Anyway, they've combed through every inch of the crime scene, and we now have an official body count.'

Dial knew a body count wasn't enough to make Eklund run

the course of emotions he had just witnessed. There had to be more to the story than that. 'How many?'

'Twenty-three – twenty of which have already been identified.'

'Is Berglund one of them?'

'No.'

'Could he be one of the remaining three?'

Eklund shrugged. 'So far we've been unable to locate Berglund's dental records, so we can't compare his teeth against those three. Obviously there's a chance he is one of the victims, but mathematically speaking the odds are against it.'

'Odds? What odds? What are you talking about?'

Eklund glanced at his notepad. 'Over the past two days, we've received calls from eight – no, make that *nine* – embassies asking for information about missing scientists. We were able to match some of those names with bodies in the morgue, but right now we have way more names than bodies. According to my notes, we have eleven possibilities for the three unidentified bodies.'

'You're right. We've got a math problem.'

'Here's the thing: figuring out how many people died in the fire is not the same as determining how many people worked in the lab. I can't tell you with certainty that Berglund is alive, and I can't say for sure that he died in the explosion. We just don't know.'

'What about the Finnish police? Any word from them?'

'They went to his house and peeked through his windows but didn't see anything out of the ordinary. Right now they're waiting on a court order to get inside the house.'

'What's the hold-up?'

'I don't know.'

'If he's dead, the Finns should want to find his killer. If

he's alive, he's a suspect or a possible target. Either way, a judge should be willing to sign the paperwork.'

'I know, but—'

'But what?'

Eklund paused, unsure how to respond to his boss.

Dial instantly regretted his tone. The last thing he wanted to do was insult Eklund by insinuating he had lost faith in his ability to direct the investigation. That couldn't be farther from the truth. 'Sorry. I didn't mean to overstep my bounds.'

Eklund nodded. 'Old habits are hard to break.'

'Still, I promised that I wouldn't interfere.'

'You weren't interfering. You were venting. Believe it or not, I've been known to snap at colleagues from time to time.'

Dial smiled, glad that Eklund wasn't holding a grudge. 'All cops do. In fact, I think I saw it during your phone call. What was that all about?'

Eklund laughed. 'That wasn't anger. That was *confusion*. I thought we were finally getting a grasp on the science at the lab. Now I don't know what to think.'

'About what?'

'Five of the victims had criminal records.'

Dial shrugged it off. 'Well, I assumed the gunmen had rap sheets, and it stands to reason that a few of the scientists got popped over the years. What'd they do? Smoke a little pot?'

'I'm not talking about either group. When the coroner ran the fingerprints and dental records of the victims, he discovered that five of them weren't scientists. They were convicted felons.'

Dial pondered that statement for a moment, his mind working through a series of 'what ifs', each more terrifying than the last.

What if the scientists were being forced to work in the lab?

What if they had stumbled across a new biological agent?

What if they planned to sell their weapon to the highest bidder?

What if the weapon was taken from the lab before the fire was set?

Dial realized the worst thing he could do was jump to conclusions, so he tried to find out more. 'Can we tie the five together?'

Eklund shook his head. 'So far we haven't been able to establish any connection between the men – except that they're felons and all of them spent time in Scandinavian prisons.'

'The same prison?'

'Nope, different – so they didn't meet inside.'

'What were their crimes?' Dial asked.

Eklund reviewed the notes he had scribbled during the phone call. 'The first was a Finn convicted of more than a hundred counts of battery and aggravated assault. He was supposed to be serving a thirty-year term. Instead, he was paroled after serving only six years of his sentence. Same thing happened with a kidnapper from Denmark. He was to spend the next twenty years inside, but he was paroled after half of that.'

'Were they paroled around the same time?' Dial asked.

'Two days apart,' Eklund replied.

'I doubt that's a coincidence.'

'It gets worse. Right about that same time, two men, a rapist and a murderer, were walking out of their respective facilities in Norway without *anyone* noticing. The prison authorities swear that the prisoners died and were cremated on site. They have no idea how they could have escaped, never mind how they could have ended up in a laboratory in Stockholm.'

'The same story at both prisons? Why don't they just shine a spotlight on themselves and announce that something fishy is going on?'

'Agreed. Someone knows something they're not telling us. These weren't so-called country club facilities. These were maximum-security installations with protocols to ensure that someone couldn't simply vanish.'

'You said five. What about the last guy?'

'An arsonist from right here in Sweden. He was transferred from Kumla prison to a psychiatric facility in the northern part of the country. Three weeks later he was released with a clean bill of health. From felon to freedom in less than a month.'

'Doesn't that strike you as odd?'

'Odd? I haven't even gotten to the odd part yet.' Eklund clenched his jaw and shook his head as if he couldn't believe what he was about to say. 'To identify the bodies, they ran the same procedure I explained earlier.'

'Rehydrating the fingertips to expose the ridge patterns,' Dial recalled.

'Right. Well, we also told the coroner to run the whole battery of testing. Given the scientific nature of the scene and our inability to say for certain that it was the fire that killed everyone, we asked for toxicology reports to determine whether they were drugged, virology reports to ascertain the presence of biological agents, you name it. If they had the means of performing the test, we wanted it done.'

'And?'

'When they examined some of the tissue samples under a microscope, they found something that goes way, way, *way* beyond odd. So much so that no one really quite knows what to make of it.'

'What did they find?'

'You might not believe this – I'm still trying to comprehend it myself – but some of their cells are still alive.'

'*Alive?* As in *living?*'

'That's what they're telling me,' Eklund confirmed. 'The fire should have destroyed them, or at the very least damaged them beyond repair, yet the coroner says he found viable tissue in some of the bodies. In fact, more than viable. He said the tissue was *thriving.*'

31

Payne and Jones had known about Kaiser for more than a decade, but they didn't really *know* him. No one did, which was one of the things that kept him alive.

Back in his former life as a supply sergeant, he had set up shop near the Kaiserslautern military community in eastern Germany. With more than 50,000 soldiers and civilian contractors, Kaiserslautern was the largest military base outside of the continental United States, but one of the trickiest to pronounce. To make things simple, American troops referred to it as 'K-town'. And the man who could get them anything was known as Kaiser.

In the beginning, Kaiser had focused on the comforts of home – items that the displaced men and women of K-town had grown to miss, whether that be American food, clothing, movies or video games. And he sold the products at a fair yet profitable price. Then, much to his chagrin, the rise of the Internet meant he wasn't the only game in town. Suddenly his clients could order almost anything online, so he was forced to shift his business in another direction.

Weapons. Smuggling. Fake IDs.

Pretty much everything except drugs.

Payne and Jones knew he operated beyond the limits of the law, but they had experienced enough during their time as MANIACs to know that even the noblest causes sometimes required the support of bullets, grenades and the occasional surface-to-air missile. Likewise, Kaiser had heard of their exploits, and he realized that men of their skills were good to know.

They had a mutual respect for one another.

Not a true friendship. More like allies.

The phone belonged to DJ, but Payne grabbed it first. He smiled at Jones, hit the correct line to answer the call, then put the phone to his ear, despite a loud protest from Jones.

Before he said a single word, he realized something was different about the call. Normal phone calls – regardless of whether they originated from a landline, a cell phone, a satellite phone, or through voice-over Internet protocol – carried some degree of ambient sound. The hum of a computer. The horns and sirens of traffic. Even the steady breathing of the caller. These were typical background noises that were layered into the signal. Even the newest noise-canceling technology left telltale traces of white noise. They were virtually inaudible, but they were not imperceptible.

This call was different. It wasn't hollow, it was silent. It was as if the caller was standing in the vacuum of space. Payne quickly realized the call was being *scrubbed* – his word for when high-tech gadgetry was used to ensure that no one was listening in. He knew the caller was running the signal through a computer, routeing the call through a series of lines and servers while at the same time erasing any digital footprint that might lead back to him.

'Hello?' Payne finally said.

A brief pause followed. 'David?'

Payne recognized the voice. 'No, it's Jon. I'm here with—'

'Put David on the phone.'

Payne was somewhat startled by Kaiser's abrupt demand. He knew they weren't friends in the traditional sense, but they certainly weren't strangers. In fact, if it weren't for Payne,

Kaiser would be missing a lot more than an eye. He would be missing the rest of his life.

Payne wondered what had changed since they had spoken last.

'It's for you,' he said, confused. 'It's Kaiser.'

Jones took the handset. 'Hello.'

'Secondary site. Sixteen eighty-two. Three. Four. Two.'

In a flurry of mouse clicks and keystrokes, Jones directed his Internet browser to a specific web address. This secondary site, as Kaiser called it, was used to screen his communications. The location, which changed at irregular intervals, was encoded on the message board that Jones had used to reach him.

The location for that particular conversation was a website that allowed people to discuss children's literature. Jones was to find the 1,682nd post in the numbered list, scroll to the third paragraph in that post, find the fourth sentence, and provide the second word. If he failed to do so, or if he took too long to do it, Kaiser would terminate the call.

Jones traced his finger down the screen. 'I authenticate . . . Mockingbird.'

'David! How are you?' Just like that, Kaiser had gone from cryptic and paranoid to warm and welcoming. 'It's been far too long!'

'I'm okay, how are you?'

'Still got my eye on the prize,' Kaiser joked.

'Which is what, retirement?'

'Forget about that. They'll put me in the ground before I call it quits.'

Jones laughed at his choice of words. He knew Kaiser wasn't referring to old age. He was referring to rival businessmen who were actively trying to put him in the ground. 'Do you have time for a question or two? I'm here with Jon, and we were wondering—'

'Please apologize to Jon for my shortness. I didn't mean to come across like such an asshole, but I have to take precautions.'

'He understands completely,' Jones said without consulting Payne. 'No offense taken.'

'Good. Now what is it that I can answer for you?'

'Well, I'm looking at a weapon.'

'I can get you anything you need.'

'No,' Jones clarified, 'I'm not placing an order. I'm looking at the actual piece. And I don't need any more. I just need to figure out where it came from.'

'What's this world coming to when someone like you is coming to someone like me for gun advice? Don't they teach this shit in the special forces anymore?'

Jones laughed. 'They do, but this gun is kind of different.'

'How different?'

'It's a one-off,' Jones explained. 'The build resembles the Beretta 92 platform, but it's a complete custom. Right down to the grip length, trigger pull, and weighting.'

'I could name fifty guys who might have put that together. Is there anything else to go on? How's the finish? Some of them are great at design but go light on aesthetics. They figure that as long as the gun fires, the look doesn't really matter. You'd be surprised how many tool marks you can find on some custom jobs. Everything from drill scuffs to swirls in the polished steel. Things like that can narrow it down.'

'No,' Jones assured him, 'this gun is a thing of beauty.'

'Well, you have to give me *something*.'

'Not only is it beautiful, it has a biometric safety.'

'You mean like a fingerprint scanner?'

'A palm-print to be exact – built into the side of the grip.'

'Mounted?'

'Nope. It's actually integrated into the gun's design. Does that narrow the field?'

'Considerably,' Kaiser answered. 'You're talking about something that combines old-world smithing with new-age technology. There's only two guys I can think of who would have the necessary skill and understanding to make something like that.'

'Hang on,' Jones said. 'If it's all right with you, I'm going to put you on speaker so that Jon can be a part of the conversation.'

'Of course,' Kaiser said.

Jones activated the speakerphone feature and hung up the handset. 'You're on with Jon.'

'Hey, Jon.'

'Hey, Kaiser. Nice chatting with you earlier,' Payne teased.

'Seriously, Jon, I'm sorry about that. I just—'

'No worries. I'm just busting your balls. I understand the need for security.'

Kaiser breathed a sigh of relief. 'I appreciate that.'

Jones got the conversation back on track. 'You were saying there are only two gunsmiths that you know of who are capable of producing a weapon like this.'

'I was.'

'What can you tell us about them?'

'Well, I have one of them on speed-dial. He's been working on a, um, special project for me over the past year. I seriously doubt he's responsible, but I can find out easy enough.'

Payne and Jones looked at each other. They both wanted to know what kind of 'special project' Kaiser was working on with one of the world's best gunsmiths. They wondered if he was outfitting a rebel army or stockpiling merchandise for a Christmas sale.

With a man like Kaiser, it could be either.

'Okay,' Payne said. 'Let's assume for the time being that it's not your guy. What do you know about the second possibility?'

'His name is Yannick Holcher, and he lives in the hills of Luxembourg.'

In some ways, the location was ideal. The Grand Duchy of Luxembourg was situated in central Europe. From there, Holcher could take advantage of a broad range of clientele from the surrounding countries. Of course, if he was as talented as Kaiser claimed, his location didn't matter. Gun enthusiasts would travel the world to possess the perfect weapon. Still, his decision to set up shop in one of the smallest countries in the world was worthy of an explanation.

'Why Luxembourg?' Payne wondered. 'There are other places nearby that would give him much better opportunities. I would have to assume the market in Munich, or Zurich, or Prague would be much, much bigger.'

Kaiser agreed. 'I'm quite familiar with the numbers, and you're absolutely correct. He could reach a far bigger audience by moving his operation. In fact, it's illegal to even own this kind of weapon in Luxembourg. Which means his clientele are mostly foreigners.'

'Not exactly the best business model,' Payne said.

'But that means nothing to him. He's not a transplant. He's a Luxembourger, born and raised. From what I hear, he has no intention of leaving.'

'Hell of a place to make a name for himself,' Jones stated.

'He doesn't care about that either,' Kaiser replied. 'Oddly, he has no interest in recognition. In keeping with that, any gun he produces is simply known as a Wiltz, named after the only town in that part of the country. Legend has it that he was born there.'

'And you think he's our man? That this is one of his?'

'The guy might be a little quirky, but he's still the best in the business when it comes to marrying tried-and-true smithing techniques with modern technological advancements. I once saw a gun he designed that had a laser sight mounted *inside* the barrel. I'm still trying to figure out how he managed to do it.'

'Sounds likes you're envious. Maybe you should have hired him instead.'

'Trust me, I tried. But he said he was all booked up, and that no amount of money could compete with what he was already being paid.'

Jones knew it was a long shot, but he had to ask. 'Did he happen to mention a name?'

'No such luck. He simply said the job would keep him busy for a very long time. Apparently the guy had ordered enough weapons to outfit a private militia.'

Payne and Jones stared at each other. If Kaiser's information was accurate, it meant that Sahlberg was in a lot more danger than they had originally thought.

And so were they.

32

The Pentagon
Arlington, VA

Randy Raskin didn't work in Washington DC. He actually worked across the Potomac river inside a windowless office in the sub-basement of the Pentagon, but due to his classified position as a computer researcher for the US military, the data he compiled frequently found its way to the White House and Capitol Hill.

Amazingly, most of his friends thought he was nothing more than a low-level programmer, working a dead-end job in the world's largest office building – because that was what he was required to tell them. But in reality he was a high-tech maestro, able to track down just about anything in cyberspace. Thanks to the next-generation technology and his high security clearance, Raskin was privy to many of the government's biggest secrets, a mountain of classified data that was there for the taking if someone knew how to access it. His job was to make sure the latest information got into the right hands at the best possible time.

Over the years, Payne and Jones had used his services on many occasions, which had eventually led to a friendship. Raskin often pretended he didn't have time for them, or their bi-monthly favors, but the truth was he admired them greatly and would do just about anything to help. In fact, one of his biggest joys in life was living vicariously through them – whether that was during their stint with the MANIACs or their recent adventures around the globe.

That included keeping tabs on them at all times.

He answered his phone on the second ring. 'Research.'

'Don't you ever take a break?' Payne asked.

'Yeah,' Jones said into the speakerphone, 'it's five in the morning. Why are you at work?'

'Some of us do have to earn our paychecks,' Raskin replied into his headset. 'Besides, if it's five a.m. here, it's one in the afternoon in Fallujah and six in the evening in Beijing. It's a big world out there, boys, and someone has to keep it safe.'

Jones laughed. 'Says the guy in the bathrobe.'

Raskin didn't smile. He was, in fact, wearing a fuzzy blue bathrobe over his normal clothes, but only because they kept his office freezing cold to prevent his computers from overheating. 'Hold up! Are you sure you want to make fun of me?'

'We always make fun of you,' Jones said.

'True, but you normally wait until *after* I do what you need.'

Payne nodded. 'That's a very good point.'

'Anyway,' Raskin said, 'why are you calling so early? To talk about DJ's *accident* – and I use that term loosely – or to discuss the gunmen that Jon put in the morgue?'

'How do you know about that?' Jones asked.

'How do you think? I designed a program that monitors millions of databases around the world. It has one specific goal: to flag the names of special forces personnel whenever they're logged into a system. Any system. Anywhere. For any reason. If someone uses his real name to make a dinner reservation or a tee time, I know about it.'

'You really care what my handicap is?' Payne asked.

'I know what your handicap is – he's sitting next to you.'

'Very funny,' Jones said.

'Actually, it was,' Payne admitted.

Raskin grinned, glad he had gotten in at least one clean shot during their conversation. 'Obviously I ignore most of the data that comes my way, but I do take an interest when you idiots decide to kill a bunch of people in your hometown. How many times have I told you guys? If you're feeling a little down and you need to go on a killing spree, stick to hobos and hookers in Third World countries. There's a lot less paperwork that way.'

'Pittsburgh PD?' Payne asked, wondering about his source.

'Yeah, Pittsburgh PD. They filed multiple homicide reports. But don't worry: they're listing it as self-defense. They won't be asking the district attorney to initiate charges, but you might still get a follow-up call.'

'Thanks for the heads-up.'

'No problem,' Raskin said as he leaned back in his chair. 'So, out of curiosity, how fast were you going when you hit that guy? Based on the video, I'd say about fifty.'

'Video? What video?' Jones demanded.

'The one where you clobber some son-of-a-bitch with a two-ton truck. That video. I've watched the footage about a hundred times.'

'Where'd you get the footage?'

'Traffic camera at the intersection just beyond the station. Security feed from Station Square across the street. High-definition satellite imagery from . . . well, technically I'm not allowed to talk about it. Seriously, take your pick.'

'How can you access a security feed?' Payne asked.

'Nowadays, almost everything is stored on a cloud-based network. The video from every individual camera is uploaded to a central computer. From there it can be accessed from anywhere. You just have to know where to look.'

As he listened to Raskin's explanation, a thought occurred to Payne: if Raskin was able to watch the Escalade ram the last of the reinforcements, maybe he could track the missing gunman as well. 'Randy, with all that footage at your disposal, are you able to track a single target?'

'Of course I can – if I know where to look.'

'We've still got one shooter unaccounted for. Darker skin, probably Arabic. I never got a clean view of his face, but I know where he was. His partner opened fire on me when I tried to leave the lower station. Unless I miss my guess, he's the leader of the operation. Is there any way you could follow him from the station?'

'Let me check.'

Payne and Jones waited as Raskin analyzed every angle of the shootout, furiously pounding away on his keyboard and pulling things from screen to screen by means of hand gestures that were detected by motion-capture cameras. It was technology that had only recently debuted in the civilian market. Inside the Pentagon, they had been using it for years. Raskin tried to work his magic, but unfortunately, this time he was unable to pull a rabbit out of his hat.

'He gets lost under cover,' he said. 'Sorry. I have him for half a block, but when he ducks into Station Square, I lose him. There's no accessible footage from inside the mall. I suppose you could try to hunt down the tapes from the individual stores, but unless he went inside a particular shop *and* you knew where to look, your chances of finding him are slim.'

Jones agreed with Raskin's assessment, but he had plenty of manpower at his disposal. He turned toward Payne and said, 'I'll send some men to Station Square as soon as the stores open. Who knows? We might get lucky.'

Raskin felt bad he hadn't come through for them. 'Sorry,

guys. I wish I could do more, but I can't work with footage that isn't there.'

'Do you mean it?' Jones said.

'Of course I mean it. If the footage isn't avail—'

'No, I was referring to you wanting to do more.'

Raskin groaned. 'Not really. It's just a figure of speech.'

'Too bad. I'm going to hold you to your offer.'

'Fine! What is it now?'

Jones grabbed the phone from its cradle – which turned off the speakerphone – and lowered his voice to a whisper so Payne couldn't hear. 'Do you think you can send me the footage of my, um, accident? I'd like to add it to my personal highlight reel.'

'No problem,' Randy said, laughing. 'Do you also want me to send you surveillance footage from the dentist's office? That door hit you in the mouth pretty hard.'

Jones flushed with embarrassment. 'How do you know about that?'

'Like I said, my system flags *everything*.'

33

The Swedish National Board of Forensic Medicine – known locally as the Rättsmedicinalverket – was a branch of law enforcement tasked with investigating the cause of death in cases of murder, fatal accidents and other 'tragic events'. Six facilities scattered across the country handled the workload, but the main facility was located in Stockholm.

Dial marveled at the interior of the lobby as the group waited to meet the coroner. Everything was polished steel, clear glass and fluorescent light. Nothing in there was organic. No wood. No wallpaper. Nothing that could incubate germs or other contaminants. There was an antiseptic feel, to be sure, but the space was actually quite comforting.

It felt safe, as if nothing could harm him there.

Dial wondered if the other lab had felt the same way.

On this field trip, Dial and Eklund had not come alone. They had decided to bring three of the scientists from the institute – Drs Miles and Norling, as well as Hedman, the engineer – to help with the investigation. They hoped that Miles's knowledge of microbiology and Norling's knowledge of seemingly everything involved in the human process would help them better understand what the coroner had discovered.

Hedman had been chosen for three reasons. First, they genuinely liked the man and respected his opinions. Second, because of his engineering background he could give them an educated opinion from a different perspective than the others. And third, he was the only one they had met at the institute who spoke in terms they could understand. The rest of the group used jargon and concepts that Dial and Eklund had a hard time deciphering. But Hedman broke the explanations into comprehensible analogies, using common vocabulary that didn't require a doctorate-level education to follow. He was their de facto translator.

'I'm sorry to have kept you waiting,' the coroner said as he appeared from the examination wing of the building. His English was flat and methodical, without inflection of any kind – as if he had learned the language from a robot. 'I trust you found everything okay?'

'I was here a few years ago,' Eklund explained. 'I knew where to find you.'

'Very good. Many visitors – not that we have many visitors per se, mainly officers such as yourself – they get confused and wind up in our business offices, which are located in a separate building.'

'Everyone, this is Björn Zander, the head of the Rättsmedicinalverket here in Stockholm.' Eklund turned to introduce the makeshift investigatory team. Zander nodded around at them all.

'Pleased to meet you. If you will follow me, I will show you what you have come to see.' Without waiting for a response, he swiped his access card through a security reader, unlocking a hallway that led into the bowels of the facility.

After a short walk, they arrived at the laboratory that was handling the victims of the explosion. As Dial entered, he caught the unmistakable scent of processed air.

'Is it supposed to smell like this?' Hedman asked.

'You smell something peculiar?' Zander replied.

'Actually, there's no scent of any kind. That's what's peculiar.'

Dial knew what Hedman meant. Air typically smelled of

something: floral oils that drifted in from the outside, chemical disinfectant, or one of a thousand other odors. Even scents that couldn't be distinguished by the nose – such as human pheromones – were still perceptible. But not in this room. The air was different here. Not stale, but empty.

'Please, forgive me,' Zander insisted. 'I am here so much that I think nothing of it. The scent – or lack thereof – is simply a by-product of the air purification system. Most systems rid the air of microbial agents, but in here we must take extra precautions. Our air is treated to remove microbes, spores and other airborne particulates. The treatment leaves the air virtually free from impurities. It can be unsettling at first, but I assure you that everything is fine.'

'I wasn't unsettled – just curious,' Hedman assured him.

'As you should be. After all, you are a man of science.'

'So,' Eklund said, trying to move things along, 'your assistant told my assistant that you uncovered some startling results in the course of your examination? Something about the resiliency of the cells?'

'Yes,' Zander said as he led them to the far side of the room. He stopped in front of a gigantic microscope and began to explain his findings. 'In ancient times, it was often reported that a body's hair and fingernails would continue to grow after death, but this has long since been explained as the mere appearance of growth due to shriveling of the tissue in the scalp and fingertips.'

Dial braced himself for a roundabout explanation of things. He couldn't imagine that any description that began with 'in ancient times' would get straight to the heart of the matter. He appreciated the coroner's attempt to provide them with the necessary background information, but he wouldn't have any problem cutting him off if he started to ramble.

'That being said, we have discovered that certain biological functions do not stop immediately upon expiration. There are secondary functions that transpire as a result of the continuing existence of bacteria in the body or the eventual loss of muscle tension. These include the release of excrement and urine, as well as the digestion of any foods retained in the body at the time of death.'

Hanna, the matriarch of the group, leaned close to Hedman and expressed herself in rapid Swedish. Eklund overheard the comment and was forced to bite his tongue to keep from laughing.

'What'd she say?' Dial whispered.

Eklund whispered back. 'She said if we were brought here to learn that people piss and shit themselves when they die, she could have saved us all the trip.'

Dial was forced to bite his tongue as well.

Zander stared at them like they were mischievous schoolboys.

'Sorry,' Eklund said to the coroner, 'police stuff.'

'Of course,' Zander replied, shaking off the interruption. 'There are also more direct continuations that occur after death. The brain, for instance, does not immediately stop functioning. When the circulatory system stops pumping blood, the brain enters a "panic mode" of sorts. Its cells struggle to find the oxygen that a person's pulse used to deliver. Synapses fire uncontrollably as the brain launches into overdrive in a final effort to survive. Only after this ultimate flurry of activity does the brain eventually succumb to the lack of nutrients.'

'Are you saying that people are still *thinking* after they die?' Hedman asked.

'No,' Zander replied. 'This activity is in no way indicative of consciousness, ability to reason, or even the capability of

perceiving the events that are unfolding. Not to sound indif-
ferent to human life, but these are little more than chemical
reactions, a by-product of the body shutting down. They are
significant only in regard to the timeline, meaning that they
occur *after* the events that precipitate death.'

'Thank God for that,' Hedman said.

'In the same manner, the central nervous system can often
radiate impulses from the spinal column to the peripheral
muscles. Twitching and spasms in the minutes after death are
not uncommon. These do not mean that the individual is in
some way still alive.'

'Your office mentioned something about cellular activity in
their report. Is that why you've called us here?' Eklund asked.
'Some of the cells from some of the bodies in the explosion
exhibited these involuntary impulses?'

'I would not have called you here for that,' Zander assured
him. 'What we have found goes well beyond the established
posthumous activity that has been documented.'

'In what ways?' Miles asked.

Zander flipped a switch on the microscope and a powerful
lamp illuminated the specimen slide that was pinned to the
stage. Next he reached over and pressed the power button on
a flat-screen display that was mounted next to the lab table.
When the screen came to life, the group could see that it was
connected to the microscope. Everything seen through the
eyepiece was now projected for them to examine.

'What do you see?' Zander asked.

Miles and Hanna stepped closer to the screen for a better
look.

To Dial, the screen simply looked like a collection of squiggly
lines against a blue background, with paler blobs dotted across
the image. He had no idea what he was looking at.

'Healthy human tissue cells,' Miles answered.

Hanna nodded, confirming his assessment.

'That is precisely what they are,' Zander said. '*Healthy* human cells. What I would like to know is . . . how?'

'What do you mean?' Dial asked.

'These are the cells from one of the victims, Chief Dial. The donor died more than a full day ago, yet these cells continue to exist. Not only that, they appear to be *thriving*.'

Hanna shook her head and gesticulated wildly as she spoke.

Eklund translated for Dial's sake. 'She says that's impossible. She says the fire alone should have damaged the cells beyond repair, and if any cells did somehow manage to stay alive in the blaze, they would have died shortly after. Without the bodily functions of the host – fresh air from the lungs, fresh blood from the heart – the cells cannot exist on their own.'

'And yet you are looking at them doing just that,' Zander said defensively. 'Feel free to choose a sample for yourselves if you have doubts, but I assure you this sample was pulled from the remains of one of your victims.'

'There's no known chemical compound, natural or otherwise, that can prolong the life of a cell in that way,' Miles argued. 'It has been discussed, but only in a theoretical sense. It's always been assumed that science of this kind was centuries away, if it was even possible at all.'

Dial cleared his throat. 'Didn't you tell me that Berglund was ahead of his time? It seems to me that you said he was a visionary.'

The comment hung in the air without a response.

Several seconds passed before Hanna broke the silence.

'Tell me more about the sample,' she said in Swedish. 'Is this an isolated discovery from a single body? A single organ? Or are these findings widespread?'

Zander answered in English. 'The phenomenon is not relegated to specific organs. Tissue samples from the skin, liver, kidneys and brain all show the same signs of cellular activity. And no, the findings were not widespread. Only a few of the victims suffered from this affliction, if those are even the right words. Five, to be precise.'

Dial groaned in realization. He knew the number wasn't a coincidence. And yet he still had to ask the question to eliminate all doubt from his mind. 'Which five?'

34

Dr Zander knew the answer to Dial's question about the identity of the victims without consulting his notes. Details like this were impossible to forget. 'The five felons.'

Dial nodded. 'That's what I figured.'

'Felons?' Hedman remarked. 'What felons?'

'We've identified the majority of the victims,' Eklund explained. 'Most were scientists, but there were also five men with distinguished criminal records. As of yet, we have no idea what role they played in all of this. We can't say for certain why they were there.'

Hanna launched into a line of questioning, but Dial had to wait for Hedman to translate.

'She wants to know if cell activity within the sample has changed over time. Was this exact number of living cells always present?'

'What does that tell us about the criminals?'

'Nothing,' Hedman answered. 'At least not directly. Frankly, Mr Dial, the presence of criminals is the least of her concerns. That is a mystery for you and Agent Eklund to solve. Her focus is on the science involved.'

'And the number of living cells tells her . . .?' Eklund asked.

Miles answered. 'It tells her whether the cells were dying off, or whether they were multiplying.'

'They were dying off,' Zander announced. 'At least at first.' He sat in front of the keyboard and tilted a nearby computer monitor so that he could see the screen. After finding the right file, the image on the large plasma screen changed as he loaded a video. 'This is a recording of the cellular activity over the course of our examination. As you can see, the cell count was much greater when the sample was first taken.'

Dial could see that the footage plainly supported Zander's claim. The image they were looking at a moment ago had only showed a handful of pale blobs; now the screen was completely speckled. Dial guessed that at least seventy-five percent of the picture was covered in the pale oblong cells.

'Watch what happens over the next several hours,' Zander said.

With a click of the mouse, the footage began to roll forward at high speed. A day's worth of video sped by in the time-compressed clip. Dial watched intently as more and more of the screen changed from white to blue.

'Do the cells always stand out like that?' Eklund wondered.

'No,' Zander explained. 'We add a blue dye to the sample before it goes under the microscope. The walls of healthy cells keep the dye from penetrating into the interior of the cell, so they show as white against the blue background.'

'And what happened when the screen turned mostly blue?'

'The balance shifted from a majority of living cells to a majority of dead cells. The cell wall loses integrity when the cell dies, allowing the blue dye to permeate the remains.'

Miles, the microbiologist, stared at the screen. 'Something kept the cells alive through the fire, but let them die afterwards. Something common to the subjects? A mutated gene, perhaps?'

Zander shrugged. 'It's impossible to answer that without a full sequencing of each subject, but the odds of probability would suggest otherwise. For an unknown genetic mutation of that type to manifest itself in five individuals from the same Scandinavian subset would be a nearly impossible likelihood.

If it were that common – present in one out of every five million people, given the populations of the relevant countries – it would have been detected long ago.'

Miles agreed with the assessment. 'Which means you believe the variable was introduced into the subjects.'

Zander nodded. 'I do.'

Eklund was a half-step behind the others. 'Introduced into the subjects? Does that mean what I think it means? The scientists at the lab were running tests on humans?'

'That's exactly what they're saying,' Hedman answered.

Eklund stared at them, incredulous.

Hedman did his best to explain. 'The world at large condemns those who would dare to use humans in the name of scientific advancement. But the truth is, such experimentation is essential to the development of science. Innovation in every field – surgical, pharmaceutical, medicinal and more – requires exhaustive studies across a wide range of subjects. There is only so much that can be gleaned from mice, rats and chimpanzees.'

Miles concurred. 'Eventually you must involve the targeted recipient. That means humans must be tested, and studied, and tested again.'

Hedman continued. 'Every medical advancement in history was tested on humanity in one way or another, but today's society only accepts it in the form of sanctioned clinical trials. However, many of the true breakthroughs came as a result of so-called "unscrupulous" behavior involving human volunteers and those willing to push the boundaries of accepted doctrine.'

Miles glanced at Hedman. 'I only question the decision to use prisoners. Why draw exclusively from that pool?'

The answer was obvious. Prisoners – especially those with lengthy sentences – were willing to do just about anything to get out of prison, whether that was risking their lives in dangerous escape attempts or volunteering for speculative medical trials. But to coordinate a program like that would require government involvement, or at the very least corrupt prison officials.

In Dial's mind, neither topic was suitable for 'mixed' company, which meant he needed to focus the scientists on a specific task, which would give him a moment to pull Eklund aside for a frank conversation about the Swedish justice system.

He pointed at the computer screen. 'Dr Zander, if you don't mind, can you play the video for my colleagues one more time? I'm sure they have plenty of questions about your discovery.'

Zander smiled with pride. 'Yes, of course, it would be my pleasure.'

'Johann,' Dial said to Eklund, grabbing his arm, 'can we talk?'

'Of course.' They walked toward the entrance of the lab, far enough away from the others to have a private conversation. 'What is it?'

'Do you understand what's going on?'

'With the science? Not really. It's all—'

'No,' Dial said, 'I mean with the prisoners.'

'Unfortunately, yes. It seems that some prisons aren't playing by the rules.'

'It fits the facts, doesn't it? They could offer freedom as a reward for participation. Not only would it ensure a steady supply of volunteers, but if anyone died in the testing, they could use their own doctors to sign off on the paperwork.'

Eklund nodded. 'Yes, it fits the facts, but for us to make accusations like that and have them hold up in a court of law, we would need a lot more proof. Scratch that. We would need proof *period* – because right now, it's just wild speculation on our part.'

Dial shook his head. 'You're missing my point. I'm not interested in the prison officials; I'm interested in the program itself. What if word leaked out about biological testing on dangerous criminals? Don't you think someone might try to shut it down?'

'You mean, like an activist group?'

'They've bombed abortion clinics. Why not a lab?'

Eklund considered the possibility.

'Or, what if it was government-sanctioned?'

'The lab?'

Dial shook his head. 'The hit.'

Eklund groaned and ran his fingers through his hair. It was a nervous tic that only appeared when the stress of his job was getting to him.

'Think about it. The building wasn't just destroyed; it was *incinerated*. In my experience, you don't rig an acetone fire for the hell of it. A fire that hot is designed to consume everything. Nothing survives. Not even bacteria or viruses. Maybe something got out of control and they had no choice but to eliminate the threat before it spread?'

'That's highly doubtful,' Hedman said, making his presence known. Dial and Eklund were so wrapped up in their conversation that they hadn't seen him approach. 'Sorry to overhear your speculation, but I'm not sure I agree with your assessment.'

'In what way?' Dial asked.

'Come take a look at what I found,' Hedman said before leading them back to the video screen. 'By my estimation, the cell count hasn't changed in nearly three hours. At the start of the high-speed sequence, the cells began dying off at an appreciable rate. You could actually see a wave of blue washing over the sample as the cell structures collapsed. But for the last few minutes the image has been static. No change.'

Everyone looked at the screen to see what Hedman was talking about. He was right. The number of remaining pale orbs seemed to have stabilized.

'They've stopped dying,' Zander remarked.

'They've stopped dying,' Hedman repeated, 'and they show no signs of cellular division. The system can't propagate on its own.' He turned toward Dial and Eklund. 'It can't spread.'

'How can a cell exist like that?' Miles asked. 'Life is a continuum. The cell should either be growing and dividing, or it should be withering and dying.'

'I've got a theory on that,' Hedman said. 'Go back to the microscope view.'

Zander ended the footage and projected the image of the slide in front of them.

'Zoom in until only one cell is visible,' Hedman ordered.

A single cell filled the screen.

'Now capture that image and select a different cell. Capture that, and move on to another. Get six or seven images for comparison.'

Zander quickly copy-and-pasted a selection of cells on to his computer screen. 'There, that's ten of them. Now what?'

'Locate the Golgi apparatus and mitochondria of each cell, and arrange them north to south.'

Zander scrolled through each image, rotating the cells to align their organelles – the internal structures responsible for the cell's life processes – per Hedman's specifications.

'Now superimpose all the images on top of one another, lining up the organelles.'

As Zander layered each new image on top of the others, Hedman's smile grew and the group watched in amazement. The organelles of the ten cells matched perfectly. Only the cell walls were different. The internal structures were exactly the same.

'Look at the spacing, the orientation,' Hedman pointed out. 'It's perfectly duplicated within each cell.'

'That sort of specificity is not found naturally. You simply don't find organelles with that level of repetitive organization,' Zander said.

'What are you saying?' Dial asked.

'I don't think they're organelles at all – I think they're synthetic,' Hedman said.

'You mean someone *built* these cells?'

Hedman nodded. 'It's why I don't consider them a threat. They can't replicate. They can't spread. The only thing they can do is follow their programming. It's nanotechnology of the highest order. Truly remarkable.'

'If they're so remarkable, why is someone so determined to destroy them?'

Hedman glanced at him and smiled. 'I wish I could answer all of your questions, but I can only do so much. After all, my specialty is science – *not* people.'

35

Payne woke to the sound of unfamiliar voices in his penthouse. The thick curtains of the master bedroom were designed to block out light, so he couldn't tell how long he had slept. All he knew for sure was that someone outside his door was shouting in a foreign tongue.

Even in the darkened room he had no trouble locating the SIG Sauer pistol that he kept in the nightstand beside his bed. He didn't need to check the chamber or the clip; he knew the gun was loaded and ready to fire.

He crept silently toward his bedroom door and twisted the knob. Peering outside, he glanced down the hallway to the living room beyond. Instead of intruders, he caught a glimpse of Sahlberg seated in front of his computer. The unfamiliar foreign voices were part of the news footage he was watching on the screen – with the volume turned up *way* too loud.

Payne smiled. His grandfather used to do the same thing.

There was *soft*. There was *loud*. And there was *senior citizen*.

Relieved, he returned the pistol to its drawer before brushing his teeth, changing his clothes, and heading toward the living room.

'Good morning,' he announced as he entered the room behind Sahlberg. He wanted to make his presence known to avoid startling the old man.

'Good morning to you too.'

'Find anything interesting?' Payne asked.

'I'm afraid not. Basically just more of the same. A fire of

unknown origin, suspicion that it was not a random act of violence. Curiosity over what was happening in this building. That sort of thing. The story is interesting because events of this nature rarely occur in Stockholm, but until the police release more information, the media has nothing new to report. They don't even know the official body count.'

'I have that information, and a list of names that I want you to look at. But first I need to get something to eat.'

'Where'd you get the list?'

'A cop buddy of mine. Where's DJ?'

'Don't mind Jon,' Jones explained to Sahlberg from the open kitchen, 'he's a little fussy until he gets going. Nothing is more important than getting him fed. I once saw him kill a man for a muffin.' He lifted a plate for Payne to see. 'Food's ready.'

Payne and Sahlberg made their way into the kitchen and found a dozen delivery containers. There were bagels, lox and cream cheese, oatmeal, fresh fruit, pancakes, eggs, and a full pound each of bacon, sausage and ham.

'I had Butch send one of the guys over to pick up some breakfast. I didn't know what anyone would want, so I had him get a smorgasbord for our Swedish friend.'

Butch Reed was the head of security at Payne Industries. Like Payne and Jones, he was former military, having spent several years serving his country in the Marine Corps before losing a leg in battle. He was one of the few people in their everyday lives that they trusted unconditionally. It didn't matter if it was keeping the building secure or sending someone for food – they knew they could rely on Reed.

'Toast and jelly would've been fine,' Sahlberg assured them. 'I hope you didn't go to all this effort for me.'

'Trust me,' Jones said as he watched Payne fill two plates with food, 'I didn't.'

'How long have you two been awake?' Payne asked as he carried his food to the same table they had eaten on the night before.

'More than an hour, less than two,' Jones replied. 'I heard the doctor get up first, and I figured I should keep him company.'

Payne had always been a restless sleeper. His inability to turn his mind off when he closed his eyes at night often kept him awake until the first streaks of light had painted the morning sky. It was the main reason he preferred to sleep in his own bed, surrounded by special drapes that could block out the sunlight.

Jones, on the other hand, had adapted well to the military lifestyle of finding rest whenever it was available. Payne knew Jones could fall asleep in the cargo bay of a bomber flying through a hurricane, surrounded by puking soldiers. He knew it because it had happened. Yet in spite of his ability to block out noise and commotion, Jones would instantly snap to attention at the slightest unexpected murmur. His ability to detect invading footsteps or the distant hum of an enemy personnel carrier while asleep had saved their lives more than once.

Given their sleep patterns, Payne had retired to his master bedroom to get some rest, while Jones had been given the living room couch to stand guard. Both realized the doctor wouldn't be able to open the guest room door without Jones being fully aware.

So far, the morning had been uneventful. Jones and Sahlberg had split a pot of coffee while rehashing the events at the incline, after which Jones had made arrangements for a proper breakfast and watched the morning news on the kitchen television while Sahlberg perused the Internet in the living room.

'You mind if we talk while we eat?' Payne asked.

'What he means is, do you mind talking while *he* eats,' Jones explained.

Sahlberg laughed. 'Of course not. There's no need to stand on ceremony. I'm indebted to you both.'

'Good,' Payne said in between mouthfuls of bacon. 'Then let's jump in the deep end. What do you know about Dr Tomas Berglund?'

Sahlberg slowly reached for his glass of orange juice. He raised it to his lips and took three long, full gulps. Then he leaned back in his chair, staring at his breakfast, not saying a word. His face was frozen in a blank, thoughtful expression.

Payne glanced at Jones, wondering if he was thinking the same thing: Sahlberg was stalling. When he spoke, *if he spoke*, they would have to take his words with a healthy dose of skepticism. Honest stories started immediately. Delays suggested the speaker was taking a moment to concoct a tale that could not be trusted with any degree of certainty.

Sahlberg could also see what Payne was thinking.

'I'm not searching for a convincing deception, Jon. I simply needed a moment to consider this new information and how it fits into this mystery.'

'So, how does Berglund fit in?'

'I'm honestly not quite sure, at least not one hundred percent . . . not yet, that is. But I assure you the pieces are coming together.'

'How so?' Jones asked.

'You asked what I know about Dr Berglund. The answer is that I know plenty. But I believe what's important is not so much what I know about him as the fact that I actually know him personally. Tomas and I are quite good friends. Or at least, I think we are.'

The news was enough for Payne to put down his fork – but

not until he shoveled one last scoop into his mouth. He wanted to dedicate his full attention to Sahlberg in order to separate fact from fiction. 'Start from the beginning.'

'Tomas is a certified genius. He is one of the finest scientific minds that Sweden has ever produced, perhaps even the best in all of Scandinavia.'

'In what field?' Jones asked.

'All of them,' Sahlberg replied. 'At least, all of those in which he takes an interest. He has studied psychology, mechanical engineering, sociology, and a variety of other disciplines. But his greatest contributions have been made in the physical and natural sciences. Chemistry, biology, even physics. These are the areas in which he truly shines.'

'How did he make a name for himself?'

'His foresight is uncanny,' Sahlberg explained. 'While others were dabbling in modern science, Berglund was preoccupied with the future. While they were constrained by the limitations of modern technology, Berglund envisioned experiments for things that had yet to be created.'

'Then he would go out and create them?'

'Sometimes. But often he would simply provide the blueprints necessary for others to realize his dreams. That was the beauty of his imagination. He was constantly pushing toward the next advancement, even while the previous discovery was still in development.'

'You said you know him. For how long?' Payne asked.

'Since the beginning.'

'Meaning what?'

'He was born in Finland, but he attended a boarding school in Stockholm on a full academic scholarship. I knew I needed to establish an early relationship with him if I had any hope of convincing him to consider my research. In the end, my recruitment proved successful, and I was able to witness his genius at first hand for many years.'

'You worked with him? Where?'

'Here in Pittsburgh, of course.'

36

Payne was beginning to understand what Sahlberg had meant when he said the pieces were coming together. Sahlberg knew Berglund. They had worked together. Someone had destroyed Berglund's lab in Stockholm on the same day Sahlberg was hunted in Pittsburgh.

That wasn't a coincidence. It couldn't be.

But something was still *missing*.

Payne needed to learn more about their connection. 'Why did you recruit Berglund?'

'Why? Because the boy was wasting his vast potential,' Sahlberg answered. 'He had all this *brilliance* – it practically oozed from his pores like booze from a drunk – and yet he had no direction in his life. The first time we met, he was hustling people in the park for money. Not robbing them, mind you, simply using his brain to exploit them.'

'In what way?' Payne asked.

'In every way,' Sahlberg said, smiling. 'Cards, checkers, chess. It didn't really matter. If it involved strategy or memorization of any kind, he had an unfair advantage. You see, Tomas has a photographic memory. You could hand him a book, and ten minutes later he could recite it to you, forward *and* backward, and in a multitude of languages. Word got around about his abilities, and people used to show up at the park to test him. That's how he made his money. He'd sit on a bench and take on all comers. Eventually he met somebody he couldn't beat.'

'You?' Jones wondered.

Sahlberg laughed. 'A friend of mine.'

Payne noticed the twinkle in Sahlberg's eye. 'You conned him, didn't you?'

'Of course I did! It was the only way to beat the lad. I bet him a substantial sum of money that a friend of mine could beat him in a game of chess. You have to understand, Tomas had the ability to play ten people at once, roaming from board to board without even pausing to think, so he jumped at the chance to play my friend for money.'

'And?' Jones blurted.

'And what?'

'And what happened next?'

Sahlberg laughed, enjoying his captive audience. 'And *obviously* my friend won, or I wouldn't be telling this story, now would I?'

'Yeah, I realize that, but . . . *how* did he win?'

'How?' Sahlberg smiled, the twinkle in his eye getting brighter. 'Oh, how silly of me! I *must* be getting old. I forgot to tell you one very important detail about my friend. I forgot to tell you his name . . . It was Bobby . . . Bobby Fischer.'

Jones gasped. '*What?* You were friends with Bobby Fischer? He's the best chess player of all time. No wonder Berglund lost.'

'Not friends, exactly. More like acquaintances. Actually, scratch that. I'd never met the man before that day. He was actually a friend of a friend, who just happened to be in town for a clinic, and we managed to arrange a game. Afterward, I made Tomas an offer he couldn't refuse. I told him he wouldn't have to pay me a cent of his substantial debt if he spent a week with me in the lab. He did the math in his head and realized it was a heck of a deal.'

'What happened after that?' Payne asked.

'I introduced him to the best scientists in the world, and he was captivated by them. After that, there was no turning back. The boy became my protégé.'

'He worked in your field?'

'At first, yes. But once he got his sea legs, I let him do whatever he pleased. With a mind like that, I'd have been foolish to put limitations on his work. He was free to pursue whatever course he deemed most interesting, and he eventually found his way.'

'Toward what?' Jones asked.

'Toward unlocking the secrets of the human body,' Sahlberg said. 'An incredibly ambitious task, I realize, but Tomas was never one to consider the impossibilities. To him, everything was attainable. Every answer was there for the taking. He simply needed to know how to find it.'

'What kind of secrets do you mean?' Payne asked. 'I assume we're still talking about things that are grounded in reality – by that I mean the *physical* universe. Berglund wasn't trying to prove the existence of a soul, or discover latent memories of past lives, or anything along those lines, was he?'

'He would have considered those pursuits to be studies in science fiction. I assure you, his research was planted squarely in the realm of science *fact*. Even if some of those facts had yet to be positively verified.'

'Then what was his focus?' Payne asked.

'Tomas was born in 1945, a year after the Avery–MacLeod–McCarty experiment showed that it is deoxyribonucleic acid that carries genetic information.'

'Deoxyribonucleic acid,' Jones repeated. 'You're talking about DNA.'

'I am,' Sahlberg confirmed. 'By the time Tomas was eight, Watson and Crick had given us the structure of the DNA molecule: the double helix that we have all come to know. While most kids his age were still learning their multiplication tables, Tomas's attention was drawn to those types of discoveries.'

Jones shook his head at the thought of someone so young being able to comprehend something so dense. 'When I was eight, the most fascinating thing in my world was learning that I could mix dirt and water to make mud. I'm building castles in the sandbox, and he was studying the building blocks of life.'

'Indeed he was,' Sahlberg agreed. 'Eventually, under my guidance, his fundamental theories began to take shape. The more he learned, the more he was certain that every weakness of the human body could be countered at the molecular level.'

'I thought the idea of gene therapy didn't arise until sometime in the seventies, but you're telling me that Berglund conceptualized it long before then?' Jones asked.

'The concept of gene therapy didn't gain widespread *acceptance* until the early seventies, but by then Tomas had already been studying the science for over a decade. As I said, he was a man ahead of his time.'

'He was interested in genes, and you were interested in cells. That's why you took him under your wing,' Payne surmised.

'While not exactly the same, our fields of interest were quite similar, yes.'

'Was he able to further your research?'

'In ways that would have taken me a lifetime to envision. The specific details are somewhat irrelevant, but suffice it to say that the suggestions he offered were so far outside the box that they would have never occurred to me. At least not on the path I had chosen. Yet in light of his explanations, his advice made perfect sense. Would I have eventually reached the same conclusions? Perhaps. But at the very least he saved me years of fruitless wandering.'

Sahlberg took another drink and set the glass on the table. He folded his hands in his lap, as if paying his respects to a dear old friend. 'I assume from this conversation that Tomas is among those dead in Stockholm?'

'We can't say for sure,' Payne replied.

'Trust us,' Jones said, 'it's not that we *won't* tell you, it's that we really don't know. All we can say for certain is that he apparently owned the facility. Let me ask you this: what was Tomas working on in Stockholm?'

'I have no idea,' Sahlberg said. 'At least, not specifically. Our conversations were always theoretical. We spoke of things in the abstract. What *might* be possible. He knew I was often awake until dawn, and he would typically call in the dead of night. I think he appreciated the sleep-deprived ramblings of an old man. It was during these calls that I would allow my mind to go to places it would not venture after a full night's sleep. It was the closest I ever got to thinking like Berglund. But we never discussed what he was actually working on.'

'When's the last time you spoke with him?'

'It's been more than two months now.'

'Is that type of gap usual?'

'No, not at all. Our calls were not an everyday occurrence by any means, but I had certainly grown accustomed to hearing from him every week or so. When he told me it might be a while until we spoke again, I was surprised, but nothing about it made me think that he was in danger.'

'He told you he needed to lay low for a bit?'

'No, he simply said it might be a while until I heard from him again. There was no implication of a threat, nor was it something I inferred from his tone. I merely assumed he needed to focus on the latest project.'

Payne walked over to his printer, opened the drawer underneath, and grabbed the list that Dial had sent to him after their conversation. He returned to the breakfast table and handed it to Sahlberg. 'Do any of these names look familiar?'

They watched his reaction in silence.

It was obvious that he knew more than one.

'They're all dead?' he whispered.

Payne nodded. 'Unfortunately, yes.'

He took a moment to absorb the news. 'What would you like to know?'

'Whatever might be helpful,' Jones said.

Sahlberg started at the top of the list. 'Viktor Eisen was a microbiologist. His area of expertise was genetics. He worked at Caltech in the eighties and nineties, at the heart of what would become monumental advancements in gene mapping and sequencing. They were the precursors to the Human Genome Project, not to mention their contribution to cloning techniques.'

Payne and Jones took particular interest in the comments. For years they had heard tales of secret, underground facilities conducting human experimentation. In military circles, the talk had always centered on biologically engineered super-soldiers – men who had been made bigger, stronger and faster. No one knew where the possibilities ended. There were even rumors of men who could see in the dark and whose wounds would heal themselves almost instantly.

Most people considered those tales to be speculative at best.

But Payne and Jones weren't most people. They knew that the reality of such technology was much closer than was generally thought.

'Stephanie Albright,' Sahlberg continued. 'She was a chemist. She was instrumental in the building of Berkeley Lab's Center for X-Ray Optics. For the first time, science could take advantage of the XUV – a subset of the electromagnetic spectrum that covers extreme ultraviolet light to low-energy X-rays.'

'And why is that important?' Payne asked.

'Light in the XUV can be used to manipulate particles at an atomic scale. Molecules and atoms too small to be altered with traditional tools.'

'Let's go back a second,' Jones said. 'You said that Eisen worked at Caltech, and now you're telling me that Albright designed an optics lab in Berkeley. What's the connection to the west coast?'

'It's not merely a connection to the west coast,' Sahlberg clarified, 'it's a connection to a very specific pipeline of activity.'

'I'm not following,' Jones said.

'Neither am I,' Payne agreed.

'All of these scientists – from Tomas right down to the last name on the list – all followed the same path at the beginning of their careers. All were lured to Pittsburgh by the prospect of funding, just as they were later enticed to California by the temptation of fame and riches. As for what drew them to Stockholm, I simply do not know.'

'I'm confused,' Jones admitted. 'I know Pittsburgh used to be the steel capital of the world, but what does that have to do with scientific funding?'

'Absolutely nothing.'

'Then what did Pittsburgh offer that other cities couldn't?' Payne answered for him. 'Jonas Salk.'

Sahlberg smiled. 'That's absolutely correct. When the polio vaccine was announced in 1955, Salk and this city were thrust to the forefront of the scientific world. Money rolled in from everywhere. It came from wealthy businessmen hoping to have their name attributed to a cure, from foundations established solely in the name of scientific discovery, from destitute mothers hoping against hope that their pennies would be the last contribution needed to finally cure whatever it was that was killing their children. The amount of money available was *staggering*. And your father was one of those leading the pack.'

'Really? In what way?' Payne asked.

'In every way. He invested a sizeable chunk of Payne Industries' capital in medical ventures. Not to mention vast contributions from his personal fortune. He also pushed his contemporaries at other companies to follow suit. He understood the implications of finding success, and he was willing to bet big. His interests were as diverse as his resources would allow.'

'If things were so good here, why did everyone leave?'

'Again, it all started with Salk. In 1963, he channeled the interest in his work – and the limitless financial backing that came with it – and established the Salk Institute in La Jolla. There he could offer the same resources with the added benefit of a southern California climate. His colleagues in Pittsburgh followed in droves. From there, they eventually branched out to other places, such as Caltech and Berkeley. Many of the others went on to their own laudable achievements as well.'

'Why didn't you follow them west?' Payne wondered.

Sahlberg smiled. 'There was no need. I had everything I could ever want right here. My lab, my house, and your father's unwavering support. I wasn't about to abandon any of it. Money and fame aren't nearly as important as loyalty.'

37

Masseri was running out of men . . . and patience.

He knew more foot soldiers were only a phone call away – his employer had given him no financial constraints and an unlimited supply of men – but superior numbers had meant very little thus far. The man protecting Sahlberg, the so-called bodyguard, had been outnumbered at the Monongahela Incline, yet he had won the battle with ease. Not only had he killed several armed men, he had forced Masseri to eliminate two more at the police station. Yes, they were all expendable assets, but Masseri wasn't comfortable with the way things were going. He was falling behind schedule. He wondered how many more delays his employer would tolerate.

He looked out over the city of Pittsburgh from the rooftop deck of his hotel. He knew that somewhere out there was the man responsible for his mission having gone awry. He was determined to understand exactly what he was up against.

Masseri pulled a tablet computer from his shoulder bag and loaded the satellite imagery of the city. It was the same feed he had accessed earlier on his cell phone, only this time the pictures weren't streaming to the device with a noticeable delay. He was looking at a recording of what the satellite had captured over the last twenty-four hours.

The video of Sahlberg from the day before was just a small part of the broad view that the satellite was able to record. It was a focused close-up of one section of what was actually available. By adjusting the zoom, Masseri could pull back to reveal the entire city. From there, he could refocus on an object by simply pushing in on a different set of coordinates.

He couldn't change the camera angle or tap into an audio feed, but he could examine any object that was visible while the satellite was recording. Using that ability, he started with the incident at the Monongahela Incline and worked backwards from there. He knew Sahlberg had made his way to the incline from his house. He also knew he had done so alone.

He wanted to know where the hero had come from.

Masseri watched himself walk stealthily, albeit backwards, towards the lower station. He watched the Escalade reverse away from the station, but not before the now-deceased driver of the sedan threw himself from the ground up on to the SUV's hood. He watched the flanking henchmen rise up from the prone position and retreat toward the front entrance as the building itself sucked in the surrounding tear gas.

Scrolling farther back and adjusting the focus to the upper station, Masseri spotted Paulsen and his partner as they emerged and took a position on the street outside. A few second later, he watched the bodyguard leave the upper station and backpedal past Paulsen.

'There you are,' Masseri said aloud. 'Now, where did you come from?'

He watched his enemy round a corner and disappear from Paulsen's line of sight. The bodyguard continued jogging backward for a few blocks before he reversed into the street-level entrance of one of Mount Washington's biggest buildings.

Masseri watched as the timestamp wound in reverse. One hour. Two. Three. The bodyguard still had not reappeared. After scanning back six hours, Masseri was satisfied.

He entered the building's address into his search engine and scanned the results. He immediately recognized the company at that location: Payne Industries.

The background check he had done on Sahlberg had listed Payne Industries as his primary employer. In fact, it appeared they had recruited him right out of college. If he had worked anywhere else after his retirement, it was not public knowledge. Whatever contributions he had made to his discipline – the likely reason for his employer's interest in the old man – had been made during his time with Payne Industries.

Though he found it odd that Sahlberg would turn to his former employer for help, Masseri couldn't deny the evidence. The bodyguard had clearly come from the Payne Industries building. Still, it seemed like an abnormal responsibility for corporate security.

He closed the program and packed away the tablet.

It was time for a field trip.

*　*　*

Masseri knew it would have been easier to follow Sahlberg and his bodyguard from the incline to wherever they went after that. Unfortunately, that wasn't an option. He hadn't dared to tail them in person with so many officers lurking around. He also couldn't use the satellite feed to track their ultimate destination. By the time they had left the scene, the satellite had completed its pass over the city and was out of range. It would be another day before it would orbit this part of the country again, which was way too late for Masseri's deadline.

With few choices left, he opted to pursue the bodyguard.

When Masseri entered the Payne Industries building, the first thing he noticed was the warmth of the lobby. It felt more like a luxury hotel than an office building. Designed by I. M. Pei, the Chinese-born American architect who was later selected to build the Louvre Pyramid, the spectacular glass atrium was accented by cherrywood paneling and a polished marble floor. Even the hardened Masseri was struck by the beauty of the sunlight as it danced through the glass ceiling like a prism and illuminated the space below.

But those feelings were fleeting.

In contrast to the warmth of the lobby, Masseri couldn't help noticing the security measures. To access the elevators, visitors had to pass through a state-of-the-art body scanner. It was the type of thing that airport administrators dreamed about. It could detect firearms and explosives through a density scan, providing a virtual X-ray that clearly outlined weapons and other forbidden items. It could pick up traces of biological toxins such as anthrax and bubonic plague. It could even use thermal filters to distinguish elevations in body temperature – signifying a nervous or excited state, a typical precursor to violent acts.

Masseri was grateful for his decision to leave his sidearm in his car.

In addition, there were a multitude of armed guards on duty. There were two security desks at opposite corners of the lobby, each with three men stationed by it. The first was there to answer the phone and direct walk-ins. The second was fixated on a bank of video surveillance monitors that covered every inch of the property. The third did nothing more than scan the room for anything suspicious.

These were not rent-a-cops. They were well-schooled, disciplined guards, who had military training in their background. Masseri knew soldiers when he saw them.

Besides, rent-a-cops wore costumes and carried mace.

These men wore Kevlar and carried .44 Magnums.

Masseri had intended to sit quietly in the lobby as if he were waiting to meet someone. Shielded by a newspaper or magazine, he hoped to take in the action without drawing attention. Once inside, however, past the mirrored glass of the outside wall that had prevented him from getting a good look at the lobby's setup, he realized his plan wouldn't work. There were no couches on this level. There was no waiting area of any kind. There was only the pair of security desks and the six alert guards, two of whom were already sizing him up.

So far, he didn't recognize any of them as the bodyguard.

In an instant, he changed his approach: instead of a businessman, he would be a confused traveler in search of directions. Committing to the ruse, he walked casually toward the nearest security officer.

'I'm sorry to bother you,' he said as he stepped to the desk, 'but it looks like I'm in the wrong place. I'm looking for an old friend. I was told he lives at this address, but this obviously doesn't look right.' He nodded toward the company name on the wall. 'Payne Industries? There's no way that this building is also the Mountvue Apartments, is there?'

'Afraid not,' the officer said. 'You're a few blocks off.'

'I didn't think this was right. I mean, I've heard of secure lobbies and doormen, but this place is like the Vatican. Does the Pope live here or something?'

The guard ignored the question. 'Have you visited the incline?'

The question burned in Masseri's gut as he considered his response.

Was the guard trying to place him from the shooting?

If so, what should he do?

Run toward the exit? Make a play for the guard's gun?

A split second before Masseri lunged forward, the officer continued his explanation. 'It's upriver a bit. You'll see signs. Head that way, and Mountvue will be on your right.'

Masseri relaxed. The officer was only mentioning the landmark as a guide.

'Oh yeah,' he said. 'I think I passed that a while ago. I'll head back that way. Hey, thanks for your help. I owe you.'

'No problem,' the officer replied.

Masseri turned and headed back toward the revolving door. He needed to learn more before he could plan his next step. There were too many questions that remained unanswered.

Was Sahlberg still a part of Payne Industries?

What did Payne Industries do that required so much security?

All he knew for sure was that he needed to speak with his employer. The game had drastically changed. It was time to renegotiate his price.

38

Henri Toulon was the highest-ranking official in his division at Interpol headquarters, and yet Sebastian James still believed he was calling the shots.

Toulon had lost track of how many times James had ordered him to do this or that, and his tolerance for the secretary general's assistant was waning. What had started as a pleasant game of annoying his greatest annoyance had quickly grown tiresome. At this point, Toulon cringed at the very sound of James's voice. His updates, once entertaining, were now loathsome.

The quicker the Stockholm case was solved, the quicker Dial could return.

The sooner Dial made it back, the sooner *he* would deal with James.

For Toulon, solving the case meant something greater than simply bringing a villain to justice. It meant his life – and his cigarette breaks – could go back to normal.

Toulon's greatest asset as an investigator was his ability to view cases from a unique perspective, which was how he had tracked down Berglund's name from insurance records long before the local police. Taking that one step further, he was willing to bypass certain security measures in order to access the online postal database for Sweden. This action fell somewhere in the grey area between *illegal* and *expected*. Any information gleaned couldn't be used for a conviction, but his search wasn't going to get him fired either.

He scanned through the location's mailing history for a full decade, but there was nothing out of the ordinary. There were no outgoing shipments from the laboratory's address, and the incoming deliveries could all be traced back to reputable supply companies. Toulon was even able to examine digital copies of receipts and confirm that the only items delivered to the lab through official channels were commonplace equipment: microscopes and slides, beakers and burners, Petri dishes and growth medium, things of that nature.

Next he examined the records that had been handed over by the local Internet service provider in Stockholm. Working on his own, it would have taken Toulon years to read through the tens of thousands of web addresses that the ISP had logged. Fortunately, he was able to outsource this duty to members of the cyber crime division. In less than an hour, they had determined that the bulk of the addresses were for email and online backup servers. These were good leads, but the necessary warrants and painstaking analysis involved in sorting through the data could take weeks, if not months. The remaining web addresses led to seemingly innocuous science blogs and research paper repositories. These were also worthy of further consideration, but they weren't the smoking gun Toulon was hoping to discover.

The real breakthrough in his efforts came with a delivery from the Swedish police. He had requested that all available video footage from within a mile of the blast radius be collected and shipped to his office. In years past, this would have resulted in boxes and boxes of VHS recordings arriving a week later. But with modern technology, the Swedish police were able to assemble a compilation of all the known footage – security video, pictures from ATM cameras, even bystander cell phone footage that had been uploaded to YouTube – and send it in a digital folder. With Interpol's high-speed servers, Toulon had access to the files within minutes of their being sent.

Toulon opened the folder and clicked on the first file, its name written in Swedish. He had no idea where it was taken from or what he would be viewing, but he ultimately didn't care. He would cycle through these clips all day and night if he had to, scouring the images for something he hadn't noticed, some clue that would help him put the pieces together.

Occasionally, he was a slacker.

But not on tasks like this.

Two hours before the explosion, a nondescript black van entered the parking lot adjacent to the laboratory. Toulon knew from the initial report that the lot required a four-digit code to open the gate. Whoever this visitor was knew the code. Unfortunately, the darkness and the tinted windows prevented a clear look at the driver or any passengers.

Five minutes after the van's arrival, it was still idling in the parking lot. When a security guard stepped outside to investigate, the occupants of the van finally surfaced. It was clear they had planned on the cameras. To combat the possibility of being identified, they wore flesh-colored masks that obscured their features. The fabric was enough to conceal their identities, while the color made them hard to notice without a lingering view.

They led the guard back inside the building, their guns held tight to their bodies so that any passers-by would not notice. They followed him through the front door with the military precision of a SWAT team entering a shootout.

Even without any footage from inside the building – it had all been erased or destroyed by the fire – Toulon knew what had happened next. The team of assassins had killed the guard and dumped his body in the elevator. Then they had disabled the elevator so that those who followed would not stumble upon his body.

Toulon glanced at the timestamp, knowing that it was during this time that the men inside were rigging the charges. For now, it was still a laboratory. In less than an hour, it would be a coffin. And Toulon was forced to watch the transformation.

Just after 2 a.m., a single man re-emerged from the building. He was still wearing his disguise as he made his way to the van and started the engine. Moments after exiting the parking lot, as it rounded the corner at the end of the block, the van passed the first car to arrive. Toulon watched in horrified fascination as the white hatchback turned into the lot and parked in the exact same spot the van had occupied only a minute before.

They drove right past him.

They drove past his van on the way to their death.

Toulon watched as more and more vehicles arrived. He could see many of their faces; most of them were smiling like it was Christmas morning. But why? It was the middle of the night. Why was everyone so happy? Regardless, it was clear that none of them sensed danger.

He scribbled a few notes before switching to the next video file. A progression of clips followed the van until it crossed the nearest bridge. After that, there was no more footage of the van. A text file inside the folder explained that the area beyond the bridge was not a commercial district. As such, there were no surveillance cameras from which to pull any additional footage.

Toulon made a note to follow up on the unmarked van. He knew it would be hard to identify without a plate number, but he held out hope that someone would remember seeing it. If he was very, very lucky, they might even recall a description of the driver.

He loaded the next video, knowing the worst was yet to come. He pushed back in his chair and braced himself for the inevitable. In a flash of brilliant light, the windows of the laboratory shattered as the heat of the explosion tried to escape. Despite the destruction it wrought, the sudden flare was captivating. A belch of flame and ash, followed by an eerie calm. A few moments later, the fire grew again, and Toulon realized that was the moment the acetone had begun to fuel the growing inferno.

His office was still. The video had no audio, and the sound of his own breathing had faded as his heart rate slowed. Toulon was transfixed in the quiet. Yet in his head he heard the screaming of those trapped inside. The desperate cries of both human and animal, pleading for mercy that would not come. He closed his eyes, but the shrieking didn't stop.

God, he needed a cigarette.

But it seemed disrespectful to smoke after watching the building burn.

Instead, he pulled out a flask from his desk and took a gulp.

Then he went back to work. He watched as the building exploded again, this time from a different angle. The view had changed, but Toulon knew the result would still be the same. He was more determined than ever to see the men responsible answer for their actions.

In his brewing rage, Toulon almost didn't see the flickering image that would turn the investigation. It was only when the footage repeated the image that he lunged for his mouse. He rewound a few seconds, then began to scroll forward frame by frame. As the initial blast commenced, the flames of the explosion lit up the waters of Riddarfjärden Bay on the far side of the laboratory. As the intensity increased, a small boat came into view. Toulon froze the image at the height of the blast.

'*Sacré bleu!*' he cursed in French.

On the bow of the boat stood a man, illuminated by the flames.

Toulon shuffled through the video files until he found a reverse angle of the ship. Taken from a camera mounted by the Stockholm Visitors Board, it was intended to capture the scenic beauty of Riddarfjärden Bay. Although it didn't show the laboratory, it prominently displayed the boat in the water nearby.

Toulon adjusted the image frame by frame until he matched the brightly lit shot he had found earlier. Then he zoomed in on the figure until his head filled the computer screen. After running a filter on the image, he watched in horror as the man's expression came into focus.

His eyes were bright, revealing his sheer excitement.

A cruel, haunting smile spread across his face.

The assassin was enjoying this.

In an instant, Toulon set about identifying the suspect on the boat. He mapped his face and entered the encoded image into Interpol's facial recognition software. If he had a criminal record of any kind, in any country, the system would find him. He could run, but he could not hide.

A few seconds later, the computer pinged and a new image flashed onscreen.

The face had been matched.

The man on the boat had been identified.

39

Masseri stretched out on the hotel bed and closed his eyes.

He longed for the silken feel of the 1,500-thread-count sheets at his own home. What passed for linen in the finest luxury hotels in America simply paled in comparison to his native Egyptian cotton.

He opened his eyes. He would be home soon enough.

Until then, there was still work to be done.

He grabbed the tablet computer from his bag and propped himself up. Before he did anything else, he needed to learn more about Payne Industries. He opened his browser and entered the name of the company. The search returned more than five thousand results. Masseri refined the terms, narrowing the scope to the company headquarters in Pittsburgh, Pennsylvania. That limited the results to just over five hundred.

He clicked the first link and began to read.

Founded by a Polish immigrant, Payne Industries has experienced unparalleled growth in the years since its inception. What was once a single man operating from the back room of his neighbor's garage is now a global enterprise with operations in more than twenty countries. Thanks to its blue-collar roots and strong sense of community, Payne Industries is consistently ranked as one of the world's most diverse companies . . .

'Well good for you,' Masseri said as he finished the passage.

He glanced down the page and skimmed through the descriptions of Payne Industries' current areas of concentration. It seemed their technology had been employed everywhere from oil fields to avionics, but there was no mention of anything that would justify the precautions he had encountered earlier that day.

He scrolled down the sidebar and tapped on the link to personnel. He was hoping it might include descriptions of the company's security force.

What he saw instead was much more interesting.

At the top of the webpage detailing the hierarchy of Payne Industries was a picture of the company's chief executive officer. It was an old photo, but Masseri recognized the man.

Sahlberg's bodyguard was none other than Jonathon Payne himself.

*   *   *

Toulon knew there were bad men in the world. Men who weren't burdened by a conscience. Men without any moral compass to speak of. Men without shame, without mercy. He had read the reports, and he had seen the file footage. He had studied the atrocities that these men had committed in the name of control, religion, or cold hard cash. He had watched them murder for sport, acts that served no greater purpose than to bring smiles to their bloodthirsty lips.

Toulon knew there were bad men.

But the man on the boat was something different.

Hendrik Cole was pure evil.

Having made a name for himself in the most unforgiving neighborhoods in Johannesburg, Cole was one of South Africa's most feared men by the time he was twenty. In ghettos that required ruthlessness just to survive, his brutality allowed him to flourish. It wasn't long before he had made the leap from local enforcer to sought-after mercenary.

Despite his reputation among his peers, it had taken a massacre in the small African nation of Benin to draw Cole's name to the attention of the world's intelligence community. Over the course of three days, Cole and his forces slaughtered thousands of men, women and children as they pushed northward through the country. Like Sherman's march to the sea during the American Civil War, they trudged toward the Niger river, carving a swath of devastation as they went. Nothing survived. The Beninese were shot, stabbed, beaten or hanged. Their livestock was consumed; their crops were torched.

Upon reaching the Niger, many of those who were trying to escape became trapped. Unable to cross, they had nowhere left to flee. There, on the banks of the river, they were mercilessly decimated by Cole and his men. The carnage was so fierce that reporters to the south noted that the Niger was tinted red in the hours following the massacre.

Perhaps the most perplexing issue surrounding the event was that no one ever claimed responsibility for Cole's actions. In an area that had traditionally known peace between its more than forty ethnic groups, it was as if Cole was simply trying to start a war on his own.

For no reason other than his personal amusement.

* * *

Masseri was rarely surprised, but this left him speechless.

Why was the CEO personally protecting Sahlberg?

That didn't make any sense!

A review of Payne's biography on the company website provided little help. Payne had held his title as CEO for less than a decade. Before that, he didn't even work for the company. That left several years unaccounted for between his schooling and his employment. Masseri wanted to know what he had done during that gap.

He opened a second tab in his browser and ran a search for Jonathon Payne.

The top hits mentioned Payne's philanthropic efforts. It seemed Payne Industries spent more time giving away money than they did trying to earn it. There were stories about sizeable donations to hospitals, universities, and half a dozen or so charities – everything from the preservation of local parks to the worldwide effort to cure cancer.

Buried at the bottom of the page was a link to a much more personal episode in Payne's life. The article recounted in great detail the adventure that Payne and his friend David Jones had survived a few years earlier. They had somehow managed to track down and uncover one of the Seven Wonders of the ancient world. What was more, they appeared to have done so with little help, and with no previous experience in the area of archeology or antiquities. In fact, the only thing these guys had going for them was their military training.

Payne was a former captain in the United States Navy.

Jones was once an Air Force lieutenant.

When asked why they had risked their lives to pursue the treasure, it was Jones who had provided an accidental clue: 'I guess we're just a couple of maniacs.'

Masseri read the line several times, focusing on the last word.

In a flash, everything made sense.

Payne and Jones weren't just soldiers.

They were MANIACs.

*　　*　　*

After the slaughter in Benin, Cole was on everyone's list. The authorities wanted to apprehend him – though some preferred to put a bullet through his brain and call it a day – while militias around the world lauded him for his cold-hearted commitment to the task at hand.

For his own part, Cole kept an uneasy balance of brilliance and insanity. He could design the perfect plan for accomplishing his goal, and then blow that plan to hell with a momentary lapse of judgment that put everything at risk. But in the end, he was almost always effective.

Toulon knew that if Cole was still in Stockholm, he would find a way to cause even more destruction. Something had to be done before he could set his sights on the rest of Europe. Still, despite Cole's unexplained campaign against the people of Benin, this didn't have the feel of a personal crusade. Toulon was confident that someone else was pulling the strings.

He brought up everything he could find on Cole. Somewhere in the police reports, bank statements and news articles was a clue as to who was responsible for his actions.

And Toulon was determined to find it.

Three hours later, he had his lead. The Directorate of Special Operations – South Africa's equivalent of the FBI – recorded communications at all of the country's major ports. They knew that criminal activity occurred at the water's edge, and they sifted through all of these recordings in the hope of overhearing something important. They had linked one particular audio file to Cole.

The conversation was in Afrikaans, a language of Dutch origin that was spoken natively in South Africa, and the voices were mumbling beneath the obfuscating noise of what sounded like a ship's turbine. Toulon did not speak the language, and he could hardly hear the words, but it didn't matter. He had access to computer programs that could remove the background noise, and resources that could translate any language or dialect in the world.

In the meantime, he focused on the two words he could understand. He ran the recording back through his system over and over, until he was satisfied with what he heard.

Two distinct words, both proper nouns.

The first was *Stockholm*.

The second was *Zidane*.

40

Como, Italy
(22 miles north of Milan)

Harrison Zidane was born in Algeria, but he hadn't lived there in decades. He had spent the majority of his adult life traveling the world in search of his next investment. Venture capitalism had been very kind to him over the years, and he had amassed a considerable fortune. He wasn't in the same league as the sheiks of Dubai, but he was close enough.

There was little on earth he couldn't afford.

The bulk of his wealth had come by means of pharmaceutical speculation. In the past he had financed numerous small companies on the verge of medical breakthroughs. When these companies had eventually made their discoveries, they drew interest from the biggest players in the industry. Over the years, Zidane had watched as his laboratories were bought by pharmaceutical giants such as Pfizer, Novartis and Bayer.

With more money than he could spend in ten lifetimes, Zidane took great pride in sharing his wealth. His contributions had funded the creation of cutting-edge scientific equipment, the development of numerous medications, and a long list of clinical trials. His most recent philanthropic effort was the building of a new hospital in Como.

To commemorate the event, the mayor held a small

ground-breaking ceremony in Zidane's honor. Nothing too fancy, just a strip of dirt and some refreshments.

The mayor spoke. 'It is with great pleasure that I offer this shovel to Mr Harrison Zidane. Without his generosity, this endeavor would not be possible.' He turned and handed the shovel to Zidane, who smiled as if he had just won a gold medal. 'Today, as we break ground on what is sure to be a world-class facility, we, the grateful citizens of Como, thank you!'

The smattering of onlookers – most of whom were from the mayor's office, the impending hospital's administration, or the media – broke into a courteous round of applause.

'It is I who am thankful,' Zidane said in impeccable Italian. 'Thankful for a community that has welcomed me with open arms and loving hearts. To the people of Como, I offer my gratitude for all that you have done.'

Having completed his rehearsed speech – he wanted to find the perfect compromise between magnanimous and sentimental – Zidane dug the shovel into the ground and smiled for the audience. Cameras clicked as he flipped the first scoop of dirt to the side and offered the handle to the mayor. Together, they lifted another shovelful of dirt from the ground. After a few more pictures, Zidane's commitment to the ceremony was over.

As the rest of the spectators mingled, Zidane made a quiet, graceful exit. He had spent the morning giving interviews and answering questions from the gathered crowd, and now that the site had been officially opened, there was no need for him to stick around any longer. As much as he enjoyed the notoriety, he simply had better things to do than spend the day sipping punch and nibbling cookies.

His limousine was parked just outside the roped-off area that marked the future site of the hospital, and his driver was waiting dutifully. Once Zidane was safely inside the limo – beyond the range of ambitious reporters, prying eyes and the glaring sun – he opened a bottle of chilled Taittinger and filled a crystal flute for himself.

It wasn't an act of celebration. The hospital project was never in doubt.

And it wasn't an act of arrogance. There was no one in the limo to impress.

Zidane simply preferred fine champagne to water.

'Where to, sir?' the driver asked.

'The harbor, please.'

'Very good, sir.'

The driver raised the partition, then pulled into traffic.

Zidane sat back and watched the charming streets pass by as they made their way toward the harbor. He remembered when he had first visited Como, back when the area was known mainly for its production of silk. Sadly – at least for those who appreciated exquisite finery – that aspect of Como's economy had been seriously weakened as foreign competitors introduced cheaper manufacturing. The silk trade had carried the city since medieval times, but now tourism was the primary industrial focus in Como.

Nestled between the foothills of the Alps and the banks of the lake, Como offered a multitude of museums, parks, theaters, churches and public gardens. The combination of natural and man-made beauty drew thousands of visitors every season. These tourists supported a variety of shops and restaurants throughout the city.

As they approached the water, Zidane tapped on the intercom button and provided further instructions. 'Keep going to the end of the harbor. Close as you can get to the farthest dock, if you will. Thank you.'

The driver did as he was told, maneuvering the limo to the edge of the roadway adjacent to the most distant pier. He parked the car and hurried to open the rear door.

'Thank you, young man,' Zidane said as he exited the vehicle. He had left the champagne flute in the back seat, but he still clutched the bottle of Taittinger.

The driver eyed his hand curiously.

'Waste not, want not,' Zidane offered. It was another of the many words of wisdom that he had valued over the years.

'Of course, sir,' the driver said.

'Here, this is for you.' Zidane pressed a yellow two-hundred-euro note into the driver's palm.

'Thank you very much, sir,' the driver said with a smile. His service now complete, he tipped his hat and made his way back to the limousine.

Zidane turned in the opposite direction and strode purposefully toward the farthest slip. Waiting for him there was the most beautiful thing he had ever seen. It was the love of his life: his *Amira*.

Named after his mother, *Amira* was a breathtaking yacht focused on opulence rather than speed. It was meant to evoke a sense of luxury, not adrenalin. There were other boats on Lake Como that were bigger and faster, but none had the *Amira*'s grace.

Standing on the lowest of the boat's three levels was Zidane's dutiful butler, a man known simply as Frisk.

'I trust everything was in order?' Frisk asked as Zidane made his way across the gangplank. His role as butler included nearly every aspect of Zidane's life, from preparing his meals to arranging his travel. If something unexpected had occurred in Como, it was Frisk who would be held accountable.

'All went according to plan,' Zidane replied. He raised the

bottle of champagne. 'Tell me, do we have any strawberries aboard?'

'The table on the foredeck has been prepared for your afternoon meal. I shall add strawberries to the menu. Also, we are ready to depart at your convenience.'

'You were able to find the organic hazelnuts?'

'Yes.'

'What about the Gruyère?'

'Yes.'

'And the salmon?'

'Flown in from the Pacific this morning, just as you requested.'

Zidane practically drooled with anticipation. He knew the ship's hold was stocked with these and other delicacies that Frisk had procured while he had attended the hospital event. 'Very good. Let's go home.'

In the last half-century, the general populace had developed a much better understanding of this region of northern Italy, due in large part to its having become the preferred destination for some of society's most recognizable and affluent citizens. The grand summer estates of famous musicians, cinema stars, fashion designers, and business moguls dotted the shores of Lake Como. Many of these properties had garnered praise the world over, appearing in magazines and movies simply to showcase their exquisite setting.

Despite this recent interest, the shores of Lake Como had been recognized for their idyllic beauty for much, much longer. Pliny the Younger had constructed the oldest villas, Tragedia and Comedia, sometime in the first century AD. The lake itself and this region of Italy had been popular among the world's aristocracy for nearly two thousand years.

For a man like Zidane, it was the logical place to call home.

41

It had been more than twenty-four hours since Cole had detonated the charges in Stockholm. Typically, he would have been halfway around the world by now, basking in the glory of his crime while putting as much space as possible between himself and the authorities. But due to the sensitive nature of this particular job, he was forced to stick around to make sure every specimen had been destroyed in the fire.

If not, he would have to plan another blast.

He had rented an apartment in Stockholm a month before the explosion, paying cash and using an assumed identity. He had needed a base of operations: a place in the same city as his targets from which he could study their every move. He would learn everything he could – the scientists involved, their entry codes, the security measures at the lab and the rotation of the guards – and then he would strike in a way that would ensure success.

Much to his surprise, he had enjoyed his time in the city. Stockholm offered a variety of food and entertainment choices – things he could never find in the jungles, deserts and mountains of his youth. He decided he could get used to the finer things in life, even if he defined 'finer things' as simply not having to kill his own dinner.

That had gotten old over the years.

From now on, Cole wanted to be a better class of criminal.

Someone who farmed out the tasks he didn't want to do.

Which was why he had brought in Masseri.

Cole had hired him based on his reputation alone. They had never met. In fact, there was no reason for them to *ever* meet. As long as Masseri did what he was paid to do, Cole didn't need to know him on a personal level. It was a relationship they had developed over many jobs in the past. As long as Masseri held true to his well-deserved reputation as a man who could find and secure anyone, anywhere, there wouldn't be any issues.

Cole saw no reason why Masseri, having been given an open budget and a handful of men he had used in the past, would have any problems apprehending an octogenarian. He had yet to meet an eighty-year-old who could fend off a trained mercenary, much less half a dozen of them. Yet Masseri had failed to check in during the past twenty-four hours.

When the call finally came, Cole was angry. 'Where the hell have you been?'

'I'm still in Pittsburgh,' Masseri answered calmly.

Both men knew there was no reason to speak in code. The minute this assignment was completed, everything – fake passports, cell phones, credit cards – would be burned. There would be nothing to tie them to either location. Their next mission would bring new destinations and new identities. As such, the only thing they avoided was the use of their real names.

'Still in Pittsburgh? With the old man?'

'No . . . not yet.'

'What's the holdup? This should have been a simple assignment. You're putting me behind schedule, and I don't like delays.'

'I don't like incompetence,' Masseri countered. 'So we're even. Neither of us got what they expected.'

'What are you talking about? The intel was sound. If you couldn't find an advantage, that's on you. Especially given the additional forces I supplied.'

'Actually, *they* were the problem. If I had handled this myself, they would still be alive.'

'What are you saying?'

'Your men are dead. All of them.'

Cole was stunned. 'How?'

'Bad intel on your part. You failed to mention the special forces.'

'Special forces? What are you talking about?'

'Does it matter?' Masseri asked.

'It does, actually. If you tell me it's someone from the Bordo Bereliler of the Turkish special forces, or the Venezuelan Special Operations Squadron, or any one of the many, *many* units in which I have contacts, then maybe there's something I can do to help. I have more connections than you could possibly imagine. I never thought I'd need to call in a favor to bring in Sahlberg, but if I have to, I have to.'

Cole regretted his words the instant he said them. He knew that no one in their line of work liked to be called out, least of all a professional like Masseri. Supporting a soldier in the field was one thing, but questioning someone's ability to finish a job was quite another.

He softened his voice and changed his approach. 'Who are they?'

'MANIACs,' Masseri answered. 'Two of them.'

'What's their connection to Sahlberg?'

'One of them is Jonathon Payne.'

'Payne?' Cole asked. 'As in Payne Industries?'

'The very same. The other one is named Jones.'

'And they risked their lives for Sahlberg? Why?'

'I was hoping you could tell me — after all, you're the one who failed to warn me of this possibility.'

Cole pondered the new development before speaking again.

Sahlberg was still his focus, but Payne would make for an interesting interrogation. Sahlberg knew the science, but Payne's secrets would certainly be worth exploring. Given its size, Payne Industries was sure to have a hand in a multitude of R&D divisions. Capturing Payne could open up a whole new world of prosperity. Cole wondered what people would pay for newfangled, cutting-edge equipment – be it a revolutionary new way to mine minerals or a plasma rifle.

At the very least, Payne's company would pay handsomely for his safe return. Hell, for all Cole knew, there might even be a bounty on him. He had heard tales of corporate espionage taken to extremes, and he wondered if there was an opportunity staring him in the face.

'I want you to consider Payne a target of opportunity. Sahlberg is the primary objective, but I will double the rate if Payne can be brought in alive,' he said.

Masseri grimaced. 'It won't be easy. I've seen what he's capable of. The old man is one thing, but Payne is an entirely different beast. I want double the rate for Sahlberg, and if I bring in Payne, we're going to split his bounty fifty–fifty.'

'Screw you! You're telling me you can't handle someone who spends his days in the boardroom? It sounds like you're slipping.'

Masseri ignored the taunt. 'Do we have a deal or not?'

'Fine!'

Cole hung up the phone and laughed. He had no intention of paying Masseri double his rate for Sahlberg. Why would he increase the bounty when it was so much easier to simply kill Masseri for his efforts?

The Egyptian was good, but so were many others.

Easy come, easy go.

42

After breakfast, they moved their conversation to the living room, where they would be more comfortable. Payne and Jones had learned a lot from Sahlberg, but the revelations about the scientist's work and his connection to Payne Industries had yet to offer any suspects. They still needed to know more if they were to figure out who had come after Sahlberg, and why.

'Does the list of victims tell us anything?' Payne asked as he settled into his favorite chair, a leather recliner he had owned for years. 'In other words, do their individual specialties add up to something specific?'

Sahlberg frowned. 'I'm not sure I understand your question.'

Payne glanced at Jones. 'DJ, help me out.'

He nodded. 'You said one of the victims was a microbiologist, another was a chemist, and so on. Think about the group as a whole. Why bring these scientists together? What could they have been working on?'

Sahlberg didn't need to review the list. He was well acquainted with their specialties. 'Unfortunately, they could have been working on *anything*. Besides the two you mentioned, you're looking at scientists from nearly a dozen other fields. Physics. Botany. Mathematics. They're all represented. There's even a geologist on the list. About the only concentration that isn't accounted for is astronomy, which means their experiments had to do with earth.'

'Great!' Jones teased. 'That means I can cancel my call to NASA.'

Payne ignored the joke. 'Think back to your recent conversations with Berglund. Is there anything that became a theme? Maybe some topic that he always looped back to?'

Sahlberg nodded. 'Tomas was obsessed with the human body – particularly its limitations. He often pondered ways to alter those limitations. For instance, what would we have to do to increase the body's tolerances?'

'Tolerances? Like heat, cold, pain – that sort of thing?'

'I suppose so, yes, but only in the sense of how those types of stimuli are processed. He wasn't concerned with external materials that could fend off these effects; he was interested in how the body could physically counter invading elements.'

'Invading elements?'

'Something foreign to the system.'

'Such as?' Jones asked.

Sahlberg thought of an example. 'Let's say a splinter of wood lodges itself in the palm of your hand. Pain receptors fire off a message to your brain, letting it know the skin has been pierced. Along the way, the message is interpreted by an area of your spinal column known as the dorsal horn. Before the brain even processes the signal, the dorsal horn has triggered a reflex that causes you to jerk your hand away from the source of the injury. Finally, the brain gets the message. It determines the severity of the event by comparing it to every impulse it has ever received and makes a decision as to how you should react. Does this injury warrant a howling scream or merely a simple wince? Does it call for tears? Should you start to sweat? What about your heartbeat? Should it be faster or slower? The introduction of a foreign body triggers all of this. And that's just the biochemical response. There are physiological effects as well.'

Payne shook his head in confusion. 'Doc, you lost me. What does any of that have to do with Berglund?'

Sahlberg explained. 'What if instead of a reflexive grimace and stinging sensation, we could delay the transfer of information? What if we could examine the injury before the brain automatically determines its severity? It would allow us to study the splinter, realize that it poses a minimal threat to our overall health, and consciously decide that the sensation of pain would be pointless. We could simply remove the offending sliver and carry on with our business.'

Jones leaned forward in his chair. 'Berglund was actually working on that? How's that even possible? You're talking about the suspension of a chemical transfer that takes mere milliseconds to complete.'

'I don't know if it *is* possible,' Sahlberg said with a laugh. 'We didn't discuss things in terms of the possible. We discussed things in terms of the theoretical. Theoretically, if you could isolate the chemical reaction of the pain receptors and interrupt it before it was relayed to the rest of the nervous system, then you could spare yourself the sensation of pain. Again, *theoretically*. Actually being able to detect the chemical reaction, isolate it, and prevent its transfer is an entirely different conundrum.'

'Isn't that the type of thing Berglund relished?'

Sahlberg nodded. 'Over the last year, we basically broke down every aspect of the immune system. He wanted to know why certain cells behave the way they do. Specifically, he wanted to know everything I knew about how white blood cells interact with the rest of the system.'

'Why you? You're not an immunologist.'

'He believed there was a connection between the perpetual cell lines I was studying and the body's immune system.'

'What was the connection?' Payne wondered.

'I have no idea. Like I said, it was just another one of his theories. The only direct question he ever asked was whether or not I believed that a perpetual cell line could be synthesized.'

'You mean created by man?'

'Yes. A man-made cell.'

'To what end?' Jones asked.

'It's only a "for instance", but if you could create a synthetic organ cell with perpetual characteristics, you could potentially manufacture replacement organs for everyone waiting on a donor list.'

'Or create a synthetic virus and let it spread throughout the world,' Jones countered.

'I suppose that's true, but it's essentially a moot point.'

'Why's that?'

'I told Tomas that synthetic cells could never truly propagate on their own. Even if you could design a machine on such a minute scale, it would lack the ability to divide. Even if it existed for ever, it could never multiply.'

Payne processed the conversation. 'You said it's *essentially* a moot point. Why isn't it *definitely* a moot point?'

'Because Tomas never accepted my answer.'

Jones jumped back in. 'If Berglund used you as a sounding board for the cellular aspects of his research – whatever that research might have been – do you think there were others he would have consulted on the rest of the variables?'

'Yes, but I'm assuming they were all killed in Stockholm.'

'What about you?' Payne asked.

'What about me?' Sahlberg responded.

'Why weren't you asked to go to Stockholm?'

He shrugged. 'I have no idea. But considering what happened, I'm glad I wasn't.'

Payne pushed on. 'For one reason or another, he kept you

at arm's length. Maybe he didn't want you or your reputation getting hurt by your involvement. Maybe he didn't want you to know what was really going on. Obviously we can't say for sure. But if *you* weren't there, isn't there a chance there were others who weren't invited as well? People who were consulted but who were never able to fully understand what Berglund was working on.'

'Maybe,' Sahlberg conceded.

'Where would we find them?'

Sahlberg gave it some thought. 'The only place I can think of is La Jolla. If that's where his plan started to form, then maybe someone out there can help.'

43

Toulon had spent the day researching his latest lead: the taped conversation of Hendrik Cole, who was heard muttering the words *Stockholm* and *Zidane* on a South African surveillance tape.

While Zidane was not a common surname, Toulon knew it wasn't unique. In fact, the mere mention of it called to mind his favorite French footballer, Zinedine Zidane. At the end of his stellar career, the aggressive midfielder had left a lasting impression in his final World Cup match. Unfortunately, the impression was that of his forehead on the chest of one of his opponents. Despite this boneheaded play and his well-deserved ejection, Zidane was considered one of the finest competitors the sport had ever known.

However, Toulon doubted that Cole was connected to *that* Zidane in any way. Instead, he logically concluded that Cole was referencing Harrison Zidane, the well-known entrepreneur, who had made billions in pharmaceutical speculation. Unsure if Zidane was a target or a suspect – or possibly neither – Toulon used his sources to track him to the Italian city of Como, where he had recently made a public appearance to commemorate the ground-breaking of a new hospital facility.

Toulon contacted the police in Como and asked them to arrange a conversation with Zidane. By phone, if necessary. By Skype, if possible. The latter would allow Toulon to watch Zidane while he answered his questions, giving him a better opportunity to gauge Zidane's reactions.

While waiting for the Italian police to track down Zidane, Toulon called his boss to fill him in on the latest developments.

'Nick,' he said, 'are you enjoying your vacation?'

'Screw you,' Dial said. 'How are things back at headquarters?'

'Running more smoothly now that I'm in charge.'

'Great. Then you won't mind covering the holiday shifts this year. They're always a nightmare, but I'm sure you'll figure out a way to deal with them much better than I ever did.'

'There's no need for threats, Nick.'

The last thing Toulon wanted to do was handle the holiday chaos. While almost everyone in the world chose to celebrate the spirit of the season, there were always a few unfortunate souls who had finally had enough by year's end. And when they snapped, they did so in grand style. Many of the most horrific crimes that Dial and Toulon had dealt with had occurred on the days between Christmas Eve and New Year's Day.

'You started it,' Dial stressed. 'But I'm hoping you have more to offer than petty insults.'

'I do,' Toulon said. 'I've been digging into the Stockholm case a bit more. Would you prefer that I begin with the good news or the bad news?'

'The good. I could use the pick-me-up.'

Toulon cut to the chase. 'I know who bombed the laboratory.'

'Quit messing around, Henri. This isn't a joking matter.'

'But I'm not joking. I know who bombed the lab.'

'Wait. Are you serious?'

'*Oui*,' he stressed. 'I pulled all the footage I could get of the warehouse and the surrounding area. Thanks to the light from the blast, I was able to spot a man on a boat in the harbor.'

'Doing what?'

'Watching.'

'Watching?' Dial growled. 'What kind of good news is that? If I was in a boat in the harbor and a building blew up on shore, take a wild guess what I'd be doing.'

'Peeing your pants?'

'Maybe. But I'd also be watching.'

'Does that mean you *don't* want to know his name?'

'Whose name?'

'The man on the boat.'

'Wait. You have his name?'

'*Oui.* I do.'

'Go on. Spit it out.'

'The man on the boat was Hendrik Cole.'

Dial groaned. 'You're sure?'

'I'm positive. I ran his image through our facial recognition software. It's a perfect match. I wish it were someone else, but it's not. It's the Butcher of Benin.'

Dial was familiar with Cole and the nickname he had earned as a result of the massacre in Africa. Of all the known killers in the world, Cole was near the top of everyone's most-wanted list. He was brutal. He was ruthless. He was unpredictable. They were qualities that served him well in his chosen field, but they made him a nightmare for others. Those who had investigated him in the past talked about him as if he were some sort of mystical snake: they never knew when, where or how he might strike next.

Dial groaned some more. 'I thought you said this was *good* news.'

'Maybe that was a poor choice of words. To be honest, I'm not sure any of this is good news. But that's the most definitive piece of information I can offer.'

'I haven't heard his name in a while. Where's that bastard been hiding?'

'The South African Directorate of Special Operations placed him in Cape Town a month ago, but between then and his appearance in Stockholm, there's no trace of him.'

'What about a list of associates? Anyone we can rattle for information?'

'You saw what he did to the last couple of guys he worked with. They're in no condition to offer any assistance.' Toulon was referring to the two bullet-ridden men who had been left to burn with the others inside the lab. 'He doesn't leave loose ends. If someone knows something about him, there's a pretty good chance he'll find them before we do.'

Dial nodded in agreement. 'Cole's already a wanted man. Every border guard in the world has him in their system, so it won't do us any good to send out an alert. All that would do is tip him off to our renewed interest. So where does that leave us?'

'Well, there's the, um, I guess let's call it the *other* news,' Toulon offered.

'Which is?'

'The South Africans lucked out and got Cole on a surveillance tape in Cape Town. In it, he's speaking Afrikaans to an unknown subject. I had one of the translators here listen to it, and Cole is talking about a job in Stockholm that has to do with someone named Zidane. Unfortunately, that's all we got. The rest of the conversation is drowned out by background noise.'

'Who's Zidane?'

'I don't know for sure, but my gut says it's Harrison Zidane. He's a billionaire venture capitalist from Algeria. He made most of his money in the pharmacy game, backing small startups with promising research and selling their products to the top companies in the world.'

Dial voiced his uncertainty. 'But Berglund wasn't a low-level startup. Neither was anyone else involved. They were established entities in the field. Berglund could have turned to any of the major players, any of the big pharmaceutical companies, and they'd throw money at him. So what was Zidane's interest?'

'I can't say there was any,' Toulon admitted. 'Their only connection is Cole, who tried to bomb one and talked about the other. As for whatever else they might have had in common, we'll just have to ask Zidane.'

'You found him?'

'He has a mansion in Como, Italy, and I have the local police trying to make contact. They cautioned it might take a while, though. Apparently many of the residents spend much of their time on the water, especially those with substantial wealth. If he's on the lake, they won't be able to reach him until he comes ashore.'

'Hopefully he can give us something to work with,' Dial said, unsure if Zidane would be cooperative. 'Let me know when you've managed to arrange a call.'

'Actually, I'm pushing for a video chat. Do you want in?'

'Absolutely,' Dial answered.

44

Toulon's phone rang just as he was about to eat dinner. He cursed under his breath, pushed his food aside, and grabbed the phone. '*Quoi?*'

'Agent Toulon?' It was English, but with a heavy Italian accent. 'This is Agent Celega, from Milan office. I call about Signor Zidane.'

'Celega? I thought Filarete was handling things.'

'Yes. Agent Filarete is here with me, but he no speak English. He ask me to call.'

Toulon rubbed his temples. There were aspects of his job that few people could ever understand. Only at Interpol would an Italian be asked to track down an Algerian in the hope of connecting him to a Frenchman to discuss – in English, of all languages – the events that had occurred at a Swedish lab. 'Very well then. Were you able to locate Harrison Zidane?'

'Yes. I calling from his house. He here now. He say okay to video chat. Please, check your computer now.'

Toulon opened the video chat program on his computer and saw an invitation to connect. He quickly sent Dial a text message, letting him know that the video chat was about to start. He also sent him a link. Thanks to modern technology, Dial could simply use his smartphone to participate. 'Okay. I'm joining the chat now.'

Celega nodded. 'I put you on with Signor Zidane.'

Toulon watched as Celega fumbled with the police-issue laptop. When the image finally stopped moving, Toulon was staring at a well-dressed man who looked a lot younger than he actually was. According to his birth certificate, Zidane was a year shy of his seventieth birthday, but he appeared no older than his mid forties. 'Mr Harrison Zidane?'

'Yes, I am Harrison Zidane. And you are?'

'Forgive me. I am Henri Toulon, assistant director of Interpol's homicide division. And I believe Chief Dial has joined the conversation as well.'

Zidane smiled with childlike delight when his computer screen split into two windows. 'I can see him now. Isn't technology marvelous?'

Dial ignored the comment. 'Hello, my name is Nick Dial, of Interpol's—'

'Homicide division.' Zidane laughed. 'Yes, that much has been explained. Tell me, Chief Dial, how can I be of service to Interpol this evening?'

'Please, call me Nick.'

'And you may call me Harrison. So, Nick, what can I do for you?'

'I would like to ask you a couple of questions.'

'Certainly,' Zidane said. 'Please, ask me anything you'd like.'

'I understand you've made a career of investing in speculative research projects, and that some of the investments have paid off quite handsomely.'

Zidane nodded, but said nothing.

'Would you agree with that description?' Dial pressed.

'I would. I have indeed been very fortunate in my endeavors.'

'And what kind of endeavors are we talking about?'

'Mainly biomedical research,' Zidane said. 'One of the companies I funded has patented a new treatment for dialysis patients that enhances kidney function. Another has reformulated existing chemotherapy regimens so that the resulting prescription is better tolerated by the patient.'

'Sounds like pretty heady stuff,' Dial remarked.

'In truth, much of the science is beyond me,' Zidane admitted. 'I don't pretend to know my way around their experiments. I suppose I simply have a knack for backing the right science at the most opportune time.'

'Let's get into that. What types of laboratories have you supported in the past?'

Zidane smiled. 'Chief Dial, there's no need to sniff around. You can ask what you'd like to ask. I have nothing to hide. You want to know if the rumors are true. You want to hear me say that I've invested millions in private flights of fancy. Am I close?'

'Mr Zidane. Harrison. No one is judging you. We're simply trying to get some information about your past endeavors.'

Zidane laughed. 'Information? Okay then. Yes, much of the research I've supported is far from mainstream. Yes, many of the things being considered by the men and women whose studies I fund are seen as unnecessary, unworthy, and quite often unattainable. And yes, much of what they do is kept far from the public eye, in large part because of how the scientific world views their investigations. But I assure you my facilities are completely legal. The research and its merit might be questionable, but the character of those I employ is not.'

Dial studied the Algerian as he proclaimed his innocence. It was clear that Zidane had been down this road before. His words were not delivered with contempt or even frustration. He was simply stating what he believed to be true. Dial wasn't sure if he was convinced by the speech, but he was certain that it wasn't the first time Zidane had delivered it.

'What about Tomas Berglund?' he asked.

'What about him?'

'Are you familiar with his work?'

'Of course. Tomas is a celebrity of sorts in the scientific community. He's famous. Everyone has heard of him.'

'Do you know him?'

'Yes, but not as well as I would like to.'

'Meaning?'

'I've tried repeatedly to lure him into a business relationship, but to no avail. He claims to have his own funding available, knocking out the legs on which my offers stood. As I have said, the science itself is over my head. The most I could put forward was monetary support.'

'Did this lead to tension between the two of you?'

'Never. And why would it? His logic was sound, as per usual. Why partner with me when he already had funding in place?'

'Did he ever tell you who was funding his work?'

'He did not. Nor did I ever inquire. Such questions are generally frowned upon in this line of work.'

'But you had theories?'

'Not particularly, no. There were simply too many possibilities. Berglund could pick up the phone and secure an eight-figure credit line in a matter of minutes. All of the big companies were clamoring for his attention. What I could offer paled by comparison.'

Dial considered the information. While he did, Zidane took the opportunity to ask a question of his own.

'Nick, may I ask why the interest in Tomas Berglund?'

'I'm afraid we can't answer that,' Toulon replied. 'It's—'

'Henri,' Dial interrupted. 'He's going to find out soon enough.'

'Nick, there's procedure to consider . . .'

'And if anyone challenges my decision, you let me worry about it.'

Toulon nodded his understanding.

Their exchange was entirely coordinated. It was a subtle version of *good cop/bad cop*, a ploy to make Zidane feel as if Dial was confiding in him. The goal was to get Zidane to reciprocate with confidential information of his own. Dial doubted it would work, but Toulon had done the legwork on Zidane and had wanted to try, so he was willing to play along.

Dial said, 'Two nights ago, there was an explosion in Stockholm.'

'Yes, I heard. It was all over the news. A laboratory of some kind.'

'Unfortunately, we believe Tomas Berglund was the target.'

'Oh God,' Zidane gasped. 'It was *his* lab? Was Tomas killed?'

Dial shrugged. 'It's too early to tell. The scene is a mess, and the body count is high. We're still in the process of identifying the victims, and we will be for some time. Strangely, his entire staff was in the building in the middle of the night. We have yet to determine why.'

'Did anyone survive?'

Dial shook his head. 'We have no idea what they were working on or who would want them dead. The only thing we have is the identity of the trigger man.'

'You . . . you know who set off the explosion?'

'We do.'

'A rival scientist?' Zidane guessed.

'I'm afraid that *is* information I can't disclose,' Dial stated. 'But he's the reason we needed to speak with you as soon as possible.'

'I don't follow.'

'Our suspect links you to the tragedy in Stockholm.'

'I . . . I don't know where you're going with this.' Zidane's face started to flush. 'How am I involved?'

'We have a recording of the suspect discussing the Stockholm job. In that recording, he mentions your name.'

'You're sure it's *my* name?'

'Clear as day,' Dial assured him.

Zidane shook his head, not knowing how to respond.

'Can you think of any reason why the man responsible for the killings in Stockholm would be talking about you in a discussion about the massacre?'

'There's . . . I . . .' Zidane took a deep breath. 'Nick, I know I have enemies, but I truly believed them to be the kind of men who were intent upon seeing me destroyed financially, not literally. As for my association with Berglund, I was his biggest fan. I stand to gain nothing in his absence.'

'Harrison, I can make arrangements with the authorities in Milan. They can take you into protective custody until we—'

'That won't be necessary,' Zidane insisted. 'I have my own security here at the estate. Take no offense, but I would prefer to put my life in their hands.'

'If that's your decision, I can't make you go with them. But until we have more control of this situation, I suggest you pass on any public events you might be planning to attend in the near future.'

'I'll clear my calendar. Thank you for your concern. I trust you'll keep me informed as new developments occur?'

'I will. Can you be reached through the computer again?'

'I'll make sure that the authorities here have all the necessary contact information.'

'I appreciate that. If there's anything you think of, don't hesitate to contact the Milan office, Henri, or me personally.'

'Understood. I hope this tragedy is solved quickly . . . for everyone's sake.'

'Thank you, Harrison. We'll do our best.'

Harrison nodded, and Celega terminated his end of the connection. Meanwhile, Dial and Toulon remained on the line.

'Well?' Dial asked as Toulon looked back at him through the camera.

'I'm honestly not sure,' Toulon said. 'He seemed forthright. He volunteered the information about the labs he supports and the outside-the-box research they conduct. And he's not lying about the legality of it all. There's nothing criminal about anything he's done in the past. What do you think?'

'I don't know if he's lying, but he definitely got flustered when we mentioned that his name had come up. Of course, that could be embarrassment, anger, fear, or a thousand other things.'

Toulon nodded. 'Should I stay on him?'

'Definitely,' Dial said. 'If he's guilty, we'll nail his ass to the wall. And if he's innocent, I want to be the one who saves his life.'

'Why's that?'

Dial laughed. 'Because the guy's a *billionaire*. It always helps to have some of them in your corner.'

45

Though he still preferred an old-fashioned corkboard to a fancy computer display when it came to organizing a case, Dial had quickly warmed to video chats – especially when he was interviewing witnesses or suspects. It wasn't as good as being in the same room as them, but it was a lot better than a simple phone call.

'Do we have a way to reach Jonathon Payne on this thing?' he asked Toulon, who was still lingering on the screen after their call to Zidane. 'We owe him an update on things.'

'Is he in your address book? If so, just click on the link.'

Dial scrolled through the names on his contact list and then hit the appropriate button. A moment later, Jones appeared on their screens.

'Hello?' Jones asked. 'Nick, is that you?'

'Hey, DJ. Yeah, it's me. I take it you can see me?'

'I see you, plus one.'

'DJ, meet Henri Toulon – my assistant director *and* a giant pain in my ass. Henri, this is David Jones – a good friend of mine and a giant pain in Jon's ass.'

Jones winced. 'I have to admit, all this "ass" talk is making me uncomfortable. It's one thing coming from a stripper. It's quite another coming from a dirty old man on a party line.'

Toulon laughed. 'Pleased to finally meet you. Despite that dreadful introduction, I've heard many wonderful things about you over the years.'

'Likewise,' Jones said. 'It's nice to meet the real mastermind of the homicide division. When are you going to start taking the credit that you deserve?'

Dial interrupted. 'Just because Jon lets you take all the credit for his achievements doesn't mean everyone operates that way. Sometimes you actually have to earn your place.'

'Wow, that's a low blow,' Jones said, pretending to be insulted. 'It's about time you stood up for yourself. I wasn't sure you had it in you.'

'Trust me,' Toulon said, 'he can be a real prick.'

Jones laughed loudly, but Dial wasn't amused. He pulled the phone close to his face and spoke directly to Toulon through the camera. 'Henri, please keep something in mind. I'm your boss and you're on the clock. Jokes are one thing; insults are quite another.'

Toulon flushed with embarrassment. '*Oui.*'

Jones sensed that Dial was just busting Toulon's balls, but based on Toulon's reaction, he wasn't one hundred percent sure. To be safe, he opted to change the subject. 'Anyway, I take it you're looking for Jon, since this is his computer and all.'

'Both of you, actually. He around?' Dial asked.

'I'm here,' Payne yelled from somewhere off camera. A second later, he was standing over Jones's shoulder in the image. 'I heard everything you said, but if it's alright with you, I'd prefer not to sit on DJ's lap during this conversation – especially after your comment about him being a pain in my ass. I don't want Henri to get the wrong idea. We're close, but we're not *that* close.'

Dial smiled. 'Point taken.'

Payne nodded toward the screen. 'Hey, Henri, nice to finally put a face to the name. And thanks for keeping Nick in line all these years.'

Toulon nodded but said nothing, still stinging from the last rebuke.

'So,' Payne said as he walked out of the frame again, 'what's on your mind, Nick?'

Dial knew it wasn't an act of indifference or disrespect. Payne simply preferred to move around while he talked. 'You still have eyes on Sahlberg?'

Jones answered. 'He's actually at the gym.'

'Really?'

Jones nodded. 'Apparently, he likes to walk after his first meal of the day. We can't let him walk outside, not with someone chasing him, so we had to come up with an alternative.'

'How about telling him to skip a day?'

'He's a creature of habit, Nick. Every day for the past century or so he takes a midday stroll. Who are we to start changing his routine?'

'What gym is he using?'

'He's using an exercise room in the building,' said Payne, who was underselling the facility. The 'exercise room' was actually a world-class fitness center. It filled an entire floor and had everything imaginable, from aquatic therapy pools to hyperbaric chambers. He figured, the healthier his employees were, the more productive they would be in the office.

'Are you sure that's wise?' Dial had visions of the elderly Sahlberg falling off his treadmill without anyone around to help him. 'Please tell me he's not unsupervised.'

Jones laughed. 'Don't worry. He's in there with half a dozen security guards. If he breaks a hip, we'll be the first to know.'

'Okay, I'll ease up. I forgot who I was talking to.'

'Speaking of which,' Payne said, 'we've got something for you.'

'You do?' Dial was a bit surprised. After all, *he* had called *them* with information, not the other way around. 'What's that?'

'Tell them, DJ.'

Jones held up the custom-designed pistol he had taken from the incline. He moved it closer to the webcam for Toulon and Dial to see, drawing their attention to the sensors on the grip. 'Remember this?'

Dial nodded. 'It's the pistol that you . . . well, let's call it the pistol that found its way into your possession. What'd you learn about it?'

Toulon desperately wanted to know the real story about the gun and how they'd got hold of it, but he was smart enough not to ask.

'You ever heard of a Wiltz?' Jones asked.

'No,' Dial replied.

'A Wiltz?' Toulon said. 'I thought it was a Beretta.'

Jones smiled. 'Good eye, Henri. It almost is a Beretta. At least it was designed with one in mind. It was actually entirely hand-crafted by a master gunsmith out of Luxembourg. A man by the name of Yannick Holcher.'

'Never heard of him,' Dial offered.

'Nor I,' Toulon said.

'And he'd probably be glad to hear it,' Jones replied. 'He's not the type of guy that's driven by publicity. I can't imagine he'd be too keen to learn that Interpol has a file on him.'

'Should we?' Dial asked.

'Probably. He's certainly at the lower end of the criminal spectrum, but there's a pretty good chance that he's supplied at least a few of the real bastards at the top end with their weapons.'

'Sounds like a name we should know.'

'Holcher isn't the villain in all of this. He's an asset,' Payne

284

said from somewhere off camera. 'He could give us the name of whoever ordered this custom piece. Whoever he is, he didn't order just the one. Seems he was hoping for a bulk discount.'

'You think Holcher will hand over the information, just like that?'

'No,' Payne admitted. 'I said he *could* give us the name. I didn't say he would. At least not until you convince him that it's the right thing to do.'

'What exactly did you have in mind?' Dial asked.

'Tell him you'll put agents on him around the clock, just waiting for the next lowlife to come to him. Threaten to use him as bait until you've arrested everyone he's ever sold to. He can either help you this one time, or you'll run off his buyers until there's no one left.'

'That's actually pretty good,' Toulon stated.

'Let's back up a second,' Dial said. 'How can you be certain that Holcher is involved? This doesn't sound like the kind of weapon he'd engrave his initials into.'

'It's definitely not,' Jones agreed. 'Holcher likes to fly under the radar as much as possible. In fact, that's why the gun is known as a Wiltz, not a Holcher.'

'How do you know all this?' Dial asked.

'We've got it on good authority,' Jones explained.

'Good authority? Whose?'

Suddenly Payne's face filled the screen as he stepped into view from the side. His stare was equal parts admonishment and surprise. 'Nick, you know we can't answer that.'

'Can't? Or won't?' Dial teased.

'Take your pick. The end result is the same.'

'Okay, okay,' Dial said, smiling. 'Let me see if I got this straight. Your black-ops connection gives you the name of the guy who made the gun that was used by the guy who tried to kill you, and you want me to track him down to get the name of the guy behind everything?'

'Exactly!' Payne said. 'Did we hook you up or what?'

Dial couldn't help but laugh. 'And, if I may be so bold, what exactly will you two be doing while I'm doing all of this?'

'We're going to Disneyland!' Jones joked.

Although Toulon had heard stories about Payne and Jones, he had never experienced their antics first hand. He had no idea if Jones was speaking in military code or if he had flat out lost his mind. 'You're going where?'

'Just ignore him,' Payne said as he put his hand on Jones's shoulder and pushed him out of view of the camera. 'We aren't going to Disneyland. We're going to California.'

'Why?' Dial asked, suddenly serious.

'Sahlberg, Berglund and several of the victims at the lab are interconnected. Before coming together in Stockholm, most of the scientists worked here in Pittsburgh. After that, they all followed the money out to California.'

'What money?' Dial asked.

'Jonas Salk's,' Jones said from off the screen.

Payne nodded. 'After the polio vaccine was released, Salk had investors lining up at his door. He took their money and founded the Salk Institute in La Jolla, California. Over the next several years, most of your victims headed west to work and/or study out there.'

'Including Berglund?' Dial asked.

'Berglund led the charge.'

Dial rubbed his neck. 'And you think there's a connection between Berglund's lab in Stockholm, your scientist in Pittsburgh, and the Salk Institute in La Jolla?'

'Yep,' Payne said confidently.

'I agree,' Toulon said as he opened a folder and stared at its contents. 'I had a chance to review Berglund's travel records, and I noticed he took several trips to California. I've got him traveling to San Diego at least a dozen times in the last two years.'

Jones appeared again on camera. 'San Diego is the nearest airport handling international flights. Unless Berglund has an unnatural addiction to the donkey shows in Tijuana – and let's be honest, who could blame him? – my guess is we'll find plenty of people in La Jolla who can give us some dirt on him.'

Dial nodded in agreement. 'Fine. I'll see if the gun lead takes us anywhere. You guys check out southern California. If you find anything, I can have someone from the FBI office in San Diego back you up. So no hero stuff.'

'Who, us?' Jones said sarcastically.

Payne pushed him aside even harder. 'Hey, Nick, before you hang up on DJ for being an idiot, can I ask you a question?'

'Of course,' Dial said.

'What's the reason you called?'

Dial shook his head, embarrassed. 'See how it is with you guys? I get so caught up with your shit that I tend to forget about my own.'

Jones popped up on camera again. 'That's because you love us.'

Dial ignored the comment and focused on the task at hand. 'I wanted to let you know we have the name of a possible suspect: a fugitive named Hendrik Cole. We have video of him in the harbor at the time of the explosion. We're pretty sure he arranged the blast.'

'Why do I know that name?' Payne asked.

'Probably from his work in Africa. He's often called the Butcher of Benin.'

Payne nodded. He was familiar with the incident. 'What's his motivation?'

Toulon answered. 'We think it has something to do with an Algerian capitalist named Harrison Zidane. He has funded several similar labs in the past, and we have Cole on record mentioning both Stockholm and Zidane.'

'Anything else?'

'Ask your doctor if he's ever heard of synthetic cells,' Dial said.

'I can answer that right now. He has.'

'You're sure?'

Payne nodded. 'I'm positive. Berglund used to ask him if it was possible to create a perpetual cell line. Synthetic cells that would propagate on their own.'

'Is it?'

'Not according to Sahlberg. He said synthetic cells can't divide, so they can't replicate. And if they can't replicate, there's no cell line. Why?'

'The coroner found synthetic cells in five of the victims.'

Payne considered the information. 'That's interesting. Sahlberg told us that Berglund had a different view on the matter. He said he never accepted the limitations of synthetic cells. It looks like he was trying to prove his point.'

46

Traveling in the Payne Industries corporate jet had become routine for Payne and Jones. To them, it was just another mode of aerial transportation to be added to a long list that included bombers, cargo planes, fighter jets, helicopters and parachutes. Though they preferred the plush amenities and quiet ride of the Gulfstream G550 over the cramped quarters and roaring rotors of a Black Hawk helicopter, the trip would have been pretty much the same: Jones would fall asleep the moment the aircraft started to move, while Payne read a book or watched a movie.

It was what they referred to as SOP.

Standard Operating Procedure.

The same routine, regardless of the situation.

Sahlberg, on the other hand, was having the time of his life. To him, the spacious private jet was the height of luxury. He had always envied the extra legroom in first-class cabins, but even the roomiest commercial airliner couldn't compete with the Gulfstream. The reclining chairs and bench seating could accommodate up to seven travelers, even on overnight trips. There was a stocked refrigerator and an array of snacks to choose from. The co-pilot was even able to adjust the satellite signal so Sahlberg could watch the Swedish news during their flight.

From Pittsburgh, they had flown west, across millions of acres of farmland, vast plains, and the staggering peaks of the Rocky Mountains. Sahlberg ignored the television screen, opting to stare out of the window at the sights below. Every so often he would mutter 'beautiful' or 'breathtaking' or something similar. It happened so frequently toward the end of the trip that Payne had to intervene, if for no other reason than his sanity.

'When was the last time you visited La Jolla?' he asked.

'It's been a few years,' Sahlberg admitted with his nose still pressed against the glass. 'I was always too busy with my own work in Pittsburgh to travel very often. And on the few occasions I found the time, I preferred heading back to Sweden.'

'So much for you being our tour guide,' Payne said.

Sahlberg laughed. 'I can barely find my toilet in the middle of the night. I highly doubt I'll be much use to you in California.'

'Speaking of,' Payne said as he pointed out the window.

As the plane descended through the cloud cover, the late afternoon sun lit up the California coastline. It truly was a sight to behold.

'Beautiful,' Sahlberg said, as he stared at the beaches below. Surprisingly, the plane went past the coast and out over the Pacific before it turned and headed south. 'Not to alarm you, Jonathon, but it seems we may have overshot our mark.'

'No,' Jones remarked without so much as opening his eyes, 'we're supposed to come in over the ocean. It keeps us out of the commercial flight paths.'

'I thought he was asleep,' Sahlberg said.

'He was. He is,' Payne replied. 'At least, most of him. He always keeps a small part of his brain awake and alert, just in case.'

'Really? How peculiar.'

It was an ability that made Jones well suited for military life, not to mention the perfect watchdog. Payne glanced out the window to check their bearings. They were already south of Los Angeles, and he watched as the industrialized port of Long Beach gave way to the sandy beaches and opulent homes of Orange County. He sat back in his chair, knowing they would touch down shortly.

Sahlberg continued to watch as a steady stream of mansions passed underneath. The last thing he expected to see was a fleet of military helicopters headed their way.

'Jonathon,' he gasped, 'you might want to see this.'

Payne stared out the window. 'No worries, they're just on maneuvers.'

'Maneuvers?'

Payne nodded. 'There's a military base not far from here. Actually, there are a couple nearby. These guys are most likely from Camp Pendleton. Farther south is Miramar. That's where Tom Cruise – I mean, Maverick – did his training for *Top Gun*.'

'Tom who?' Sahlberg asked.

'Short guy, great teeth.'

Sahlberg shrugged. 'A friend of yours?'

Payne laughed; obviously Sahlberg wasn't familiar with the actor or the film. 'Not really. DJ and I played him and Goose in a sweaty game of beach volleyball once. We kicked their butts, and they stopped taking our calls.'

'That's because Goose died,' Jones added.

Payne nodded solemnly. 'That's right. He did.'

'I'm sorry,' Sahlberg said, missing the joke.

'Not to worry,' Payne assured him with a laugh. 'We still have some close friends at both bases. In fact, we know the commanding officer at Pendleton. DJ and I fought with his son in Afghanistan. We saved his life on more than one occasion.'

'But not Goose. No one could save Goose,' Jones said with

his eyes still closed. 'The poor bastard. He didn't stand a chance.'

Worried they had taken the joke too far, Payne directed Sahlberg's attention out the window, pointing at the twin-rotor helicopters that were flying in formation below them. 'Those are Boeing Vertol Sea Knights. They're used to transport heavy machinery. They're not carrying anything now, so they'll probably redirect toward land at some point soon.'

As if on cue, the three massive helicopters broke toward the shoreline, dipping low and skimming across the water as they headed in the direction of the beach. Sahlberg watched in utter fascination as three tank-like vehicles emerged from the surf to meet them.

'Those are 7As – amphibious assault vehicles,' Payne said.

They watched as the Sea Knights deployed towlines and hovered just long enough for the soldiers on the ground to attach the lines to the 7As. In less than a minute, the three Sea Knights pulled back in unison, their cargo now swinging safely below. 'They'll head inland, drop the 7As, and swing back out here to repeat the drill.'

'Amazing,' Sahlberg muttered.

Payne smiled. He knew the drills were amazing to most people in the world. But to the men and women of the armed forces, they were simply doing their job.

'We're about to make our final approach,' the captain informed them over the loudspeaker. 'We'll be on the ground in less than five.'

'DJ, we're here. Time to get up,' Payne said.

'I heard the man. There's no need to shout,' Jones said as he tilted his chair to an upright position. 'By the way, those assault vehicles were 7A1s, not 7As. If you're going to entertain our guest, at least give him the correct information.'

'Says the guy who slept through the whole flight.'

'You said it yourself, I never sleep.'

'Good point.'

Due to the small size of their aircraft, they were able to bypass the heavy air traffic of San Diego International Airport, landing instead at the smaller and less congested Montgomery Field. It was a few miles north of the city center, and La Jolla was only a short cab ride to the west. As they taxied to the hangar, the captain came on the loudspeaker again.

'The control tower has informed me that your transportation has already arrived. It is waiting for us on the tarmac.'

Payne frowned. 'Transportation? What transportation?'

'Did you call ahead?' Jones asked.

'No,' Payne said as he glanced out the window and spotted a black town car. A burly chauffeur stood at its side. 'The driver looks like a bear.'

Jones cursed as he unbuckled his seat belt. After a long nap, it wasn't the response he had hoped to hear. In a flash, he lifted the cushion off the bench seat. Hidden underneath was a private arsenal. He selected a pistol and handed it to Payne. Then he chose one for himself.

'Wait!' Sahlberg said. 'Don't do anything rash! I think they're here because of me.'

Jones nodded. 'That's why we're going to shoot the bastards.'

'No,' he pleaded as he stepped in front of the duo. 'You don't understand. I let them know we were coming. They're here to help. They're not a threat.'

'What do you mean?' Payne demanded.

Sahlberg tried to explain. 'Just because I've never been here doesn't mean I don't know people who live in the area. You have friends at Pendleton. I have friends in La Jolla. People who can help our cause.'

'Scientists?' Jones asked.

Sahlberg nodded. 'Yes.'

'Friends of Berglund?'

'Some of them.'

'That's what I thought,' Jones said as he checked his ammo. 'Jon, I'll head out first—'

'Wait!' Sahlberg shouted. 'What are you doing? I told you I know them.'

'Maybe,' Payne said, 'but you don't know their intentions. What if they're mixed up with Berglund and the lab in Stockholm? What if people are following them to get to you? Do you know the burly guy next to the car?'

Sahlberg shook his head.

'Then how do you know it's safe?'

'I guess I don't.'

'You're damn right you don't,' Jones said angrily. 'We've been in the plane for five fucking hours, and in all that time you never said a single word about your colleagues in California or a town car at the gate. If you had, we would have had a security team search him before we even landed.'

'Sorry, I didn't know.'

'Didn't know what? That you were in danger? Is that what you were going to say? Because I find it hard to believe that a genius like you is struggling to grasp the situation.'

Sahlberg sensed that Jones was too upset to reason with, so he turned his attention to Payne. 'Jonathon, I didn't tell you about them because I didn't know if they would show.'

'Them? Who's them?' Payne demanded.

Sahlberg didn't know what to say. 'I can't . . . I'm not allowed . . .'

'Spit it out!' Payne ordered. He had come to like Sahlberg quite a bit, but right now they weren't seeing eye to eye. 'Tell

294

me who they are, or I'm going to shoot the driver where he stands. And if you don't believe me, think back to the incline.'

A strained look spread across Sahlberg's face. It was obvious he wanted to answer, but something was preventing it. 'Jonathon, listen to me. *Please* listen to me.'

Payne took a deep breath. 'What?'

'If I asked you questions about your military career – probing questions about specific missions like that one in Afghanistan where you saved your commander's son – would you be allowed to tell me everything?'

'No.'

'Why not?'

'It's classified.'

Sahlberg stared at him, allowing his eyes to do some of his talking. 'Same situation here. There are certain things I can tell you, and some I can't. Not because I don't want to, but because I *can't*. Men like you and David – you *have* to know what that's like. The lies. The secrets. You can't let people in unless you have permission to do so. Right now, I don't have permission.'

Payne clenched his jaw and nodded.

He hated surprises. Especially when his life was on the line.

But he had been in the game long enough to recognize the truth. It didn't mean he liked being deceived, but he believed what Sahlberg was saying.

'When will you get permission?' he asked.

'Hopefully now,' Sahlberg said as he glanced out the window. 'You have to trust me on this. They mean us no harm. They can help us. Just let me talk to him alone.'

'Not going to happen,' Payne said as he jammed his gun in his waistband. 'I'm heading out first. If I get any bad vibes, I'm getting back on the plane and we're leaving. If everything checks out, I'll signal and you can join me. Understood?'

Sahlberg nodded, but said nothing.

Jones stared at his best friend. 'I'll give you cover.'

Without waiting for a response, Jones found a hidden seam in the rug and pulled it back to reveal a trap door. Payne knew that Jones could drop to the tarmac without being seen, shielded by the rear wheels. Hidden there, he could provide cover if anything went wrong. While Jones scrambled into position, Payne stepped off the plane and made a beeline for the town car.

'Mr Payne,' the chauffeur announced. 'Welcome to California. My name is Stanley. I will be your driver for the duration of your visit.'

His tone was pleasant, inviting. If he was packing a weapon, Payne could not see it.

He continued. 'I was told there would be three passengers. Was this information incorrect?'

'Stanley, I get the sense you're just doing your job, which is the only reason you're still alive. But you have to understand my position: I don't know you or your employer.'

He smiled. He could see that Payne's adrenalin was surging, that he was a coiled snake, ready to strike. 'I assure you: you have nothing to fear. We're here to help.'

'*We?* Who is *we?*' Payne asked forcefully.

His smile grew even wider. 'Mattias didn't tell you?'

'No, he didn't tell me! Who the hell is *we?*'

Just then, the tinted back window was lowered, which forced Payne to pull his gun. Had he spotted a weapon of any kind, he would have emptied his clip into the driver and the back seat while Jones did the same from his position near the plane. However, the face that appeared in the window was possibly the least-threatening one that he had ever seen.

The occupant of the car was a cheerful old man, with dark

leathery skin that looked like a saddle that had been left in the sun for too long. What little hair he had was sheer white, and he combed it left to right in order to cover his scalp the best he could. He looked like a Muppet – a grinning, withered Muppet.

He spoke with a Spanish accent. 'Don't blame Mattias. He did what he was supposed to do. He kept our organization a secret.'

Payne lowered his weapon. 'What organization is that?'

'The Einstein Group.'

47

Payne stared at the old man like he was crazy. 'The Einstein Group? Never heard of it.'

The old man grinned. 'That's because our members are good at keeping secrets. Isn't that right, Mattias?'

Payne turned and saw Sahlberg standing behind him. Left unguarded, he had taken it upon himself to exit the plane and approach the conversation. Between the hum of the engines and the assumption that Sahlberg would stay on the plane, Payne had never heard him coming.

'That's correct,' Sahlberg said. He turned toward Payne to apologize. 'I'm sorry, Jonathon. I couldn't talk about the group until they gave me permission to do so. As I said on the plane, I'm hoping that's what they're here to do – to give me their blessing.'

'It is,' confirmed the old man. 'But not like this. Please, join me inside the car, where we'll have some privacy. We'll have plenty of time to talk on the way to the mansion.'

'The mansion?' Payne asked.

'I'm sure you'll love it. It was designed by Frank Lloyd Wright.'

Sahlberg didn't wait for permission. He practically skipped toward the car, greeting the man inside like a long-lost brother. 'It's good to see you, Juan.'

'You too, Mattias. It's been years!'

Sahlberg glanced back at Payne. 'Don't just stand there, my boy. Come here and meet Juan Carlos Gambaro. He is our group's most senior member, and one of the smartest men this world or any other has ever seen. Juan, this is Jonathon Payne.'

Payne waved but didn't approach the car.

Too many thoughts were racing through his head.

The chauffeur opened the car door for Sahlberg, who climbed into the back seat, where he talked with Gambaro in rapid Spanish. If he didn't know better, Payne would have assumed Sahlberg had grown up in Spain instead of Sweden. Gambaro laughed loudly – *so* loudly Payne was afraid the old man's dentures were going to fly out of his mouth and land on the floor.

Payne cursed under his breath.

Sahlberg was forcing his hand.

He didn't like it, but he was too curious to turn back now.

He raised his open hand and patted the top of his head. It was a signal to Jones that it was safe to join him. If he had tapped his closed fist against some part of his body – his leg or shoulder, for instance – Jones would have wounded his target in the corresponding area. And if Payne had pressed a closed fist against his head, Jones would have taken a kill shot.

Jones saw the signal and emerged from his hiding place behind the rear wheels of the plane. He jogged over to Payne's side. 'What's going on?'

'We've been invited to meet the Einstein Group.'

'The Einstein Group? What the hell is that?'

'I have no idea. Sahlberg is going to explain along the way.'

'The way to where?' Jones asked.

'The mansion.'

'The Playboy Mansion?'

'Doubtful.'

Jones shrugged. 'A boy can dream, can't he?'

'Dream later. We need to get our things.'

Payne and Jones ducked back inside the plane to grab their bags and provisions. That included ammo, two Smith & Wesson M1911 pistols, a short-barreled Mossberg shotgun, and a prototype Barrett sniper rifle that could be disassembled to fit neatly inside an inconspicuous briefcase. It was a gift from the Barrett family themselves, who considered Payne and Jones dear friends.

They also took a moment to change their clothes. Not because they were underdressed, but because their cotton shirts would do them no good in a firefight. Just to be safe, they pulled on specially designed polo shirts that had been woven from Kevlar fiber. This next-generation fabric couldn't stop a high-caliber bullet at close range, but it could certainly deflect a ricochet and would keep a direct hit from cutting through the body. They might suffer a massive contusion or even break a rib, but the wound would not be fatal. Just as importantly, the shirts didn't look like flak jackets. To the casual observer, they appeared as typical attire.

Still unsure if the Einstein Group could be trusted, they positioned themselves inside the car accordingly. The town car was an executive model, allowing Payne and Jones to sit in the rear seats, with Sahlberg and Gambaro facing them in the second row. Throughout the trip, Jones kept his pistol aimed at the back of the driver's head, though the gun was shielded from view by the briefcase on his lap. This was his way of staying safe without insulting his host.

They made their way toward the mansion. Sahlberg smiled as he watched palm trees zip past the window. He seemed more at peace now than at any other point of their time together.

Meanwhile, Payne was the exact opposite. 'Tell me about the Einstein Group.'

Gambaro leaned forward in his seat and drew close to his new friends. 'How familiar are you with Albert Einstein?'

Jones shrugged. 'Probably the most important scientist in the twentieth century. He completely revolutionized the way we look at modern physics.'

Payne nodded. 'E equals MC squared.'

'Oh, and he had a crazy Afro. Looked like a Chia Pet, only white.'

'All true,' Gambaro said, laughing, 'but let's go back a little farther. Before he won the Nobel Prize, Albert Einstein was making ends meet by offering private lessons in mathematics and physics. One of his pupils was a man named Maurice Solovine, a philosophy student. The relationship soon became a friendship, with Einstein and Solovine spending countless hours discussing the nature of philosophy. They quickly added Einstein's neighbor – a mathematician named Conrad Habicht – to the conversations. For more than two years, the group met regularly at Einstein's apartment in Switzerland to dissect the pre-eminent books written about philosophy and mathematics.'

'You're telling me the Einstein Group has been around since then?' Payne asked.

'No,' Gambaro answered. 'At least not in its current form. The original group – Einstein, Solovine and Habicht – only lasted a few years. And they weren't known as the Einstein Group. They referred to themselves as the Olympia Academy. In their close-knit group, they were free to discuss anything, everything, without fear of ridicule. It was in this way that

Einstein believed the biggest breakthroughs would materialize. And he was right.'

'How so?' Jones wondered. 'You just said the group only lasted a few years, and I've never heard of the other two.'

'The Olympia Group disbanded in 1905, but that didn't stop Einstein from seeking out the top minds of his day. He would continue to meet with other scholars until the day he died. Always in private. Always without publicity.'

'People like who?'

'Robert Oppenheimer when he was working on the atom bomb. Watson and Crick while they searched for the structure of the DNA molecule. And Jonas Salk as well.'

'But Einstein died fifty years ago,' Payne said.

'Man dies, but the spirit lives on,' Gambaro said philosophically. 'In Albert's case, the spirit was to push the boundaries of accepted science. To challenge the limits of our accomplishments. He may have been the most celebrated embodiment of this ideal, but he certainly was not alone. After his death, others took up the mantle and led the charge into the unknown.'

'And the financing?' Payne asked.

'There are people in the world who do not need their investments to produce returns,' Gambaro explained. 'Wealthy individuals who are willing to offer their resources in exchange for simply knowing that they contributed to the evolution of science.'

48

Wiltz, Luxembourg

Yannick Holcher was the kind of source that Interpol agents dreamed of. Someone who could shed light on countless criminal organizations around the world. Someone who could crack dozens of cases and give them the upper hand in future investigations as well. Someone who could give them insight into the bombing in Stockholm and the abduction attempt in Pittsburgh.

In Dial's mind, it was a once-in-a-decade opportunity.

One that required a delicate touch.

His delicate touch.

Dial left Sweden in the middle of the night and arrived at Wiltz Noertrange airfield well before dawn. Two men greeted him when he stepped off the plane: Benoit Faber, an officer from the Grand Ducal Police, the main law enforcement agency in Luxembourg; and Pierre Blanc, an NCB agent from Luxembourg City, which was an hour to the south.

To avoid unwanted attention, they climbed into Blanc's unmarked sedan and made the short trip to Holcher's house under cover of darkness. Dial wasn't much of a historian, but he knew that this stretch of land was the site of the largest and bloodiest battle of World War II, known to many as the Battle of the Bulge. More than 100,000 people had been killed, injured or captured in the German offensive that lasted more than a month and extended into the mountains of Belgium and France. It was too early in the morning for irony, but Dial couldn't help but think that it was an interesting spot for a gunsmith to call home.

Was that the reason Holcher chose to live here?

If so, he was one sick bastard.

Dial didn't know what to expect as they approached the property. During the flight from Sweden, he'd imagined a prison-style compound with high walls, barbed wire and hostile guard dogs foaming at the mouth. Not rabid, just really hungry. So he was stunned – and a little disappointed – when Blanc turned down a long, wooded path leading to a scenic farmhouse that looked like it belonged in a fairy tale.

He glanced at Blanc. 'Are you sure this is right?'

'*Oui.*'

'Yannick Holcher lives here?'

'*Oui.*'

'Come on. This looks . . . *peaceful.*'

Faber, a local officer, cleared his throat in the back seat. 'Pierre is right. This is the Holcher farm. We are in the right place.'

Dial grunted his surprise. Maybe the police were right and Payne was wrong. Maybe he'd been given some bad information from his black-ops connection.

'How do you want to play this, sir?' Blanc asked.

Dial answered. 'You guys stay out here. I'm heading in alone. I think he'll be more receptive if he's dealing with me and only me.'

'What should we do out here?' Faber asked.

Dial shrugged. 'Beats the hell out of me. I brought you here as backup. Nothing more. If my life is in danger, you have my permission to come inside and save the day. Otherwise, I honestly don't care what you do. Play with the cows or something.'

Blanc laughed, but Faber didn't.

And Dial couldn't have cared less.

He left the car and approached the front porch with extreme caution. Not because he was worried about being shot, but because there was an untethered goat eyeballing him from twenty feet away. He knew those creatures would eat anything, including the credentials he held in his hand. Paranoid, he stared at the goat while he knocked on the door.

The first round was soft.

The second round was louder.

The third was loud enough to wake the chickens.

Finally, a middle-aged woman cracked open the door.

'*Bonjour?*' she said through the gap.

Dial's French wasn't perfect, but it was passable after years of working in Lyon. 'I'm sorry to bother you at this hour,' he said as he held up his credentials, 'but I must speak with Yannick Holcher. It is an urgent matter.'

Given Holcher's profession, Dial could only imagine what sort of weapon was currently aimed at him from behind the door.

'Can this wait until later?' the woman asked in French.

'It cannot,' he stressed as he held his identification even higher.

She strained to read it. 'Interpol?'

'Yes – I mean, *oui*.'

'You would prefer English?' the woman asked as she opened the door. Dressed in a bathrobe and slippers, she was the only person in sight.

'If that's okay with you. I'm not always sure about my French.'

'Your French seems good with me.' She nodded toward the kitchen. 'Coffee?'

'Please,' Dial answered. She led him to a spacious kitchen and offered him a seat at the sturdy, weathered table. He thought it was decidedly humble for a family whose weapons demanded staggering prices on the open market.

'What is it that you need with my father?' she asked as she set the kettle on the stove.

'Yannick is your father?'

'He is,' she replied. 'I am Josephine.'

'Nick.'

'Nick from Interpol – who has come to ask questions at four in the morning. So what are your questions?'

'Your father has made some interesting weapons.'

'That isn't a question.'

'And the people who bought those weapons used them to attack a colleague of mine in cold blood. He's lucky to still be alive.'

She folded her arms in front of her. 'Still not a question.'

He forced a smile. 'Have you ever been arrested?'

'Pardon?'

'See, *that* time I asked a question, yet your response didn't improve. That leads me to believe that I need to have a conversation with your father instead of you.'

She shook her head. 'Not going to happen.'

'Josephine,' he said calmly, 'this isn't a hard decision for you to make. I came here quietly, in the dead of night, hoping to reach an agreement with your father. I'm not looking to cause problems, I'm truly not. But with one phone call, I can have a thousand agents descend upon your farm like locusts. It will be loud, and it will be messy. We will tear apart every inch of this property and interrogate everyone for miles. If only half of what I hear is correct, your father will spend the rest of his life in prison and your neighbors will never treat you the same. Or . . .'

'Or what?'

'Or you can wake your father for a short conversation.'

She took a deep breath before settling into the chair at the head of the table. 'I'm afraid that's impossible. I tried to wake my father two years ago from his afternoon nap. It didn't work then, and it won't work now. You're welcome to try, though. He's buried out back in the flower garden. Shall I show you the grave, or do you want your agents to find it on their own?'

Dial furrowed his brow. 'He's dead?'

'Yes.'

'Yannick Holcher is dead?'

'You can ask me a thousand times – my answer will not change.'

'We have no record of his death at Interpol.'

'That's because I didn't tell Interpol, or anyone, for that matter.'

From the tone of her voice and the look in her eyes, Dial knew she was telling the truth. 'How'd he die?'

'Parkinson's,' she said, bitterly. 'First it took his hands. Then it took his legs. Then it took his life. Toward the end, he wanted to die.'

Dial wondered how a gunsmith could work with a crippling disease like Parkinson's. Even with the best drugs and therapy, it would be impossible to build world-class weapons without an extra set of hands. And then it hit him – the reason Josephine never reported the death of her father. The reason no one knew he had even been sick. And most importantly, the reason they were making guns so far away from the public eye.

He leaned back in his chair and nodded. 'I'll be damned. *You're* the craftsman. Not your father. *You.*'

'I am now,' she admitted with a shrug, 'but it wasn't always that way. My father was the best gunsmith in the world. He could take a hunk of metal and turn it into a work of art. But when his hands started to go, he had nowhere else to turn. Thankfully, I was shooting before I could walk, studying his designs before I could read. Over the years, he taught me everything he knew. All the tricks, the nuances that made his guns such prized possessions.'

'*Illegal* possessions, I might add.'

She waved off his comment. 'What is legal in our country may be prohibited in the next. We cannot be held accountable for that. Technically, by the laws of our land, we have done nothing wrong. Our facility is registered. We have the requisite manufacturer's license, and we do not sell to the citizens of Luxembourg. Besides, many of our weapons are sold as collectibles. In many parts of the world, they qualify as art.'

'Full auto pistols? Suppression barrels? You call that art? You know there's no legitimate reason to request such modifications. You think these guys were hunters? Let me tell you, the only places you hunt with something like that are city streets.'

'Like I said, we have no interest in what becomes of our products.'

'Well I do,' Dial countered. 'If you'd like, I can dedicate my life to shutting you down, or you can help me find some of the criminals you've sold to. In exchange, I swear to keep your name out of things. No one will ever know the information came from you. Furthermore, you can keep pretending that your father is still running things – which I assume is important to some of your Middle Eastern customers. After all, who would want to buy a gun from a girl?'

She knew he was right. 'Which criminals?'

He smiled. 'Let's start with the bastard who attacked my

friend. His men were armed with Beretta knockoffs with bio-metric palm scanners.'

'Biometric palm scanners?' she asked, confused. 'You're joking, are you not? We have never dealt in such things. You must be mistaken.'

'Josephine,' he said with a laugh, 'I thought we were *finally* beginning to understand each other. You do me a favor, and I do you a favor. Unfortunately, that only works if you hold up your end of the bargain. Remember, one phone call from me and your business disappears.'

'Do not move,' ordered a voice from behind him. The demand was followed by the unmistakable click of a pistol being cocked.

'Natalia!' Josephine shouted. 'What are you doing?'

Dial turned slowly to see a younger version of Josephine standing behind him. It was obvious that Natalia was Josephine's daughter. It was also obvious that she knew how to handle a gun, based on her steady aim and perfect stance. Of course, that made sense, given that her mother was one of the best gunsmiths in the world.

'Lower your weapon,' Dial insisted.

'Why are you here?' Natalia demanded.

'Natalia, he is from Interpol,' Josephine explained in French. 'He has only come to talk. We have done nothing wrong. Please put down the pistol.'

After a few more seconds of posturing, Natalia uncocked the hammer and holstered the weapon. As she did, Dial caught a glimpse of the same biometric palm scanner that Payne had discovered on the gun in Pittsburgh.

'I must apologize for my daughter,' Josephine said. 'You came to our farm in the middle of the night. A stranger she did not know. She was merely trying to protect me.'

'Heir to the family business?' he guessed.

Josephine nodded. 'She has been studying the craft since she was a child.'

'Oh, I'd say she's been doing a little more than studying, haven't you, Natalia?' He pointed at her holstered weapon. 'That grip sure looks familiar.'

Natalia looked down at her weapon.

'Natalia, what does he mean by that?' Josephine asked.

Natalia tried pulling her sweater over the holster, but the gun was simply too big to be concealed.

Josephine stepped forward, pulled back the sweater, and drew the gun from its holster. She examined the grip, immediately recognizing the palm-scanning technology that Dial had just mentioned. 'Natalia . . . what have you done?'

'It is nothing. A custom order. I do them on my own.'

'Your job is to take orders and see they have been shipped,' Josephine argued. 'You are not ready to design your own line, and you have no right to alter my creations!'

'They aren't buying your creations! They are buying my modifications!'

Dial reached under his jacket and unholstered his own gun. Then he slid his hands under the table, just in case Natalia panicked. 'Let me see if I got this straight. Your mom makes the guns, but you make the changes before you box them and send them off?'

Natalia answered his question with a subtle nod.

Dial laughed at the absurdity of the situation. He couldn't believe that one of the most respected arms dealers in the world was a defiant teenager.

'Why are you laughing?' Natalia demanded.

'Natalia, be quiet,' Josephine said.

He continued to laugh. 'Your customers are going to love

this. So will your competitors. And so will my friend. I forgot about him. He's gonna be pissed when he finds out her custom order almost got him killed.'

'She is only a girl. She stays out of this!'

'Of course,' Dial said as he nodded to the empty chair to his right, 'but only if she sits down and tells me everything I want to know. In fact, that statement applies to you, too. By the time this conversation is over, the three of us are going to be the best of friends. But before we get started, I need you to do two things for me. First, I want you to hand me that gun . . .'

Josephine, who was riding a crest of emotions, glanced down and realized she was holding her daughter's gun so tightly that her hand was turning white. She apologized for the oversight and placed the weapon on the table in front of Dial.

'Thank you. You were making me nervous,' he said.

She nodded. 'What's number two?'

He smiled at her. 'Where's that coffee you promised me?'

49

The car crested a small slope and stopped near a meticulously groomed wall of shrubbery that shielded the property beyond from the prying eyes of those on the street. Between the road and the hedge was a wide iron gate: another deterrent that ensured privacy.

Payne watched as Stanley lowered the window and pressed his hand against a scanning device. A series of six lights lit up in turn – the first for his palm, then one for each of his fingertips – and Payne could hear the distinct ping of the magnetic locks disengaging. The electric gates retracted, allowing access to the driveway.

As they drove past the protective blockade of landscaping, the back half of the magnificent estate came into view. Though no stranger to prime real estate, Payne was impressed with the natural design. The multi-tiered structure was a collection of distinct bungalows. In the center was a larger main area. Together they appeared to Payne as southern California's opulent version of a quaint bed and breakfast. They passed a small fountain in the middle of the driveway's roundabout and pulled up next to the building's stately entrance.

'Let me show you around,' Gambaro said with a smile.

Payne, Jones and Sahlberg exited the car and followed.

On the other side of the carved wooden doors, they found a warm, inviting lobby with floor-to-ceiling glass walls that faced the back half of the property. Payne could see more bungalows lining the rocky bluffs and a perfectly manicured lawn that stretched more than two hundred feet. At the far end was a patio that overlooked the pounding surf of the Pacific Ocean below.

'Holy crap,' Payne whispered to Jones. 'Frank Lloyd Wright outdid himself on this one. I might need to buy this place.'

'If you do, please hire me as the pool boy.'

'Pool? What pool? I haven't seen one yet.'

'Me neither,' Jones admitted, 'but let's be honest, I'm not going to clean it anyway.'

Gambaro led them to the second floor, a trip that took nearly a full minute. At the top of the stairs, the landing opened on to a rooftop terrace dominated by a massive circular table. It was like something out of Camelot, only with ocean views. Seated around the table were an elderly woman and two men who were considerably younger.

'Welcome,' the woman said without standing. 'I am Rita Dawson. And you are Jonathon Payne and David Jones, correct? Come now, which is which?'

They could tell from her accent that she was Australian, and based on her sunglasses – which were oversized and opaque – she was also blind.

'Jon Payne, ma'am.'

Rita turned toward the sound of his voice. 'Ma'am, is it? No need for formality. Rita is fine.'

'David Jones,' Jones announced.

'Very pleased to meet both of you.' She smiled and turned her focus toward Sahlberg. 'Mattias, how long has it been?'

'Too long,' he answered as he stepped forward and kissed her on the cheek. 'You're as beautiful as ever, my dear.'

Rita blushed as Payne and Jones looked on. 'Please, everyone sit down.'

The younger men extended their hands in greeting as Payne and Jones approached the table.

'Charles Fell,' said the first, his words tinged by his Welsh heritage.

'Benjamin Grossman,' the second added with an Israeli accent.

'Tell me,' Rita asked, 'what has Juan Carlos told you of our little collective?'

'Enough to get us started, but clearly not everything,' Payne replied.

'Then you have more questions?'

'We do.'

'By all means, fire away!' she implored. 'We have nothing to hide. If we did, we wouldn't have brought you here in the first place.'

'Let's start there. Where are we? What is this place?'

'This is one of the properties we own – a sanctuary where our members can find peace and quiet and, if need be, isolation. The rooms are all self-sufficient, but there are also communal areas such as the kitchen, library and media room. And of course the outside facilities: the pool, spa and sunset patio.'

Jones smiled at the mention of the pool. 'Sounds like a pretty good deal.'

She nodded. 'Our intention is to provide a stress-free atmosphere for our visitors. The more serene the environment, the more comfortable the guest. The more comfortable the guest, the more they can focus.'

'Focus on what?'

'Whatever issue they've come to tackle,' she said with a laugh. 'Our members represent a wide range of disciplines from countries around the world.'

'And they can just show up whenever they're in town?'

'Of course. They are welcome here, or at any of our other residences.'

'How many properties do you own?'

'Several. In the United States alone, we have the west coast bungalows here, a ranch in Colorado, houses in Chicago, Seattle and New York City, a collection of villas on St Thomas in the US Virgin Islands, and a breathtaking place in Malta.'

'How does someone join the Einstein Group?'

'Members must be invited. And invitations are extended only to those who have demonstrated a significant contribution to their field or fields.'

'Tomas Berglund was a member?'

'Yes.'

'What about the lab in Stockholm?'

'What about it?' she asked.

'Was it an Einstein facility?'

'No,' she answered. 'The first we heard of it was after the explosion. It had nothing to do with our work.'

Jones spoke up. 'That doesn't make any sense. A facility of that size, with all the prominent names working there – how could he keep something like that a secret?'

'It would take an effort,' she admitted. 'But the question that concerns us isn't *how* he kept it a secret. The thing that worries us is *why*.'

Payne and Jones exchanged nervous glances.

Rita continued. 'For the last three decades, Tomas Berglund has been one of our most treasured assets. His brilliance in the area of practical application was unlike anyone we have ever seen. His creativity was never challenged, but his impulses grew to be somewhat of a concern.'

'Meaning what?' Sahlberg asked.

Grossman cleared his throat. 'No disrespect, Dr Sahlberg,

but you certainly realized that Tomas didn't always agree with the ideals of our institution. In particular, the ways in which we disseminated information to the general public.'

Jones laughed. 'In other words, you have a bunch of secrets.'

Grossman nodded. 'Tomas felt we should be more open with our discoveries. He argued that we should always look to push the pace of scientific advancement. We agreed with the latter sentiment – in fact, we like to think we were the motivating force behind many of the greatest scientific advancements of the past century – but we challenged his notion of how to share this information with the world at large.'

Fell explained. 'New discoveries and new technologies often need to be released in a limited stream to protect humanity from itself. For instance, our scientists have developed a cure for the common cold. We've had it for several years now. However, if we flood the market with this product, there's a chance the rhino-viruses and coronaviruses – the two most common cold viruses – will mutate into something more problematic. If we're not careful, coughs and sniffles may be replaced by bloody noses and lung tumors.'

'No thanks,' Jones said.

'And Berglund didn't agree?' Payne asked.

'Tomas pushed for research we did not necessarily feel was in the best interests of mankind. The more we attempted to steer his endeavors back toward projects we were comfortable with, the more palpable his frustration grew.'

'This is true,' Sahlberg confirmed. 'Tomas was frustrated by the methodical pace of the group. He would often reach out to me in the middle of the night in search of an understanding ear. Typically I could calm him down and make him realize that these were small concessions when compared to the greater good.'

Payne grimaced. 'I'm not trying to be difficult, but what gives you the right – any of you – to determine what anyone should or should not be researching?'

Rita answered. 'We have a responsibility to protect the world from the misuses of our collective knowledge, do we not? It is a tenet we have held to since the beginning. Without it, we are doomed to a similar fate as Oppenheimer. Having realized the magnitude of his atomic bomb, he said, "Now, I have become death, the destroyer of worlds."'

Jones groaned. 'Let's hope that isn't what Berglund had in mind.'

50

Payne studied his hosts, trying to get a sense of their mood. 'When was the last time any of you heard from Berglund?'

Rita pointed at Sahlberg. 'Mattias talked to him roughly two months ago. As for the rest of the group, it's been closer to three months.'

'Why did he pull away?'

Gambaro shrugged. 'We aren't sure why – nor do we know what he was doing. And that's what has us worried.'

Fell nodded. 'Someone of his skill, with his abilities, must be handled with care.'

Grossman agreed. 'Monitoring his activities is essential.'

The comment upset Sahlberg, who pounded the table in frustration. 'He's not an experiment to be handled or monitored. He's a man – a brilliant one at that. His thoughts are his, not ours. We have no more right to them than to the blood in his veins.'

Payne put his hand on Sahlberg's shoulder and patted it gently. He wanted to quell the rising emotions before things got out of hand. 'Everybody just take a deep breath. I can see where you're all coming from, and everyone has a valid point.'

Jones spoke next. 'Mattias is right: a man is entitled to think whatever he likes, without the need to answer for his thoughts. However, the fear felt by the rest of you is justified. I think we would all sleep a little more soundly if we knew exactly what he has been working on.'

'What have you done to find him?' Payne asked.

Rita answered. 'Inquiries were made, but we were forced to do so delicately. We are not, as you might have guessed, a group that welcomes publicity. It was our hope that someone as recognizable as Tomas would be unable to fly under the radar for very long. Unfortunately, it seems we have underestimated his skill set. Apparently he is as talented at avoiding detection as he is in other areas. In fact, we were hoping you might be able to help us.'

'With what?'

'Filling in some of the missing details.'

'We can do that right now,' Payne said. 'We know that Berglund was running human trials in Stockholm. The coroner located synthetic cells in several of the fire victims.'

'So,' Gambaro said, 'we're no longer dealing in hypotheticals.'

'I'm afraid not. The cells are very much a reality,' Sahlberg said. He went on to describe how his research in immortal cell lines might have influenced Berglund's experiments. For the most part, the science was way above Payne and Jones's understanding.

'Does that technology pose a threat?' Payne wondered.

'That depends upon his intentions,' Rita offered cryptically. 'If Tomas was studying ways to prolong life, I imagine there are those who would stop at nothing to obtain his research.'

'How does a synthetic cell prolong life?' Payne asked.

Sahlberg answered. 'If he can somehow overcome the limitations of a synthetic cell's inability to replicate, then he could effectively design a human body that would flourish for an unnatural period of time. Synthetic cells would be immune to the ravages that destroy natural cells. Cancer and other diseases would not be a concern. What's more, the natural processes that determine a cell's life cycle would not exist. The cell could be manipulated to grow to a certain point, and then it would simply stop growing. With nothing to kill it off, it could remain that way for ever.'

'You're talking about immortality,' Jones stated.

'Yes and no,' Grossman replied. 'No one can say for sure what the neurological impact of immortality might be – the reality of never ageing beyond a certain point may drive a person insane – but Tomas's research was aimed at extending human survival.'

Jones shifted uncomfortably in his seat. 'I'm starting to see why you guys liked keeping track of Dr Berglund.'

'Then I'm hoping you'll assist us further,' Gambaro said. 'Based on your experience with the MANIACs, you are particularly suited for the task at hand. We can finance your endeavor in any way that you choose, so long as there is no direct association with our group.'

Jones stared at Payne, who stared right back. Neither needed to be psychic to know what the other was thinking. Their operations with the MANIACs were classified above top-secret. How in hell did the Einstein Group know about their training?

'You guys work fast,' Payne said with a laugh. 'Granted, I kind of figured that your group had government connections, but still . . .'

Rita cocked her head to the side and faced Sahlberg. 'You didn't tell him?'

Sahlberg shrugged. 'I didn't know I could.'

'Tell me what?' Payne asked.

'His file, please,' Rita said.

Fell raised a briefcase off the floor, opened it, and removed a manila folder. He slid the folder across the table to Payne.

'Jonathon,' he said in a comforting voice, 'you're a legacy. We've been following your career for quite some time.'

'I'm a *what?*' Payne demanded.

He whipped open the folder and stared at its contents with a mixture of excitement and confusion. On top was a black-and-white photograph of four people sitting around a table, their glasses raised in a toast. Payne recognized the man in the middle as Jonas Salk. To his left was a much younger Mattias Sahlberg. Next to him was a sighted Rita Dawson. And to Salk's immediate right was a college-aged Andrew Payne.

'My father?' Payne asked incredulously. 'My father wasn't a scientist.'

'No,' Rita explained, 'but he was a visionary. He understood that scientific discovery comes with a cost – a *literal* cost, one that can be measured in dollars and cents. He realized that most investments would never see returns, not when financing projects on the fringe of known science, but he endorsed these attempts regardless. He supported projects like the polio vaccine and others that were dismissed as flights of fancy. Without him and those like him, the Einstein Group would be little more than a debate club.'

Payne furrowed his brow. 'My father was still an undergrad at Pitt when the polio vaccine was announced. There's no way he could have financed Salk's research.'

'Not alone,' Sahlberg agreed, 'but don't underestimate his powers of persuasion. Your father took it upon himself to approach every big-money family in the Pittsburgh area in his search for support. And in the forties and fifties there were quite a few big-money families in the area. He convinced the Carnegies, the Rockefellers, the Mellons and the Heinz family – not to mention all of their friends on Wall Street – to support Salk's work.'

'You're too young to remember the magnitude of Salk's

discovery,' Rita explained. 'When the polio vaccine was announced, the news swept over the country like a joyous wave. Radio programming was interrupted to broadcast it. Those who had televisions were able to watch the announcement live. Remember, this was an era when even presidential addresses were taped and then broadcast at a later time, so a live feed was extraordinary. Shops and department stores relayed the news across their loudspeakers. Businesses closed so that employees could go celebrate. Even judges suspended their trials so that they could rejoice.'

She smiled at the memory. 'But what I remember most was the sound of the church bells. They rang from coast to coast, loudly trumpeting the defeat of the horrible plague that had affected so many children. All of it thanks to your father and men like him. It was his first contribution to our cause, but it certainly wasn't his last. In our circles, everyone would come to know and respect him. Turn it over. Read the inscription.'

Payne flipped the photo over and saw a handwritten note. The writing was scribbled and unsteady, but still legible.

Dear Andrew,

Thank you for your tireless efforts in dedication to our goal. Though the world may not come to know your name, you will never be forgotten by those behind the scenes. When the millions of mothers pray in thanks for the salvation of their children, know that it is you to whom they are thankful. May the world bring you as much happiness as you have brought unto it.

Yours very truly,
Albert Einstein

Payne handed the photo to Jones before turning to Sahlberg for an explanation. 'You're telling me that my father *knew* Albert Einstein?'

Sahlberg nodded. 'They met a few days before the polio vaccine was announced on April 12, 1955. It's a good thing we visited when we did. Albert died six days later.'

'You introduced them?' Payne surmised.

He nodded again. 'We took the train from Pittsburgh to Princeton. It was the least I could do. Besides, it was hard to say no to Albert when he wanted to meet someone.'

'That's pretty cool,' Jones admitted.

'Pretty cool indeed,' Sahlberg replied.

Rita continued from there. 'So you see, Jonathon, you have been under our *microscope* for quite some time.' She laughed at the pun. 'For many years, it seemed as though your chosen path might never cross with ours. But now it seems as though they were fated to intersect. We could use someone with your training and expertise. Someone like you and David.'

Payne glanced at Jones, waiting for his response.

All Jones could do was laugh. 'It's freakin' Einstein, dude. How can we say no?'

51

Twenty minutes had passed since the meeting on the terrace had ended. Sahlberg and Rita had gone to the outdoor patio at the far end of the lawn to catch up on old times, and Gambaro had retired to his room for a much-needed nap. Meanwhile, Payne and Jones were starving. Grossman and Fell led them into the kitchen and told them to help themselves, which was a huge mistake considering Payne's enormous appetite.

'So,' Payne asked as he raided the refrigerator, 'did you guys draw the short straws?'

'I'm not sure I follow,' Fell replied.

'I imagine the membership roll of the Einstein Group is a lot longer than you two and the elder statesmen. Why were you chosen to babysit us?'

'You're correct about our numbers,' Grossman answered. 'Historically, we've tried to keep our membership to a hundred members or so.'

'One hundred?' Jones asked. 'That seems awfully small, given the tasks you've undertaken.'

'We didn't set the number,' Grossman explained. 'It is merely a product of our evolution. In the past, the group has allowed more members, but the resulting conflict of personalities and ideals proved unmanageable. And since revoking membership is simply untenable, it created issues for quite some time.'

'Why can't you kick someone out?' Jones asked.

Fell answered. 'The knowledge gained by entering our ranks

is as powerful as it is broad. The risk of that knowledge being misused – be it without our consent or against us – outweighs the advantage of dismissing a member. A difficult personality is preferred over a disgruntled, perhaps vengeful, individual.'

'If dying is the only way out, the vetting process must be intense. I can't imagine what kinds of hurdles you have to clear before you're invited in.'

'It is a complicated progression of approval, I assure you.'

'So,' Payne wondered, 'when this is all over, what happens to us? Neither of us are scientists or mathematicians, and neither of us have cured any diseases.'

'Not true,' Jones insisted. 'I once got a rash at a whorehouse. I was so embarrassed I stole some penicillin from a medic and treated that shit myself.'

Payne rolled his eyes. 'As you can tell, we're just a couple of soldiers whose lives have taken some interesting turns along the way.'

Fell smiled at the comment. 'The same could be said for me. I served in the Royal Marine Corps of Her Majesty's Armed Forces before I found my true calling.'

Jones sized him up. 'Imagine that – he's a bootneck.'

Fell laughed. 'It's been quite some time since I've heard that term. And I have to admit, I'm kind of glad. It's not the most flattering name.'

Jones pointed at Grossman. 'What about you? Did you serve?'

Grossman shook his head. 'Not a soldier. Just a Jew.'

Fell laughed at his colleague's dry humor. 'Ben's comment is more revealing than you think. It actually answers your original question.'

'Which question is that?' Payne wondered.

'You wanted to know why the two of us are on babysitting duty. The truth is, we volunteered for the job.'

'Really. Why?'

Fell explained. 'If you turned us down, I was fully prepared to press upon your sense of duty as a former soldier. And if that failed, Ben was going to guilt you into it.'

Grossman nodded. 'That's what my people do best.'

*   *   *

The patio at the far end of the property offered striking views of the rocky coast below and the blue waters of the Pacific Ocean. Though it had been years since Rita could see the sunset, she still enjoyed feeling the warmth of the setting sun on her face. She had come to this spot often enough to know when the shifting winds were signaling the last streaks of light across the sky. The breeze no longer swept against her face. Now it gently pushed her toward the cliff.

It would be dark soon.

The two things that protected her from falling into the sea were a small stone ledge and the man sitting next to her on the bench. It was a seat that was normally reserved for Gambaro, who often joined Rita for this nightly ritual. Tonight, Sahlberg had taken his place.

They had met at a symposium in New York City not long after he had arrived in the country. He had traveled from Pittsburgh to attend; she was studying in New Jersey at the Institute for Advanced Study, one of the few lucky enough to be mentored by Albert Einstein himself. There was an instant romantic spark between the two of them, but they pushed those feelings aside in order to pursue a long-term intellectual relationship.

It was one of the best decisions they had ever made.

Eventually, it was Rita who had pressed for Sahlberg's admission into the Einstein Group. Though there were no ranks, Rita was held in the highest regard among her peers. Not only was she a vocal member of the group, she was one of the few who had personally worked with Einstein before his death. It was a distinction that carried a lot of weight.

Years had passed since they had chatted in person, but their chemistry was still obvious. As they huddled together, the warmth of their bodies countering the chilly summer breeze, a feeling of ease drifted over them. Sahlberg looked skyward as the stars began to twinkle. He lolled his head back as far as it could go to observe the sky above.

Instead, he saw a face staring down at him.

A face he knew.

A face he'd hoped he would never see again.

Omar Masseri clamped a gloved hand across Sahlberg's mouth, stifling his yell before it even began. With his other hand, he plunged a syringe deep into Sahlberg's jugular vein. The shot of Propofol rendered Sahlberg unconscious in a matter of seconds.

Unfortunately for Masseri, he had only brought a single dose of anesthetic.

As Sahlberg's grip relaxed in her hand and his body began to slump away from her, Rita knew something was wrong. She reached out for his shoulder; instead she felt the powerful arm of someone lowering Sahlberg to the ground. She drew a breath to scream, but Masseri was faster. He thrust his fingers under her chin, choking off her airway.

She couldn't breathe, much less call for help.

'I'm sorry about this,' he whispered.

He dug his grip into her carotid artery, inducing brain ischemia: as the blood vessels in her brain dilated, the sudden shift in blood pressure caused her to lose consciousness. He gently laid her on the warm cement of the patio before rigging his escape by tying the rappelling lines to the concrete bench. Confident that it would support the combined weight of their descent, he pulled Sahlberg into a kneeling position, then wrapped the tandem rig around Sahlberg's waist and shoulders, securing the safety straps between his legs. The final step was to lower his own body over his target's by means of a backwards bend – a move that only a yoga instructor could appreciate – allowing him to link their harnesses.

As Masseri rolled to the side and then pulled himself to his feet, Sahlberg dangled from his back like a toddler. After securing the harness to the line, Masseri stepped over the ledge and dropped into the darkness below.

52

The instant Rita regained consciousness, she screamed for help.

Payne and Jones hurried through the glass doors that separated the main hall from the lawn and broke into a sprint. They spotted her in the yard, stumbling toward the house. She had fear on her face and bruises on her neck.

Payne reached her first. 'Where's Mattias?'

'He's gone!' she cried.

'*Gone?* What do you mean, *gone?*'

'Someone took him!'

Payne scanned the yard but saw no movement of any kind. With weapon in hand, he charged forward toward the bench, the last place Sahlberg had been seen. Jones waited with Rita until Fell and Grossman arrived a few seconds later.

'Take her inside and alert security. No one leaves the house until we've cleared the grounds. Is that understood?'

'I can help,' Fell insisted.

'You're right, you can – by following my orders.'

Fell nodded. 'Understood.'

As Payne approached the bench, he could see that the rappeling line was taut, which meant someone was still using it. He peered over the edge, but his view was blocked by a rocky outcropping some twenty feet below. Without a moment's hesitation, he grabbed the rope in his hands and used it to lower himself down to the ledge. There was no harness, no safety line of any kind. It was only Payne's upper-body strength that kept him from tumbling to his death.

When he reached the ridge, the rest of the journey came into view. Far below him, two shadowy figures were about to make the final drop to the beach. Payne could see their destination: a small seaplane anchored just off shore. He leaned as far out over the cliff as he could, hoping for a clear shot at the plane's engine. He fired once but missed.

He steadied himself and aimed again, but he knew it was a next-to-impossible shot with his pistol. That wouldn't have been the case with his sniper rifle. Using the Barrett and its Trijicon optics, he could have accurately gauged the distance and overcome the outside factors of wind drift and the effect of the waves. Unfortunately, that gun was still in its metal case in the house. There was no time to get it now.

He fired twice more with his pistol.

This time he hit something.

The silhouette closest to the wall looked up and spotted Payne on the narrow ridge. He quickly drew his own weapon and started firing.

Rocks splintered all around Payne as Masseri's bullets missed him by inches. Making matters worse, he knew he couldn't return fire. There was too great a risk of hitting Sahlberg in the exchange. For the moment, his only choice was to pull himself back to the top of the precipice. He grabbed the rope with both hands and began his ascent.

Thirty seconds later, he reached the top of the cliff. He was helped to his feet by Jones.

'What were you shooting at?' Jones demanded, unable to see anything below due to the ledge and the fading light.

'There's a plane anchored along the shore. I tried to take out its engine.'

Suddenly the seaplane roared into life. This time it was Jones who reacted. He ran further down the lawn, as far as he could go until he reached a thick wall of shrubbery that signaled the end of the property, and tried to read the registration numbers on the side of the plane. Gray smoke poured from beneath the plane's manifold, but it wasn't enough to stop the aircraft.

'Anything?' Payne yelled.

'He's smoking but Oscar Mike,' Jones shouted back.

It was military slang. Oscar Mike meant *on the move*. It was Jones's way of saying the seaplane was still able to take off. Thankfully, it also reminded Payne of his options.

He pulled out his phone and dialed the commanding officer at Camp Pendleton, who he had emailed on the flight out to let him know he would be in the area. 'Colonel Smith, this is Jonathon Payne . . . Yes, sir, I told you I might call . . . No, sir, the honor is all mine . . . I hate to ask, but I need a favor. I need to borrow a Yankee, and I need it right now. I've got an unknown runner carrying one of ours, flying southbound from my location, and pursuit is essential . . .'

He paused as he waited for a response.

Jones hustled back to his side.

Payne covered the mouthpiece on the phone. 'Where are we?'

Jones glanced at his watch. Along with the time and date, it also provided an array of information such as ambient temperature, elevation, and global positioning coordinates. He read off the longitude and latitude, which Payne relayed into his phone.

Thirty seconds passed before he got his answer.

'Yes, sir. Thank you, sir. The honor is still mine.' He grinned and hung up the phone. 'We've got ten minutes. They're sending a Bell Venom to pick us up.'

Jones laughed. 'Just like that?'

Payne nodded. 'I guess saving his son's life finally paid off.'

'It's about time,' Jones said as he remembered the incident in Afghanistan, 'because his kid is a real asshole.'

53

The Bell UH-1Y Venom, known by soldiers as a Yankee, touched down on the lawn and was quickly boarded by Payne and Jones. Not only had Colonel Smith come through with their transportation, he had provided a gunner as well, just in case. Hovering above them was their support craft, a Bell AH-1 Cobra attack helicopter.

Payne strapped on the headset to hear the gunner's explanation. 'Captain Payne, the colonel insisted on the Cobra. It's the best he could do at such short notice, but we can have Apaches in the air by zero one hundred if needed. Your call.'

'I hope it doesn't come to that,' Payne replied.

The pilot pulled back on the controls and the helicopter lifted off the lawn. He pointed it south – the same direction the seaplane had traveled – and gunned the throttle. In an instant the aircraft were roaring across the water in pursuit.

'We've got your aircraft on radar,' the pilot informed them. 'Looks like he's limping along, trying to make a run for the border.'

'Can you catch him before he gets there?' Jones asked.

'It'll be close,' the pilot answered.

Two minutes later, the Mexican border came into view, and there was still no sight of the plane.

'Sir, he's entered Mexican airspace,' the pilot confirmed. 'Looks like he's set down about ten miles beyond the border.'

'Show me,' Payne insisted.

'Sir, we don't have authorization to follow beyond the NOLF

at Imperial Beach. We need a certified flight plan in coordination with the Mexican government to pursue any farther.'

Payne was familiar with the protocol. NOLF stood for Naval Outlying Landing Field, an auxiliary field used to handle overflow air traffic. Apart from being essentially the largest helipad in the country – it was often labeled the Helicopter Capital of the World – Imperial Beach was also the southernmost occupied point along the west coast. Beyond it was roughly a mile of wildlife refuge and then the US–Mexico border. Flying farther than the field at Imperial Beach risked straining relations between two governments, whose border was already guarded by razor wire and armed patrolmen.

'Show me the plane, or get out of the chopper,' Payne stated bluntly. He turned toward Jones. 'You can fly this thing, right?'

'Affirmative, Captain,' Jones deadpanned. 'Can the pilot swim?'

'We're about to find out,' Payne answered.

The young pilot didn't know Payne or Jones personally, but the colonel had instructed him to defer to their instructions. He also knew sincerity when he heard it. Rather than risk a cold, dark swim to shore, he decided it was in his best interests to proceed with Payne's request. He dimmed the cabin lights and dropped the Yankee only a few feet above the water. 'Be advised, we are continuing our present heading.'

In response to his statement, the Cobra dipped low and took a lead position in front of the Yankee. Without its running lights, which had been turned off the moment it had crossed into Mexico, the attack helicopter was virtually invisible against the dark sky.

Fortunately, the undocumented trip into foreign territory didn't require them to travel far. They spotted the seaplane as they rounded a small point a minute after crossing the border. It had landed near a small bay and had ridden the swell all the way to shore. The high walls of the coastline and the desolate beach meant there was nowhere for anyone to hide and very little chance they could have made an escape in the brief time since their arrival.

The Cobra swung wide to face the seaplane. It hovered in front of it, each weapon in its arsenal trained on the fuselage.

'Set us down alongside,' Payne said.

'Negative,' the pilot replied. 'I can't touch down, sir. Not on Mexican soil.'

The pilot was doing his best, given the circumstances. Flying into foreign airspace was one thing, but landing there was something else. He was willing to fly them in, but he worried that putting his Yankee on the sand constituted an invasion.

Payne understood the distinction. 'Drop us in the water. We'll come up from the rear. Put us directly behind him, the blind spot where he can't see us coming.' He opened the cargo door and grabbed the M60 machine gun from the gunner's hands.

The rotor wash from the hovering Yankee caused a tornado of foam and spray. In the center of it, Payne and Jones jumped into the waist-deep water. Once they were clear of the skids, the pilot pulled the helicopter back to a tactical position above the seaplane.

Payne was surprised to see the pilot of the seaplane in the doorway as they crept into position. His arms were raised in surrender and he was shouting something, but his cries could not be heard above the rotors of the helicopters. Jones pulled the pilot to the ground as Payne cautiously peeked inside.

The plane was old and rickety. There were no seats, only loops of rope bolted to the interior wall for people to hold on to. Payne had seen this type of aircraft before. It was known as a coyote plane. The pilot would pack it full of illegal immigrants – each of whom had paid a hefty sum for the privilege

– and smuggle them across the border into the United States. Sometimes the planes made it to land, but more often than not they touched down far off the coast and the passengers would swim ashore.

That was if they were lucky.

Payne had heard horror stories of pilots who, rather than risk being intercepted by the United States Coast Guard or other authorities, would simply fly miles out to sea and force their cargo into the water. Sometimes they wouldn't even land the plane.

Today, however, there was no one on board.

'Where are the passengers?' Payne demanded.

'*No entiendo*,' the pilot insisted. '*Qué está pasando?*'

Jones was the more language-oriented of the two. He did his best to translate. 'He doesn't understand what you're asking. He's not sure what's happening.'

'Ask him about the two men from the beach. Where did they get off the plane?'

Jones translated the question and the pilot's response. 'He says they never got on the plane. He left them on the beach.'

'What? Why would he do that?'

A moment later, Payne had his answer.

'He says that was the plan. That's what he was instructed to do. Wait for the man to come back down the rope, and when he gave him the signal from the beach, he was to take off and fly back to Rosarito. He only made it this far before the engine gave out.'

Payne was stunned. They had been tricked.

Masseri and Sahlberg had stayed behind on shore.

It was a risky plan, letting the plane leave as decoy.

But it had worked.

* * *

Masseri smiled. He had watched the plane take off from the relative safety of a cave at the edge of the rock wall. He had heard the arrival of the military helicopters, and he had laughed as they sped out across the sea, giving chase. Only after they had flown out of view did he deploy the small Zodiac he had hidden in the caves at the base of the cliff. The inflatable boat and its engine were prepped in under five minutes.

After loading his unconscious cargo, Masseri sped off into the darkness.

Now that he had secured his target, he could finally breathe a sigh of relief. He knew his mission was still not complete. He understood his ruse with the seaplane would only guarantee a head start, but for the first time in a long time he was comfortable with the situation. He was once again in control. He could dictate the next step. As long as he safely delivered his quarry, he was free to do as he pleased.

Masseri stared at Sahlberg and wondered why he was so important. The plan had been to keep him sedated with a steady stream of narcotics, but now Masseri wasn't so sure.

It would be a long trip to where they were going.

He might enjoy the conversation.

And some answers.

54

Payne and Jones loaded the Mexican pilot into the helicopter while the gunner looked on with shocked disapproval.

'Relax,' Jones said, 'he's my gardener.'

It didn't have the calming effect that he had hoped for. The gunner nodded, but the glance he shot the Yankee pilot wasn't one of reassurance. It was more like, *first a foreign incursion, now they're taking prisoners!*

As Jones secured the seaplane pilot, Payne grabbed the Yankee pilot by the shoulder. 'Take us back to the estate.'

The Yankee pilot nodded and tapped his headset, indicating that Payne should put his on as well. 'It's the colonel. He needs to speak with you.'

Payne grabbed his headset, flipped it over his head, and adjusted the microphone. 'Colonel Smith . . . I understand, sir, and we're en route now. You'll have your birds back within the hour . . . Yes, sir, heavy by one extra . . . Yes, sir, *my* responsibility, not yours . . . Sir, I need another favor. Our target is still missing. I need radar imagery of the original pickup location, starting ten minutes before our departure . . . It was a misdirect, sir. The target sent us after a decoy. The target and his cargo were extracted through other means, and I need to know how . . . Thank you, sir . . . Yes, sir, never again, sir.'

He pulled the headset from his ears and groaned.

'What was that all about?' Jones asked.

'I think we're starting to wear out our welcome,' Payne said.

'*We?* What the hell did *I* do?'

Payne ignored the question. 'Call Randy. See if he can get us pictures of the abduction.'

The gunner no longer wanted any part of this adventure. He had no idea who Randy was and wasn't sure if the abduction they were referring to involved the Mexican pilot they had just grabbed south of the border. If so, the last thing he wanted was to be caught on film.

'Should I be worried, sir?' he asked Payne.

'About what?'

'All this, sir.'

Payne stared at him. 'That depends. Did you *see* anything, marine?'

'No, sir. Not a thing, sir.'

'Then you'll be fine,' Payne assured him.

Meanwhile, Jones used his cell phone to call Raskin. It was tough to hear inside the chopper, but they couldn't risk talking to him over the chopper's radio.

'Research,' Raskin answered.

Jones skipped the pleasantries. 'I'm currently in the belly of a Yankee, heading toward shore. You remember the old man from the incline?'

'Of course.'

'He's been taken.'

Raskin started tracing the call. 'From where?'

'We came to Cali to meet with some colleagues of his, and someone snatched him from the property.'

'While you were there?'

'Yes.'

'How's Jon taking it?'

Jones looked at his friend. The veins in Payne's neck pulsed in anger and frustration. 'How do you think? He's pissed.'

344

'What can I do?' Raskin asked.

Jones gave him the same coordinates that had been given to Colonel Smith at Camp Pendleton at the start of the rescue mission. 'Use your birds to zoom in on that position. You should see an expansive waterfront property with a rooftop patio and a long, narrow lawn.'

Raskin zoomed in until he found the property. 'I've got it.'

'Good. We need to know what kind of activity has transpired on the beach below and off the coast over the last hour. I mean satellite coverage, marine traffic, Coast Guard reports, everything.'

'Looking for anything in particular?'

'Two men. Our man and the man who took him. Last seen on the beach.'

'Got it.'

'You're going to see a plane and two helos leaving the site. You can disregard them. We used the choppers to track the plane, but the old man wasn't on board. It was a decoy.'

'Please tell me you didn't steal the helos.'

'Never,' Jones said with a laugh. 'Well, not this time. Pendleton loaned them to us. Trust me, it's all semi-legit.'

'I'll call you when I have something.'

Jones hung up and updated Payne. 'He's on it.'

'Good.' Payne pointed at the seaplane pilot. 'In the meantime, find out who hired him.'

Jones relayed the question and then the response. 'He says he never got a name. The target is about six feet tall, dark complexion, medium build. His instructions were to deliver him to the shore, then wait for his return. When the man signaled, he was to fly back to Rosarito, just as he said before. He said it was easy money.'

Payne cursed. 'It sounds like the same guy I saw outside the incline. He must have followed us out here.'

'How?' Jones wondered.

'Who knows? Maybe he's got a contact inside the group. Or maybe he tracked our jet.' Payne balled his hand into a fist and pounded the side of the chopper. It was a flash of emotion that Jones rarely saw. 'As of now, it doesn't matter.'

Payne put his headset back on. 'How long till we get back?'

'Almost there, sir,' the pilot answered.

'Don't take us to the house. Drop us on the beach below.'

'Yes, sir.' He jerked a thumb back at the Mexican. 'What about him, sir?'

'Take him to the stockade. I'm sure immigration would like to have a word with him.'

The pilot nodded his understanding and pointed to the ground up ahead, indicating that they were nearly there. A minute later, Payne and Jones were exiting the Yankee. They had borrowed a couple of flashlights to search the narrow strip of beach, but they found nothing useful.

As the fruitlessness of their efforts began to sink in, Payne's phone started to ring. He glanced at his caller ID and saw a blocked number. He naturally assumed it was Raskin, calling with an update. 'What do you have for me, Randy?'

'This isn't Randy,' the voice explained. 'But I do have something for you.'

'Who is this?' Payne demanded as he signaled Jones to trace the call.

Jones dialed Raskin's number and cut him off before he could offer his customary greeting. 'Randy, trace Jon's phone right now. I don't need a name, just give me the location.'

In his basement office on the other side of the country, Raskin pounded away on one of his keyboards in a frantic attempt to locate the caller.

'My name is not important,' Masseri said. 'What is important is that I have your friend, and I'm willing to give him back to you in one piece.'

Payne cut to the chase. 'Name your price.'

'I'm afraid it's not that simple.'

'Everyone has a number,' Payne insisted.

'If I wanted money, I could simply deliver Dr Sahlberg to those who hired me. I assure you the sum they are willing to pay is more than enough for me to live comfortably for quite some time. No, money is not the issue.'

'Then what do you want?'

'I want your expertise,' Masseri said cryptically. 'I will return Dr Sahlberg in exchange for services rendered.'

'What services? What do you want me to do?'

'Not like this. Not over the phone. Let's discuss your opportunity in person. Be at the center of the Charles Bridge in Prague. We can discuss the finer points then.' Masseri laughed and gave him a specific time. 'Obviously, any attempt to alter this arrangement will be met with certain unpleasant consequences. *Na shledanou*, Jonathon.'

With that, he disconnected the call.

'Tell me you got that,' Payne said to Jones.

Jones held up a finger, letting him know that Raskin was still working his magic. 'Sorry, Jon. He couldn't complete the trace. The call was way too short, and the caller bounced the signal around the globe before he routed it to your cell.'

Payne signaled for Jones to hand over the phone. 'Did you get anything at all?'

'Jon? Is that you? Sorry, man, I don't have much. This guy is really good. About the only thing I know for sure is the manufacturer of the cell phone. It wasn't made in America.'

'Big shock there.'

'Or Japan.'

'Now we're getting somewhere.'

'It was actually made in the Czech Republic. The company is headquartered in the Mala Strana district of Prague. This particular brand of phone has a distinct signature.'

'You're sure?'

'Positive. Also, the caller signed off with *Na shledanou*. That translates to "goodbye" or "see you soon" in Czech.'

Payne grunted in surprise. Typically, the last thing he expected from men like the kidnapper was honesty. Then again, why call him out of the blue and risk getting caught? After all, he had made a clean getaway with Sahlberg.

'Randy, what do you have for transportation?'

'Is tomorrow too late?'

'No, that will work.'

Raskin worked his magic, cross-referencing the data that appeared on his various monitors. 'If you can get to Washington before noon, I can get you a ride with the 87th Airborne to Ramstein in Germany. We can work on the rest of the trip while you're en route.'

'That works. I'll be in touch.' Payne disconnected the call.

'What works?' Jones asked.

'Pack your shit. We're going to Prague.'

55

For more than a thousand years, the narrow streets of Prague had seen conflict and celebration, great wars and prosperity. The history of the region was rich with stories of everything from the Holy Roman Empire to the suppression of the communist movement. Today, its heritage was recognized throughout the world, and the city had become a heralded tourist destination.

Payne took a deep breath as he approached the Charles Bridge. It was currently filled with tourists.

If everything went well, no one – apart from those directly involved – would ever know about their rendezvous. But if things went badly, he knew his adversary would not hesitate to add his personal touch to the violent history of the city.

Payne stepped on to the stone bridge and readied himself for anything. He knew Jones was somewhere nearby, poised in a makeshift sniper's nest. Even though he trusted his friend's ability to come to his aid from five hundred yards away with one expertly placed shot, he also understood the reality of the situation: the bridge was virtually indefensible. It was a wide-open space with nowhere to run or hide. If things went badly, Payne's best option would be to jump from the bridge into the waters of the Vltava river.

After that, he'd be a sitting – make that *swimming* – duck.

He hoped it wouldn't come to that.

Payne knew that if need be, Dial could bring the vast resources of local law enforcement with a single phone call. They could blanket the area with police officers, shutting off the mercenary's escape routes as they methodically tightened their grip on the area. Unfortunately, he also knew that taking such action most likely meant they would never see Sahlberg again. The man who held him, whoever he was, was not new to the game. He would certainly see to it that Sahlberg paid for Payne's betrayal.

It was a risk he was unwilling to take.

Of course, it took some effort to convince Dial to stay out of things. Payne reminded him that Interpol had no authority to investigate this matter, and that any action on Dial's part would have to be explained and defended long after his return to Lyon. By then, there was no telling what might become of the suspect, since he would be subject to Czech law.

You don't want red tape. You want results.

And I want Sahlberg.

Stay out of my way, and we'll both get what we want.

Payne walked to the center of the bridge and stood with his back to the railing. He scanned the vendors, who were still setting up shop for the day. He took note of the artists attempting to capture the beauty of the early morning sky, painters and photographers focusing on the banks of the river as the sun illuminated the buildings of the Old Town. He studied everyone nearby, burning their faces into his memory while searching for trouble.

Deep inside, he knew *he* was the one in trouble.

One false move, and he was dead.

If given his preference, he would have chosen somewhere far from civilization. He was accustomed to the confines of thick jungles and the burned-out remnants of villages, places where he could duck and weave to safety. Here, he felt thrown into a different world: a Cold War game of dead drops and clandestine exchanges of information.

He was a soldier, not a spy.

His radar was on high alert when a young boy on a bicycle parked beside him on the bridge. The boy clumsily dismounted the bike, which was far too big for him to handle. It would be a few years before his feet would be able to reach the ground while sitting on the seat. Yet it didn't seem to bother him. He smiled excitedly as Payne eyed the bunches of wrapped flowers in the oversized basket between the front handlebars.

'Sorry, kid, I don't need any flowers,' Payne explained.

The boy nodded at the mention of flowers, the only word he understood. Before Payne could stop him, he had carefully selected a particular bundle and handed them over with the same joyous look that most children reserved for Christmas morning.

Payne reached into his pocket for a few *koruna*, realizing it would be easier to simply pay the boy than to argue over unwanted flowers.

The boy held up his hand and shook his head wildly. No matter how much Payne insisted, the boy refused his offering. Instead, he mounted his oversized bike again – nearly falling twice as he did – and waved as he sped off in the opposite direction.

It took Payne a moment to realize that this wasn't merely

a random act of kindness. The boy was actually a messenger. Wrapped around the collection of stems was a note. Payne unfurled the paper and saw a map with arrows leading him across the bridge and ending at the Old Town Square. Underneath was scribbled a single line: *Bring the flowers*.

Payne studied the map to get his bearings. He wondered how many people besides Jones were currently staring at him through a sniper's scope.

He covered his mouth and said, 'Old Town Square.'

The message was picked up by his radio mic, which was tucked discreetly into his ear, and transmitted to Jones in his sniper nest.

'Copy that,' Jones said as he unscrewed the sound suppressor on his rifle. 'Walk slow. I'll need some time to get into position.'

*　*　*

The Charles Bridge connected the Lesser Quarter of Prague with the more picturesque Old Town. As Payne walked, several elaborate statues cast their gaze upon him and the other tourists that filled the streets. He passed through the arch of the Charles Bridge Tower, signaling an end to the bridge and the start of the Old Town, and followed the twisting path laid out on the map, stepping through the shadows of structures built upon ancient ruins, traveling routes once used by knights sworn to protect the land, passing the remnants of what had once been spectacular gothic architecture.

Finally, after a short jaunt made longer by his deliberate pace, he reached the Old Town Square. Sitting at a round table underneath a wide umbrella was the man Payne had come to find. The same man he had seen outside the incline station in Pittsburgh.

They stared at each other across the square. Payne glared,

his body tense, while Masseri raised a water glass in a toast, a sinister smile creeping across his face.

Payne dropped the flowers and cautiously made his approach. Reaching the table, he stood opposite Masseri. 'I got your message.'

'I see that you did. Perhaps you would enjoy something to drink?'

Payne wanted to strangle him. 'Can we cut the crap?'

Masseri nodded with a slight chuckle. 'Please, sit down. We have many things to discuss. Tell me, is this your first visit to Prague?'

'How could that possibly be important?'

'It took me a great number of years to allow myself any form of pleasure while on assignment,' Masseri said, paying no attention to Payne's response, 'but I quickly discovered what I had been missing. Time is an important commodity, more valuable than any metal or precious stone. To waste it is a sin more heinous than all the others.'

He pointed to the empty chair across from him.

Payne reluctantly took a seat.

Masseri smiled. 'Look around you. Take it all in.' He drew a long breath to punctuate his point. 'The mishmash of styles, all telling the story of this square. Church after church after church. Look at them all. Romanesque abbeys. Gothic cathedrals. How many souls do you think have passed through these monuments?'

On any other day, with any other company, Payne would have gladly discussed Prague and its architectural beauty. Though not a historian, he could see why millions of people visited the city every year. Charming, vibrant facades enveloped them in all directions. Church spires rose mightily into the sky. In the distance, the Prague Orloj – the oldest functioning astronomical clock in the world – was mounted on the southern wall of the Old Town City Hall.

Today, he simply wanted Masseri to get to the point.

'Right now,' he said, 'the only souls I care about are Dr Sahlberg's and my own. We can talk about the rest when I'm sure he's safe . . . and out of your reach.'

56

Masseri grinned at Payne and slid a folder across the table. 'Thirty miles to the east, you will find a facility – a laboratory – in the woodlands near Rakovnik. It was once a military stronghold, a structure that passed through the hands of the various occupiers of what was then Czechoslovakia. The Nazis. The Soviets. And so on. Trust me when I tell you that it has seen its fair share of atrocities. It has been retrofitted to meet the needs of today's modern science.'

Payne ignored the folder. 'What are they studying there?'

'The experiments are not important,' Masseri countered. 'At least not to me. What is important are the men supervising the facility.'

'You owe them?'

'Quite the contrary: they are the ones who owe me. In exchange for the delivery of your Dr Sahlberg, they have agreed to pay me a rather exorbitant sum.'

'You have Mattias. Why not collect your money?'

'I received a better offer – one that pays more and allows your friend to keep his life. I believe that is what you Americans refer to as a "win-win".'

'They're planning to kill him?'

Masseri smiled. 'I see no other alternative. Once they've obtained the information they seek, there's no need to keep him around. The risk is too great. And the death of an elderly man can be easily explained – not that they're worried about that sort of thing.'

'What is it that Mattias knows?'

'That doesn't concern me. All that matters is that someone is willing to pay more to keep him alive.'

'Who?'

Masseri smiled. 'In due time, Jonathon, in due time. Tell me, what of the facility?'

'What do you mean?'

He pointed at the unopened folder. 'I want to know the likelihood that you can raid the compound and kill those in control of it, of course.'

'You want them dead?'

'It seems like the cleanest way to accomplish the goal.'

'Just like Stockholm,' Payne stated.

Masseri scoffed at the notion. 'I assure you I had nothing to do with Stockholm. In fact, by eliminating this facility, you will have your retribution against those responsible for the destruction of the Stockholm laboratory.'

'You mean, the men supervising this lab—'

'Yes! They are the same men that deemed the Stockholm facility a liability.' Masseri paused, letting the information sink in. 'Don't worry: you're not being sent to kill everyone, only the men with their fingers on the trigger. Their deaths will restore the balance. An eye for an eye, as they say.'

'I don't kill for revenge,' Payne said.

Masseri laughed. 'Your past actions would prove otherwise. Or can you justify every special forces killing as a necessary pre-emptive strike?'

Payne kept his cool and refused to take the bait. He would have liked nothing more than to explain the difference between revenge and justice in painful, bone-cracking detail, but it would have to wait. Right now, as much as he hated to admit it, this man was the best lead he had.

He opened the folder and glanced at the photos inside. 'Why kill them? Why not blow the whistle and let the local police handle the dirty work?'

Masseri shook his head. 'You must understand, the first rule of a double-cross is to ensure that those you are about to betray are not left standing. Contrary to your righteous claim, revenge is a powerful motivator for most. If I don't eliminate these men, then I am forced to live in fear of their reprisal. And I have neither the time nor the desire to do that. Once this act is completed, I can walk away for good. Free and clear to spend the rest of my days as I see fit. I've done terrible things, but that time has passed. You can facilitate my retirement, Jonathon.'

Payne smirked. 'I can do that right now . . . with a bullet.'

'But you won't. And do you know why you won't? Because my death means Sahlberg's death too. It's as simple as that.'

'Why use me? Why not do this yourself?'

Masseri leaned back in his chair. 'The second rule of a double-cross is to make sure you're as insulated from the front line as possible. Normally, this rule would be super-seded by my need to make sure that the job was done effectively, but in this instance I've been granted a reprieve. I have you.'

'In other words, you're a pussy.'

'No,' Masseri said, 'my particular talent involves the apprehension or termination of a single objective. I creep into their lives and pounce when they least expect it. Your skill set, on the other hand, is eliminating multiple targets in a hostile environment. Overwhelm the opponent with brute force. I have every confidence that your abilities will serve you well in this situation.'

'Lucky me.'

'No, lucky *me*,' Masseri stressed.

He couldn't have hoped for a better scenario. If Cole managed to kill Payne and Jones during the assault, Masseri would simply turn Sahlberg over to the South African as planned. He would be rewarded with his original fee, and the status quo would be maintained. However, if Payne successfully wiped out Cole and his men, Masseri was free to collect a larger fee from the other party seeking Sahlberg's safe delivery. After that, he could give up this life and disappear for ever.

As long as he controlled Sahlberg, he controlled his own destiny.

The situation was already a win-win, so what harm could it do to push for a little extra? With Cole dead, there would be no more looking over his shoulder.

Payne studied the contents of the folder. They included little more than a map of the compound and pictures of the men he was to kill. 'Which one is Hendrik Cole?'

Masseri twitched at the mention of Cole's name. 'You know he's involved?'

Payne stared across the table. 'I do now.'

'Very nicely played. But no matter, his identity was to be revealed during this conversation. The first picture is of Hendrik. He is at the top of the list. The others all take their orders from him. They are no less dangerous, just considerably less wicked.'

'I'm familiar with his reputation.'

'You have no idea,' Masseri countered. 'The Butcher of Benin doesn't do it justice. The man is vile through and through.'

'Given the source, is that supposed to scare me?'

'It is not my intention to scare you. Rather, I want to be clear what you're up against.'

'If I do what you ask, if I kill these men, what assurances do I have that Mattias will be set free?'

'You have my word.'

'Not good enough,' Payne insisted.

'Then perhaps this will suffice.' Masseri opened his briefcase and withdrew a small electronic tablet. He handed the device to Payne. 'Press play.'

Payne tapped the arrow on the screen and a preloaded video began to roll. It was of a middle-aged man seated at a desk. In his hand he held the previous day's edition of *Czechia Today*, one of the country's newspapers. In the military, this was known as proof-of-life documentation.

As the camera focused on the man's face, Payne began to recognize him. He had seen his image in the file that Dial had forwarded to him, although the man on the screen looked like he had aged ten years in the last two months. When he spoke, he confirmed Payne's suspicion.

'I am Tomas Berglund, and I need your help.'

Payne paused the recording. 'You've had him the whole time?'

'Keep watching,' Masseri replied.

Payne restarted the video and listened as Berglund explained the situation.

'When they destroyed my laboratory in Stockholm, I knew they would eventually go after Mattias. They were smart enough to find our communications and were untrusting of my pleas that he knows nothing of my research. To protect his life, I have made an arrangement with the very man they sent to locate him. Now that Mattias is safe, there is only one more thing that must be done. The men who destroyed my lab must be dealt with. It is the only way to end this madness. It is the only chance we have to walk away.'

Berglund leaned in to the camera. 'Please, you must trust me. I beg of you, help me. Help Mattias. Help us all.'

57

Payne had committed to the rescue mission, but he had no intention of going through with things until he'd spoken to Jones about the particulars. He had his own opinions as to how they should proceed, but he always gave Jones the opportunity to make his case.

They met in the billiards room of the Café Louvre, which was less than a mile to the south. Over the years, this famous café had played host to some of the greatest minds of the twentieth century. It was a favored haunt of Franz Kafka in the years preceding his most influential works. Later, as a professor at the Prague German University, Albert Einstein himself frequented the establishment as a regular guest of the German Philosophical Circle, a Tuesday night round table of the city's academics.

Jones was aware of its history, which was why he had chosen this spot as their meeting place. He thought it was only fitting. 'That was a smart move by him, meeting under the umbrella. If I hadn't beaten you to the square, I'd never have found you. As it was, I still didn't have a shot.'

Payne nodded. 'He's not stupid, I'll give him that. He knew what he was doing.'

'And what *was* he doing?'

'He was offering us a job,' Payne replied.

'What kind of job?'

Payne handed Jones the tablet with the Berglund video. 'Here, see for yourself.'

Jones watched the recording in disbelief. Once it had finished, he used the device to pull up a picture of the *Czechia Today* newspaper. He flipped between the website and the image on the video, comparing the headlines. Once the date was confirmed, he found a picture of Berglund on a scientific blog. Then he compared the image on the Internet with the man in the video – the aged, downtrodden man – and concluded they were one and the same.

He nodded. 'I'd say this is legit.'

'Me too.'

Jones tried to wrap his head around everything. 'So, let me get this straight. We eliminate the men operating this rogue lab outside of the city, and in return he'll hand over Mattias?'

'That's the offer,' Payne said.

'Yeah, that's the offer, but I'm still not sure why he's making it. Why doesn't he just kill them himself? He knows them. He could walk right up behind them and turn out their lights before they even knew what happened. Why does he need us to do the dirty work?'

'That's a good question,' Payne admitted, 'which is exactly why I asked that very thing before our meeting ended.'

'I heard you ask the question, but I didn't hear his response.'

'He said he'd found someone better to do the job. Us.'

Jones nodded. 'The man has a point.'

'I thought so too.'

'Out of curiosity, who hired him to begin with?'

'I couldn't get a name. He's not willing to give it up.'

'Or he doesn't know himself,' Jones offered.

'That was my thought too.'

'You know, we're going to need that information before this is all done, right?'

'I do. But right now we can only deal with the

information we have. We can focus on the rest later. One thing at a time.'

'What else do we know?'

Payne answered. 'For most of the last year, Dr Berglund was working on a secret project here in the Czech Republic. He was the lead scientist at the Rakovnik facility. The place was his to run as he saw fit. Despite all that, two months ago he quietly set up his own laboratory in Stockholm, recruiting a hand-picked collection of scientists that he knew he could trust.'

'Why the second lab? What were they studying?'

Payne shrugged. 'No one seems to know. Best guess is some offshoot of the research being done in Rakovnik. It would explain all the secrecy. Berglund was trying to keep it from the people funding the lab in Rakovnik.'

Jones nodded in understanding. 'You don't sink money into a research facility just to watch your lead scientist walk away and start his own lab. You need a return on your investment. To make that point, they buried the Stockholm laboratory and everyone who worked there.'

'But not Berglund,' Payne stressed. 'Killing him would serve no purpose, since he was the genius behind the science. They needed him to run the lab in Rakovnik, but what they didn't need were loose ends. So when they found out about his late-night calls to Mattias, they were afraid he had shared too much with his mentor.'

'Why didn't they just kill Mattias?'

'They couldn't. They needed to find out who else he might have told. Which is why our new friend was hired to bring him in alive. They need to know what he knows.'

Jones groaned. 'After that, he's as good as dead.'

'Fortunately, Berglund is a pretty smart guy. *Stupid*, for getting involved in this, but smart nonetheless. He realized Mattias was a target and made a side deal with the assassin that I met in the plaza for double his original fee. Now the only way to protect Mattias is to eliminate the men in control so the asshole can walk away free.'

'On the plus side,' Jones added, 'it sounds like cutting them down will liberate more than a few scientists being forced to work against their will.'

'Look at you,' Payne replied, 'ever the optimist.'

'We're going to need Nick's help,' Jones said. 'If we're going to rescue the right people, we need to know who to shoot and who to save.'

Payne held up the folder. 'I have pictures of the bad guys.'

'Maybe, maybe not. Who knows if we can trust his intel?'

'True, but . . .'

'But what?'

Payne knew what Jones was insinuating: they had friends in high places that might be able to offer some answers. 'You actually want me to call the director of the homicide division and ask him to send us some photos so we know who to kill?'

Jones grimaced. 'I think it's *whom*.'

'What is?'

'I think it's *whom to kill*, not *who to kill*.'

'What?'

'Your sentence—'

'Yeah,' Payne snapped, 'I get it. Actually, I take that back: I *don't* get it.'

'Well, you see, in that particular sentence—'

'No, dumbass, I get *that* part. The part I don't understand is why you're pointing out flaws in my grammar when you should be focused on the sentiment of my statement.'

'Whoa! Whoa! Whoa!' Jones teased. '*You're* the one who butchered the English language, but *I'm* the dumbass?'

'At least we agree on *that.*'

'Here's something else we can agree on: you're afraid to ask Nick for help.'

Payne objected. 'You know damn well that isn't the case. I ask Nick for help all the time.'

'Then what's the problem?'

'The problem is we normally call him *after* we've killed someone, not before.'

Jones smiled. 'That's a very good point.'

'I thought so.'

'In that case, maybe we should handle this without his help.'

'That's all I'm trying to say.'

'Good idea,' Jones said as he stood from their table. 'And since it was your idea, I think you're the one who needs to call Nick to tell him the bad news.'

'What bad news?'

'That we're about to kill some people, but he's not invited.'

'I don't think I'll put it like that.'

Jones laughed and patted him on the shoulder. 'Say it however you want. Just say it quick — like ripping off a Band-Aid.'

'Wait. Where are you going?'

'While you're breaking his heart, I'm going to take a piss.'

* * *

Dial, who had arrived in Prague that morning, had reluctantly stayed away from the rendezvous at the Charles Bridge, but as more and more time passed by, he was wondering if he had made the right decision. As it was, he had paced back and forth so many times in the lobby of the Mamaison Hotel in Prague that other guests were wondering if *he* was actually a psycho killer.

He sure sounded like one when he answered Payne's call. 'Where the fuck have you been? I could have walked to the bridge and back twenty times since I heard from you last.'

Payne winced. 'Don't worry, I'm fine.'

Dial took a deep breath and tried to relax. 'Sorry, Jon. I'm glad you're fine. It's just, I'm not used to this waiting-around bullshit. I'd rather be on the front line with you.'

'I'm sorry to hear you say that.'

'Why?'

'Because I got a lead that you can't pursue. At least not yet.'

'Meaning what?'

'Meaning exactly what you think I mean.'

Dial read between the lines. 'Jesus, Jon, I don't like this one bit.'

'I know you don't, but this is the way it has to be.'

Dial groaned. 'The cop in me wants to hang up right now before I hear another word. The friend in me wants to help you out in any way possible.'

'I'm cool with either. Do what you have to do.'

'I haven't hung up yet.'

Payne smiled. 'In that case, I need some pictures.'

'Pictures? Of what?'

'Of all the missing scientists – the ones who *weren't* killed in Stockholm.'

'Why? Did you find more bodies?'

'Just the opposite. I got confirmation that they're still alive. They're being forced to work at a second lab. We know where, and we're going after them.'

'Is Sahlberg there?'

'Doubtful. But Berglund is.'

'Wait! Berglund's alive?'

'As of yesterday, yes.'

'Jon, you don't have to do this. There are professionals who can handle this. Give me an hour, and I can round up the top men in the Czech police.'

'No offense, Nick, but you won't find a SWAT or rescue team that can do the job that DJ and I can do. We specialize in this kind of thing. Quick, clean and effective.'

'And no red tape,' Dial reiterated.

'Now you're getting it,' Payne replied.

'Jon, I'll send you everything I have. Pictures and names of the scientists we believe were working in Stockholm and a three-dimensional mock-up of the facility that some of the tech guys put together. If the scientists are studying the same things, maybe the layouts of their laboratories are identical too. It will give you an idea of what you might find there. Which levels house the equipment, the test animals, that sort of thing.'

'That'll help.'

'If you think of anything else, just say the word.'

Payne nodded. 'I'll call you when we're done.'

58

Rakovnik, Czech Republic
(40 miles west of Prague)

In the early twentieth century, the forests outside Rakovnik were an ideal location for a military installation. The territory was far enough removed from the social, economic and bureaucratic center of Prague that its inhabitants could operate without fear of interference. Those in command in this remote area governed autonomously, without the oversight of central command. As such, the atrocities committed there throughout the years went largely unnoticed.

It wasn't until after World War II and the end of the Cold War that many of the stories surrounding the facility began to surface. By then, the complex was an abandoned mess of crumbling brick and overgrown courtyards. To most, it was little more than a reminder of a bygone era. A period in history that was better left forgotten.

The locals saw it as an eyesore.

Zidane saw it as an opportunity.

He realized that the thick, sturdy walls could be resurrected to their former glory with only a fraction of the investment required to build them from scratch. He saw a self-sufficient compound with its own electrical and water treatment plants. Perhaps most importantly, he saw acres of undeveloped land on all sides of the grounds, a buffer zone that ensured privacy.

The former military settlement deep in the woods was far from prying eyes, yet it was close enough to Rakovnik – and the services enjoyed by its more than fifteen thousand residents – to entice those scientists who insisted they couldn't leave the comforts of civilization.

It was the perfect place for a laboratory.

A lab to study whatever he wanted.

In the waning light, Jones stared at the facility through a pair of high-powered binoculars. He noted that only a single story was visible above the ground. The rest of the structure had been dug into the earth. Rumor had it there were tunnels that went for miles.

Although Payne had been the leader of the MANIACs, it was Jones who had a special gift for tactics. As such, the assault had been his to plan. He had chosen dusk not because of the fading light. That logic was sound if they were fighting out in the open, but today's battle would take place inside. Instead, the decision to proceed at this hour was based upon Masseri's note that most of the guards would be eating dinner. Jones wanted to take full advantage of any edge he could find, and having his opponents gathered in one place was a good start.

To aid their cause, Berglund had provided a description of the security measures used at the facility. There were no cameras or booby traps – nothing that would provide a record of the men and women who worked there or expose the true nature of the building. As such, the main deterrent the team had to overcome was a series of locks.

The front entrance and interior doorways were secured by magnetic locks that could be temporarily disabled with the swipe of a keycard. Fortunately, Berglund had stolen one of the cards from an unsuspecting guard and had smuggled it to

Masseri, who in turn had made multiple copies and placed them in the folder he had given to Payne.

Of course, Payne had no way of knowing if they would actually work until his ass was on the line and he was standing outside the compound's front door.

He took a deep breath and swiped the card.

The door opened with a soft click.

'Main breach,' Payne whispered as he entered the building. The mic in his ear relayed the news to all the members of his team.

'Copy,' came the reply, 'on your go.'

As much as they hated the thought of involving Dial or the Czech police in the assault, Payne and Jones had no qualms about bringing in outside help. To strengthen their numbers, they had turned to the vast network of former commandos now living abroad.

Men they had met in battle.

Men they could trust.

Two phone calls later, they had successfully recruited three men to help. Each was ex-special forces, and each lived within an hour of Prague. In fact, two of them were roommates. Though none of them were ex-MANIACs, they had been stationed with Payne and Jones in the Middle East and had heard stories about their exploits. The chance to help them out and to shoot some bad guys was an opportunity they couldn't pass up.

The soldier who lived alone – a demolition expert in the Navy SEALs – was known to his peers as Rapture. His call sign was given to him because of his ability to create end-of-days-type carnage. His main responsibility was to level the electrical sub-station on Payne's order.

Rapture could do that in his sleep.

When the time was right, they hoped to use the loss of power to their advantage. The problem with the strategy was the possibility that the power outage would render the magnetic locks inoperable. If the interruption unlocked the doors, everything would be fine. But if the doors were stuck in the locked position, they would need another way to open them.

Enter Hulk and Rhino, two hard-partying ex-Marines who could bulldoze their way through anything in their path. Though they were known as human battering rams, they were also good with knives and guns. Their main job was to evacuate the innocent scientists. If they happened to kill some guards along the way, so be it.

That being said, if anyone was going to get hurt, Payne and Jones wanted to make sure they were first in line to take a bullet. That was why they planned to handle the riskiest part of the mission personally. Their job was to find and eliminate Hendrik Cole.

Payne led the men down the first corridor of the building, peeking into every room but finding nothing but empty offices. They had no way of knowing if these were an elaborate ruse to fool visitors, but it was clear that whoever worked there had gone home for the night.

After ensuring the area was clear, Payne and the others used the stairwell to descend to the next floor. They were halfway there when the smell told them what they were about to find. Their senses were confirmed when they saw the test subject storage level. Every wall was lined with built-in cages of all shapes and sizes. A third of the spaces were empty, but the cages that were full contained the same assortment of animals that had been found in Stockholm.

Only here, they were very much alive.

Pigs squealed and dogs barked at them as they made their

way across the floor. Jones vowed right then and there to make sure these creatures were cared for. He knew they had a job to do before he could worry about saving them, but he also knew he would be haunted by their faces if he left them behind. Nothing deserved to suffer for being what it was born to be. *Nothing.*

At the end of the row, a trio of chimpanzees stared out at them from behind the bars of their cages. There were no cries, no howls; only the forlorn faces of three animals already resigned to death. Jones could see the intelligence in their eyes, and he felt his normally iron stomach begin to turn. So much so that he had to do something right then and there.

'Hold up,' he whispered to Payne.

Payne glanced back. 'What's wrong?'

'*Them.* I have to free them.'

'What? Why?'

'*They're* from Africa. *I'm* from Africa . . .'

'No you're not. You're from Pittsburgh.'

'Come on, man. Just these three.'

'I swear to God, I don't get you sometimes.'

'That's 'cause *you're* not from Africa.'

Payne rolled his eyes. 'Be quick.'

Jones smiled and opened the cages. Then he directed the chimps' attention toward the main entrance. 'Go that way, guys. Toward the trees. Run like the wind.'

Hulk and Rhino glanced at each other, confused.

Then they turned and pointed at the door as well.

The chimps squealed their thanks as they bolted for the exit.

'Okay,' Jones said, laughing. '*Now* we can go downstairs.'

In contrast to the other floors, the third floor down was bustling with activity. Through the small window in the stairwell door, Payne and Jones could see an assortment of laboratory and computer equipment, with each station attended by at least one scientist.

Along the far wall they could see a small area that was being used as a guard post. Its cinderblock walls were only three feet high, with wide panes of glass rising to the ceiling. The cordoned area extended awkwardly into the main room, a hastily constructed afterthought to be used as an observation point.

Inside the cement and glass box that jutted into the primary space was Hendrik Cole and seven of his men. They were laughing over plates of spaghetti and meatballs, blissfully unaware of the threat bearing down on them.

Payne glanced at Jones, who in turn nodded toward Hulk and Rhino. Payne swiped the keycard through its receiver, disengaging the door's lock. Then he contacted the fifth member of the assault team, who was waiting outside. 'Rapture. You there?'

'Here, sir,' he replied.

'Game on.'

59

Rapture smiled when he received the order from Payne. Then he did what he did best: he unleashed a series of explosions that utterly decimated the power station. In a flash of fire and a shower of sparks, the entire facility went dark. Before anyone else could react, Payne and his assault team burst through the doorway of the laboratory's main floor.

'Fire!' they screamed as loud as they could.

They had learned from experience that this distress call transcended language barriers. It was one of those words that elicited an immediate response, regardless of the situation or the location. Within seconds, the warning was being translated and relayed throughout the room. Startled scientists pushed toward the exits in a calm and orderly fashion. Even in near darkness, the evacuation of the building had started better than Payne and Jones could have hoped. It wasn't until the battery-powered backup lights switched on that all hell broke loose.

That was when the real panic started.

As the flickering lights began to illuminate the room, the invading men could no longer remain hidden. Payne and Jones had broken for the guard station the instant the room had gone dark, but they had only made it halfway to the door when the glow of the backup lights gave away their advance. One of the scientists screamed at the sight of two armed soldiers streaking across the room. Then another. And another.

Before long, everyone was screaming.

Cole charged out of the guard station with his weapon raised. He spotted Payne in the midst of the chaos and opened fire. He didn't care about collateral damage. All he cared about was killing the intruders. Payne launched himself sideways into a pack of scientists. They crashed to the floor like bowling pins as broken glass rained down on top of them.

Other guards joined in, and before long, automatic weapons were shredding the laboratory. Jones and his squad returned fire while shrieking scientists crawled their way toward the safety of the stairwell. Payne twisted around and yanked one of the women he had saved behind the solid base of a specimen table.

'See him,' he said as he pointed to Hulk, 'he's here to get you out.'

Now sobbing, the young woman summoned the courage to rise to her knees and scurry toward the door.

From his position on the floor, Payne could see other scientists cowering behind anything and everything to protect themselves from the chaos around them. 'Go now!' he yelled. To reinforce his demand, he rose to his feet and returned fire.

His first volley caught one of Cole's men in the stomach, and he crumpled to his knees. A second later, a headshot from Rhino splattered the wall with grey matter. When Jones silenced another guard with a shot to the neck, the rest of the men cowered inside the guard station, ducking for cover behind the concrete walls and an overturned steel table.

Spaghetti and meatballs covered the floor.

Together Payne, Jones, Hulk and Rhino were able to lay down a suppressive wave of gunfire, allowing the remaining scientists to crawl their way to the exit.

Hulk stepped farther into the room, determined to help

Payne and Jones, but the duo cut him off before he could make good on his intentions.

'We'll handle this,' Payne insisted between bursts of gunfire.

'Get the scientists out of the building and to the rally point,' Jones directed.

'But sir—'

'Now! That's an order,' Payne barked.

'Yes, sir,' Hulk replied as he backpedaled toward the exit.

Payne watched as Hulk and Rhino disappeared into the stairwell. From here on out, it was just him and Jones against whoever was left cowering behind the conference table.

They ducked low to reload.

'What are you thinking?' Payne asked.

Jones raised his assault rifle. 'I'm thinking maybe we should have brought a little more firepower. Is it too late to call Kaiser?'

Payne smiled. The M4 in his hands was compact and efficient. It could easily shoot through the steel table, but it didn't have the punch to drive a bullet through a concrete block. If they wanted Cole and his men, they would have to flush them out.

As he considered their options, two of Cole's men rose from their positions and began firing wildly in Payne and Jones's general direction. In the spaces between shooting, Payne could hear the squeak of rubber soles against linoleum tile. He knew that Cole was trying to escape. The men weren't really trying to hit Payne and Jones; that would merely be an added benefit. Their actual intent was to cover Cole's retreat.

'Jon!' Jones yelled above the din.

Payne turned to see his friend pointing toward the second stairwell at the far end of the floor. He watched as Cole and two of his henchmen disappeared through the exit.

'Rabbit?' Jones asked.

Payne flexed his trigger finger. 'Rabbit.'

Jones slung his M4 over his shoulder. He crouched like a sprinter in the starting blocks and took a deep breath before bursting from his stance. His head held low, he darted between tables and equipment stands, ducking and weaving his way across the room.

Like greyhounds chasing the racetrack hare, the gunmen's aim followed Jones as he ran. As they turned away from him, Payne sprang from his crouch and unloaded a full magazine into the unsuspecting pair. They fell, unable to catch their breath as the air escaped their bullet-ridden lungs. Confident that his friend was no longer in danger, Payne stepped over each man and ended his life with a single round.

'Clear?' Jones asked.

'Clear,' Payne replied.

Jones rose to his full height as Payne raced by him in pursuit of Cole. Jones followed him into the second stairwell, where they had a decision to make. The exit was above them, but bloody palm smears on the wall indicated that someone had made their way down.

'You go up,' Payne said. 'I'm going to check out the basement.'

'See you outside,' Jones replied as he raced up to the next level. He kicked the door open and ducked behind the wall as shots ricocheted around him.

The goon waiting for his arrival had just missed his best opportunity.

Jones stepped through the door and aimed his rifle where he expected his opposition to be, but there was no one visible in the gloom. All he could see were the animal cages he had passed on the way in. Row after row of mice, rats, cats and more. All of them riled up from the panic and noise and fear. They, more than men, could sense danger.

Suddenly Jones saw a shadow dart across the room.

Two more joined the hunt, moving more quickly than humanly possible.

Another shot rang out, this time missing Jones by mere inches. He returned fire with a spray of bullets from his M4 and used the commotion to adjust his position, creeping around toppled transport cages that were now strewn about the room, trying to locate his target. He steadied himself and listened, hoping that his quarry would give himself away.

What he heard instead sent a chill down his spine.

The man's scream was shrill. A horrified shriek like the wailing of a banshee. It was followed by two rapid gunshots, then a sickening, gurgling plea for help.

Jones stepped forward cautiously, unsure of what he would find. As he came upon the gunman, he realized that shooting him would have been an act of kindness.

But he wasn't in the mood to be kind.

A dead chimpanzee lay at the man's side. He had killed it with the pistol that dangled from his limp hand. The other two chimps were busy dismantling the man's face. His eyes and ears had been removed, and his throat had been torn open. Jones could see from the man's wounds that he was close to death, as the carotid artery had stopped spurting blood into the pool that had gathered around his head. Now it was just a trickle.

'Got what you deserved,' Jones muttered as he retreated toward the exit, not the least bit concerned about the angry chimps. He had set them free earlier, and they had cleared his way. He knew they wouldn't attack him from behind.

'Headed for the surface,' Jones announced.

'Copy that,' Rhino answered. 'You have eyes on Panther?'

'Negative, Rhino. Panther, do you read?'

But Payne did not respond.

60

As Payne entered the basement, the acrid scent of burned flesh and noxious gas stung his nostrils. He had seen pictures of the crematorium used in the Stockholm laboratory, but this was different . . . very different. This was something straight from the horrors of Auschwitz or Dachau. Here the incinerator was virtually the entire floor – a long corridor of flamethrowing nozzles that could be sealed at either end.

The chamber was open.

And gas was venting into the room.

A cough from somewhere in the distance pulled Payne's attention from the gas that was spreading throughout the basement. Then he heard loud, labored breathing.

Following the wall of the incinerator deeper into the basement, his rifle at the ready, he found the source of the sound as Hendrik Cole emerged from the shadows at the far end of the floor. Blood seeped from a gunshot wound in his abdomen.

Cole wouldn't survive the night without medical attention. Payne knew it, and Cole knew it too.

He laughed at the sight of Payne. 'I'd put the rifle down . . .' He pulled Tomas Berglund into view. He looked terrified. '. . . Unless you want us all to burn.'

Payne knew he was out of options. He could feel the air thickening with the flammable gas used to fuel the incinerator. If he fired his M4, the muzzle flare would ignite the room, turning the basement into a raging inferno.

'Masseri gave us up before you killed him?' Cole asked. When Payne didn't respond, a surprised smile spread across Cole's face as he began to understand the truth. 'You didn't kill him, did you? He *led* you here.' He laughed at the thought.

'And I'll bet you thought assassins were trustworthy,' Payne taunted.

Cole shrugged as blood seeped from his gut. 'Good help is hard to find. I guess I'll just have to make better decisions in the future.'

'What makes you think you have a future?'

Cole pounded on the metal wall. The hollow echo of the tunnel behind it resonated throughout the room. 'Always give yourself a way out.'

Payne lowered his rifle. 'You better run fast. I'll be coming.'

Cole opened the steel door and pushed Berglund into the tunnel. He lingered in the doorway for an extra second. 'Actually, you're the one who better run fast.'

As he pulled the door shut behind him, he lobbed something back into the basement. Payne immediately recognized the device as a flash-bang grenade. It wasn't normally lethal, but he knew that the white-hot spray of burning magnesium that would erupt from the canister was sure to ignite the explosive vapor hanging in the air.

He cursed and broke for the stairwell, trying to outrun the flames. As he sprinted up the stairs, he felt the air rush past him as the exploding grenade drew in the available oxygen before exhaling in a mighty roar. He turned a corner and slammed a door, flames nipping at his heels. By the time he was at the top level of the compound, the fire had reached the main lab. Freshly fueled by the chemicals, the flames devoured the top two stories of the building just as Payne charged through the exit.

Jones watched as his best friend dove for cover a split second before the front entrance of the building was destroyed by the explosive force of the escaping fire. He ran forward and dragged Payne from the reach of the flames. As he did, he could smell the acrid stench of burned hair and cloth. He looked down to make sure his best friend wasn't on fire.

'Jon,' he demanded, 'are you okay?'

Payne opened his eyes and shook his head, clearing the ringing in his ears. 'They got away.'

'Who?'

'Cole and Berglund. They got out through a tunnel in the basement.'

Without saying a word, Jones used a series of hand gestures to notify Hulk and Rhino of the development. In response, the two soldiers took off into the woods surrounding the compound. Jones helped Payne to his feet, and together they stumbled toward the crowd of rescued scientists that had gathered a safe distance from the building.

'What of Herr Cole?' a man asked nervously in a heavy German accent. 'He is dead?'

'I'm afraid not,' Payne answered. 'He made it out.'

'Tomas?' a woman's voice shouted.

'He made it out as well,' Payne assured them.

A murmur of relief ran through the crowd.

'Does anyone know where the tunnel under the building ends?' Jones asked.

A slight man in his fifties stepped forward. His accent gave away his Swiss ancestry. 'I'm afraid none of us were permitted into the basement. Only Mr Cole and his men were allowed on that level. We know nothing of a tunnel, or anything else that took place down there.'

From the tone of his voice, Payne and Jones could tell that the scientists understood the implications of what happened in the basement. No doubt they had sent countless test subjects to the lower level for disposal. How that was accomplished and who was in charge of the actual disposal was a mystery that none of them were eager to uncover.

A third man, younger than most and of Asian descent, approached the group and spoke to them in a language that neither Payne nor Jones could understand. The Swiss scientist nodded his agreement with whatever the man was talking about.

'Doctor . . .' Jones said, looking for the Swiss scientist's name.

'Yuler,' the scientist offered. 'Roger Yuler.'

'Dr Yuler, what's he saying?'

Yuler explained. 'He says that a tunnel makes sense. It explains the sudden arrival of our patient, even at the oddest of hours.'

Payne frowned. 'Your patient? What are you talking about? I thought this was an experimental facility.'

Yuler shook his head. 'We are studying experimental sciences, but this is a *medical* facility. Though we are limited to specific areas of treatment, I assure you that our sole intent is to offer aid.' His tone was now defensive, as if he were trying to justify the secretive nature of the compound, even though they weren't working there by choice.

'I'm confused. What were you treating?' Payne asked.

'Cancer,' Yuler replied.

'That doesn't explain *this*,' Jones chimed in. 'A lot of people are treating cancer. And they aren't doing it at gunpoint inside a secret laboratory in the middle of nowhere.'

'A lot of people *are* treating it,' Yuler agreed. 'But I assure you that no one is treating it quite like we are.'

'Keep talking,' Jones pressed.

'Cancer is, at its basest level, a mutation. A cellular anomaly that turns the body against itself. Its causes are broad and varied, but the treatment is almost always the same: remove or reduce the affected areas, counter the secondary infections and other ailments with pharmaceuticals, and hope that the cancer retreats into a state of remission.'

'You've come up with something more effective?' Payne guessed.

'Not me personally,' Yuler replied. 'I was merely a consultant. Tomas Berglund is the true mastermind behind our therapy.'

'Which is what?' Jones asked.

'Rather than treat the effects of the cancer after the cells have mutated, Tomas envisioned a method of preventing the abnormalities altogether.'

'How?' Payne asked.

'Nanotechnology,' Yuler answered. 'He developed a microscopic vessel – essentially an artificial cell – that could not only eradicate cancer cells, but could also seek out other, precancerous cells before they could transform into something life-threatening. These synthetic entities could actually be programmed to detect the precursors of the cancerous formation: chemical flags that signal the forthcoming malignancy.'

'You could wipe out cancer before it even existed,' Jones stated in fascination.

'Theoretically, yes, with a high enough dosage. But delivering enough of the agent to search every part of the body proved impossible. The immune system interprets the introduction of that many foreign bodies as an all-out invasion. The resulting defense is more than the body can handle.'

'The therapy ends up killing the patient,' Payne summarized.

'Yes, but only when we attempted to immunize the *whole* body. By concentrating the therapy to one organ or another – in other words, *localized* treatment – our methods proved almost one hundred percent effective. In clinical trials, the primary concern was not the conflict between the treatment and the immune system; it was establishing guidelines for a proper dosage. Fortunately, there are a number of factors to guide us. In real-world applications, a patient's family medical history would be considered.'

'So, localized treatments were working on your patient?' Jones asked.

Yuler shook his head. 'Unfortunately, they were not an option. When our patient came to us, his cancer had already metastasized throughout his body. Our only option was to alter the primary course of therapy.'

'In what way?' Payne wondered.

'We first allowed the nano-cells to locate and eradicate the known cancers. Then, to stop his body from destroying itself, we reprogrammed a second batch of nano-cells to destroy his white blood cells, lymphocytes, T-cells, and all his other defenses.'

'You replaced his immune system?'

'We did.'

'And now your technology is the only thing keeping him alive.'

'It is,' Yuler admitted. 'And the effects are finite. The nano-cells cannot replicate, nor can they function in perpetuity. If the inoperative nano-cells are not continuously flushed out of the system and replaced by new nano-cells, something as innocuous as the common cold would have devastating effects.'

'Jesus,' Jones mumbled under his breath.

Payne remained focused. 'That explains the *what*, but what about the *who*? Someone went to great lengths to establish this facility and keep you all here. We need to know who it was.'

Yuler agreed. 'Our patient was Harrison Zidane.'

61

As a young man, Zidane had worked for an industrial radio-graphy company owned by his father. His job was to transport canisters of material used in X-ray technology – the derivation known as iridium 192 – to and from the various facilities that produced and utilized the radioactive isotope.

During one of his deliveries in northern Africa, a canister of iridium somehow fell from his truck. It was discovered by two children, who played with it for five days before presenting it to their grandmother. Unfortunately, the radiation damage caused by the iridium led to severe chemical burns in the case of the children, as well as thyroid and breast cancer in several relatives and neighbors. At the time, it was assumed the kids must have pried the canister open or it had been damaged when it had fallen from the truck. After further study, it was determined that the company had improperly contained its product.

The family had been exposed to the iridium for less than a week.

Zidane had been transporting the element for more than a year.

His contact with the radiation had been intermittent, but the sum total of its effect would make itself known. By the age of forty, Zidane had undergone a multitude of biopsies to remove tumors throughout his body. By fifty, he had been diagnosed with a wide variety of cancers. Though he had managed to evade an immediate death sentence – the cancers were fought with aggressive surgery and intensive chemo-therapy – the doctors did not give him much time.

Determined to live, Zidane used the modest inheritance from his father's estate to finance anything that might discover a cure for his ailments. Along the way, his efforts made him a vast fortune and eventually led him to Tomas Berglund, who gave him something much more important than money.

Tomas Berglund gave him hope.

*　*　*

Payne and Jones had saved many scientists at the laboratory in Rakovnik, but they had failed to deliver the two things they had promised Masseri: Tomas Berglund and Hendrik Cole.

With nothing to trade for Sahlberg and no idea where to look for Cole, they were forced to strike a new deal with Masseri. They knew they couldn't put their trust in him entirely – after all, he had double-crossed Cole – but so far he hadn't led them astray.

He had told them where to find the lab.

He had told them where to find Berglund.

And he had told them where to find Cole.

They hoped Masseri could help them again, which was why they reluctantly agreed to meet him in Prague. The same café as before. This time, the three of them together as the nightly festivities of the Old Town Square carried on around them.

Payne realized this would be a renegotiation, so he did his best to establish his position as one of strength. 'It looks like you've lost your leverage.'

Masseri scoffed. 'How do you figure that? I still have Dr Sahlberg.'

'True, but how do you plan to collect? Cole's not an idiot. He knows exactly how we found him in Rakovnik. If you try to deliver Mattias, he'll cut you from ear to ear.'

Masseri smiled. 'In that case, Sahlberg is no use to me. I guess I'll leave him to rot.'

'He's of plenty use to you,' Payne insisted. 'He's the only thing keeping me from leaping across this table and crushing your windpipe. I want him back.'

Masseri smiled. 'I want double what Berglund was offering. In exchange, I will tell you where I have hidden Sahlberg.'

Payne shook his head. 'Not a chance. I'm not altering our previous deal. I retrieve Tomas Berglund, and you hand over Mattias.'

'How do I benefit from that?' Masseri asked.

'We're still going to kill Hendrik Cole.'

All things considered, Masseri knew it was his best option. He couldn't turn Sahlberg over to Cole. Not now. Not after his double-cross. Cole would kill him on sight. And if he couldn't strong-arm Payne into paying for Sahlberg – and it certainly looked like Payne had no intention of paying a ransom – then at least Cole's death would keep him from looking over his shoulder for the rest of his life.

His only other option was to kill Sahlberg, dump his body in the river, and disappear for as long as possible. But as he looked into Payne's eyes, he knew the MANIAC would stop at nothing to avenge the loss of his friend. Killing Sahlberg would be a death sentence.

'What do you need from me?' Masseri conceded.

Jones answered. 'We need a location. Where would Cole take Berglund for safe keeping?'

'He doesn't want to keep him safe. He wants to trade him for cash as quickly as possible. And guess who benefits the most from Dr Berglund's continued existence?'

'Harrison Zidane,' Payne answered.

'Exactly,' Masseri said with a smile. 'If Cole grabbed

Berglund, it's safe to assume that he has every intention of getting the most value for him. And it's rather obvious Zidane has the deepest pockets and the most motivation.'

'You think he's taking him directly to Zidane?'

'That's what I would do,' Masseri said. He leaned forward to make his point. 'Harrison Zidane is in no condition to stray far from home. Until the hospital he is financing in Como is completed, he needs to remain in close proximity to the laboratory you destroyed or to his villa on the lake. He went to the lab for treatments, but Berglund went to him for checkups.'

Jones considered their options. 'I'm guessing you've seen his place in Como. What kind of security are we talking about?'

'Zidane keeps his own security force on hand at all times. Ex-Mossad, British SAS, former special forces, and so on. And that's just to guard his artwork. There's no telling what changes he'll make once he hears about Rakovnik. And this time, you won't have the element of surprise. He and his men will be waiting for your arrival.'

*   *   *

If Cole headed directly to Italy, there was no way for Payne, Jones or Dial to beat him to Lake Como. He simply had too much of a head start. Fortunately, Dial didn't need to be in Italy to mobilize his troops. He managed that with a phone call.

Though they had no power to make arrests, there was nothing in the Interpol charter that prevented them from observing suspects. At Dial's insistence, NCB agents from the Milan office were patrolling the waters of Lake Como before the sun came up. And their timing couldn't have been better. Had they waited even fifteen minutes longer to follow Dial's order, they would have missed the small powerboat as it slipped into Zidane's private dock at dawn.

The agents watched as three men stealthily made their way

from the water to the house. The first was the driver of the boat. The second was Tomas Berglund. The third – the injured man pushing Berglund as he stumbled up the steps to the villa – was Hendrik Cole. They were greeted by a throng of security personnel, each carrying the kind of firepower seldom seen on men protecting exclusive waterfront estates.

'They've arrived in Lake Como,' Dial told Payne and Jones as he disconnected the call from the Milan office. 'They're at Harrison Zidane's house. And your informant was right about the guards. The property is protected by at least ten heavily armed men.'

'I'd prefer heavy men with no arms,' Jones cracked.

'Me too,' Payne admitted.

Dial frowned. 'Guys, I'm worried about your safety here. If you approach from the front, the guards can take you out long before you reach the shore. Not to mention anyone who happens to be in the water at the time.'

'Who said anything about the front?' Jones asked as he pulled out his tablet computer and showed Dial several images of the back half of Zidane's property. It consisted of a sheer rock face that extended several hundred feet in the air and protected the villa like a castle wall.

Dial looked at him like he was crazy. 'You can't be serious.'

Jones deadpanned. 'I'm always serious.'

62

Saturday, 27 July

Zidane's villa on Lake Como abutted the steep slopes of the Italian Alps. Cut into the rock, the house perched magnificently above the water's edge. The location offered stunning views of the lake. It also made the estate inaccessible from the rear.

At least for *most* people.

Thanks to satellite images from Randy Raskin, Payne and Jones realized that the security detail at Zidane's house was focused on the lakefront. The guards kept a watchful eye on the water, but they left the back of the property – the sheer cliffs of the mountain – virtually unattended.

Jones decided this was the best way in.

Plus, it would be a hell of a ride.

Payne stood at the edge of the Boeing C-17's cargo ramp and peered out into the night sky. Had it been a few hours later, he would have been able to see the curvature of the earth from this height.

'You remember how to do this?' he teased.

'Like riding a bike,' Jones replied.

'Since when do you ride a bike at thirty thousand feet?'

'Okay, it's nothing like riding a bike,' Jones admitted. 'It's a hell of a lot longer fall to the pavement.'

While on active duty, they had often used HALO jumps – High Altitude Low Opening – to infiltrate hostile territory.

This dangerous maneuver allowed them to deploy from more than five miles above the lake – far too high for either them or their aircraft to be noticed by guards on the ground. They would freefall to the top of the mountain peaks before opening their chutes at the very last minute.

If all went as planned, they would be able to halt their descent somewhere on the rock face above the house. From there, they would anchor climbing gear and make their final approach by means of a rappeling line. It was exactly the type of high-risk, high-reward endeavor that Payne and Jones had come to miss as civilians.

The light in the cargo hold flashed green, and Payne looked at Jones. It was now or never. They only had a small window of opportunity to make their jump before the C-17 had to reroute back to Aviano Air Base. They wouldn't get a second chance. Their current heading could be explained as a training exercise. A second pass would draw the attention of the Italian air force.

They stepped off the ramp and plummeted into the void.

Adrenalin surged through their systems as they fell faster and faster. By the time they reached terminal velocity, the muscle memory they had honed during their countless previous jumps kicked in. They tucked and rolled as needed, correcting their course to stay on target.

At five thousand feet they released their chutes. There was a sudden jerk as their parachutes filled with air, followed by a graceful glide to the rocky cliffs below. This was the part that Jones had been waiting for.

They skimmed the rock face below as they descended, searching for anything that would serve as a foothold or any place they could anchor a clip. After several hundred feet, they finally managed to land on the vertical wall.

As they secured their climbing rigs a few hundred feet above the property, Jones could only grin. He hadn't been entirely sure that they would be able to cling to the smooth slope of the mountain, even after their fall had been dramatically slowed by their chutes. For a split second, he found himself wondering if the hard part of the assault was already over.

'What are you smiling about?' Payne asked.

Jones laughed. 'I honestly didn't know if we'd be able to stop up here. I was afraid the wind off the rock face would take us out over the house.'

Payne could only shake his head. 'Now you tell me.'

'I didn't want to scare you.'

Both men knew that gliding down to the villa under a para-chute would have led to a slaughter – *their* slaughter.

'Next time, I'm planning the mission.'

'Next time?' Jones said as he set an anchor in the rock. He tested it to make sure it was secure. 'Let's hope there *is* a next time.'

'There will be,' Payne assured him, suddenly all business.

Jones nodded in reply. He grabbed a small infrared flashlight and aimed it at the hillside on the other side of the lake, where the third member of their team lay in wait.

Rappeling down the sheer face of the mountain would require Payne and Jones to use both hands on the line. While in motion, their rifles would be slung over their shoulders and their pistols would be holstered. If they were spotted, they would be defenseless – save the possibility of swinging wildly to dodge the gunfire from below. To counter this disadvantage, they needed a sniper on the opposite side of the ravine to cover their approach.

Though they would have preferred Hulk or Rhino watching their backs, neither man had the long-range shooting ability of Masseri, who had willingly volunteered his services. They didn't trust him, but they ultimately decided to accept his offer, knowing full well that he was highly motivated to kill Cole and as many of Zidane's men as possible. After all, if Tomas Berglund didn't walk out alive, Masseri wouldn't see a payday of any kind.

Masseri was watching the slope above Zidane's house through his night-vision scope. Jones's flashlight wasn't visible to the naked eye, but the optics on Masseri's sniper rifle picked up the flash as if it were a standard bulb. He watched Payne and Jones begin their descent before he fixed his crosshairs on a guard at the front of the property.

He waited. And waited.

Until the time was right.

Then he squeezed the trigger.

The guard's head exploded like a water balloon, spraying those around him with a colorful burst of blood. The other guards scrambled for cover as they fired wildly toward the lake, unsure where the shot had come from. Two seconds later, Masseri added to their confusion by killing another, this time with a shot to the neck.

The men were well trained and well armed, but they were unprepared for this type of assault. One by one Masseri took them down, smiling as he did. Even firing from the opposite bank across the windswept lake, his accuracy was flawless.

By the time Payne and Jones had landed on the roof, Masseri had eliminated five of Cole's men. As reinforcements poured from the house, Payne and Jones shot at them from above while Masseri continued to pick them off from a distance. Caught in the kill zone between three experienced shooters, Cole's guards were hopelessly outmatched.

Payne watched as one overwhelmed henchman literally spun

in circles, aimlessly shooting in all directions. Like a well-armed Tasmanian devil, the soldier tried to inflict as much damage to the surrounding area as he could. Unfortunately for those around him, he managed to shoot not one, but two of his fellow guards. In the end, a member of his own team took out the spastic shooter. It was friendly fire that had become defensive fire, a necessity of the moment.

When the carnage ended, fourteen men lay dead on the patio.

'I think someone made it back inside,' Jones pointed out.

'I saw him too,' Payne replied.

They dropped to the patio below and surveyed the damage. If the satellite images and the NCB patrols were correct, the security force was comprised of fifteen men. That left one still unaccounted for. One guard and Cole, along with Zidane and Berglund. Even if Cole could fire a weapon in his condition, Payne liked their odds much better now than he had done a few minutes before.

63

Payne and Jones stepped inside the house cautiously, one scanning high and to the right, the other covering low and to the left.

The house was warm and inviting. In the main sitting room, two massive, overstuffed leather couches were arranged around a driftwood coffee table. A mahogany bar stood in the corner. Row after row of top-shelf liquor was displayed in glass cabinets on either side. Above the fireplace was a projection screen that spanned the width of the chimney. Beyond that, tall bay windows looked out across the length of the lake.

'Here,' Jones said as he aimed his rifle at the floor.

Behind the farthest couch lay the final guard. He was struggling for breath, a gaping hole in his back where Masseri's bullet had torn through him.

Jones crouched low and pressed a finger to the man's neck, checking his pulse. A moment later he shook his head.

Payne nodded and stepped deeper into the house.

They made their way down a long hallway lined with photos. The story of Harrison Zidane, told in pictures. School graduations. Big game fishing. Posing with politicians and celebrities at various awards ceremonies. All the best moments of his life were represented.

They passed offices and bedrooms, each furnished with the trappings of opulence. Fifteen-hundred-dollar Aeron desk chairs. Four-thousand-dollar Charlotte Thomas bedding. Priceless works of art on every wall. No expense had been spared.

They continued toward the farthest door, checking each room as they passed. When they reached the end, they found a spacious library that had been transformed into a makeshift treatment center. Payne had seen intensive care units that were less equipped.

The first person they spotted was Tomas Berglund. He was standing in the back half of the room in front of two large canisters of oxygen and a third filled with an unknown gas. He had a terrified look on his face, a reaction to the chaos he had heard unfolding outside.

Beside Berglund was Harrison Zidane. One of his hands was resting on the desk in front of him, as if he needed its support to remain upright. His other hand was at his side, partially obscured by the desk itself. His skin was pale, but his eyes were bright and hopeful. He showed none of the fear that Berglund exhibited, as if gunfights were commonplace on his property.

Payne and Jones raised their weapons, but both knew they couldn't risk a shot. Not without the possibility of their bullets going through Zidane and rupturing one of the tanks behind him.

'Where's Hendrik Cole?' Payne demanded.

'Dead,' Zidane replied. 'I am told he was wounded in Rakovnik and that he didn't survive the trip to Italy.'

'Did you see him die?' Jones asked Berglund.

'My face was bound in some sort of covering,' Berglund answered. 'I could not see or hear anything until we made it to the villa. But I have not seen him since we arrived.'

'I know that men in your profession cannot be certain of anything until you see the body for yourselves,' Zidane stated, 'but I am afraid that in this instance such a meeting simply cannot be arranged. Cole's remains were disposed of en route.

No one but the men involved could give you an exact location, and I am afraid they are now dead as well.' Zidane nodded toward the carnage that was strewn about his patio as he sat down at his desk.

Payne lowered his weapon as Zidane placed both hands where they could be seen.

'Cole's death was inevitable, really,' Zidane continued. 'He was never part of the long-term plan.'

'Which was?' Payne asked.

'A partnership,' Zidane said. 'One that would bring us unimaginable wealth, not to mention extra years to spend it.'

Jones laughed. 'You need to check your meds. I think you've lost your mind.'

'Actually, my friend, I never lose.' Zidane flashed his best smile. 'I am offering the chance of a lifetime. The breakthroughs Tomas has made will revolutionize the human body. No more disease. No more weakness. The perfect machine, customized to your choosing.' He glanced at their weapons. 'Imagine the military applications. The healthiest, most advanced fighting force the world has ever seen, with the ability to heal themselves on the battlefield.'

'You're talking about super-soldiers,' Payne said.

'Exactly! With this technology we can create an entire army of such men. There's no limit to what people would pay for such an advantage. Your military. Mine. The rest of the world. We could sell the technology to the highest bidder, then we could tweak the science and sell it again.'

'Immortality to the highest bidder,' Jones concluded.

'While *we* control the balance of power,' Zidane stated.

'Who is we?' Payne asked, egging him on.

'Your company and mine,' Zidane smiled. 'The power will remain solely with us.'

Payne smiled and lowered his weapon. 'In that case . . .'

Zidane moved to congratulate the men he now saw as his partners. 'Excellent! I knew you could be convinced. Believe it or not, Jonathon, we are a lot alike. We come from wealth, yet we yearn for more.'

Zidane offered his hand to seal the deal, but Payne used it against him. He gripped it hard then squeezed it harder until Zidane fell back into his chair. As he did, the smile on Payne's face turned into a menacing scowl.

Payne glared at Zidane, his hold still firm. 'You're a sick son-of-a-bitch responsible for the death of dozens of innocent people. You and I are *nothing* alike.'

Zidane's face grew pale as his reality began to sink in. For the first time in his life, he had met someone who could not be swayed by money or power.

'How long do we have?' Payne asked.

'What do you mean?' Zidane replied.

Payne squeezed until he could feel Zidane's knuckles begin to pop. 'How long . . . *do we have?*' Payne demanded.

From the moment Zidane had sat down, Payne had sensed his ploy. Zidane was stalling. He was buying himself precious minutes, waiting for whatever was to happen next. Payne had sensed exactly what was going on, but he'd chosen to take advantage of it. If Zidane was going to offer information about his master plan, Payne was willing to listen. Now that he had heard enough about Zidane's grandiose vision, all he wanted to know was how quickly reinforcements would be arriving.

A moment later, he had his answer.

Payne and Jones knew they had to move the moment they heard Masseri's voice through their earpieces.

'You guys have company!' Masseri announced. 'A yacht just

pulled up at the dock, and whoever's on board is in one hell of a hurry.'

'Can you cover us?' Jones asked.

'Negative,' Masseri answered. 'The boat is blocking my shot. It's directly between me and the house. You're on your own.'

With a jerk of his arm, Payne pulled Zidane to his feet. In the same motion, he spun Zidane around and pinned his hand behind him. 'The stairs to the boathouse, *now*!' Payne ordered as he pushed Zidane in front of him.

Jones grabbed Berglund by the belt and ushered him after Payne and Zidane. It wasn't an act of aggression, but it was forceful enough to let Berglund know that Jones's directions should be followed without question.

Payne and Jones were in charge.

Berglund needed to trust them if he wanted to survive.

64

Payne knew from the reconnaissance file that Raskin had produced – which included everything from satellite footage to construction blueprints – that the house had a stairwell just off the main hallway leading down to the boathouse. As they pushed through the lower door, Payne saw what he was looking for. The boathouse stored a jet boat in its covered dock. Payne smashed the lockbox mounted on the wall nearby with the butt of his gun and tossed the keys to Jones.

'Get them out of here,' ordered Payne, whose main priority was bringing Berglund to safety and Zidane to justice. He would stay behind and cover their escape to make sure they got away.

'You're taking a later train?' Jones asked.

'Not quite,' Payne said as he pointed through the open waterfront doors of the boathouse. 'I'm taking one of those.'

Jones turned to see the opulent yacht that was parked alongside Zidane's dock at the front of his estate. Two WaveRunners were suspended in cradles on the aft deck. These high-speed personal watercrafts could be lowered to the lake by a small crane that was also used for loading palates of food and other supplies.

'Nah, man, screw that!'

'Screw what?'

'You get to zip out of here on a water Harley, and I'm stuck chauffeuring a white dude across the lake like I'm Morgan Freeman in *Driving Miss Daisy*? What kind of racist bullshit is that?'

'First of all, you're Morgan Freeman *with a gun,* which is pretty bad ass.'

'True.'

'Secondly, I'm your commanding officer, and I say—'

'Wait! You're my *what?* I hate to break it to you, but we're retired.'

'*Retired?* We just jumped out of a military plane and shot a squad of armed men. That doesn't sound like retired to me.'

Jones growled as if he were going to turn the situation into a standoff, but only for a moment. As much as he loved to give Payne a hard time, he knew when to relent.

'Fine!' Jones snapped as he jumped into the open bow and shoved Zidane toward the front of the boat. 'But *you're* driving. That's right, Miss Daisy, I'm your worst nightmare. I'm Hoke with a fuckin' gun.'

Payne laughed as he pushed the boat away from the dock.

'No funny stuff,' Jones warned as he tapped the steering wheel with his pistol. 'Head north, and don't stop unless I tell you to. Understood?'

Zidane nodded.

'What about me?' Berglund asked.

'Stay low and stay out of my way,' Jones replied.

'I'll try.'

The boat was not designed for safety; it was made for excitement. Its gunnels were no more than eighteen inches above the water and offered little protection to hide behind. Even slouched as low as he could go, Berglund's head and shoulders were still exposed.

'You've got ten minutes to catch up,' Jones shouted to Payne as the boat floated toward the open water. 'Any longer and I'm coming back to save your ass.'

'From what?'

'From yourself.'

Payne smiled and retreated toward the door as the jet boat's engine roared to life. A moment later, Zidane dropped the throttle and the boat rocketed forward like a dragster at the starting line. The sound was so loud it attracted the attention of every surviving guard on the property, which was exactly what Payne had been hoping for.

The more he killed on land, the less he would have to worry about on water.

Payne steadied himself at the bottom of the stairwell. The passage was narrow, forcing people to descend one at a time. It was the perfect chokepoint for Payne to lie in wait.

When the door finally opened, three of Cole's soldiers hustled down the tunnel in succession. Payne peeked around the bottom corner of the stairwell and opened fire. His first bullet caught the lead man in the throat – an instant kill shot. In the close quarters, the remaining men were unable to raise their weapons in time. Payne leveled his pistol and squeezed the trigger again. The second man fell dead and tumbled forward, which left the third standing in the clear. Payne fired once more, and the confrontation was over a few seconds after it had begun.

Payne took a deep breath and checked his ammo. As he did, he heard the distinctive roar of the jet boat moving farther and farther away. Payne assumed everything was fine until he heard a second engine rumble to life. Then another. Then two more. Suddenly concerned, he sprinted back into the boathouse and peaked outside toward the source of the sound.

In front of the mansion, four more WaveRunners were being launched from a hidden hold in the stern of the yacht. Payne cursed loudly as he watched four gunmen speed away in pursuit of Jones's jet boat. He knew that with three passengers on board, it wouldn't have the speed to keep its distance from the lighter, faster WaveRunners.

His friend was about to be out-paced, out-manned, and out-gunned.

*   *   *

In the early-morning light, Jones could see Zidane's villa growing smaller and smaller in the distance. They were almost a mile away, but they were by no means safe. Not yet. Not with four WaveRunners closing in on them.

'We can't outrun them,' Jones announced.

'Of course not,' Zidane replied in a smarmy tone. 'You're only prolonging the inevitable.'

'I don't need the commentary,' Jones shouted back. 'Just keep driving.'

He knew Zidane was right. The WaveRunners would eventually catch them, and when they did he would have no choice but to engage in a one-sided firefight from a boat that offered very little protection.

Jones heard the telltale *pop-pop-pop-pop-pop* of an automatic rifle, but the riders in pursuit were unable to compensate for the WaveRunners' heaving motion as they sped over the swells and whitecaps on the lake. A series of tiny splashes erupted in the water to the side of the jet boat as the bullets fell harmlessly wide of their target. Another round whizzed by overhead. Range was not the issue for the high-powered assault rifles; it was their aim that could not be controlled.

In the midst of the gunfire, Jones watched as the lead soldier suddenly tilted his weight and veered sharply. The action caused the nose of the watercraft to dip below the surface, which in turn forced the rear into the air. A massive plume of water sprayed from the vehicle and soaked the two soldiers to his left. He then repeated the action in the other direction and doused the soldier to his right. Now that he had everyone's attention, he swung his gun from one side to the other, squaring the men in his sights while violently shaking his head.

'Why'd they stop?' Berglund asked as he brazenly stuck his head up to see what was happening behind him. Ever the scientist, he deemed the reward of knowledge greater than the risk of being shot in the face.

'One of them just figured out that if they shoot Miss Daisy, they'll be going home without a paycheck,' Jones explained. 'But don't worry, they're still trying to kill *us*.'

'On the contrary,' Zidane said. 'Tomas is of great importance to me. His life is to be spared at all costs. I'm afraid that the only person they're trying to kill is *you*.'

65

Jones studied the men in the distance. He knew they wouldn't risk shooting their employer, and he knew he could use that to his advantage. If he let them get in range, he could end their pursuit once and for all. 'Slow down. Bring them closer.'

Zidane was a smart man, and he quickly figured out what Jones had in mind. He also realized this was probably his best chance to get away. Rather than slowing down, he forced the throttle into neutral, pulled the key from the starter, and dove over the side of the boat.

Jones started cursing before Zidane even hit the water.

But what could he do?

With the boat now bobbing lifelessly, the soldiers would attack in a matter of seconds. He knew there wasn't enough time to dive in after the keys, and without Zidane's presence on the boat, he and Berglund were sitting ducks. Jones pulled the scientist to the floor and prepared to make the best of a bad situation.

Zidane laughed at the sudden turn of events.

But his joy didn't last.

Just as the soldiers opened fire, a sleek gunboat cut between them and their prey. The gunboat's .50 caliber guns made short work of the WaveRunners, pumping round after round into the overmatched mercenaries. Compared to the armored gunboat, the personal watercraft were little more than toys – toys that could be easily shattered at the whim of the biggest kid in the playground.

Today, the biggest kid was Nick Dial.

Thanks to Dial's persistent urging, the Italian State Police had eventually agreed to provide their assistance. Jones had known they would be out there, somewhere in the water. He simply needed to buy enough time for their arrival and then give them a reason to get involved. Whatever reservations they had were put aside the moment they saw four men raining automatic rifle fire upon a defenseless vessel.

As the gunboat circled the wreckage, Zidane finally conceded defeat. With Jones's gun trained at his head, the billionaire swam slowly back to the jet boat.

'Nice try,' Jones admitted, 'but did you really think I was alone out here? I might be pretty, but I ain't stupid.'

Zidane pulled himself on board and stumbled around the boat, shaky on his feet from the shock of what was happening. In his wildest dreams, he had never imagined his legacy would end like this. He thought he would live in comfort for many more years, a rich man who could buy his own immortality. Now everything he had done would be for naught.

He had spent a fortune to prolong his life, but in that moment, he wanted to die.

A minute later, his wish would be granted.

Jones waved his arms to signal Dial, who was now standing on the bridge of the gunboat taking stock of the scene. Dial could only shake his head at the bodies in the water.

'You really need to stop taking our calls,' Jones said.

'Last time I make that mistake,' Dial replied.

As they laughed in unison, a single shot rang out across the lake.

The round from Masseri's rifle traveled faster than the speed of sound.

There was nothing they could do.

By the time they turned around, Zidane was already dead.

*   *   *

As he made his way across the grounds, Payne had no idea what to expect. He sprinted around the small cove that protected the boathouse and ran into the clear. But instead of a waiting army, all Payne found were the littered bodies of the men he had already encountered. It appeared that everyone in the second wave of soldiers was on the water.

There were no signs of life on the yacht, either. It simply sat at the end of the pier, dark and motionless. Despite its uninviting appearance, Payne ran to the end of the dock and leapt aboard, landing softly on the aft deck. In less than a minute he had positioned the crane and attached the sling underneath one of the WaveRunners.

A minute later he would have been in the water and racing to the aid of his best friend.

Unfortunately, Hendrik Cole had other ideas.

After the incident in Rakovnik, Cole had been forced to make a detour into Como before arriving at the villa. There he had met a local doctor who was able to treat the injuries he had sustained at the lab. Normally the first to fight, he had decided to rest on the yacht while Zidane's men handled the security breach on the estate, but all that changed when he heard the whirring of the crane. Cole left his berth to investigate and spotted Payne on the deck.

In a flash, he knew his recovery would have to wait.

He had to act fast to keep the element of surprise.

Ideally, he would have preferred to shoot Payne in the back of the head and be done with it, but he had no idea where Jones was or what other reinforcements were lurking nearby. This forced Cole to kill Payne in a much more personal manner.

And because of the whir of the crane, Payne didn't hear him coming.

One moment he was hoisting the WaveRunner from its cradle, and the next he was being slammed violently into the watercraft.

In the collision, Payne's gun fell from his belt and slid off the deck into the water below. It was followed by a thunderous crash as the WaveRunner broke loose from its lifting straps and toppled over the side of the boat.

Cole relished the opportunity to murder someone as revered as Jonathon Payne. Driven by a surge of endorphins, he was oblivious to the ache in his gut. Even if Cole had known that the staples closing his wound had pulled loose, it would not have stopped him. He might never get a second chance. He wasn't about to pass it up.

Cole reached into his scabbard and withdrew a large, machete-like blade. It was razor sharp, with a cutting edge on the front side and deep serrated teeth on the back. The tip was narrow and pointed. It was a weapon capable of stabbing, slicing, and sawing – and Cole had experience with all three methods of death.

In response, Payne pulled his bayonet from its sheath. It was only a third the size of Cole's custom sword, but it had proven its worth throughout Payne's career.

Without saying a word, the two men circled each other like wrestlers, both waiting for the right moment. Cole struck first, swinging at his opponent's neck. Payne ducked the attack and countered with a swipe across Cole's thigh. The cut drew blood, but it wasn't crippling. Cole stepped back, then half-smiled, half-snarled as he struck again. This time it was a downward-looping motion, as if Payne was a chunk of wood that Cole intended to split. Payne was able to intercept the blow with his knife, deflecting Cole's weapon to the fiberglass hull. Shards flew before Cole reversed the direction of his swing, jerking the serrated teeth in the direction of Payne's forearm.

The bite of the blade found its mark, and the saw-like points tore the flesh from Payne's arm as he winced in agony.

Cole laughed with delight.

Payne took the knife in his opposite hand as blood soaked the arm of his long-sleeved shirt. In an act of mockery, Cole also changed his grip, tossing his weapon from one hand to the other. Despite his injury, Payne now took the offensive. He sprang forward and delivered a series of stabs, swipes, and swings. Cole deftly deflected each attempt, his grin growing with each missed opportunity. Catching Payne off-balance, he lifted him off his feet and slammed him to the deck. But he did not attack. He simply stood over Payne, relishing the moment before allowing him to scramble to his feet.

Payne held his wounded arm to his chest. Blood streamed off his elbow and pooled on the polished deck around him. His breathing was heavy and labored; his eyes were dull and sullen. He had the look of defeat. It was the moment Cole had been waiting for.

He raised his weapon and charged his target, attempting to run him through.

But Payne's vulnerability was just a ploy.

He sprang to life and sidestepped the bull rush at the last possible moment. As Cole passed by, Payne struck him several times in rapid succession. The blade of his bayonet punctured Cole's lung, stomach, and kidney. The doctor in Como had done his best to repair Cole's wounds, but Payne now sliced through the Butcher with his brand of surgical precision.

This time, Cole would not recover.

If left alone, he would be dead in a matter of minutes.

But that wasn't soon enough for Payne.

Taking no chances, he wrapped the line of the deck crane around Cole's neck then shoved him toward the railing. With a swift kick, Payne sent Cole's body swinging out over the side of the boat like a prized shark at the end of a long voyage. Blood drained from his wounds into the water below as he struggled for a last gulp of air that wasn't to come.

Eventually, the body went limp as Payne staggered away.

Epilogue

Jones racked the balls for a game of billiards at Café Louvre in Prague while Payne selected a cue. Sahlberg sat on a nearby barstool, nursing a well-deserved beer.

'You know this is the only way you'll ever beat me, right?' To drive home his point, Payne nodded toward his bandaged arm, which was resting comfortably in a sling.

'Give me a break,' Jones said. 'We both know you're an expert at one-handed sports. You certainly get enough practice.'

Payne chuckled at the crude innuendo.

'Is this safe?' Sahlberg asked.

'Is what safe? Playing pool?' Jones asked.

'Being out in public,' he clarified.

It was a fair question, given the week he had just experienced. He had gone from a breathtaking sunset in California to the confinement of a Czech root cellar in less than twenty-four hours. He had remained drugged and locked away in the dank basement, subsisting on raw vegetables and dried meat, for days. Just as he had begun to lose hope of rescue, he had been freed by one of Masseri's accomplices without an explanation of any kind.

Released near the Charles Bridge, he didn't know where he was or how long he had been missing. Nor did he know the identity of his captors, or if anyone was looking for him.

Fortunately, a Czech policewoman spotted him and told him that Interpol had plastered his image across the city's precincts. The next morning, he was reunited with Payne and Jones, who filled in many of the missing details about Berglund and Zidane.

'Mattias,' Payne said with a gentle pat on his shoulder, 'drink in peace. I assure you, we're safe from Masseri. He knows that if he comes after us, he's a dead man.'

Sahlberg nodded his understanding, remembering their earlier conversation. Payne had explained that he had military connections all over the world, and that if he and Jones were killed, another member of their team would pick up the fight. Masseri would be hunted down without mercy, and he knew it. There'd be no place on earth he could hide.

Jones changed the subject. 'Did you get a chance to talk to Dr Berglund?'

Sahlberg smiled. 'I did. He seemed in very good spirits, all things considered.'

'Keep an eye on him,' Payne advised. 'He might take a turn for the worse if he starts to believe that he was responsible for the deaths of the scientists in Stockholm. You have to do everything you can to steer him clear of that line of thought. Have you figured out if he'll be coming to Pittsburgh with you?'

'Actually,' Sahlberg said, 'we'll be headed to La Jolla when he's finally free to travel. I spoke with several members of the group earlier this morning, and they're eager to hear about Tomas's discoveries. Perhaps, as a group, we can formulate the best course of action.'

Jones walked to the table and grabbed his beer. 'Zidane wasn't wrong, you know. With that technology, you can name your price.'

'But at what expense?' Sahlberg asked rhetorically. 'What price do we pay for upsetting the natural order of things?'

Payne smiled. It was the response he was hoping to hear. 'Like I said, just keep an eye on him. Guilt has a funny way of sneaking up on you.'

'So does Nick Dial,' Jones said with a nod.

Payne turned and spotted the final member of their celebration, who was making his way through the crowded room. They raised their beers in salute.

Dial couldn't help but smile. 'It's about time you showed me the respect I deserve. Next time, I want you to bow as well.' He approached Sahlberg, his hand extended. 'Dr Sahlberg, we haven't been officially introduced. Nick Dial.'

'Mattias, please,' Sahlberg answered as he shook Dial's hand. 'Very nice to meet you.'

'You too.'

'I hate to be bold, but what can you tell me about Tomas? How much trouble is he in?'

'Hard to say,' admitted Dial, who had spent several hours with Berglund in order to establish a timeline of the past few months.

But some things were abundantly clear.

Zidane's first priority had been to save himself. The Rakovnik laboratory had been designed as his own personal hospital. Everything there was geared toward keeping him alive. Berglund, on the other hand, wanted to determine how his technology could be used for the betterment of the public in general. To do that, he had to secretly break away from Zidane.

This had ultimately led to the laboratory in Stockholm, which was where several of Berglund's most trusted colleagues prepared the technology for clinical trials. They even went behind Zidane's back and used his own connections without his knowledge to procure human test subjects – namely criminals, all of whom had terminal illnesses. When a warden at one of the correctional facilities began asking too many questions, Zidane found out about the facility and was furious. He was spending his personal fortune to extend his life – not to help a bunch of dying felons.

That was when he gave the order to destroy the lab.

Payne rejoined the conversation. 'Mattias, if there's one thing I'm sure of, it's that you want Nick in your corner. I challenge you to find anyone with a greater sense of right and wrong.'

'While I will certainly take the compliment, I have to tell you that it's not my case,' Dial replied. 'It never was . . . at least not officially.'

'Who's handling things?' Jones asked.

'Johann Eklund, one of our Swedish agents. And he's the right guy for the job. That sense of right and wrong? He's got it. Trust me, he'll be fair.'

'So where do you go from here?' Payne asked.

'Back to Lyon.'

'How bad is it going to be for you?' Jones asked.

'Not bad at all. Like I said, I was never officially involved. Agent Eklund broke the case on his own. He gets all the credit. And he's not telling anyone the secret of his success.'

Jones raised his glass. 'To Eklund and his secrets.'

'And ours,' Payne said as he nodded toward the back of the room.

Sahlberg turned and glanced in that direction. He immediately laughed when he saw the framed picture on the billiard room wall.

It was a photograph of Albert Einstein, pool cue in hand.

A smile on his lips and a twinkle in his eye.

Acknowledgements

It takes a village to raise a child, but it takes a lot more than that to publish a book – especially when the person writing the book is the village idiot. (I figured I'd make the joke before Payne & Jones had a chance.)

Anyway, here are some of the people I'd like to thank:

Scott Miller, Claire Roberts, Robert Gottlieb, Stephanie Hoover, and the whole gang at Trident Media. They sold this project before it was even written.

Ian Harper, my longtime friend/editor/consigliere. He reads my words before anyone else – and then reads them again and again until they're perfect.

Vicki Mellor, Emily Griffin, Jo Liddiard, Jane Morpeth, and everyone at Headline/Hachette UK. They took my story and turned it into a book. And then they printed, like, a million copies and shipped them all over the world.

All the fans, librarians, booksellers, and critics who have enjoyed my thrillers and have recommended them to others. If you keep reading them, I'll keep writing them.

And last but not least, my loving family – because they are the ones who have put up with me the longest.